The Last Dying Light

The Last of the Romans: I

The Last Dying Light

A NOVEL OF BELISARIUS

WILLIAM HAVELOCK

Copyright © 2020 by William Havelock

All rights reserved. No part of this book may be reproduced or used in any manner without written permission of the copyright owner except for the use of quotations in a book review. For more information, address: william@havelockbooks.com

Book cover design by Dusan Markovic
Maps by Cyowari

ISBN: 978-1-7379808-0-3 (hardcover)
ISBN: 978-0-578-75540-3 (paperback)
ASIN: B08FZKSBL3 (ebook)

www.havelockbooks.com

For Vicky. Thanks for believing.

Ah! vainest of all things
Is the gratitude of kings;
The plaudits of the crowd
Are but the clatter of feet
At midnight in the street,
Hollow and restless and loud.

But the bitterest disgrace
Is to see forever the face
Of the Monk of Ephesus!
The unconquerable will
This, too, can bear; —I still
Am Belisarius!

~Henry Wadsworth Longfellow (1807 – 1882 C.E.)

CHARACTERS

Aetius	Long-dead general of the Western Roman Empire, Attila's nemesis
Ajax	A Roman street thug
al-Harith	Heir to the Ghassanid Kingdom
Alypius	Roman centurion in Tauris
Anastasius	The aged Roman Emperor
Antonina	Young Roman aristocrat, daughter of Basilius
Archelaus	An *excubitor* and leader of a Thracian *banda*
Ascum	Alani *ballista* commander, serves the Cappadocian Army
Attila	Long-dead Khagan of the Hunnic Empire
Baduarius	Ostrogoth, leads Belisarius' spearmen
Basilius	Former East Roman consul, chief advisor to Justin
Belisarius	General of the Cappadocian Army
Bessas	Armenian, leads Belisarius' cataphracts
Cephalas	Greek, spearman of the Thracian Army
Dagisthaeus	Ostrogoth, brother of Baduarius, a tribune under Belisarius
Fastida	A chief of a Gepid village
Germanus	Justinian's cousin, who serves in the Thracian Army
Godilas	General of the East Roman armies, and a close friend to Justin
Hormisdas	The Pope in Rome
Hypatius	The eldest nephew of Emperor Anastasius
Ildico	Attila's final bride
Isaacius	A Jewish soldier in the Thracian Army
Jabalah	King of the Ghassanids

John	Belisarius' second-in-command
Justin	Lord of Anastasius' *excubitores*, *dominus* of Varus and Samur
Justinian	Justin's nephew and close advisor
Kavadh	*Shahanshah* of the Persian Empire
Kazrig	Khagan of the Avars
Leo	Long-dead Pope, met with Attila
Liberius	A senior advisor to the Emperor
Marcellus	An officer of the excubitores
Mariya	Princess of the Ghassanids, King Jabalah's daughter
Mundus	An experienced centurion of the Thracian Army
Narcissus	Leader of Singidunum's garrison
Narses	Theodora's chief spy and advisor
Nepotian	A wealthy Roman senator, and Solomon's father
Odoacer	Chieftain who overthrew the last Western Roman Emperor
Paulus	The Roman Emperor's Minister of the Treasury
Perenus	An exiled Lazic prince, and Varus' second-in-command
Petrus	An aged Roman priest
Pompeius	A nephew of Emperor Anastasius
Probus	A nephew of Emperor Anastasius
Procopius	Imperial scribe and historian
Rosamund	A captured Gepid pagan and healer
Samur	A Herulian slave to Justin, Varus' only sibling
Sembrouthes	Commander of Aksumites guarding Princess Mariya
Shaush	Prince of the Avars, eldest son of Kazrig

Simmas	A commander of the Hun *foederati*, brother to Sunicas
Solomon	A young Roman aristocrat, son of Nepotian
Sunicas	A leader of the Hun foederati, brother to Simmas
Theodora	Justinian's betrothed
Tribonian	The Roman Emperor's Minister of Laws
Troglita	A centurion in the Thracian Army
Tzul	Kazrig's warlord
Varus	The narrator, a Herulian, and a slave to Justin

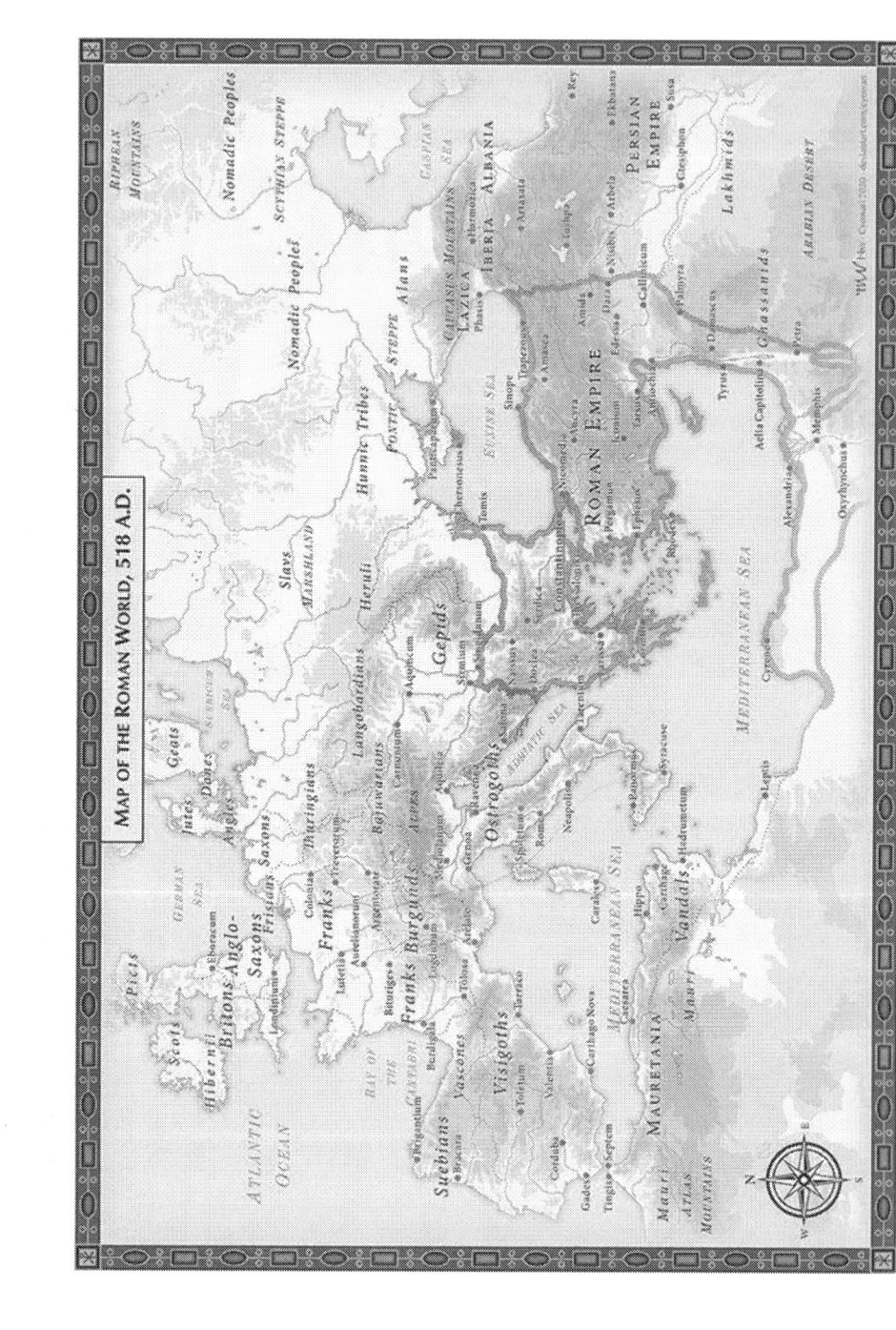

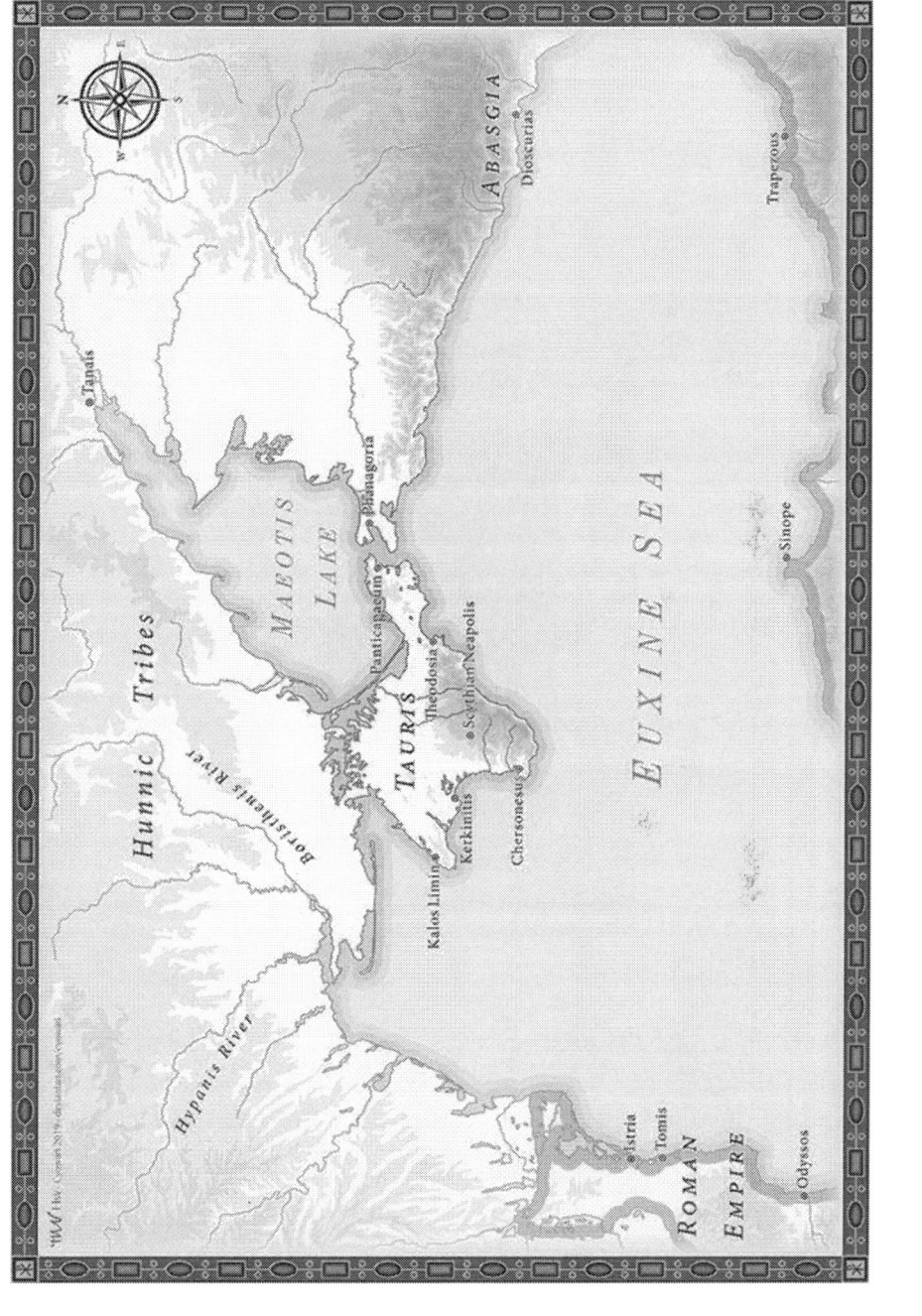

PROLOGUE:
THE CHIEFTAIN

THE OLD CHIEFTAIN WHEEZED blood as he sprawled in the dirt. His horse had perished long ago, its heart pierced by a lance from the enemy riders. Thousands of others, most his own kinsmen following him in the attack, lay dead or twitching along the plain. He had been a warlord for so many years, had won victories against so many kingdoms, that the crushing weight of sadness surprised him, made heavier still by the knowledge that the entire calamity was his fault. Years ago, when he was a child, these city dwellers ran in fear of his people, yet now, so many years later, they had come in force to kill all the chieftain's people.

Though age and injury had diminished his hearing, the chieftain could sense the enemy horseman advancing in a regular, almost impetuous canter. He tried to rise, yet gaping wounds had robbed his legs of their vitality. He was no stranger to death, for he had brought many to the Dark God's abode over far too many summers to count. He had even boasted of it. Yet there was no such boldness now, only a desperate impulse to escape the stone-faced soldier who slowly crested the horizon.

As paralysis trickled up his thighs and into his stomach, the chieftain surrendered, light-headed and sick. He gazed at the yurt just a short ride from his position, yet knew even that destination was beyond the limits of his remaining strength.

As the horseman drew nearer, all the chieftain could do was draw his sword—the legendary blade that had embodied his father's pride and won many victories over their blood enemies—and sit in feeble defiance.

The Last Dying Light

The horseman dismounted and knocked the sword aside with his own. He stared into the chieftain's eyes, his face grim yet triumphant as he loomed over his enemy's broken body.

"Please…" The chieftain spat blood as he tried to mouth the words of his enemy's language. He stole one last glance at the yurt, overcome by the bottomless grief known only to those who fail such duties of life and death.

The horseman did not reply. He took his enemy's sword and drove it into the chieftain's chest. The chieftain gaped as the blade punctured his heart, the final act of pain and mercy leaving him breathless, numb, open-mouthed. His vision darkened; now he saw only the eyes of the horseman, already trained on their next target. The chieftain's pain ebbed, and the world dissolved around him.

IMPERIUM

Many years ago, I was young and strong. Now I am neither, and I cannot think the wisdom of years is a proper remuneration for the loss of one's youth. Winters grow harsher, friends succumb to hunger or illness, and all the things once held with pride decay to ash.

So many dead. So many friends, lovers, sons, daughters, kings, and queens, departed and gone. Sometimes I think fate has left me as the last emblem of a dying era, yet the priests assure me it is God's will that I am still here, and that He still has work for me to do in His name. When I think of friends who perished long ago, I cannot help but feel that He chose poorly.

It does not bother me that the world I helped to build will fade away, but that those much better than me will be remembered in infamy, or not at all. Even old enemies are recalled fondly, not for their prowess in causing pain, but for their conviction, as they loved deeply, fought selflessly, and believed wholeheartedly in the cause of Rome and Justinian. The Eternal City is in the debt of so many of these legends but owes none more than Flavius Belisarius—the king without a crown, the last of the true Romans, who marched obediently through a valley of certain death for the vanity and pride of his emperor.

To me, however, he was simply a friend, and the greatest man I have ever known. He, above all others, deserves love and praise, yet jealous hearts will never allow such adulation.

It is because of this, to forestall his ignominy, that I seek to honor his memory with this tale. My age-addled brain will certainly recall some things incorrectly, which the scribes will rewrite to their own aggrandizement, yet I will tell it the only way I know, as the truth of a man I loved. Back to a time when I was still young, and

The Last Dying Light

my sword arm true, invested with all the dreams that youth may hold in a world that offers nothing but suffering, hardship, and, for the fortunate, comrades to share the burden.

BONDAGE

M<small>Y FIRST MEMORY IS THE</small> smell of blood. The singers tell of battlefields and rivers drowned in the gore of the vanquished, but their tales rarely mention that awful scent: a metallic, pungent odor that infests the mouth and nose for hours and leaves the ground stained far longer. That smell, so indelible, is the first thing I remember as I search through the fog of my earliest memories. That, and the screaming.

I do not remember much else of the events that led to my enslavement to Constantinople. One blessing of age is the dwindling awareness of the horrors of childhood, the misfortunes of pain and poverty buried as the hourglass of life trickles full. I cannot recall my mother's face or my father's voice; my parents exist only as formless shadows at the precipice of my memory. All that was known is that we—myself, along with my younger brother Samur—were the only survivors of an East Roman raid that brought on our childhood bondage to Constantinople.

It is fitting, then, that my story begins with a death. Rather than the filth and mud of a dying barbarian tribe, however, this death took place in Constantinople's Great Palace, where the old emperor wheezed his last moments in the purple. Emperor Anastasius possessed no strength to move his limbs, and in between violent hacks, managed only the faintest whisper to his advisor Basilius, who nodded in silent understanding at the monarch's will.

"Boy." The skeletal courtier beckoned to me. "Go to your dominus and summon the Emperor's nephews to this chamber. Hurry now!"

I scurried to the door and found my dominus, Justin, on the other side. An older man with thinning hair streaked white, Justin nevertheless showed no sign of his many decades of life in his sharp eyes. They missed nothing, yet still held a particular kindness that I had come to know in my time as his slave. Once I had left the imperial sickroom, he closed the heavy wooden door with one hand and placed the other on my shoulder.

"What did the Emperor want with you, Varus?" Justin asked in Heruli, the language of my childhood.

"To bring his three nephews to his sickbed," I said. Despite my scant dozen or so years, I could sense something unusual was underway at the Imperial Palace.

Shadows danced from Justin's face as his steel-gray eyes fixed upon a nearby brazier, whose low embers did little to cut through the darkness of the marble hallway. The old general rubbed his gnarled hands together in silent contemplation and shivered against the cold that crept through the arched palace windows. Despite the light of the dying flames, Justin's features seemed to darken as he considered my words.

"They are fools," he said under his breath, "but likely the only legitimate heirs to the throne. Go and summon them to the Emperor, but keep me apprised of anything you hear."

I nodded, taken aback by the intensity of his tone. The disdain in his words was unusual—this was a man who had dedicated so many years of his life to the Emperor's will, after all—yet who was I to question Justin? A barbarian slave with long-dead parents is not afforded the luxury of opinion, and if he does indulge himself and speak his mind, he will not live long to enjoy it.

Yet I had rarely felt that nagging sense of fear that other slaves carefully hid behind masks of subservience. Justin had been a fair master and had provided opportunities typically enjoyed only by the wealthiest aristocrats of Constantinople. My brother and I were far luckier than the endless hordes of other slaves brutalized by whips lashing their backs and chains rubbing their ankles until they were bleeding and raw. Still, despite Justin's generosity, or perhaps because of it, I knew better than to question him, or even be suspicious of him.

Most remember Justin only as Justinian's patron, and later, as his puppet, but the truth was something else entirely. Justin was a hard man, yet he knew how to reward those he led and listened to wise counsel. He paid his soldiers with strict regularity, reimbursed local peasants and towns for their food and forage during his campaigns, meted out swift justice against lawbreakers in his armies, and treated noble cavalry and humble spearmen alike with respect and dignity. Justin had no children of his own, but he lavished his nieces and nephews with his own wages and delivered an unparalleled education and military training to the young servants and slaves he kept as attendants. Justin was a rare good man in an age beset by fools—fools such as the three I was now sent to fetch. Justin was not wrong about them.

The marble floors echoed with my footsteps as I climbed to the princes' apartments. Frescoes of the Savior and His Apostles covered the long walls, their imperious poses as grand as they were stern, but their faces melancholy; their eyes seemed to follow my every movement, and it made me uneasy more than reverent. As I neared the upper floors, the princes' clamor drowned out my steps throughout the vaulted halls.

Sounds of revelry rang to the rafters; I would undoubtedly find the Imperial princes in a drunken stupor. Though wealth and extravagance were well-known to the ruling elite, these three men lived a particularly soft existence of an overindulgence of wine and other unsavory appetites. I knocked on their door and entered. My greeting was a mixed stench of sour wine and stale vomit, as well as a half dozen young women in various stages of undress.

"What do you want, slave?" croaked Hypatius, the eldest of Anastasius' nephews.

Wine dribbled down his chin over patches of unkempt beard, staining his tunic a deep red. "Speak, mongrel, or remove yourself from my presence."

I dared to raise my eyes to meet his gaze. "The Emperor wishes you to attend him in his sickroom in the lower rooms of the palace."

"Why? For what purpose?" Hypatius demanded, a hint of indignity in his voice.

"He is dying. That is all I know."

Dismissed with a limp wave of Hypatius' silk-covered arm, I was only too happy to leave the princes behind. I walked back into the hallway, sucking in air mercifully cleaner than within the filthy rooms of Anastasius' heirs. The palace was empty, the pungent stench of mortality pervading the once-bustling Imperial halls. Even the small army of palace slaves, always in the shadows, took additional pains to remain unseen throughout the palace, although whether this was from the foul sickness that emanated from the Emperor's rooms or through a justified fear of assault and rape by the royal nephews was unclear.

Though I had not suffered such ill treatment myself, some slave girls and younger boys had asked me to intervene and alert Justin on their behalf. Justin heard my tales and promised to take appropriate action, yet the nephews never appeared to suffer any serious consequences from the excubitor commander's remonstrations. On more than one occasion, Justin charged *me* with keeping my fellow slaves safe from the princes' lustful grasp; it seemed even he was powerless to prevent that most wicked of aristocratic sins.

And so, amid a persistent aura of fear, only Basilius and Justin moved confidently along the palace's marble hallways. However, in Anastasius' final days, even they huddled near corner braziers, basking in their warm glow as they shared news of our monarch's lingering demise. My previous command completed, I returned to my dominus, approaching discreetly as the two spoke in hushed yet urgent tones in the darkness.

"I understand your words, Basilius," Justin said, "but if the Emperor wants to choose his heir in some unorthodox manner, then we have no choice but to respect his wishes."

"Foolishness," Basilius said. "You think that your rigid sense of honor will protect you when Hypatius takes the purple? Or one of the others? They'll have your throat cut on their first evening of power, and send my corpse after yours."

"Nevertheless, I swore an oath," Justin said with obvious irritation. "Anastasius is my Emperor, regardless of whether his decisions are sensible or just."

"Excubitores," Basilius muttered. "Justin, listen to me. All our hopes and plans have led to this. You have one chance! I'm not asking you to defy Anastasius, just to be liberal in your interpretations of his will."

Justin said nothing, but lifted his hands over the dying embers of the nearby fire. Orange flames flickered light over his emotionless face, his brow lined from decades of duty and worry. Ignoring Basilius' fidgeting, Justin took his time to summon a response, as though gathering a final piece of information critical to his judgment.

"You've spoken with the others on this?" Justin asked. "The priest?"

Basilius nodded excitedly. "Godilas and Liberius both agree, and the priest was eventually convinced. This is our final chance, Justin. It must be you."

With a sigh, Justin nodded. "Very well, but I will execute the Emperor's wishes in my own way."

"Naturally," Basilius said. "But it must be done now, while we still have the initiative."

My dominus nodded again. His eyes darted to the shadows, an old soldier's instincts warning him of my return. "Varus, I know you are here. I have a job for you and your brother." I hurried to his side.

"You'd trust this to a slave? Perhaps you are just as mad as Anastasius." Basilius' whisper was tinged with danger.

Basilius' thin frame and thinner hair made him appear frail, yet he was anything but. In truth, he was perhaps one of the most powerful men outside of the Imperial Family, having served as consul and personal advisor to the Emperor throughout Anastasius' long reign. Rich robes displayed his status as a senior minister; the cloth alone would fetch more silver than five years of a spearman's wages.

"I'd trust Varus with my life," Justin said tersely, holding Basilius' gaze.

Basilius sneered but did not speak against the old general. Though I knew that he had faith in my dominus' judgment built over their many years together, I did not yet understand the gravity of the situation they had thrust me into.

Justin pulled me into a small side office, barred the door from potential interlopers, and handed over a sealed scroll. He explained what was required of me: I would delay the nephews long enough for Samur, my brother, to arrange three benches. Two larger ones would be placed near the Emperor, with one smaller and farther away such as to be unlikely to be chosen by the rotund princelings. My task, then, would be to spy on the meeting through a narrow gap in the walls that, though far too small for any grown man, was perfect for a young boy.

"That's stupid!" Samur cried, moments after I told him of Justin's orders. "Arrange furniture so that three drunk perverts can fawn over their uncle? I'd rather not."

"No, you're the one being stupid, Samur! Don't you understand?" I cried. "The old emperor is going to die, and one of them might become the new one unless we obey our dominus."

It made little difference to Samur who wore the purple, but the silent threat of a whipping for disobeying Justin was persuasive enough. Samur was still young—nine years of age to my twelve—yet even then, he possessed a wiry strength equaled only by his sense of mischief. He scuttled off with Justin's scroll to the Imperial sickroom, where, in his boyishly high voice, he begged forgiveness for intruding and presumably set off to his task.

As Samur disappeared, I heard the nephews thumping and bumbling down the marble stairs toward the main antechamber of the Emperor's private quarters. Hypatius, Pompeius, and Probus had hastily redressed in colored and perfumed robes that most Roman nobility would consider feminine, the princelings' soft silks contrasting against the coarser wool and linen favored by the Emperor's ministers. Next to Justin's rough tunic and white cloak of the Emperor's elite guards, the nephews' garb made them look almost foreign.

I stopped them, begging forgiveness for my intervention and asking that they wait while their beloved uncle finished an evening prayer. Pompeius sighed at this indignation, while Hypatius and Probus beckoned for seats to support their ponderous girths. Even the short trip down the stairs strained the brothers' physical capabilities; their soft bodies were often lifted to the main level with a wrench and pulley system that required three slaves to operate. I bid them to wait but a moment, and that their uncle would call for them soon.

Not long after, Samur returned from the Emperor's chambers and winked—success. I then instructed the nephews to enter and seat themselves near their uncle, who wanted to speak with them in his hour of need. They composed themselves, rose deliberately to their feet, and strutted inside, while I snuck into the servant's passage just a few doors away, toward my listening post.

One lesson I learned early in bondage was the Roman distaste for visible servants. Other than the more paternal interactions with

Justin, Samur and I received little kindness, frequently scorned and humiliated by the wealthy palace children, although my dominus' reputation usually protected us from the harshest treatment. Yet even still, I was unwilling to shield myself with Justin's favor too frequently, and kept well away from the court nobles unless summoned.

Keeping unseen was, fortunately, a simple task. For every main passage or doorway for a wealthy merchant or patrician, an unimposing and disguised servant's entrance or sleeping quarters stood not far off. Aside from bed slaves or a body servant, the nobility could go an entire day without a glimpse of their inferiors, left to assume that their meals were prepared and night soil disposed of by magic. Our hidden comings and goings were assisted by tiny peering holes within the walls, which, although designed for slaves to know which rooms were occupied by their masters, made eavesdropping far too easy for a motivated slave child.

Though I was often set to scraping dung, or washing soiled clothes, or cleaning and disposing of the occasional corpse that had given up the ghost in one of the palace's hundreds of rooms, eavesdropping was the only duty that I truly loathed. Even the indignity of the slave's collar was less painful, for the cruel japes and taunts of the wealthy Roman children were small in comparison to the evils that their parents enacted in the privacy of their rooms. Not that I reviled the *act* of eavesdropping, per se; Samur and I had shared many a stifled laugh as we peered silently upon one of our classmates attempting to sing in a horrendous pitch or listened excitedly to tales of notable Romans from centuries ago.

Yet for every spy mission that brought us joy, dozens more terrible scenes burned themselves in our memories. At Justin's command, Samur and I bore witness to every manner of brutality that a person may inflict upon another. On many occasions, we had discovered one minister or another cracking a spouse or lover with wooden canes or closed fists, the cries of their victims muffled by the thick walls. Once, I spied upon a murder, the attacker darkened with rage and lashing out with a hidden dagger. But it was the torture and rape of slaves, many recently captured along the Empire's frontier and ferried back to Constantinople for purchase, that sent me the sharpest terrors in the night.

One such incident had never left my mind. At roughly ten years of age, I had been ordered to spy upon the Emperor's Minister of the Laws and found the plump and balding man chaining a black-haired girl to a wall before inflicting his will upon her. She was no more than fifteen or sixteen, her frayed garment ripped from her frame, exposed to all manner of unwanted force. Yet it was not until she begged for mercy in Heruli, my own native tongue, that my hands began to shake. Those familiar words earned a heavy crack along her ribs as the minister commanded her to abandon such a heathen tongue. With bile in my throat, I wept.

Justin set things to rights soon thereafter. He nearly always did. However, he rarely asked for such services from me after that incident, and called me into his private chambers to explain the evil that I had witnessed. It must have been difficult to make sense of the world's injustices to a mere boy, yet Justin had prepared well for such a task, expounding on the importance of holding fast to righteousness and order even when others fell short. I know that I nodded, and indeed I agreed, yet that girl's pleading always remained on the edge of my memory, mixing with other, distant screams from another woman—my mother, I assume. That girl's pain will weigh on my soul until the day that God finally does remove me from this life. Until then, I beg her forgiveness. I did not even know her name.

But that day, when Justin asked me to spy upon the Emperor and his nephews, I knew it was no light, gossipy task. Stomach churning, I snaked through a servant's hallway until at last I squeezed under several beams and opened the peephole into Anastasius' death chamber.

Samur had accomplished his task. The two fatter nephews were taking their seats together on a shared bench on the Emperor's left, with another sitting at the foot of his bed. Off in the right corner sat an unoccupied chair, far too small for any of the three of them to sit comfortably, with just the hint of a thick scroll poking out of embroidered cushions.

"Beloved uncle," Hypatius broke the silence, his tone smacking of insincerity and indolence. "How may we ease your mind in this darkened hour?"

Anastasius sputtered out thick globules of phlegm, now dotted with spots of blood that stained his neckline crimson, a grim echo of his nephews' own wine-soaked clothes. "Have any of you received my message?" he asked slowly, in a voice much deeper and larger than his small frame seemed capable of producing.

"Message?" Hypatius asked. The other two shrugged and muttered to themselves. "Yes, Uncle, we came to speak with you as you commanded."

Anastasius chuckled sadly. "Never mind, never mind, you may leave."

Visibly irritated, yet all too grateful to take their leave of a dying man, the nephews waddled out. As one passed my hiding spot, I heard him murmur his incredulity at such a time-wasting fool's errand before all three left the dying Emperor alone with his thoughts.

Then, the most remarkable thing happened. Old Anastasius, who generally gave little attention to the affairs of others and much to the collection of gold and silver, wept like a child, his thick sobs interrupted by lengthy coughing fits, lung-deep rasps that attested the illness' hold on his life. As Anastasius wept, he called out to God, Jesus, and whichever saints would hear him.

"Oh, Lord, I have sinned and fear the torment that awaits me. If a rich man would have difficulty passing into the Kingdom, how would you treat one that offered nothing of his people but beggary and loss? I beg forgiveness for my transgressions, which I feel around me like hungry shadows waiting impatiently to collect their dues."

Anastasius sputtered again in a greater fit than before, still unaware that his confession was being witnessed by one he thought so little of in life.

"The one good act I can perform before the end of my life," he continued, "is to bow to your will. The first man that appears on the morrow in my presence will be your choice for the purple, and I will obey that selection. I have no other recourse."

With that, I knew I had heard it. I jumped back and rushed to Justin's chambers, where he and Basilius sat in silence, waiting for news.

"Yes, Varus?" Justin asked.

I told them everything: the dismissal of the nephews, the unclaimed deed to overlordship of the Empire, and most of all, the last confession and promise of the dying ruler. Both listened intently, their faces gradually brightening. Though the Emperor's words were clear, I held little understanding of their importance for my dominus or his associates. Basilius, however, quickly shed light.

"This is our chance," he said to Justin. "For all of his faults, the old man is pious enough to believe that such a scheme would please God. We must bar the doors until daybreak, and you must be the first to enter with his morning meal."

Visibly shocked, Justin looked from me to Basilius. "I'm a tired old man myself," he said, "and have no claim or education with the throne. I wouldn't perform any better than Anastasius, and I'd likely be killed within a fortnight of my ascension."

Basilius shook his head. "The throne is only supported as long as the military backs it. Your soldiers here and in the field will

The Last Dying Light

ensure our success. Many emperors of the past understood this well."

"Yes, but they were also killed with alarming frequency by their friends and servants and left the Empire in ashes and ruin," Justin countered.

"There are no other real challengers, and we will not make the same mistakes as the usurpers of history," Basilius said. "It must be you, or one of those cretins will take power and have us all murdered for a night's entertainment."

Shadows danced over their faces as the brazier's embers burned low and coated the walls and ground with soot and ash. After a time, Justin sighed deeply and nodded. He bade me to depart and wake him an hour before dawn, and thus the plan was set. I instructed a night servant to wake me in a few hours, and descended to my quarters in the bowels of the palace, asleep as soon as my head hit the straw.

A few hours later, Samur shook me awake, not trusting the other servant to properly execute orders to a manner he deemed necessary to keep his brother in the continued favor of our dominus. The outer hallways were still dark, but Samur had lit a few tapers that revealed folded clothing and sandals along the edge of my mattress. Samur had always feared the black void of a closed room and often cried out fearfully in his sleep, and would have slept with the candles lit if I had not reminded him of the risk of fire. Now, it is hard to imagine being grateful for something as insignificant as a handful of wax tapers, yet then, for those in our position, even these were luxuries. Our windowless room was bare; we owned nothing to decorate the smooth stones of the walls. Still, the fact that the two of us even had our own room, however small, was a minor miracle. Justin made sure that we slept in comfort and security, and for that I could not grumble.

I took a torch from outside the room and walked through the empty servant's hallway toward Justin's quarters. Even in the darkened haze of night, the Imperial Palace was normally a buzzing hive of activity underneath the elegant imperial rooms and halls, yet now they stood hollow with eerie silence. In the wing of guest chambers, Justin's room was almost as sparsely decorated and furnished as our own, the feather bed and stuffed pillows the only indication of the old warrior's accumulated wealth. I gently nudged my snoring dominus awake and prepared him for the day ahead.

That day began no different from the countless I had lived before. Crisp winter air promised another dry and bitter afternoon along the Bosphorus Strait, sending drafts through the palace grounds. While the palace itself lay still, Constantine's city bustled with noise and movement even in its waking hours. Hundreds of thousands of people brought dozens of spoken languages, cooked foods, and religious houses within its walls, yet those same people brewed a horrifying smell throughout the streets, laying growing numbers of dead, victims of plague or a brigand's knife. The palace grounds were surrounded by multiple layers of interlocking fortifications, although the city was so vast that a merchant could spend a year navigating Constantinople's countless alleys and stalls and never come in contact with the palace or its guardsmen. I spent many mornings looking out through the palace balconies into the Sea of Marmara, and that morning could have blended in memory with so many others. But it would not, and has not faded from my mind even now, for it was that morning that my dominus, a humble outlander turned Roman general, became ruler of all.

A door slammed. I ran to the Emperor's chambers in time to see Justin walking out of Anastasius' room. He looked at me, twitched a smile, and requested I bring two scribes and as many witnesses from the Imperial Council back to the Emperor. Justin sighed and sat heavily on a nearby bench, where he drew his sword to gaze at the whorls and outlandish runes that adorned the blade's length. It was a beautiful weapon, easy prey for any young boy's attentions, and I found myself sorely tempted to sneak my own private glance of those indecipherable symbols. Yet I dared not risk Justin's ire; my survival and life of relative comfort balanced upon his love and trust for a barbarian child birthed along the distant northern plains. I would not annoy him.

Still, even at a distance, I could see it. The hilt was forged as a dragon belching the sword's blade from its mouth; its wings formed the crosshatch and its tail snaked down to the steel and bone pommel. As a small boy, I lusted after that blade with every fiber in my body, but I never would touch it. Justin only drew the blade in times of greatest melancholy or distress.

"Everything is going to be different," he said softly, more to himself than anyone else.

And so it was, for all of us.

THE ASCENSION OF JUSTIN

THE AILING EMPEROR DIED just a few nights later. Justin's coronation immediately set the Roman government to rights, with old military comrades and government councilors alike swarming their new ruler with requests for gold and slaves to finance any number of construction projects or business ventures across the Empire's provinces. Justin addressed each with the gravity that had made him famous as a general, and he always ended each day weary and joyless. Yet even as dark circles began to sag under his eyes and flesh melted from his already thin frame, he always found the vigor to smile and pat me on the shoulder when I appeared.

Going about my duties, I often found the new emperor in private conversation with his nephew, Flavius Petrus Sabbatius. A lesser-known soldier, Petrus Sabbatius was rumored to hail from peasant origins along the Illyrian coast, yet benefitted from a close bond with his uncle, who had paid for an extravagant education that surpassed even that of the children of the Imperial Palace. I can recall Petrus Sabbatius as a young man who, though polite, remained distant and cold, never meeting my eyes or deigning to ask my name.

By the time of Justin's ascent, Petrus Sabbatius had grown well into manhood. After my dominus named him as the heir to the imperial throne, he adopted a new name for himself—Justinian. Despite Justinian's youth and quarrelsome reputation as a statesman, none questioned the honorific, save Justin, who hinted his annoyance at his nephew's haughty assumption of the offered privileges.

There was truth to both sides. Indeed, Justinian was wily and shrewd, but what gave him his power was that the new Emperor Justin, for all his virtues, was unlettered, and could not so much as write out his own name. As such, not a single missive reached Justin without his nephew reading it first, and Justinian undoubtedly reframed their contents to fit his own purposes. It was not uncommon to see the two huddled together in the darkest hours of night, administering to an empire that spanned three continents, with only a host of burning candles to cast their shadows across the palace's marble pillars.

Despite Justin's days now brimming with taxing duties, he still found time to supervise the education and training of his foundlings, including myself and my brother. Some councilors wondered why the lord of millions, the heir to Caesar, would waste an education on barbarian slave boys over a new crop of Greek prefects, but none dared to question him. So it came to pass that Samur and I, along with a handful of others, were all given lessons in writing, Greek and Latin, and early training for combat. Justin also insisted that Samur and I train our fluency in Herulian and Hunnic, the latter a tongue spoken within many of the Empire's elite bands of barbarian warriors known as *foederati*.

Only two subjects were denied us: the Christianity practiced in Constantinople and anything of statecraft or governance. The former was prohibited due to Justin's staunch deference to Pope Hormisdas in Rome, and it was natural that his slaves should follow his example. The latter was a more cynical refusal; by law, slaves were denied the right to an education that could empower them to ascend to government official. More so the better, for I did not want to become some ink-stained clerk tallying shipments of grain at the city's harbor. Such men ground through their years in a resentful slog, hardly venturing more than a few thousand paces beyond the stone boulders at the city boundaries.

Rather, my desperate hope was to become a warrior. I constantly imagined myself wearing Justin's interlocking scaled armor with the Imperial banners flapping against the breeze. It was a hunger that grew more gnawing, yet less likely to be sated, as the years went on, for no commands within the Roman army would accept slaves. Even the lowliest positions of undertrained and poorly armored *limitanei* border guards were available to freedmen only, with slaves only fit to dig latrines or attend to the personal needs of camp officers. Nevertheless, in Justin's first year as emperor, I had gathered the courage to seek his blessing for such a position, but he merely shook his head and promised that my time would come.

So, rather than pursue my desire of soldierly glory, I submitted to Justin's insistence that Samur and I first take full lessons under Petrus Marcellinus Felix Liberius, one of the Empire's most experienced ministers, who took few pupils and would rather be left to his own schemes. Some men whispered rumors that Liberius was so old that he was a childhood friend of Romulus Augustus, the last boy emperor of the West Roman Empire. Others further alleged that the two had been lovers, for no one could recall Liberius in the company of women. Liberius scoffed at such inquiries into his youth as foolish prattle, telling us that wagging tongues wrought unhappy ends. He came to spend his days either advising Justin to throw all courtly flatterers and eunuchs into the Black Sea or educating the Emperor's foundlings.

"Too much for an old man with a bad bladder," Liberius had often said, "yet this damned city has few enough men that can read, and the Emperor always requires what poor counsel can be made available."

For despite this false humility, Liberius had the strength and vigor of one far younger, and indeed loved to trick others into thinking him a feeble, brain-addled fool who had outlived his usefulness. When I asked why, Liberius only grinned mischievously and told me it kept irksome little boys from asking too many questions.

At our first meeting since Justin's ascension, Liberius hobbled into our classroom, took a seat, and stared off into the distance as if in a trance. It was hard to tell how long we sat in a fearful silence, not daring to interrupt our teacher, yet we were worried that this was just another test of character, bravery, or something else that made sense only in the old man's mind. Samur squirmed in his wooden seat, and some of the older students shot amused glances at one another, making crude faces and tossing small pebbles to one another when they deemed Liberius not paying attention.

That contest was interrupted by Basilius' daughter, Antonina, who often sat as the uncontested ruler of the palace's children and foremost instigator of misbehavior. Clad in similarly expensive garb as her aged father, the eighteen-year-old Antonina took pride in flashing her sapphire silks or the intricate golden chains that decorated her arms and throat. Such boldness, bolstered by such wealth, won her the favor of many of her highborn classmates, either out of genuine admiration or out of a desire to curry favor with the daughter of a senior Imperial minister. Antonina looked upon my brother and me as undeserving interlopers into this privileged assembly, but her scorn was returned in kind: Samur was known to place tiny nails on her favorite schoolroom bench or loosen its legs before she sat.

That morning, for whatever reason, Antonina took a small, smooth pebble into her hand, drew back her arm, and threw it right at her venerated teaching master. It bounced off Liberius' chest and onto his desk in a clatter so faint that it may have easily been mistaken for the creaking of the palace walls.

Liberius, who had been paying us no mind, now shuddered to attention.

"Samur, stop fidgeting!" Liberius cried, his trance disappeared. "I can't abide fidgeting. It looks as though you're doing something unseemly—*and* in public." He drew a deep breath. "As I was saying before I was so rudely interrupted, it is preposterous that we continue to refer to ourselves as the heirs of the Roman Empire. Most of our esteemed government men cannot speak Latin without difficulty, and Rome has long been absent from Constantinople's rule in lieu of the Goths that we look down upon. Our lands shrink piece by piece each summer, and our people starve and die off in greater numbers each winter. Who can we call truly Roman anyway? Most of your parents were not even born in Italy, yet you claim a kinship with the Italians of the old Empire. We are neither Roman nor a true empire, but a collection of poorly behaved cities that quake at the thought of the barbarian wrath waiting at our every frontier." Antonina did not miss the insult to her father, Basilius. She replied in her haughty voice that the Eastern Empire was always the greater of the two, and that our lands were rich in gold and manpower, and so on.

"The Herulians"—Antonina smirked in my direction—"the Vandals, the Goths, the Persians... it makes no difference. We are the superior race, and will live on for thousands of years to come."

Liberius smiled. Then, too swiftly for Antonina to move, he hurled the pebble straight between her eyes. She shrieked. Tears of humiliation welled in her eyes, and she sputtered the beginnings of a protest sure to be rife with the indignation only a scorned noblewoman was privileged to speak. Yet Liberius gave her no chance.

"I've been to Rome, and I've seen what the tribes can do against our perfumed soldiers," he said calmly. "Rome has been trounced countless times by the Huns, the Franks, and the Gepids. Persians pace at our borders, hungry to devour what remains of Rome's east. The Goths and the Vandals both ravaged the Eternal City like it was no more than a pliant whore, and the Goths still rule with the Senate under its heel, the Roman men as their slaves, and its women as their playthings. Even if he never enjoyed the spoils of Rome's conquest, Attila nevertheless led to our destruction. In the years since, we've only shrunk in size and grown in fear."

The Last Dying Light

Liberius took a breath. "And if you ever strike me again, Antonina, I will grab you by that pretty collar and throw you headfirst onto those dung-riddled streets you so love to disdain."

Samur, brightening at the rout of his hated Antonina and the mention of his much-admired Attila, sat at attention. "But, master, if the Huns were such fierce enemies so many years ago, why did their empire crumble so quickly, and why do they serve us now?"

Liberius laughed heartily. "Now I've definitely proven my point. A Herulian slave takes upon a shared sense of history with his Roman captors." He looked intently at his pupil. "Well, Samur, we have one advantage that the Huns and all the other barbarian tribes do not. Can anyone tell me what that magical gift might be?"

Silence fell. Most students avoided their teacher's gaze, unwilling and unable to give the answer. Some of the bolder ones tried varying answers—gold, slaves, history, and even the favor of almighty God—which won them no more than a disdainful look. Even Antonina attempted a guess—"the love of the common people?"—which Liberius seemed to delight in scoffing at. Still, when no correct answer came, our visibly saddened teacher insisted on more answers.

"Civilization," I said at last. "Civilization, and the belief in protecting civilization."

Liberius stared me down, trying to unsettle me with his flinty eyes.

"Correct, Varus. Civilization." His tone was gruff as he began a slow turn of the room. "The Huns, and all the other tribes that followed, value only strength. Attila knew this and leveraged both brutality and an unbreakable will to forge an empire that stretched from Gaul to Media. The Huns, Goths, and others value bloodlines, and they propped up the less fortunate offspring of past conquerors, yet their holdings quickly evaporated after the death of their great leaders. Without civilization, all that remains is darkness, where lands fall into chaos and honest men turn into bandits or worse. Such a system is fragile beyond words, yet it keeps the darkness at bay and allows us to build a world that our children may inhabit unburdened by nightmares of death and screams."

At Samur's desk, he paused.

"Attila's strength united the tribes to defy Rome and proved just how fragile true civilization is. We continue to lose more of Rome's heritage each day, and any attempts to shore up our resources and maintain what we have left is like pissing into the wind—fleeting, messy, and doomed to fail."

With that, Liberius moved on, yet I did not. My mind remained on Rome's fall from grace. Attila had died some sixty years ago or more, without ever advancing on Rome, yet dozens of the Hunnic leader's vassal tribes still savaged the lands and kept the Eastern Empire as an incomplete piece of a formerly great whole. It was widely known that the Huns themselves collapsed under the weight of their own conquests: Attila's sons, unable to hold their people together, had disintegrated into smaller and smaller tribes along the northern plains. Some Hun clans did remain loyal to Attila's family years after, but it was rumored that the last of Attila's progeny perished years ago.

Despite their history, Anastasius had welcomed Huns into his Roman army as both officers and common soldiers alike, albeit in units that separated them from their fellow Romans and other barbarian tribesmen. The growing need for professional soldiers and the declining recruitment of Eastern Roman citizens had forced many emperors, now long dead, to abandon the old legions in favor of a new military structure, one that embraced new combat tactics and enlisted these men, men of barbarian tribes long known to be hostile, as footmen, horsemen, archers, and naval commanders. I had to suppose that if Julius Caesar could glimpse what the Roman armies had become, he would neither recognize nor be able to command such a force.

There was also a need to reduce the staggering expense of armoring, equipping, and feeding tens of thousands of soldiers and sailors throughout the provinces. With only the broken and rusted armor, the Emperor's field armies and limitanei border guards had traditionally relied upon plunder from enemies or outright theft of the local population for personal enrichment. Only the Emperor's elite guard, the excubitores, received the best iron and leather procurable, their expenses covered by the Imperial Treasury. Prior to his ascension, Justin had been the commander of the excubitores, and he bore the interlocking layers of polished iron proudly, despite his advanced age.

As I reflect, I realize it is essential to understand that few in the Empire's armies at that time retained the privilege of personal wealth or patronage from one with such resources. Though the Empire could call upon over a hundred thousand armed men to its defenses, few of those men resembled the disciplined and trained soldiers from the time of Augustus or Trajan, nor did they share the common morale that propels soldiers to utmost heights of personal sacrifice. Instead, our armies were demoralized and uncoordinated; individual generals brandished local power and even paid out silver coins in exchange for the loyalty of junior officers and spearmen alike. Though all pledged an oath of allegiance to the Emperor, Justin had worried as much about the pressure of invasion at the Empire's borders as he did that those within those borders would rise in rebellion. None ever did, as I now know, yet Justin's closest advisors had always been certain a revolt was close at hand, calling for reform after reform to return the army to the disciplined glory of the legions of Pompey or of Caesar himself.

Though I sought Liberius' praise through apt attention, it was weapons instruction with General Godilas that caught my boyhood longing. Godilas was one of the Emperor's closest confidantes and a veteran of a dozen campaigns along the Ister River. Godilas had a face striped with battle scars and a body that was steadfastly burly, even after decades in the service of Rome. Where Liberius was responsible for strengthening our minds, Godilas molded the boys into warriors for Rome's future armies.

Liberius was a serious and sober taskmaster, but Godilas frequently turned to drink and had a penchant for joviality around those under his tutelage. He worked his pupils from the time of their arrival until well after sunset, hurling bawdy jokes and drinking from his wineskin. Occasionally, Godilas would even chaperone his pupils on a riding lesson outside the city's famed double walls, though such sojourns were limited to a single day. Even astride a horse, Godilas hid a wineskin in his pack and gulped it down as he trotted along.

"Don't ever follow my example, boys," Godilas cautioned one day. "A soldier's first job is to fight with a clear head, even if most of them choose not to."

When one of the other boys asked why he sought to break this sacred rule, he had only replied that if we had seen the things he had, we would understand all the better. Hypocrisy be damned.

Samur and I both loved our time in the training yard. Now, many years later, I understand the necessity and seriousness involved in hardening boys for future service in the army, yet in my youth I saw it only as a game. A game that I excelled at from my very first attempts, no less, which was even better. I was always broad and tall for my age, and the years of work under Godilas only chiseled me into a bigger, stronger athlete. We began each practice by wielding blunted swords against wooden soldiers crudely shaped in the image of a Persian Immortal, with our master-at-arms pacing closely behind to criticize each misstep or undisciplined thrust.

"Pierce and jab, boys! You aren't cutting wheat with those blades!" Godilas would shout as he walked, stopping only to criticize those trainees who clasped two hands around their mock swords. "A Roman soldier is only as strong as the shield to his right and the spear to his left. That means if you cannot shield your comrade to your left, you are dead, and he is dead, and the wall is dead. So stab! Quick cuts, lads, and no chopping at those Persian bastards."

Where my muscled form grew stronger from Godilas' instruction, Samur's smaller, lither build—though it would later make him deadly fast in a fight—turned him into the target of the burlier boys in the training yard, none of whom felt camaraderie with a barbarian foundling. Samur never complained at their aggression, and indeed, it rarely amounted to much more than an overzealous tussle after an individual fight had long finished. He just grinned in bloody indignation and fought on.

However, by the end of Justin's first year on the throne, the minor bruises turned more dire, and I would often find my brother sobbing on his bed with a host of angry welts on his body and face. Though visibly pained, Samur rarely asked for any assistance, and never spoke the names of his attackers. Instead, his eyes flared with a raw hatred, a desire for real revenge. The helplessness I felt left a sour taste in my mouth as I tried to sleep. I tried, too, to ignore Samur's moans of pain, but could not stop occasionally rising to offer aid that I knew would be promptly rejected.

A few years later, however, when I had reached the age of seventeen, Samur's injuries became impossible to ignore. As I was leaving one of Liberius' lectures on my way to the training grounds, I heard a moan from a small meeting room in the western end of the palace. Inside, I found Samur bleeding onto the marble floor, his shield arm bent askew and his breathing rattling with bloody spittle that betrayed at least one broken rib. I shouted for help in a panic, yet I was able to make out one word in the low moaning of my brother, "Solomon."

That bastard. Of all the cruel entitled Roman children trained in the Emperor's palace, Solomon was the cruelest, and therefore their natural leader. Bull-headed and broad-shouldered, Solomon rounded up sycophants thanks to his family's position in the Imperial Court and his sponsorship by Justinian. But he was also a treacherous coward, and God help me, if I had known then the anguish he would eventually cause to the world, I would have cut his throat as a boy and tossed his body into the Golden Horn. Other than Justinian, I doubt many would have minded.

That afternoon, with Samur barely able to speak, I raced to the practice field, guessing where Solomon might be, and indeed spotted him across the yard, surrounded by a half dozen fellows, laughing and gesturing lewdly. A couple of years my senior, Solomon had acquired a formidable physique, and bore the aquiline nose and pointed jaw typical of Rome's Italian families.

Solomon brushed a thick, dark mass of hair from his sweat-strewn face as his eyes met my own at a distance. I could see him smirking as he scratched at his scalp.

Godilas, meanwhile, had been in the midst of yet another lecture on proper sword and spear technique, and concluded with barked orders to pair up for sparring. Still intent on Samur's tormentor, I ran toward the corner of the training yard where he chuckled with his comrades. Our fight was set: Godilas, thinking this little more than boyhood rivalry, threw training swords at our feet. Still smug, Solomon whirled his blade around as if to show that I was no match for him.

"I'm going to beat the shit out of you, slave. Then you can join your bastard brother," he said, so low that only he and I could hear. His haughty grin disgusted me.

I grabbed my own sword as Godilas gave the signal. Solomon shouted and swung his blade with a long, arcing slash that would have beheaded a small ox. With that, he had already lost.

In a pitched battle, as with individual fights, underestimating your adversary means death. Solomon was a sizeable youth, larger even than I, who stood a head and a half taller than most grown men. He assumed he could cut down a Herulian savage with brute force alone.

But his blow was slower, clumsier than a true swordsman's. I caught his blade plumb near the hilt of my own. The force of the blow rippled up my arm and through my shoulder, numbing my hand in a manner that nearly saw the hilt slip from my weakened fingers. I whirled beneath our interlocked tournament swords, jamming the iron-sheathed rim of my shield against Solomon's throat as I emerged. Shock flooded his face; the blow of the shield knocked him backward. Stumbling, he choked for air as I delivered a flurry of blows at his legs and trunk. He feebly raised his blade, stumbling backward, wheezing painfully. The look in his eyes was as real a plea for mercy as I'd ever seen from him, but it was no use.

I thought of Samur's twisted body lying in its own lifeblood, and mercy became impossible. My vision went white at the edges, and a giddiness overtook my body that seemed to slow the passage of time itself. I lunged my shield and sent Solomon's legs swinging wildly. He dropped his own shield, still staggering, and I drove my sword arm toward his calves and flank, raining blows with the blunted blade.

"You bastard!" I screamed, deaf to his whimpers. "You gutless bastard!"

He lifted his sword, a sign to yield, yet I did not stop, not even at the crunch of broken bones. Openly weeping now, Solomon lay prostrate and unarmed on the training sand, and I raised my own weapon to deliver a blow that would have sent my enemy straight to God's mercy.

Yet before I could, someone flung me to the grit of the ground.

"Did you not hear me, Varus?" Godilas cried. "That's *enough*!"

Godilas pinned me down, lest I rage up once more, as one of the other boys fetched the medic. Solomon had collapsed in a heap of blood, bruises, and the stink of loose bowels and fresh piss. Palace guards ran onto the sands and half carried, half dragged me to Godilas' private rooms, where they were careful to lock the door behind them.

At the familiar sound of the key twisting in the bronze lock, the truth set in, and any lingering bloodlust was drowned in a horrible wave of realization. Even in the training yard, no slave could beat a patrician bloody without consequence. And Solomon was a patrician's patrician, his family one of the oldest and most elite to claim Rome's ancient heritage.

If they were merciful, I would merely be condemned to the copper mines in Arabia—a fate that generally meant death after a few excruciating years of deprivation and pain. Worse, with his protector gone, and anger against us stoked, Samur's torment and beatings from Solomon's friends would surely increase. Strangely, however, it was not the punishments that struck me hardest; I was most ashamed that Justin and Liberius would scold me as a savage unworthy of the civilizing influence of Rome or their favor. I'd brought this suffering upon myself, and now those I loved would suffer from my choice to bloody a Roman citizen whose only crime—beating a slave—was legally no crime at all.

Perhaps an hour later, Godilas unlocked the door and sat down at a squat desk along a corner of the office. The old general ran his hands through his thinning gray hair. Solomon's blood still stained his tunic, and sweat poured down his scarred temples and cheeks.

"Well, Varus." Godilas sighed. "Let's get out of here."

"Lord?" Surely this was some sort of trick.

"The Blues are racing today," Godilas said. "Aren't you a supporter?"

I nodded. For whatever reason, my master-at-arms was not punishing me but, curiously, escorting me to a chariot race. It seemed a miracle. Justin's priests had often lectured on the goodness of God in delivering the wicked, and in that moment, I believed them absolutely.

Wordlessly, I followed Godilas out, his gait relaxed, mine stiff and fearful. I was deathly afraid that this was some sort of trick, that I was being duped into a jail where Godilas could deposit and leave me forever. Instead, he led me down one of the winding passages that connected the palace to the Hippodrome, where he unbolted the door and beckoned for me to follow him through the palace door and into the Emperor's personal box—Justin detested the races, I knew, but allowed his inner circle to take full advantage of his seats. Though the day's races had not yet begun, the din of a rancorous crowd was already swelling in the massive horseshoe-shaped circus. Godilas stopped near the door and gorged from his wineskin.

"That sound has a different meaning in battle, Varus." His face was grim.

"Lord?"

He sighed, his gaze slack, and I knew he was gathering the words for one of the battle stories his pupils lusted to hear and he reviled telling.

"Six years ago, Anastasius sent a division of spearmen to challenge a Hunnic war band that threatened border villages along the Ister River. Justinian, a man with no battle experience and little patience for strategy, was given command. We marched in full armor for two days and nights, stopping only to evacuate our bowels and eat our rations." Godilas took another deep drink of his wine.

"After fording the river, when our spearmen were on the brink of collapse, they came. Howling like wolves, they emerged from the forest and trapped our war band against the river, except in greater numbers than expected. Rather than a small raiding party, the Huns had recruited Herulian and Gepid raiders to join them in setting an ambush, which Justinian blindly walked right into. We formed the defensive square, yet still they came, wailing and screaming like demons. The sun was nearly set, so a few of the Hun outriders threw flaming torches just out of our reach, illuminating our shields and marking gaps in our lines for their horse archers to fire upon. We dropped by fours, by fives, and still they fired hell upon us. I was hit in the shoulder—the arrow cut through my mail like soft cheese—but I counted myself lucky. So many others were dead or dying slowly from wounds that would never heal."

"Lord, I…"

Godilas silenced me with a hand. "When all seemed lost, and the lines started to break, and I was sure that day would be my last, a horn sounded in the distance."

As if on cue, horns blared along the Hippodrome track that signaled the next teams of riders to take to the sands. Godilas scratched his chin and took an aggressive swallow of his wineskin, seemingly unwilling to continue. Yet as the noise of the track mounted to its normal roar, he concluded his tale.

"That is when a previously unknown Illyrian barbarian named Belisarius led a *banda* of Roman cataphract cavalry straight into the Hunnic lines." Godilas' rumbling tone took on new energy as his eyes gazed into the distance. "Armored in those thick iron scales of theirs, the cataphracts broke the barbarian alliance. Belisarius himself struck down the rabble's leader. It was over in moments."

The empty wineskin fell to the marble. Godilas was drunk. "If it weren't for a fortunate scouting party from a nearby Thracian outpost, we would have all died on the banks of that river."

His stare was deep, sad, a stare that had taken in so much. "It doesn't matter where you came from, Varus. Roman, barbarian, slave, noble… it makes no difference. If you have the patience and skill, a man can pull victory from an otherwise ignominious defeat. You have the heart of a lion and the craftiness of a wolf. You just need a cooler head."

I stared at him, unsure how to respond to something not only so intimate, but so potentially treasonous; slander against the Emperor's nephew was punishable by death. Godilas said nothing further, absorbing the cheers from the Hippodrome as he rested a palm along the palace doorway. He opened the door to a wave of thunderous noise from the crowd, and we entered the Emperor's box. Several bejeweled and lavishly garbed men and women were already inside, chatting busily near the front railings, so Godilas led me up to a seat near the rear. He bade me to sit and disappeared back into the tunnel leading to the palace, leaving me in the supervision of yet another of the Emperor's councilors.

"Godilas mentioned that you were the fastest swordsman he had ever seen." It was Liberius, sitting alone just behind me. "His mind may be broken, but I wouldn't bet against his knowledge of blades."

For all his complaints of old age, Liberius could somehow move silently and invisibly, even in a crowd. He rose from his seat, came to sit gingerly next to me, and placed his beloved staff on the ground with a chuckle.

"Fast, but brutal," Liberius said. "No wonder. Solomon probably deserved it, the little shit he is. Always falling asleep in my lectures and pandering to his cronies."

How my teacher knew of my transgressions so quickly after I'd committed them, I did not know. Liberius was a man who prided himself in knowledge, from learned scholars and whispering spies alike. And in the Imperial Palace, the only privacy to be found was inside one's own head.

"But, Lord, I do not understand…" I stammered. "Why am I not being punished? Why was I brought here?" My voice cracked shamefully as hot tears threatened to trickle onto my cheeks. "I nearly killed a citizen. Slaves are put to death for far less."

"If there's anything that you students refuse to learn, it is that the old rules are dying." Liberius gave a pointed sigh of exasperation. "You cannot expect to receive equal respect with the Emperor or his family, but otherwise? A man is what he makes of himself, whether he bears a famous name or not. Besides, how would Solomon's father take the knowledge that his darling son soiled his trousers in a fight with a Herulian slave, even if he was one of Justin's foundlings?" He grinned. "Say nothing more of this—it is resolved. Though I would advise you to avoid mauling any of your peers for at least a month."

As the charioteers took their marks, my teacher put an arm around my shoulder, leaving me only more confused as to my standing. The crowd, a churning mass of blue and green, cheered for their respective teams with such fervor that the roar was felt more than heard, even in the covered Emperor's box. The Blue Faction was generally supported by wealthy aristocrats and businessmen—with a few notable exceptions—and typically were the favored teams of the Emperor. Consequently, the Greens held the loyalty of everyone else: the common workers, the slaves, and the poor. Every man in the city held loyalty to one team or another, and even the most destitute beggar had a trinket to signal their favorite charioteer.

Indeed, so popular were the races that the Imperial Court subsidized the events, distributing gifts of salted meat and ripe fruit to spectators—less out of magnanimity or sporting camaraderie than as a means to soothe any disquiet over things like high taxes and the ceaselessly looming threats of pestilence and war. Supporters of various team factions were even invited to voice their desires to the Emperor's ministers. The Games were a rare channel where free citizens mingled easily with their noble overlords. Merchants and wealthier artisans among the Blues might seek trading rights or an abatement on Imperial tariffs on their goods, while the laborers, dockworkers, and farmers pled for relief from their toil. All such requests were funneled through Justinian, who strategically granted or ignored the entreaties based on how important he deemed the plaintiff to the broader goals of the Empire.

The Last Dying Light

Yet the boisterousness of the political jockeying was nothing compared to the pounding fury of the chariot races. For each circuit, eight four-horsed teams assembled at the starting line as the crowd screamed and chanted with riotous anticipation. Sweeping purple banners unfurled along each of the Hippodrome's U-shaped walls, the center display marked "S.P.Q.R.," a ceremonial holdover from centuries ago, when matches all began with a salutation of the Senate and People of Rome. Then, trumpets blasted in unison and ushers hushed the crowd's booming shouts as tens of thousands of heads turned toward the Emperor's box, where the editor of the races would hold forth, proclaiming the Emperor's glory and generous sponsorship of this show of athleticism, whether or not the Emperor's chair was occupied. That day, skeletal Basilius stood from the editor's position and waved the crowd silent, but not before throwing a private wink at someone—a richly dressed and younger woman who I couldn't help but notice stood distinctively apart from the collection of older statesmen and ministers. She smiled politely at Basilius, her back straight and chin high despite the heavy jewels at her hair, ears, and throat.

"He's loving every moment of this," Liberius whispered to me. "Justin eschews the games, yet Basilius profits from them."

While I wanted to think the races had some sacred, or at least righteous, purpose for the Roman elite, Liberius was correct. For every four coins earned at a brothel or gambling house, Basilius took one for his purse, even though, as the Emperor's closest advisor and an envoy to a host of Imperial trading partners, his fortune was already considerable. To me, he was the opposite of old Liberius, who never sought personal gain, even when doing so would allow him to flaunt his healthy disrespect for most Imperial ministers and flout the court customs he so loathed. In my older age, I understand that profiting from the vices of others is to be expected, and is not even repulsive given certain circumstances. Yet in my youth, I saw Basilius only as a leech on a dying world, unaware of the dreams that he shared with my dominus, Liberius, or Godilas.

Villain or no, Basilius filled the cavernous Hippodrome with a deep, rich voice that told of the Empire's great virtue. No other civilization in all the world could build such architecture, he exclaimed, or fill it with the greatest athletes in the history of sport. Basilius extolled not only the Imperial Court, but also our benevolent Emperor Justin, who loved his people so that he bestowed these merriments upon us.

Yet after the expected paean to the Empire's power, Basilius' speech took a turn for the unexpected. "I have invited a great friend of my family and the Emperor himself, the young Theodora"—he gestured to the raven-haired woman to his right and paused for effect—"to give the starting signal in the glorious name of Emperor Justin, and the people of Rome!"

At the sight of Theodora, the crowd erupted. She gracefully edged to Basilius' side, lifted a slender arm to the heavens, and brought it down in a bejeweled fist. All eight chariots shot forth, whips cracking at the horses' backs as every charioteer muscled his way through the pack. Pillars of dust plumed behind pounding hooves, and chariot wheels strained and rattled at their hubs. Death and dismemberment were close at hand, waiting only for one false move, one slippery grip or faulty step, yet nothing could disrupt the sheer, untamable joy of thousands.

Unlike those thousands, Liberius had his eyes on the woman with raven hair, the unexpected honorary editor. This, then, was Theodora. There had been rumors that a former actress by that name had bewitched Justin's nephew Justinian, but this woman was no pox-scarred wretch or a lewd slattern told of in gossip. No, the true Theodora was astonishingly different from the stories; even a ways away, I could see she carried herself with a natural sureness that crackled any room alive. As Liberius took her in, she laughed at one of Basilius' comments, then turned to meet my teacher's gaze, her deep-green eyes unblinking and locked on his. After several moments, she smiled and returned her attention to the race.

"As I said, Varus, everything is going to be different," Liberius said, as though resuming a speech stopped only seconds ago. "You will be cast aside unless you can realize a greater ambition for yourself. You will never be an aristocrat, but any man can make a name for himself in battle."

Any man except for a slave. Then, as now, Romans did not allow slaves to enlist, preferring the service of freemen or those barbarian conscripts. The fear was that the well-trained slaves would be too docile to fight within the shield wall, while the impudent would simply seize their freedom and escape. Even in the Empire's darkest and most desperate days of invasion and civil war, military slaves were relegated to the dull and the grueling, like galley slaves manning the oars. No slave was permitted to raise a weapon in battle, and battle was the only path to glory.

Yet whether Liberius considered these conventions in his reasoning, I could not say. He scowled as Basilius attempted to flatter and impress Theodora, who brushed his forays away—decisively, though not unkindly—as she watched the races intently from her seat. Casting a glance about the box, Basilius spotted my teacher—or, more precisely, spotted an opportunity to cut short his doomed conversation with his lovely guest of honor.

"Liberius!" Basilius said jovially. "I never knew you as one to favor the Games."

Basilius' sapphire cloak billowed in the wind that swirled inside the box, a colorful display of support for his favored Blues. My teacher, by contrast, wore his typical black wool. Justin had often remarked that, with his black hood and wild beard, Liberius dressed the part of a parish priest, lacking only a clergyman's tonsure and meek tongue to complete the disguise. Of course, no one could be further from a soft-spoken man of God; Liberius had a flair for the dramatic, and no love for anything beyond sound philosophy and wicked mischief.

"I've only come here on business, which has been completed," Liberius said tersely. "I must attend the Emperor, who has no time for these games. However, I know you will be so kind as to watch after my pupil Varus here."

Basilius wrinkled his nose, an expression that brought to mind his daughter Antonina. "Liberius, I'm not so sure…"

"Of course he can sit with us!" The cheerful voice came from none other than Theodora, who patted the empty seat beside her. "Come sit next to me. This race seems poised to be a memorable one."

Liberius flashed a rare smile at my newfound friend. "I leave you with Theodora, Varus. Heed her words, and do not return to the palace until the races have concluded."

Taking his leave, he slipped back into the tunnel toward the palace, and I dutifully scurried to Theodora, who, if she noticed Basilius' sighs of annoyance, showed nothing on her face. All was drowned out by the thundering chariots below, besides; from the front row, I had a full view of everything: the scores and scores of bodies crammed in the stadium's benches made somehow tiny, the aisles adorned with dozens and dozens of sculptures of the old, false gods and goddesses of early Rome. The white marble of the circus glowed in the afternoon sunlight, its splendid candor marred only by grit and sand roiled by hooves and wheels. Samur had often, and rightly, called the Hippodrome a great mouth, hungry for the easy meal of a few thousand Roman bodies. Rival gangs within the Greens and Blues needed little provocation to turn violent; a good race almost guaranteed a half dozen bodies would need disposing of by day's end.

As we watched, Theodora's perfume washed over me, hinting at the sorts of citrus fruits I had cut and served to the Emperor. She smiled at me, and up close I saw how stunningly white and straight her teeth were, contrasting to the decayed maw of most Roman citizens and the crooked display within my own mouth. "What do you think, Greens or Blues?"

"Blues, of course, my lady." I grinned, perhaps showing too little reservation in answering my social superior.

"Of course! I'm not so optimistic today, though." Theodora laughed. "What is your name?"

"Varus, Lady, of the Herulians."

"Varus?" Theodora's soft mouth gave my name—once barbarian, now Romanized—a gentle shape. "Are you attached to the foederati?"

"No, Lady," I said softly. "I am a personal slave to the Emperor Justin."

"Well, I won't tell if you won't, Varus." She winked and took my hand.

I was a boy who grew up around coarse warriors and callused scullions. Theodora's was the softest skin I had ever felt, her fingers so slight and delicate that I was sure they would break like glass under the slightest pressure. She was slender in figure, yet her voice revealed a deep strength that no one fragile could possess. "The Blues will need all the noise they can get today, no matter whose chest it resonates from." She offered a reassuring pat to my knuckles. I was mystified: who was this woman?

Rising cheers swept away any further talk as, down below, the race careened into a ferocious conclusion. The charioteers had run several lengths, and now—and only just now—were the swiftest amongst them breaking from the pack. Three vied for the lead: two Blues, one Green.

The favorite was unmistakable. "Pe-re-nus! Pe-re-nus! PE-RE-NUS!" cried the mass of Green spectators in impressive unison.

From what I could see of him, this Green charioteer was far younger than his Blue competitors, who trailed by just half a length. The Blues cracked their whips hard, and blood oozed from their animals' flanks, yet the horses pushed onward with only a whinny of pain, faithful to their masters' command. The Blues were gaining.

"That Green driver, Perenus, is an exiled Laz prince from the Old Kingdom of Colchis—did you know?" Basilius nodded at Theodora, eagerly seizing on an opportunity for the lady's attention. "A fine rider, surely, yet he's only a boy, unwanted at his uncle's court. They say he doesn't even use the lash on his horses for fear of hurting them. Clearly naïve."

"I would argue that makes Perenus wiser than our own charioteers," Theodora said. "But I am only a young woman, and perhaps too naïve to know the difference."

"Hmph." Basilius opened his mouth again, shut it, and fixed his attention back to the match.

As if on cue, the Blue riders had whipped their chariots to sidle up by Perenus. Only a handbreadth apart, the outer Blue driver cracked his leather whip across Perenus' horses, snapping thin red stripes into the beasts' white hides. The other driver rammed the side of Perenus' chariot again and again, finally knocking him off balance and nearly sending him tumbling into the dust. It was opening enough: Both drivers now hammered against the Green, over and over and over. Wood splintered in all directions as the young Lazic driver scrambled for his footing.

Locked together, Perenus and the Blues hurtled down the track as the Games' flag bearer signaled the final lap of the race. Seeing their champion ravaged by the detestable Blues, Green supporters flung half-eaten food and empty cups onto the track, and the more inebriated fans shouted threats of violence that were soon made good. Shoves turned to fistfights , dustups into wails of pain and injury, and all stoked hot anger that spilled across several rows. All the while, those few sober Greens kept up the chant of "PE-RE-NUS! PE-RE-NUS," hoping to will the charioteer to his feet.

The Last Dying Light

It would be daunting. The twin Blue carts did not relent their attack, leaving Perenus only a perilous one-handed grip away from a fall and a broken limb or even broken neck.

Now the final turn was at hand. The one Blue racer reared back his whip and lashed Perenus' arm, and his grip was lost. The other rammed Perenus' chariot again, this time with a crash hard enough to knock him off his feet, off the driving platform entirely.

A hush fell, so quickly and entirely that one could still hear echoed cheers from just moments ago. These days, many who were there recall what happened next differently. But from the near-perfect view of the Emperor's box, it seemed like Perenus floated an arm's length above his chariot. Either from sheer instinct or blind luck, Perenus flailed his arms forward and *caught* the horses' reins! He pulled to the left, landed hard on his feet—his horses keeping pace—and leaned into the final turn of the race. The silence sundered as the Greens erupted with applause and cheers. Even Basilius mouthed a silent expression of awe. And even I, a boy avowed to the Blues, could not help but marvel.

Far ahead of the five other competitors, the three leaders completed the turn in a deadlock. Perenus fed on the crowd's energy as he urged his exhausted horses forward to a tiny but noticeable lead. His win—a Blues loss—was imminent. The Blues driver closest to the audience wall signaled his partner: another collision against the Green chariot. They sped closer, drew closer, and at three or four armlengths from Perenus, launched to crash, both at once, into their adversary.

Perenus should have died. Any other, less fortunate, chariot driver would have taken the impact of two carts at full speed and been fatally crushed, and anyone paying attention expected as much. But Perenus, somehow, knew better. He anticipated his rivals' move. As they drove inward, he reared back on the reins, pulling his horses to an abrupt halt. The two Blues skimmed past, colliding into one another in a direct and devastating hit. The outer driver's chariot, unstoppably propelled, catapulted its driver against the inner wall. Body and cart exploded in a mist of wooden shards, metal spokes, and blood. It is said that a few lucky fans were able to pry teeth from a nearby stone wall, to keep in commemoration or to sell to a more ghoulish enthusiast. The inner driver fared only slightly better, as he was ejected from his platform and trampled underfoot by the few horses remaining on their feet. He lived, as I found out later, although he was never again able to chew his own food or relieve himself without assistance.

Unscathed, Perenus diverted his beloved horses around the wreckage and across the finish line to the thunderous euphoria of Greens across the stadium. He lifted his arms in triumph and shouted to the heavens, only fanning the chants of "PE-RE-NUS!" to a frenzy, as those who, only moments before, were convinced their champion was doomed now rang with celebration. Perenus, the prince and victor, grabbed a Green flag and carried it through his victory lap, stopping before the Emperor's box to salute the valor and achievement of Emperor Justin.

Basilius and Theodora nodded and waved back politely, yet the crowd had no ears for the Emperor. "Greens! Greens! PE-RE-NUS!" only grew louder as few left their seats and turned joy into revelry. Others cheered the victory, *"Nika! Nika!"* Though I knew better as a slave than to express such emotions, I jumped in my seat, clapping my hands together as I gaped in wonder at the Green rider. Theodora laughed and patted me lightly on the shoulder, the touch of her fingers burned into my memory even into my old age.

"An unfortunate display, my lady," Basilius said after Perenus swung his chariot into another victory lap.

"I cannot disagree more, my lord Basilius," Theodora put in lightly. "He may be a Green, but that charioteer put on a marvelous race, and outnumbered as well! I think I would like to meet this Lazic princeling."

Basilius stroked his chin, looking skeptical. "That may be unwise, my dear. The mob is often riled up in the aftermath of the Games, and this race will give them plenty to celebrate."

For all his distaste for the Greens—indeed, for most people under his station—Basilius was not wrong. Rome had been infested by armed gangs on each of its hills and collegia for centuries, yet Constantinople had largely been spared this plague until Anastasius' reign, and by Justin's first years, small riots and fits of lawlessness ran rampant in the city slums after a race; even several *bandae* of dedicated spearmen could not quell them.

"If you will not accompany a lady in need, good Basilius, perhaps Varus will attend me instead?" Theodora put forth, and fixed her eyes upon the racing track below as Basilius formed his reply.

Basilius had been routed. He would not be able to sway his less-than-pliable guest, and he knew it.

"Very well." Basilius scowled. "Take Varus and two of my guards. The Hippodrome crowds will have little respect for their betters after such a match."

Bowing to Basilius Theodora and I rushed out of the Imperial box and down the marbled Hippodrome steps, the armored swordsmen behind us could barely keep up in their efforts to separate Theodora from the pockmarked and impoverished masses below.

I pressed through the clinging stink of thousands of bodies, shadowing Theodora with a mixture of shared excitement and sinking guilt. From her first words to me, Theodora had awakened a need to see what a mysterious character such as she might further offer—not any sort of carnal need, but a need born of wonder at her charm. There was a sense, at her side, that any small action or trivial choice could lead to a greater adventure. Yet, though I longed to follow Theodora, each of my steps was dogged with the issue of my brother's welfare. Somewhere in the palace, he lay lonely, his body racked with pain. At the same time, the lady could not travel safely through the city on her own, not tonight. So I resolved to return to Samur's side immediately following Theodora's return to safety. But as we reached the lower levels of the Hippodrome's benches, it was clear that any choice I'd made was forfeit.

A few rows from the bottom, a flowing throng of more belligerent civilians seethed before us, still drinking outrageously oversized tankards of strong ale sold by the more enterprising gangs in attendance. Alone, I could have disappeared into the crowd, into safety, but if I did so now, I would leave Theodora one protector short when she would need all she could muster. The sounds of Samur's feeble cries fled my imagination as another danger reared its head—a danger to Theodora most of all.

It was Theodora's gift to be unmistakable, unmissable, and here that gift was made a curse. That one of the braver or a more inebriated racing partisans would be eager to grope an expensively dressed woman was all but guaranteed. The steel behind us dissuaded such boldness, yet near the bottom of the Hippodrome stands, a careless Green flung a full cup of ale into the air, which landed at my mistress' feet. Whether the insult was deliberate or just drunken foolishness, I could not know; what happened next was far less uncertain.

Disregarding consequence, the guard closest to Theodora unsheathed his sword and cut downward in one fluid motion that cleanly severed through the flesh and bones of the offender's wrist. Blood pulsed through the open stump, the man's wounded screeches more animal than human. These cries, and the sight of fresh blood, stirred up Blues and Greens alike, and soon gang members brandished knives and clubs without reserve. One such rogue jumped behind the offending guard, cut his throat deep enough to sever bone, and left him to collapse in his own lifeblood and the grime of the arena's aisles. Other spectators filled the space where the guard stood, cutting off the steps we had descended.

The Last Dying Light

Instinctively, I picked up the guard's bloodied sword. "Run! We need to run, now!" I screamed at Theodora, her lovely face drained white.

Riven by the sight of gore, dozens of Greens and Blues nearby roared in indignation, pressing closer to our position. Whether by drunkenness or true enmity, several fights broke out among the divided spectators, with others pointing and screaming at Theodora.

Ignoring all propriety, I grabbed Theodora's arm and edged down the remaining steps. Behind us, our remaining guardsman protected our escape and followed soon after. I held tight to the lady's arm, thinking only of her safety; such a gross breach of decorum would easily justify an extended flogging, especially for a slave who'd just that afternoon bloodied one of his betters, but in the face of looming violence, the pretentions of a slave seemed a small thing indeed. And so, spotting a narrow opening through the swirling crowd, I hauled Theodora forward and forward still, until I could lower her to the rough sands of the racetrack.

Some threw empty cups at us, and more than a few yelled threats, which in turn only encouraged more drunken rioters to follow us in hopes of getting in some robbery or a murder to round out their night's festivities. I knew, again, that Theodora made sumptuous prey for poor citizens, who could live for years on the spoils of cutting her throat and stealing her jewels. In her deep-blue dress, she was hateful to angry Greens who saw in her wealth the cause of their own poverty, the Empire that gloated of its splendor and golden riches manifested in one finely dressed woman.

It was one such pursuer who cost us our last remaining guard: a Green who had dislodged a statue—Mars, the old god of war—and thrown it, crushing the guard's sword arm and chest. He was dead before he fell onto the dust.

Theodora leaned for her slain protector, but I tugged at her arm once more.

"This is my fault!" she cried. I remember, even amid the chaos, that her painted and shadowed eyes showed more rage than fear.

"Not now!" I yelled over the roar of the mob, which was more eager than ever to come for us now that our guard was bludgeoned dead. "We need to get out of the arena!"

Theodora nodded briskly, and we hurried toward the charioteers' exit, which mercifully stood open even after the racers' exodus; they had fled, rightly, at the first sign of violence. Slipping through the worn wooden doors, we wormed through the covered hallways on the other side, unsure if the noise behind us was the footsteps of fortune-hunters set on our capture or simply other drunkards taking full advantage of the debauchery. We skirted past the Hippodrome's stables, which were empty save a few horses abandoned in panic, their coats half brushed and cleaned. Following torches on the walls, I led Theodora to a servant's exit and into a small alley. The pungent odor of horse dung was thick and awful, yet not unwelcome, as it discouraged curious bystanders from following us.

I guided Theodora past the dung heaps and into an adjoining alley, glimpsing her pained expression. At our hurried pace, her feet must have been worn raw against her thin sandals; the hem on her luxurious blue dress was already stained by whatever ill humors it had brushed against. Yet she made no complaint, nor any sound at all to register the indignity of her swift descent from honorary editor of one of the most memorable chariot races in generations to fugitive dodging horse shit and rioters. Instead, she followed me closely through a maze of the servant's alleyways to the nearby Hagia Sophia. Safety, surely, would be found in the house of God.

"Bitch!"

A gang leader, and behind him, a rush of followers. One of the Blues ran ahead of the rest and swung his club at my head. Instinct took over: My blade bit deep into his wrist, severing the man's hand

and sending him careening away in a mist of blood and screams. Not waiting, I pivoted and charged into the enemy closest to Theodora with a lunge that would have made Godilas weep with pride. I pierced his shoulder, then lashed out at another, a squat and shaggy-haired creature whose clothing had been stained by caked sweat and sour wine. He was at the end of my reach, too far to stab, yet the tip of my blade still carved into his jawline, sending him howling back.

My head swam with the same giddiness of thrashing Solomon on the practice grounds that morning. Not all warriors experience such a rush, but those who do tell of a feeling of invincibility, when time slows to a crawl and no enemy dare come close to you. I had fought only within the confines of a training yard, and now all the fatigue, emotion, and lingering concern for Samur temporarily faded away, survival and victory my only objective. Now, unlike in my bout with Solomon, I kept my mind clear, heeding Godilas' warning. *A cooler head* indeed. I would come to experience this near-inhuman burst of vigor many times in my life, yet it was this time I remember most, as it would be the closest I'd ever come to certain death. Until the very last, anyway.

However, my battle joy ended abruptly with a club to my left shoulder. As I struggled to fend off my attacker, I tested the usefulness of my left arm, which burned with pain but was movable—unbroken. My attacker reared back for another strike as Theodora jumped on the man's back, stabbing him repeatedly in the neck until he collapsed to the ground. At the sight of the slaughter, one of the remaining Greens dropped his blade and dashed out one of the church's windows and into the street.

All alone, the gang's leader picked up the dropped blade, now holding a knife in each hand. I slashed at him to push him backward, but he first dodged, then attacked, slamming into my injured shoulder with his full weight and sending me toppling into a marble column. He drew back his arm, knife poised to soar toward his target—Theodora—when the alley door burst open in a spray of splinters and chunks of wood.

An arrow sailed from the entrance, catching the last attacker high in the chest. Dumbstruck, the knives fell from his hand as he sunk to the floor, a low gurgling sound emanating from his throat as he struggled to breathe. *Danger.* I jumped upright with my sword in hand and inserted myself between Theodora and the door, fully convinced that the next arrow would send me sprawling onto the ground with my dying enemy. I have never been more prepared to die as in that moment, either from the foolishness of youth or the desire to please a woman who would have fared better on her own than being tied to me.

A heavy boot kicked the remaining scraps of the door open. Six armored Roman soldiers filed into the narrow church entrance. That was the first time I laid eyes upon Flavius Belisarius, and truthfully, he did not look the part of a conquering Roman hero. His face, awash in sweat, was plain and otherwise unremarkable save his clean-shaven jaw and close-cropped hair, as many forwent such vanities as unnecessarily painful and imprecise. However, most striking was the kindness in his face, a quality I later learned made him enormously popular with the masses. Despite his unadorned appearance, he struck a strong figure of youth in his armor, and commanded obvious respect from the surrounding soldiers.

"Lady Theodora, young master, are you both all right?" Belisarius' voice was deep and confident as he inspected the carnage and low flames now growing around the church.

"I am safe and unharmed, thanks to Varus' courage," Theodora said. "But I am confused, Lord Belisarius. How did you come to find us here?"

"We can speak more once we have reached the safety of the palace." Belisarius was nothing but courteous, his eyes still fixed on the rising flames threatening to engulf the church. "This fire is about to grow beyond control, and the gangs are still looting and fighting on the streets near the Hippodrome. Both of you, stay close to my men, and the mob will likely ignore us altogether."

Theodora took my arm. I dropped my bloodied sword onto the church grounds and fell in with Belisarius' men. We exited into the alley, and from there slipped through a different door to the arena that led to the second level. From that vantage point, I was able to glimpse a half-empty Hippodrome, littered with bodies and filth along its rows, and minor fires flickering near the exits. Several statues to Jupiter, Mercury, and Mars had been broken by those seeking stones to throw, while the stairs swam with blood and excrement, leaving poor footing for those still struggling to depart. Farther in the distance, the roof of the Hagia Sophia was ablaze so furiously that nothing but embers and ruin would remain upon the morrow. Then and now, our priests love lecturing about the horrors of Hell, yet I cannot imagine anything in the life to come worse than the chaos of a riot in this one.

Our forward guards pushed their shields against more belligerent members of the crowd, forcing us back to the Emperor's box and the private passage to the Imperial Palace. Belisarius escorted us through the palace and into an empty meeting hall, instructing us to wait for the others to arrive. Exhausted, I sat in a cushioned chair, where fatigue enveloped my body, and I almost fell asleep until Theodora brushed me to attention.

"How is your shoulder?" she asked, clearly worn from the day's exertion.

"Stiff, but it feels fine now," I lied, hiding the pain that still shot up my arm and into my chest. "My lady, I have to ask…" I summoned all the boldness I could muster. "Who are you? How did you get here?"

"I am what I am." Theodora laughed. "Though I admit, I was not always considered worthy enough to be here. I suppose you heard rumors that I have kept residence in Basilius' household over the past few months?"

I nodded, although I did not mention that most such stories had painted her more as a crook-backed harpy than the young woman who stood before me.

"Well, that is only partially true, and I am sure the rest will become obvious soon enough."

Emboldened, I pried further. "And the dagger? Those men—"

"Was that your first time taking a life?"

"Yes, Lady." It was the bluntness of her question that made me finally comprehend the gravity of what had transpired in the church.

My chest burned. My victim's face rose again in my mind, eyes wide and tongue lolling in a mask of death. The urgency of the fight had left no time for reflection that I had taken up a weapon and slain my enemy, erasing all that he was and eliminating all that he would have done if our paths had not crossed. I did not fear the consequences, for any in the palace would firmly approve of my defense of the lady Theodora. Even so, it felt as if a sodden blanket had been lain over my shoulders, and I offered a silent prayer that God might forgive my violation of his law. Whether it was murder, self-defense, or even service as a warrior mattered little, for the conclusion was the same, irrevocable: I had become a killer of men.

"A woman does not survive long in the city without the willingness to get dirty. I was not always dressed in these beautiful—well, once beautiful, now ruined—clothes, and until recently I was piteously alone in this vast city. To my mind, doing what you must to survive gets easier as long as you do *only* what you must. And not a *step* farther," she emphasized. "The knife was given to me by my mother, but I had to learn how to use it on my own."

With that, Theodora stood up and kissed my cheek. "Thank you, Varus. I believe that you saved my life."

I blushed, and Theodora laughed her pleasant laugh once again. Her gratitude leveled me; even if her rumored past as a common actress were true, she was a noblewoman, and no noblewoman had ever lowered herself to speak to me, a palace slave. More than the act of speech, however, was what she said to me—a compliment to my skills when she clearly needed no help of mine to stay alive in that, or any other, dire situation. I came to know that Theodora possessed several innate gifts, but above all else, I took away that she was a hardened survivor.

A knock interrupted us, and Justinian strode in with several attendants. "My love." Justinian rushed toward Theodora, anxious and clumsy as a youth. "Did they harm you? Are you all right?"

"Yes, Petrus," she said. His childhood name. "Varus made sure of that."

Justinian gave me a sideways glance. "If I hadn't ordered Belisarius to watch you from the upper levels, you could be dead by now!"

"You had him stalk me even in the Hippodrome?" Theodora said, feigning outrage. "No wonder he found us so quickly."

Justinian raised his hands in protest. "Only because I can't bear the thought of you being unprotected, *dulcissima*. Now, if we could speak further in private…"

Theodora gestured politely for me to leave, asking that I visit the healers before falling asleep. I agreed and left the pair to their own discussion.

Dulcissima… Sweetest? Justinian having Theodora followed? My mind raced. I had no understanding of why one of the top councilors of Rome would take such an interest in in one rumored to be base-born, even if she was beautiful. Moreover, I did not understand why such a woman would also serve as editor to the Hippodrome races alongside one of the haughtiest men I had ever known: Basilius. Theodora, it seemed, cloaked everything in mystery.

And then—then there was Samur, who remained in the care of the palace healers, the depth of his injury unknown to me. I swore to find him, not sure where he had been taken to convalesce, and took only a brief moment of rest to gather my thoughts. Such worries, as well as the overwhelming press of the day's changes, swam in my head, and I returned to our shared chamber, where I foolishly collapsed in a heap on my straw mattress, my promise to find Samur already broken from oppressive fatigue. Within moments, the world went black.

I awoke to an annoying prodding at my side, and a breathtaking soreness in my left shoulder. My body resisted waking for a few moments until Samur's voice broke my daze.

"Wake up, Varus! Come *on!*"

"Samur?" I mumbled. "You're better already?" Consciousness was slow to revisit me in our windowless room.

In truth, my brother still looked terrible: yellowed bruises across his face, his arm in a sling. Even these injuries, however, could not erase that mischievous grin. "The surgeon said my arm will heal fully, and I should be back to light training in a couple months. Anyway, a messenger came and left this for you."

He dropped a sealed note at my side, the wax indicating the arms of the Emperor. Sobered, I shot upright despite the pain in my arm, broke the wax, and unfolded the letter from my dominus, the Emperor of the East Romans. I skimmed past the obligatory salutations and commendations to the monarch until I caught my name. There, I stopped, dumbstruck.

> *It is by the Emperor's command that you, Varus, the Herulian slave, aged approximately seventeen years, are to be freed from the bonds of slavery and are granted the rights to full Roman citizenship. This is done at the turning of 523 years after the birth of our Lord and is effective upon receipt.*

The Last Dying Light

Below the decree was a thin, spidery postscript. *Come to the Imperial chambers two hours before sunset today, and tell no one.*

I folded the note, eased into my tunic, and belted my coarse leather pouch, tucking the letter inside. There were no words.

Samur broke the silence. "Well, what did it say?"

THE PACT

Just before the appointed time, I began my ascent to the Imperial chambers, unsure of the purpose of such a meeting or what could come next. Many in later years have asked how I reacted to such abrupt and unexpected news, doubtlessly expecting my joy at such freedom, yet in truth I walked forward merely moonstruck. In the turning of a single day, I had beaten a senator's son to near death, sat in the Emperor's box at the Hippodrome, evaded crowds and looters with a woman of rising importance in the Imperial Court, and was granted freedom after a lifetime of bondage to the Empire. More than anything, more even than joy, I felt uncertainty, even fear, for I had no knowledge of any life outside that as the Emperor's slave. My heart fluttered at the thought of liberty, yet my cowardly stomach soured at the thought that my dominus, who had provided for me these many years, freed me only to free himself of that burden.

Whatever my conflicting emotions—curiosity, excitement, anxiety—they all joined in common to drive me to the Emperor's chambers as the sun drew low on the horizon. Those thinly scratched words, *"tell no one,"* only added to my curiosity and anxiety as I climbed the marble steps, especially since I knew their author. It was unmistakably Liberius' handwriting, another mystery amid a day of mysteries.

Questions swirled. Why was I not banished for assaulting Solomon? Why was I suddenly freed? Who truly was Theodora, this lowborn woman who had come to occupy the attentions of Justinian and Basilius? And, most pressingly, why had I been summoned to my former master and teacher? Thus confused, I knocked upon the doors of the Emperor's private chambers, alone.

The Last Dying Light

The door creaked open, spilling light from the many hanging lanterns inside. These chambers were no secret to me—indeed, in Justin's first years as the emperor, I would light these candles myself—yet now I felt this place was utterly foreign, with nothing familiar to comfort me. It was too late to turn back, however, so I steeled my nerve and approached the robed figures within.

I recognized them immediately. Aside from a handful of servants, the room's only inhabitants were Emperor Justin and Liberius, along with one of Justin's many hunting dogs that had taken up residence in the palace's kennels. It was commonly believed that Justin loved dogs more than people, for he only appeared fully at ease around his hounds and away from the garish display of corrupt prefects and self-serving councilors that dotted his Empire. He favored the great Molossian hounds from Epirus, which served equally well as household pet and battle-ready companion for infantry.

Justin, clad in rare silk of deep violet and gold, scratched his dog's head as I entered. "Ah, Varus, good. I hear that you did not seek the help of our physicians, which is certainly to be corrected. Yet first, congratulations are in order for your freedom."

"Highness, I'm deeply grateful," I said. "Believe me, I am. Yet I can't help but ask why? Why now? What did I do to deserve this?"

"What he means to ask is whether you are sending him away for good," Liberius translated, his eyes reflecting the dancing flames of a low brazier.

Justin stroked his chin, as if carefully crafting his response. Seven years in the purple had aged him dramatically, transforming him from a vigorous and decorated general into a weary figure of melancholy. Once gray, his hair hung lank and bone white about his brow, leaving much of his scalp exposed and speckled with tiny broken veins. Even worse was his skin, spotted with age and creased in frailty. His gaze lacked the intensity that had marked him as leader of the excubitores under Anastasius, and he spoke slowly and only after long pauses to conserve his energy. My former dominus and current benefactor was a ghost of his former self, and by this point, even he knew that death, though always an inevitability, was now a looming prospect.

"Ah, well, the answer to your real question is yes, I am sending you away, but no, I am not sending you off alone. If you agree, anyway… for freedom grants you the right to choose."

"Highness, I don't follow…"

"Varus, I should have freed you years ago," Justin said. "I grew fond of you, and your brother, and I came to view you as the children that I was never to sire myself. So I am sorry, Varus. I let my own weaknesses blind me to what was truly best for you."

Such displays of emotion were rare for a onetime warlord of the Roman Empire. "You know as well as I that you will never gain status in government," he went on. "No matter your competence, these patrician families are still so steeped in their resentment of tribesmen. However, the service of a good sword is never refused, no matter the arm that wields it. I've kept most of the world's horrors and hardships out of your life, and until yesterday, I'd like to think I succeeded."

Out of breath, he looked to Liberius. In his robes as black as pitch, Liberius was the antithesis of the Emperor—simple instead of gaudy, hale instead of flagging, wicked and improper instead of solemn and dignified. Most of all, his instincts were rogue whereas Justin's submitted to his sense of honor.

"If you agree, you will be enlisted in the Roman Army once your shoulder has healed," Liberius stepped in. "You can refuse, and live the life of a free, educated young man, and go with our blessing and our assistance. Or you can accept a more perilous fate and take up arms for Rome."

And there it was. My future, laid out in two divergent paths. The former would likely lead to wealth and comfort, and perhaps even a family to follow my traditions as I lived and bicker over my treasures when I died. The latter would be a life of pain and exertion, with a violent death its likely end. Yet it promised the chance, the sliver of possibility, for a glory that would see my name live forever.

"I do not want you to decide until after our meeting," Justin said. "Listen and hear what we want to achieve. What we have waited our entire lives to put into motion."

"Indeed, if I may," Liberius interrupted, no sign of deference in his voice. "The representatives are all assembled in the Great Hall."

Justin nodded, and the two left together. At Liberius' signal, I followed the pair down a flight of stairs leading to the entrance of the Great Hall. Outside of some of the ancient buildings in Rome, the Hall was rumored to be one of the largest in the world, able to shelter several hundred men without the discomfort of cheek to jowl. As we approached, guards threw open the massive bronze-sheathed oak doors, and a crowd of no fewer than a hundred prefects and soldiers, all standing in wait for Justin's arrival, greeted us.

I scurried to an empty corner seat as Justin sat at the head of a long wooden table, with Liberius to his right. From there, I peered out at the room and gawked: Countless lanterns and torches made this immense hall almost as bright as the midday sun. Though I had attended this room countless times before, the looming display always brought me to pause, the thousands of candles casting an ominous glow upon the frescoes that adorned the walls. Busts of long-dead emperors lined the walls, their painted eyes gazing with cold unfeeling at the assembly.

To my surprise, I did glimpse one friendly face as my eyes met Theodora's at the far end of the hall; she offered the smallest hint of a smile and wave in my direction as she sat next to Justinian. Aside from Theodora, no women were present at this meeting, not even the Emperor's own wife, Euphemia. Some delegates near me grumbled at this breach of decorum but fell silent beneath Liberius' heated gaze. From the rafters hung banners of each of the provinces and army battalions that held allegiance to Constantinople, the Imperial Eagle and cross displayed beside tribal wolves, foxes, and other beasts both real and mythic.

On the Emperor's left, skeletal Basilius helped Justin take his seat by moving the Emperor's ponderous robes over the gilded bench. The Emperor signaled that the others, too, should sit, and a hundred chairs all creaked in unison. All conversation ceased. I presumed whatever the Emperor's proclamations might be were unknown to all in the room, save perhaps the Emperor's closest advisors. I heard only the uneasy shuffling of impatient men and the panting of another of Justin's dogs, which had found its way to the Emperor's feet as if to spite the solemnity of the occasion.

Unlike moments ago, Justin now glared with the raw intensity of a younger man. He took his time drawing out the tension in the room, breathing deeply and stretching out the anxious anticipation from his men—for why had the representatives and military commanders of each province been summoned to an audience with the Emperor? What grand pronouncements were to come?

At last, the Emperor signaled for several slaves to unfurl a massive scroll down the middle of his table, revealing a map of the Empire's current holdings and the many tribes and kingdoms at the periphery. Several near the center gasped: The map was impressive, charting thousands of miles of territory lined with stone roads and Roman cities. Surrounding each province were darker Latin markings that signified the many tribes and armies that bordered the Empire, from Persia in the east, to the Vandals in Africa and Libya, to the Gepids, Heruli, and Huns to the north. Holding his gaze motionless, Justin at last spoke.

"This meeting is long in coming, yet is proven all the more necessary by yesterday's events. Our Empire, given to us by Pompey and Caesar, Scipio and Sulla, is dying of a sickness in the soul." Justin's voice, too, was firm and unwavering.

"That sickness is derived from many causes—conflicts in faith, poverty, criminality—yet all derive as branches of a single tree. That tree is our shameful lack of purpose."

More rustling at the end of the hall. The braver attendees shot the Emperor irate glances, offended by the caustic statement. But Justin would not yield, and he slammed his fist onto the table, sending cups of wine spilling onto the floor.

"Our ancestors understood that honor and glory to Rome was everything. This demanded we expand into new lands, conquer new peoples, and build new wonders that would make children hundreds of years from now crane their heads in awe. If we do not build, we die. If we do not conquer, we die." He allowed us a moment to reflect, then raised his voice to a roar. "If we do not expand, we die!"

Any grumbling in the crowd hushed. With all his reserved strength, Justin pushed himself to his feet, and all followed suit. "For too long, I have watched our boys cower in defeat. For too long, we have lost one town after another, surrendering our citizens to be raped and killed at the hands of savages. Too long! But no longer."

He walked carefully along the table. Basilius offered his arm, but Justin shrugged him away. "We will rebuild," he said, drawing closer to the table's center. "We will reform our laws and bring back untold riches to the people. The common people, who need so much and have been neglected for so long." At the center, he stopped and seemed to face down every man in turn. "We must rebuild our empire. We must take Carthage, we must take Ravenna, we must take Rome!" With that, Justin unsheathed a heavy knife from his robes and slammed it home—the center of Italy.

The knife quivered, then stilled, upright. The room was utterly silent. Not even Justin's beloved dog stirred, and the rest of us stood as statues as Justin strode back to his chair. "We must not fail. I will not let us fail." He paused, still standing. "I am not long for this world, and it will be up to the youth in this room to carry out our dream to retake our home. This work will take many years, yet I, while I still have the authority to do so, will begin this great undertaking with four pronouncements."

Now presented tangible goals, action to be taken beyond the lofty ideals of an old man, the representatives sharpened their attention. Scribes scratched dark ink onto scraped vellum parchment, writing carefully, though mistakes in transcription were inevitable.

"First, I levy the creation of new battalions of cavalry and infantry in the regions of Thrace, Syria, Cappadocia, Macedon, and Egypt. New commanders will be selected on merit."

At this, the military commanders banged their appreciation on the table; more attention, and a greater salary to go with it, was imminent. At this, I perked in interest, coming to understand Justin and Liberius' desire to reform the Empire's armies back to a time of strength and honor. More importantly, it offered true opportunity to shift the trajectory of my life, and rise beyond what station I had been condemned to throughout my youth.

"Second, I name my nephew, Flavius Petrus Sabbatius, my heir. He will take your oaths of fealty at the conclusion of this meeting, and will form a new government of councilors to begin reforms domestic and martial." Even louder shouts erupted at this pronouncement, but these were not all of support. Justinian had his faults, but he was undeniably a resourceful and dedicated man. Yet such men are often despised by those who cannot themselves achieve success. At the time, I held little regard for Justinian, my youthful ignorance finding him as just another opportunist offering to relieve the vast burdens of Justin's throne.

"Third, I decree that any male patrician may legally marry a woman of any station in life, giving her his name, title, and membership in his noble household in the event of his death."

Only murmurs at this, calming the din. The wealthy and honored patricians naturally wanted to bar commoners or outsiders from diluting fortunes or political power, but it was immediately clear why this departure from tradition was to be put into practice.

The Emperor's darkened eyes and weary gaze now fell upon Theodora. "Last, I announce the betrothal of my nephew, Flavius Petrus Sabbatius, to the lady Theodora, represented by Councilor Basilius." The youthful vigor was back in his voice. "May God grant them many happy years together."

Though some more conservative members of the delegation hissed, most delegates cheered rancorously. Theodora's beauty and charm had easily won over the younger delegates and military commanders, who saw her as someone closer to themselves than any rigid and powdered lady of proper upbringing. Basilius beamed in triumph, and I could easily understand why: With Theodora as Empress, he would enjoy near unlimited Imperial support. Yet Basilius' triumph was eclipsed by the lady herself, who smiled broadly as she tried to cover her laughter. I beamed at Theodora's delight, for although the woman was still a mystery, I could not help but feel drawn to her, a rare individual who had shown me kindness instead of indifference.

"Go, and tell the prefects in each of the provinces and commanders in the field what I have said here, and make it so. In this, we cannot fail. We must not fail!" Justin slammed his fist onto the table one last time.

At that, all cheered wildly for the old man, any objections or confusion temporarily sidelined. Some shouted his name, which soon filled the hall and echoed out into the night beyond the palace. Others bellowed the old Roman victory cheer *"Roma victrix!"* Justin had given them purpose and hope, something that had been missing for far too long. We would build, we would expand, and we would conquer, or all perish in the attempt. By God, even I was swept up in the euphoria, and just like that, my decision was already made.

The Last Dying Light

RITE OF PASSAGE

A FEW MONTHS LATER, I LEFT Constantinople's city walls for the first time. It was the day of my deployment. Though I had grown familiar with the city's filth-encrusted streets and its dwellings swollen from overcrowding, I had never stopped to consider what sort of life lay outside of the capital's walls. True, I had heard of peoples and lands far from our own from Liberius' lessons or the words of a writer long deceased, but going to see them with my own eyes had never seemed a real possibility. Thoughts of open grass, deep woods, and distant and near-legendary snowcapped mountains all fed my excitement, even as I knew, deep down, that such freedom came at the price of enlistment. I was now enmeshed with the Roman Army, and what that would mean, I did not know for certain. Nevertheless, it was a jubilant day, and a promising time for many in the Empire. Change was fast approaching.

Though Justin remained as the figurehead of the court, since his pronouncement, he only involved himself in the most important decisions of government. Justinian, meanwhile, had used his newfound power to raise his own councilors and protégés in law, tax collection, and even with military appointments—although, through Basilius, Justin still exercised some authority there. One appointment of note was that of Belisarius, who was raised to generalship over new Roman armies in Cappadocia. I still knew him only from our rescue at the old Hagia Sophia, yet I knew many approved of his rising fortune. Basilius had even betrothed to the new general his daughter, my old classmate, Antonina, who for all her faults was a rare beauty, at least outwardly. To my mind, where Theodora had a golden soul to match her physical radiance, young Antonina's figure still masked a bored, spoiled child who had delighted in tormenting the palace slaves.

The Last Dying Light

Though such excitement would have heaped new obligations upon the palace slaves and attendants, the new life awaiting me meant I paid little mind to the sweeping changes of Justin's government. I was excused from further palace duty, but my excitement at gaining entry to the hallowed class of Rome's warriors did little to dissipate the toxic gnaw of shame: Samur would not share in my newfound freedom. Worse, his still-healing face was fixed with smiles and encouragement at my sudden fortune, his eyes bright and his words honeyed as he told me of the glories that I would surely achieve—even unto my day of departure.

"When do you think you'll be back?" Samur asked innocently, staring intently at a stone path near my departure gate.

"Half a year, maybe more?" I shrugged, my cheeks burning despite the cool breeze in the air.

"Maybe they'll let you write?" Samur's voice was full of sickly cheer that contrasted his usual mischief.

"Maybe," I agreed. "I'll come back as soon as I can. If anything happens while I'm gone..."

"I'll handle it," Samur said sternly, a rare flash of cold fury on his face. "Just keep yourself alive, and don't let these Romans forget who you are."

"Never," I swore. "And with the coin I earn, I'll free you as soon as I can."

Samur smiled weakly, bruised and swollen fingers rubbing his eyes. He shuffled forward and wrapped his thin arms around my chest with some difficulty. Despite the curious eyes of onlookers taking notice of our overfamiliar exchange, I returned the gesture, even touching my forehead to the peak of his scalp as I towered over him.

"I'll pray for you," Samur whispered. "And I'll be waiting."

Poor Samur. If I was a poor Christian, he was a worse one, and even now I cannot be sure which god or gods he entreated that day.

All I know is that before we parted, hot tears pattered against my linen shirt, and that afterward, Samur bustled away from the gate and back toward the palace, his slave collar reflecting sunlight as he disappeared.

Wordlessly, on the back of a donkey given to me by one of Justin's councilors, I passed beneath the city's double outer walls for only the second time in my life, and the first in my living memory. Built by the long-dead Emperor Theodosius when the Western Empire still had its own sovereignty, these walls stood higher than four grown men, the cut and dressed stone several cubits thick. The inner wall nearest the city was protected by an additional outer wall, which, while a bit shorter, was considerably stouter. Every hundred paces were further fortified by extended fighting platforms, where a company of archers could fire down upon an attacking enemy. At the gate, I passed the papers detailing my commission into the army to the guards. Their curiosity and job requirements satisfied, the massive iron-and-wood doors creaked open, and I rode outside the city of my childhood.

A mere day's leisurely ride separated me from the city's walls to my intended encampment, an efficient journey over miles of neatly trimmed and dressed stone roads built and maintained with the same mastery as the city's walls. Even six centuries after the death of the original Caesar, his roads still connected the old provinces with the Eternal City, though their upkeep would startle their original builders. Yet even in the days of Justin's reign, they sped the pace of groups so that two laden ox-wagons could ride abreast of one another without difficulty. For a single traveler, it was more than adequate to bring me to my camp many times faster than over unpaved ground.

I rode on. The sun grew great in the sky, and then, as it waned at last, I glimpsed the purple banners of one of many forts that defended the Great City's perimeter. The East Roman Emperor billeted all but their excubitores in these palisade outposts, both to serve as a line of defense outside of the city's walls and to prevent an unruly general from sowing discord within the city proper. This was all the better for a young recruit, as the crisp air and expansive grasslands granted a refreshing reprieve from the cluttered and dung-riddled streets of Constantinople.

The sentry hailed me to approach, then glanced at my documents with an appearance of interest. I was unsure if he could make sense of the letters on the page—indeed, odds were he could not—yet he spent several moments looking it over and ran his fingers over the wax seal placed by Emperor Justin himself. Satisfied, the sentry nodded, and I entered the fort, handed off my mount to the stable master, and hesitantly made my way to the commander's tent.

Like Justin, Archelaus, the commander of the fort, was one of Anastasius' older excubitores, who enjoyed his elite status by retaining command over one of the more profitable forts outside of the city. Armed patrols were empowered to search all wagons and caravans that entered the city; wise travelers and traders knew to offer gold or silver to guarantee the soldiers' blessing. While officially illegal, this practiced ensured a fort's commander received a regular tribute that could triple their annual wages—a practice that made *Komes* Archelaus one of the wealthier officers in the Roman Army.

As a komes, Archelaus had a personal command of two hundred men, not counting a collection of servants, armorers, and any of the camp followers who seemed to cling to any serious gathering of soldiers the world over. Unlike the looming stone fortifications that made the capital city, this was a rough mixture of earthworks and wooden palisades the height of a mere two men. The palisade was reinforced to allow for fighting platforms every twenty paces and gave archers protection from outside attackers. Fighting platforms gave a clear view from the fort's hilltop, where the Roman road ran within thirty paces of the fort's entrance.

Several banners billowed in the wind, with the largest and tallest signaling the golden eagle of the Emperor, its wings outstretched in a manner of the legions of Marius and Caesar. The squadron itself had no discerning flag, as this banda was stationed here only for a training camp, but Archelaus' personal sigil of a coiled viper on a green field could be clearly seen alongside the Emperor's double-headed eagle.

Archelaus was known as the snake of the army—a namesake he portrayed in his own sigil. He liked to joke it stood for his ability to strike fast in battle, yet even before my departure from Constantinople, I had heard of his shifty and unpredictable behavior both within and outside of a fight. I do not wish to make the man seem some sort of imp—no man could rise so high in the Roman Army without treating his men well and gaining prowess in warfare—yet I would be lying if I denied any apprehension at greeting my new commander.

Inside his tent, Archelaus was arguing with one of his younger centurions. The komes spoke of the need to "beat the humor out of the new recruits," which was met with mild yet firm resistance from the centurion.

"It does no good to hit the men for cheek, sir," the centurion replied, deferential yet unyielding. "They show promise with the sword and spear all the same."

Archelaus glanced up to the latest intruder at his tent door—me.

"Do as you think best, Mundus," Archelaus said, waving an indifferent hand. "But I don't want to hear anymore laughing at the end of drills. They should have no energy for foolishness, understand? Dismissed."

The centurion Mundus nodded, hailed his superior officer, and brushed past me to leave me alone with the Viper himself. Candles flickered, casting shadows that reminded me of the Imperial

Palace's long hallways, and gave me an opportunity to get a better look at the banda commander.

Archelaus was a squat, thickly muscled warrior, with a forked black beard that gave his face a natural grimace. As an excubitor, his military kit was far finer than any I had seen, with polished interlocking scale armor that covered him neck to mid-thigh beneath a crimson cloak. A black-plumed helmet rested on the table near his straw bed, and an impressive array of weaponry lined the walls. While even then I was large for my size, I felt small in the gloom of his commander's quarters, a feeling that his considerable physique did nothing to alleviate, nor did his demeanor as he read that I was here as his latest pupil for military training.

In the many years that would follow, I would meet many who shared Archelaus' predilections for raw violence. Hard years and long campaigns rarely made a man gentler, nor did the tendency to gorge upon the sour wine that was always in abundance in a military camp even when food had long grown scarce. Though Archelaus shared the temperament of thousands upon thousands of Roman soldiers who came before, he also possessed a shrewdness that set him apart from his less-inventive peers. Alone, such a quality would have been a boon to the world, yet raw acumen alongside unfettered cruelty rarely fostered anything other than devastation for anyone in the way.

Yet that day of our first meeting, I knew little of the banda commander beyond his epithet. After reading, Archelaus grunted and tossed the parchment onto his bed, a sorry thing of old straw that teemed with lice and stank of sweat and old wine. Unrepelled by the odor, Archelaus collapsed onto it and drank from a skin hidden at the foot of the bed. Nervous and unsure of proper decorum, I stood stock-still until his eyes met mine.

"The fuck do you want?" he bellowed.

I stammered something, tongue-tied and unable to think of a proper retort. Archelaus did not bother to offer me an opportunity.

"You start tomorrow, so I don't want to see your shit-eating face tonight. Go."

Clumsily, I saluted and rushed through the tent's flaps and back into open air, free of the noxious odors of what I could only guess were weeks of drunken debauchery by the squadron commander, as if no servants were willing or able to clean it. It was not until moments later that I realized that my breathing had quickened and my hands were tremoring uncontrollably—a surprise given the far worse treatment I had received as a slave to Rome. Off to my side, someone chuckled—Mundus, the centurion Archelaus had dismissed prior to our encounter.

"Don't worry, lad, he's not always like that," Mundus said with a slight smile. "And don't worry about him overhearing us. This time of night, he gives no shit to anything other than getting violently drunk."

I nodded and again stammered an introduction, unsure why he would speak to me in such familiar terms.

"The last batch of recruits arrived yesterday evening," Mundus explained, gnawing at a brick of twice-baked bread that had long been a staple in the army. "There might be space for you to bunk in barrack four. It may not look like much, but it's a warm bed in a wooden hut that will seem like a wet kiss from Jesus compared to your tents on the march."

Mundus showed me to a storehouse and asked the quartermaster for a recruit's kit: a rough wool tunic that covered one from the neck to the knees, a pair of nailed leather boots, and a faded crimson cloak that looked more like a horse blanket than military attire. He then took me to his own tent—a surprisingly warm and clean dwelling in comparison to Archelaus' sorry home—and offered a crust of the same hardened bread alongside a ripe red apple the size of a fist.

"Many a man has joined the army for the promise of a regular feeding and holds no shame in that at all," Mundus said, "but by the size of you, you don't look like you've gone hungry in some time. So why are you here?"

I decided upon the truth.

"Because the Emperor asked me to."

The grizzled centurion gave a belly laugh. Where Archelaus bulged with muscle, Mundus had a lean, hard physique. I found out later that he was only five or six years older than myself, yet the heavy lines of his face, thinning black hair, and wild beard looked to have seen far more than twenty-five years. More at ease, I explained my position a bit further, changing Mundus' laughter into light bemusement.

"So, you've met the Emperor?" Mundus asked, seeming unsure whether to believe the boasts of some scrap of a boy who had almost pissed himself in the commander's tent not an hour previously.

I told him that indeed I had, both Anastasius and Justin, although I served as a personal slave only to the latter, prompting several questions about life at the Palace.

"I've never even seen an emperor," the centurion said, "although I've fought their wars and killed their enemies since I was old enough to hold a blade straight. You're a lucky one, Varus. I'm not sure that this life on the hard ground is a life for you. These men are outcasts, delinquents, and men too down on their luck to act normal in polite civilization. You won't get any special treatment here, and you'll work to the point that your body may just rather die than deal with another day's march."

Rather than deflate my hopes, Mundus' words stirred a desire within me to prove myself hard enough to make a name for myself in this banda; indeed, that may have been his intent all along. I would get to know him well in the years to come, yet even then I could see Mundus was a genuine soul amid a ragged collection of killers and thugs. Still, caring nature or no, this warning was a real one. I will never forget the horrible agonies of training, which made my time in Godilas' yard seem like a proper rest.

We talked a bit more of the Palace, of Justin, and of army life, until the last slivers of light disappeared into the horizon, when he showed me to my barracks for the evening. Most of the men inside were already deep in slumber, snoring and farting in a cacophony of the restful sleep that comes from a day's hard labor in the field. I found an empty bunk, threw down what few possessions I had at the foot of the mattress, and collapsed. My last thoughts were of Samur, and I mouthed my own prayer that God would see him safe for whatever fate awaited him alone in the Emperor's care.

The Last Dying Light

THE LEAST OF ALL MEN

I AWOKE TO AN INCESSANT poking at my chest. "Awake, awake!" the strange voice rasped in Latin. "Come now, we haven't much time."

I wanted nothing more than to lash out at this unannounced nuisance, yet I urged my eyes open. It was still dark outside, with only the slightest hints of dawn on the horizon. Mundus had not mentioned when the day's training began, yet since all the others still slept on their straw, it would seem that this intruder was not a military man himself. In the heavy gloom, I made out an old man in a loose robe, with large eyes that seemed weary, almost annoyed at the lot in life God had provided him.

"Up and dressed, Varus. We have much to discuss."

I had not seen this old man the day prior, and I knew Archelaus would never allow someone without any martial aspirations to stay more than a few moments within his rampart. So I could not fathom what sort of person this might be. My curiosity gave me just enough energy to pull myself upright, dress in my new attire, and walk through the cool predawn air to where my visitor awaited.

His dirt-strewn and torn black robes belted with rope, the old man was warming his hands by a fire lit by the sentries returning from their evening patrols. His face was a curiosity—beardless and cragged with a heavy brow and white cropped hair with a peppering of gray. He was a plain man—neither ugly nor handsome—and had only a heavy wooden cross hanging from his neck to decorate his body. If I had passed him on the road, I would have assumed him to be another poor beggar, yet his stock-straight stature and soft hands betrayed a more privileged life than one of toil.

The Last Dying Light

He greeted me with a low acknowledgment and gave his name as Petrus, a Roman priest. Such traveling priests were common along the roads to Constantinople, yet this particular priest was no medicant, but sent expressly by Emperor Justin to serve as my personal chaplain.

I could not help but be wary of such lofty intentions in so lowly a place as a training barracks. "Recruits don't even have servants, let alone a personal priest."

A sliver of light bled across the horizon, yet darkness still ruled the encampment, and only stiff, tired sentries were yet awake. The old man rubbed his hands against the cold, his wrinkled skin as thin as the finest parchment in Constantinople's libraries. He studied my face and frowned. "You are smaller than I expected."

He left me no time for a response, as he raised a bony finger. "The Emperor wishes you to maintain your education and devotions. I will attend to you each morning before your training begins to make this so."

I groaned. I had already grown anxious anticipating the tolls of training, and this arrangement would impose on what little time I'd have for rest. My former dominus, the Emperor, curiously fixed upon my tutelage in Latin Christianity, did not intend to leave me entirely independent, despite my newfound freedom. Surmising my annoyance, the priest sighed lightly, rubbed his dark eyes, and led me to his swaybacked gray mare.

Father Petrus reached into a dark leather satchel loaded to the point of visible strain. Yet it was remarkable: Oiled until it reflected a soft sheen even in the darkness, the bag had been handled with care and was marked only by an engrained crosshatched *Chi* and whorled *Rho*, an homage to Christ the Savior, identical to the Emperor's personal seal and that indelible profession of faith first borne in battle by Constantine long ago.

From this bag, the priest retrieved a thin iron chain and a bronze cross. He delicately placed them into my hands and folded my fingers shut.

"Your friends in Constantinople have seven gifts to return to you," the old man mumbled. "God willing, you shall receive them in due course. They will help make you the man you were always meant to be."

He stopped, drawing heavy breaths after the exertion of his pronouncements.

"The first is a simple cross of bronze," he said, his voice now as stern as his gaze. "This is my gift to you. May it remind you that even as the world falls to darkness, faith will guide you to victory beyond that of any sword or spear."

I stared at the old man, whose hands were still wrapped firmly around mine, as the outline of the cross and chain dug into my palms. Dumbstruck, I nodded, and he bade me depart before the day's training began. Later, I thought of many questions to ask him, yet then I only watched him shuffle away toward a private tent near the officers' section of the encampment. Sluggish from disturbed sleep and the overwhelm of this demand, I returned to my bunk and fell into a daze, still clutching the priest's gift as the world faded around me.

My rest was limited. A cacophony of horns soon blared throughout the encampment, calling the recruits to training. Men stirred in the barracks, bleating protestations of the sore bodies bestowed on them by life in the Roman Army.

The thin wooden door of the barracks burst open, smashing its iron latch against the wall. I beheld the figure of Mundus, his stony face empty of the warmth from the evening before. Hooded soldiers flooded in behind him, brandishing cudgels that they smacked against our bedposts.

"On your feet, whelps," he barked. "The last of you dressed and in formation will be shoveling shit for a new latrine until sundown." The threat spawned a flurry of activity, with all us men stumbling in the dark to don their prescribed sandals, tunic, and cloak as the cudgel-bearing soldiers spat scorn and hatred into our faces. The man who bunked above me tripped on his cloak and smashed his face into a wooden post, swearing a soft oath and spitting a mist of blood.

My new brothers bore the motley appearance of a dozen tribes and peoples sourced from the nearby region, though all spoke enough Greek to understand and obey their centurions' orders. There were auburn-headed Epirotes, their bodies famously attuned to mountain fastnesses for centuries. There were striplings of the impoverished inland towns of Macedonia, all of whom claimed a spurious connection to fabled Alexander. There were even several tall and ruddy Sclaveni, a pagan tribe from beyond the Ister River, whose young men occasionally accepted Roman military service in return for the promise of plunder and slaves. Yet most were black-haired Greeks from nearby Thrace, their Greek as coarse and unrefined as their beards. None were Heruli, however, leaving me few easy friends among the malnourished and grimy recruits.

Under Mundus' keen gaze, we scurried into formation in the training yard, where I could only guess at my place. Seeing my rising panic, one of the other recruits hurriedly directed me into a space in the orderly ranks. Other buildings emptied of their men, until four lines of fifty men stood at attention, still save for the light billowing of cloaks in the faint breeze carried from the distant Sea of Propontis.

We stood this way a good while, fearful of even stealing a glance toward the officers parading along the periphery of the lines. The last remnants of darkness faded from the sky as the sun rose, shrouded only by the barest of clouds. The faint breeze whipped up with rising force, promising an ever-colder day despite the warmth of the sun's rays. I dared not shiver, nor did any other recruit, all of us unwilling to acknowledge the cold that sapped at our energy as we waited, motionless.

Soon enough, the centurions took their places at the end of each line. Toward the front of the formation, a senior officer with a black-plumed helmet walked the length of the lines, arms bulging under the leather and metal that covered his body. As he approached my area of the ranks, I made out the face of Komes Archelaus, who evidenced no trace of the alcohol and bile that caked his tent the day prior. He maintained a deliberate pace, somehow inspecting each man without acknowledging their presence. After multiple silent circuits, Archelaus faced the ranks.

"At all our borders, savages are panting like dogs to take your food, gold, and women. They grow stronger each year, and many have already begun probing for openings into our lands. And God help me, the only thing stopping them are you lot."

He snarled and began pacing again, this time with a sense of anger at the indignity of his situation.

"The legionnaires from the days of the Caesars were *men*, not a bunch of boys still stinking of their mother's teats. The mountain tribes laugh at us when they steal our wheat and rape our women. And I am supposed to hold them off with *you*?"

He spat at us, venom in his gaze that matched the scorn of his words. His pace quickened, his hobnailed sandals pounding into the training ground dirt as he flung criticisms at individual recruits on their manner of dress, stance, or lack of a properly stoic Roman gaze. Still, Archelaus paused at each victim for but a moment. Until he reached me.

"I do not *fucking* believe that the recruiters allowed you into my army. Only a dung-eating catamite would arrive in my training yard with no helmet," Archelaus roared, deep veins raising from his neck and forehead.

My heart froze in white-hot shame. My helmet, though a dented and poor bronze skullcap reserved for recruits, lay forgotten in a bag just a few short paces away in my bunk, safely away from the vituperations of Archelaus.

"Yes, I remember you." Archelaus edged his face closer to mine. "You're the slave that came from the Imperial Palace yesterday. Tell me, boy. Did you get this posting by pleasing the Emperor? I will *not* abide catamites in my army, boy, that is simply unacceptable. If you want to suck cocks for your dinner, Adrianople is only a few days ride away."

Heat flushed my face, but I bit back the urge to strike. My restraint had limits, however, and the honor of my former dominus could not go undefended.

"Sir, I am no slave, and the Emperor—"

Archelaus drove his fist into my stomach, hard. I gasped, and when I doubled over, he rapped my spine with a staff. My knees gave way, and I crumpled into the dirt.

"Do *not* speak until you are spoken to, recruit. In this army, I am your lord and master until you choke blood and favor us with your overdue expiration." Archelaus spat again. "On your feet, immediately."

Slowly, I pushed myself upright, retaking my position on the line. Archelaus decried my every motion, waiting for another excuse to strike again. Despite the pain streaking throughout my body, I stood firm and locked on to my commander's eyes.

"Well, men, we have a new addition to our banda, a soft palace slave who thinks himself better than us. Let's put that to the test. Training swords." Archelaus signaled, and an attendant retrieved a sheaf of wooden blades.

Such swords, meant for instruction, lacked the heft or sharpness to kill, yet from my fateful bout with Solomon, I knew they could gouge eyes and splinter ribs with the proper handling.

"Cephalas, take this slave," Archelaus commanded, summoning a thin Greek from the line to face me. A small boy handed me a wooden blade, modeled on an old-fashioned gladius from the earliest days of the Roman Empire. I gave the blade a few slow, arcing slashes, getting a sense of its balance and weight.

The ranks parted and formed a jagged circle, and Cephalas approached. He was harelipped and slack-jawed, dribbling spittle onto a coarse beard as he approached. Yet his eyes possessed an intelligence that most would have overlooked due to his deformity, and Liberius' lessons echoed in my mind that there is more to a man or woman than the accident of their birth. Indeed, despite that intelligence, I could tell he was a raw fighter with little training or skill.

Cephalas raised his sword to his chest. Though plenty capable of countering blows, the gladius was notoriously a blade whose strength rested in its tip rather than its edge—a piercing weapon for soldiers locked in the shield wall. I dropped my stance, knees bent and arms loose, as Cephalas closed the remaining distance between us. My breathing slowed as I tightened my gaze on Cephalas' movements.

He raised his arm in a wide slash better suited to cutting wheat than single combat. I dodged easily, and his chop to my head bit nothing but air. Cephalas grunted and jabbed again, but this I parried, backing up just a pace to retain strength and momentum and forcing him to overextend.

Frustrated, Cephalas threw another quick jab, followed by a lunge that was as clumsy as it was predictable. I dodged again and hefted my wooden blade down upon his leather-wrapped forearm. I raised my blade to his throat, and he dropped his own, unceremoniously ending the match.

"Disappointing, Cephalas!" Archelaus bellowed. "He is not even Greek! A barbarian! A child could have toppled you into the grass with the skill you demonstrated today." Rubbing his arm, Cephalas handed the tourney sword back to Archelaus' attendant and rejoined the ranks.

The Last Dying Light

Archelaus surveyed the circle of men, hands at his waist. "Barda, Glycas, take a position with shields. It seems our slave has more skill than I expected."

Two other Greeks stepped from the line and grabbed their armaments. A slave boy handed me a circular wooden shield, worn and dented by hundreds of strike marks from previous training bouts. I fastened the straps to my left forearm and tested the shield against the blunt edge of my wooden gladius. My opponents glanced between each other and me as if deciding who would attack first. Eventually, the two Greeks ambled forward, their movements noticeably cautious.

Their movements suddenly quickened as the two recruits moved to my flanks, seeking to find me off balance in an already uneven duel. One struck at my sword arm, and the other at my opposing leg, then both loosed a flurry of blows that sought to leave their target unable to do more than cover and cower.

Yet their blows were weak and predictable, their technique contemptable compared to the skills I'd learned from Godilas. After a few additional exchanges—to better anticipate their movements—I hopped backward. Barda slashed forward and stumbled into empty air. With his eyes wide in alarm, Glycas lunged forward to assist his ally, but I turned the blow aside, unbalancing him then bashing him with the iron boss of my shield. Dazed, Glycas stumbled backward to hoots and jeers from the rest of the recruits.

Barda, now my sole enemy, backed into a defensive position, the bulk of his body behind his shield and his sword pointed forward; of the three I had yet faced, he was by far the best trained. Barda stepped forward and entangled me in a clashing dance of wooden blades. He put up an admirable attack, but soon he flagged, betraying the inexperience of a raw recruit. Despite Archelaus' jibes to the contrary, thanks to Godilas, my body had been hardened over the years to the swords and spears that littered the Imperial Armory. At last, I edged forward, forcing Barda into a desperate defense until I finally knocked the sword to the ground and won his surrender.

"Pathetic," Archelaus spat. "Fine, I'll show you whelps how to beat a cur myself."

The komes tugged his helmet tight over his head, grabbed a training sword and shield from one of his slaves, and bounded forward. For all the previous evening's drunkenness and malodor, Archelaus gleamed in his excubitor's armor, the rattling of tiny iron scales muffled by thin strips of leather, there as protection from a wayward spear tip or an unlucky arrow. Archelaus grimaced beneath his helmet as he roared forward, fluid as a serpent, and leveled the blade at my chest.

He lashed out a storm of blows faster than any I had yet seen. I managed to fend off any palpable hits, yet had no room to launch any attacks of my own. Archelaus pushed forward, forcing me incessantly to the edge of the crowd in a dance of footwork and will.

As he struck, he laughed. "What are you? Hun? Heruli? Goth? All of you mongrels look the same to me."

In the limited respite his taunting allowed me, I noticed it: an ever-so-slight limp as Archelaus transferred weight onto his sword leg. But no sooner had I glimpsed that weakness than he leaned to his right, his shield pressed closer to his chest and sword swaying nigh imperceptibly away from his body. It was but a fleeting glimmer of weakness, a momentary lapse well disguised as Archelaus continued to shift from one foot to the other.

But I had seen it all the same. As Archelaus again shuffled onto his sword leg, I lunged, shoulder firm against my shield's upper rim, at his chin. He nearly avoided the unexpected blow with a sidestep left, but it was not enough. My shield cracked against his exposed jaw. Archelaus' head snapped back with the impact, his plume shaking.

The Last Dying Light

The komes stumbled, pure rage in his eyes. The taunting stopped. He unstrapped his shield and let it fall to the ground and grabbed at his mouth, which was now trickling blood onto his excubitor's scales. His fist tightened around the sword's pommel, and he lunged at me once again, his bloodlust stoked by injured pride. Yet this time, he did not intend to humiliate, but to injure.

He struck again and again, but my shield caught the worst of his frenzy until he grabbed its rim and wrested it from my grasp. Resentment burning off him like smoke, he slashed at my now undefended left.

The crowd had grown deathly quiet, the hooting and laughing gone. It was all I could do to parry. Each strike sent shocks rippling up my sword arm and numbing my hand. I thought if I protected myself long enough, the exercise would end, and I could return to safety.

Archelaus slashed downward in a sweeping arc, which I met with all the force I could muster. Our blades met in a violent crack, stuck in midair, in mid-blow. With all my might trained on the swords, I did not see Archelaus' fist.

Knuckles smashed into my nose, and I was undone as much from the force as from the surprise. Pouncing, Archelaus drove a knee into my gut and another fist into my back, and I sprawled at his feet. The fight was over.

"That's why you wear a helmet, slave," Archelaus grunted, dropped his sword, and stalked away from the dueling grounds.

My nose oozed blood, and I choked and spat. A web of arms lifted me upright as the ranks reformed, with Mundus' voice mumbling into my ear to steady myself, and to slow my breathing. Yet thick gore still poured from my nostrils, and I fought back tears of pain as my commander went about his inspection of the ranks as if the disruption of our bout had never happened. The komes stopped every few paces, berating a recruit for some small transgression or another, until he completed his circuit and returned to the front of the formation.

"None of you are soldiers, but a sad collection of fuzz-faced infants that the Empire has deemed worthy to dispose of. I've fought on the border, and if you think you can survive an attack from the tribes, let alone a pitched battle, you are fools as well. My job is to shape you into men, lean and hard for the Emperor to send to where godless savages need killing. Defy me, and you will be punished. Fall short of expectations, and you will be punished. Quit, and you will be punished. Survive training, and you may even live long enough to gain some measure of profit in service to the Empire... however long that may be."

Archelaus gestured for his team of slave attendants, who took up boiled leather bags that sagged under the weight of their contents. Hand over hand, the bags were deposited at the front of the formation, until they formed a great mound that reached half the height of a man.

"I am determined to break you of your softness." Archelaus' thin lips creased into a cruel grin. "A Roman soldier should be able to march, in full gear, for a half day's journey without stopping for any reason or infirmity. This bag includes the standard weight of a Roman pack. You will run to the next camp and return tomorrow morning. See your centurions for further instructions."

As he walked off, men grabbed at the bags and circled around their officers. The centurions barked instructions, with one exclaiming, "Any man who opens his pack without orders will be whipped!"

Still dazed, I rose to my feet, grabbed a pack, and found Mundus, who had been herding his recruits into a small audience to give his orders. He explained that we were to trot, as a unit and in full gear, to the coastline on the Euxine Sea. At this pace, it was expected to take half a day's exertions. Komes Archelaus had already positioned a sentry at our destination point—known only to the centurions—where the unit was required to take a Roman banner as proof of our accomplishment. Then, Mundus informed us, we would camp near the beaches and return to the fort before nightfall on the following day.

Each of the individual units exited the gates, eager to put the training yard behind them and leave more time for a rest before a long journey back. Mundus placed us two abreast until we, too, departed. I looked back one last time as the gates slammed behind us. There, with his sentries, Archelaus was gazing over the battlements as his unbloodied recruits hurried off into the distance. At the rear, Mundus yelled a command to begin, and our unit quickened to the required pace that would take us all the way to the sea.

Though I soon regained full balance and clear vision, even the casual gait of the run saw my face throbbing and my nose pounding and sore. I sent every breath through my mouth, yet the bitter taste of copper made me gag and spit after a certain number of strides.

My formation partner beckoned for my attention, clearly worried whether I was fit for such exertion. In truth, the march was hardly more than a brisk walk, yet even that light motion seemed enough to keep my nose from healing properly, or even calming its pain. Shrugging, I feigned a smile that sent thick globs of gore into my mouth, and glanced at the unfamiliar figure of the man who would share the next day's march with me.

"Not the best day I've had, that's for certain," I sputtered, still intent on my breathing.

"Aye, but it's still morning!" He chuckled. "And at least Archelaus didn't snap your neck. Something to be grateful for."

His features were largely concealed by the dented bronze helmet worn by all new recruits to the Roman Army, a device intended to signal a lack of status as much as offer a modicum of protection against attacks such as those that Archelaus delivered onto me. A coarse black beard jutted beyond its cheek-guards, making his head appear far too large for his slim body. Tanned skin gave him the look of a foreigner to Thrace, yet with his flawless Greek and shrouded appearance, I could not immediately place his origins.

When asked what brought him into the army, he chuckled again and explained that he had come into some trouble at the Hippodrome. "It was the army or prison," he said, "and I thought a bit of adventure would be better than rotting away in a cell."

The men in front of us laughed as they trotted forward, keeping two paces of separation to prevent the ranks from crashing together.

"I'm not sure this is much different!" the man before me said. "I've been to prison, and the food is about the same as here."

The man to my right grinned and shot back, "The only thing I miss is silence at night. Instead I'm stuck with you lot, a bunch of stinky, farting, snoring cows that were scrapped from Hades' arse."

More caught on and joined the banter—a racket that drew Mundus' ire. Mundus ordered silence down the line, or else he would quicken the pace until we lacked the breath to speak any further.

After some time, we parted from the squared Roman roads, our column snaking into the soft Thracian grasses that led toward our destination along the Euxine Sea. The pliant earth, while not the uniform surface of the stone roadway, was still easy to traverse in the hobnailed sandals of a Roman infantryman. The other columns that had also departed for the march had long separated from view—most far behind, with one column farther ahead. The farther we traveled, the less idle joking and talk ran down the lines. Mundus shouted changes in direction at certain intervals, and gradually the column devolved to the mute trudge known only to those who have walked a great distance without stopping.

To keep my attention away from my bruising face and my growing itch for cool water, I let myself daydream and think of those who I had left behind. How was my dominus, who had fallen into such poor health these last few months of his weary reign? What was he planning with Liberius, my teacher? Most of all, I thought of Samur, and hoped that he would learn to defend himself without his brother for protection. I was confident that the Emperor would let nothing serious befall him, yet I was all too wary of what a vengeful Solomon might do to heal his wounded pride.

Melancholy settled over me. I began to doubt whether I had chosen this commission wisely. In my first full day as a recruit, I had done no more than make a fool of myself and make an enemy of my camp commander. I was no longer a boy, but lacked the prizes of true manhood—a household, a wife, even any serious promise for a worthy future in service of Rome. All I possessed was my freedom, given to me by a sick man who had long outgrown his unruly barbarian servant. Yet even that gift now seemed a poisoned chalice—I was free, but as an outsider, I was the lowest of the low in an army with too many enemies skulking in the shadows. If I did not die—or worse, become crippled by—the exertions of training, the odds were that I would die in some far-flung skirmish, deprived of both a famous name and comrades who would stop to burn my body and send word to my brother that he was now alone in the world.

These dark thoughts were occasionally broken up by the rising pains from my body, which was slowly rebelling against the continuous grind of the march. The leather straps of my pack had begun to dig into my shoulders, chafing my flesh raw with sweat, salt, and friction. My feet had begun to throb, and my legs tightened and screamed for reprieve. Thankfully, the swelling in my nose had subsided, but even so, breathing came only with difficulty as we trudged ever onward. Mundus had not mentioned how far our destination was, yet based upon the motion of the sun toward the western horizon, we should have been nearly there. Rest was not far.

Sure enough, a swathe of blue colored the distance, and a cool sea air blew toward us. Noises of relief and ecstasy rippled throughout the ranks, and even I joined their cheers as one of Liberius' stories flashed before my eyes.

"The Sea! The Sea!" I called out, laughing with a distended tongue that craved the cooling relief of water.

"So it is," said my partner. "Were you a fisherman or something?"

"No." I chuckled. "It's from Xenophon."

"Never heard of him. Was he the fisherman, then? A friend of yours?"

I shot him an incredulous look. Silence, I decided, would be preferable. The brisk sea breeze billowed sweetly against our faces. Sounds of slow and lazy waves filled my head, renewing my vigor, and I concentrated on planting one foot before the other, heedless of the growing pain. Others muttered similar expressions of hope as the salty air billowed through our ranks, yet none showed the same joviality of the early stages of the morning march. On Mundus' orders, the column fanned out into two long lines, and we finished the final miles on sand and pebble beaches. When Mundus called the column to a halt, the recruits fell to the ground, many with groans of pleasure at their finished labors.

My marching companion sat near me, massaging his calves and fussing over one of his feet. "The damned sandals aren't a good fit, and I've been running for the last few miles in a bloody gulch of a boot."

With no bandages or healers nearby, the best I could offer was to clean the wound with the salty water from the Euxine Sea. We abandoned our helmets and gear and walked to the high-water mark of the current tide. I examined him carefully—he seemed familiar, yet he had not served in the palace or with any lords or generals who sought the Emperor's attention. I supposed it was time to introduce myself, and so I did—having no great family name beyond a tribe I had no memory of—as Varus the Herulian.

"Perenus, of the Lazic people," he answered, visibly pleased to have at least one other non-Greek to share the tribulations of physical training.

Perenus. The sound of that name, a name I'd heard chanted and screamed, unleashed a flood of memories that, though only a few months old, seemed a lifetime ago. My fight with Solomon, lectures from Godilas and Liberius, guiding Theodora through a riled mob and a burning church, and of course, the chariot-racing champion of the Greens…

"Perenus," I repeated, half stupidly. "I saw you win at the Hippodrome not five months past. And when you said you ran into trouble at the Hippodrome…"

"Blamed for the whole godforsaken riot." Perenus grinned, his crooked teeth flashing in delight at the recognition of his achievements. "Rather than gold or women, my prize was to choose either prison or the spear."

As we waited for Mundus' instructions, Perenus offered further details of his path to the coastline of the Euxine Sea, gulping fresh air after each sentence. Destruction from the Hippodrome riots had rendered much of the city a smoking ruin, and would cost thousands of pounds of gold to repair. Perenus, a foreigner and driver outside of the aristocratic Blues, was an easy target for public scorn and blame for such chaos. He shrugged after telling his story, brushing aside any loss of wealth or status as he cleaned and dried his wounded foot, which was still bleeding copiously.

When Mundus gave the command to unpack and set camp, the men abandoned any remaining sense of decorum and tore at the heavy packs that burdened their every step on the day's march. I grabbed two of the accursed packs, one for me and the other for Perenus, and headed back toward the seashore. As I did, sounds of protestation, even fury, arose throughout the camp. One after another, the men were discovering the contents of their burdens.

Rather than supplies of precious food, water, and makeshift tent material, our bags were stuffed with sand and fist-sized stones painted a bright red. All packs, including those I carried, were cursed with this misfortune. I scanned the recruits and found Mundus reading over a small scroll that had been sealed in his own pack, his face flaming with barely checked frustration.

As the camp's dismay threatened to boil over into violence and mutiny, Perenus returned to my side to take in the shock. He fished one of the red stones from his pack, swore loudly, and dropped the useless pack to the ground, wincing.

The incredulous din softened as Mundus, hoarse from a day of shouting formation commands, attempted to get his soldiers under control. Men gathered around him—some sitting, others pacing with an unusually frenetic energy given the day's march. Mundus held up a scarred and muscled arm, and when we quieted enough to hear, he explained.

He confirmed what we had already known—none of us was equipped with any of the supplies necessary to make nightly camp. Mundus assured us he was no exception to this hardship, which had taken him by surprise as it had the rest of us. The letter, written the day before by Archelaus, had left simple instructions. The packs, with all of their stones, must be returned to camp.

A wave of confusion spread throughout the men, who in their fatigue had already sought desperate relief from their waterskins. Others, like Perenus, had suffered minor wounds and abrasions that required rest and bandaging. One man, who undoubtedly had never lived near the sea, asked if anything could be done to make the nearby water potable, and Mundus replied that those desperate enough to drink that salted water would go mad, or worse. Others asked if we might prevail upon any local river or stream. Another still volunteered to lead a hunting party for wild game in hopes of finding and slaughtering such animals with whatever rocks and sticks might be found.

Mundus shook off all suggestions as fruitless. He cleared his rasping throat and croaked, "Lads, the only option left to us is to go back the way we came. It is not likely that we should come upon any civilians, let alone those who could care for all of us. We should also not expect to meet with any other detachments from the training camp, as each were given separate staging points to encamp along the Euxine Sea. Even if we did, they will be in the same predicament, and as unable to help us as we would be unable to help them."

Protests rose again, yet Mundus thundered in his deep centurion's cadence for silence, hoarseness notwithstanding. "The sun will set in a few hours. If we leave in the next few moments, we will make it to camp in darkness and avoid the worst of the heat. Delay will only make us weaker and less able to make the journey back." Mundus waited to ensure he had the men's attention. "Do your best to prepare for the return to camp. We *will* make it back, I promise you."

Some still offered complaints and feeble ideas of finding water and shelter, but most had grimly accepted their fate. Men everywhere massaged knotted calves and stiff joints, already thinking to the journey ahead. Someone suggested that we empty the bags of their rocks and sand, carry them most of the way, and refill them closer to camp—none would be the wiser.

"Won't work," Perenus remarked. "Look at how the rocks are painted. We would never be able to replace them."

"We could at least dump the sand," Glycas, my onetime battle foe, said helpfully. "Save weight for the trip back."

Perenus shook his head again. "The sand keeps the stones from jostling around, and the bag more manageable. A little extra weight is well worth the cost if it means an easier time marching back."

"Indeed." Mundus nodded at my newfound friend in a kind of gruff approval. "Perenus has it. Repack your bags and prepare to depart."

Heeding Mundus' command, I attempted to help Perenus fasten his boots to better fit his bruised feet, yet had no recourse for the blood that pooled from the open cuts and onto the coarse leather of his leather straps. My face still stung, and a metallic taste flooded my mouth, yet thankfully I had no serious injuries to my feet or legs. Some suffered similar bodily woes—deep cuts from bootstraps as Perenus had, overextended calf and thigh muscles, and even swollen and likely broken toes from walking into a stone hidden in the endless sea of swaying Thracian grass. Even those not injured panted and lolled with dry mouths and paste-covered tongues, complaining of headaches and dizziness and the lack of lifesaving water.

Even so, Mundus left little time for discussion and corralled us back into formation. The centurion's own face was flecked with sweat and salt, yet he betrayed no weakness as he paced through our lines and inspected all for their fitness for travel. Satisfied, or at least resigned to the ragged reality of our war band, Mundus signaled to start.

The sun had dropped from the sky, yet dusk remained some time off; hidden rays still illuminated the grasslands ahead of us. Even so, ominous clouds had begun to form from the southeast, scattered cotton-white bolls that later grew to thicker and darker grays. Not long into our return march, they darkened over the sun altogether, bestowing a reprieve from the heat that had burned away what little vigor our water-deprived bodies still retained.

In the distance, a violent dagger of light speared the ground, followed by a growling crash of thunder. Many crossed themselves, while others made signs to placate any one of the pagan gods whose cults stubbornly persisted in hinterland hamlets. Many emperors had sought to stamp out such resistance and prevented pagans and Jews from taking up many positions of authority throughout the provinces, but an already overstretched and undersupplied army could not afford the luxury of discharging the faithless. Instinctively, I reached for the bronze cross that had been Father Petrus' gift, cursing inwardly that I seemed to share others' superstitious fear of lightning.

The last slivers of sunlight disappeared behind a wall of gray and black. Lightning fired to the earth nearer and nearer to us, the rumbling thunder a crackling sound, like a great tree being split in half. I shivered despite the humidity, the hair rising on my neck and arms as the dark expanse turned brilliantly bright with each bolt, revealing the churning skies above. On the vastness of the grass plain, we had no cover to take—had we even the time to do so—and so our ragged column could only push onward. Those inclined to pray did so, while others merely kept a wary eye to the skies. I gave a few words of prayer, then grinned at the thought of Samur, who above anyone would have relished the unfettered chaos of weary, dizzy men on foot, stones clacking in their bags, whispering to God for safety from thunder. Perenus cocked his head—I must have had a strange look on my face—and I shook my head in casual dismissal.

The grunting and groaning increased as we went, either from nagging injuries, new injuries, or the constant need for food, water, and rest. Up the column line, men limped and panted despite the casual pace, while others hunched over from the weight of their useless packs. Despite his best attempts to mask his discomfort, Perenus soon joined their ranks, wincing from a cut foot that only bled worse as we marched on.

Yet that was our one command—do not cease the march. Years later, I can see the wisdom in Mundus' orders, which at the time seemed simply cruel. Yes, at the time, I cursed my centurion as my limbs screamed for relief and the rolling thunder crashed overhead, desiring nothing more than a brief respite from our travails. Yet, given our weakened state, even a few moments of rest would be catastrophic. The weakest of the men would likely not be able to go on, their bodies spent, and the column would be forced to halt one final time without water or shelter. In Mundus' eyes, stopping meant death—even in Thrace, which was well within the borders of the Empire and should have guaranteed our relative safety. Our only real option was onward, and though my fatigue-maddened mind could not parse the depth of the strategy, it still retained the ability to obey, and to survive.

The men did what they could to alleviate their basic needs. A musk of piss hung heavy in the air, rising from streams of wet dirt left in the wake of a recruit. Soon enough, men were shitting themselves, leaving piles of dung that littered the path of our progress. Even surrounded by open air and stiff breezes, the acrid smell of human filth grew overpowering to the point that breathing itself was an unwelcome process. And still, thunderbolts arced around us, lighting the path forward as we fought the need to collapse and clumsily dodged the foul leavings of those marching before us.

After an eternity of hours, several men gave out. Their bodies had quit from the sheer scale of exertion. Even Perenus was teetering, his foot already forming dense blisters that leaked blood onto the grass. I threw his arm over my shoulder, taking some weight from his flagging leg. We grunted encouragement to one another, urging ourselves onward and forbidding moments of weakness to tempt us to a halt.

As the lightning grew more frenzied, the swollen air broke at last, and heavy droplets smacked into our helmets. Soon, a torrent of water fell around us. Men cheered and overturned their helmets, collecting what precious liquid they could in the bronze and leather caps. Even here, the march did not stop, with Mundus croaking orders to push forward at all costs. Yet it was easier now, if only a little; the storm had broken the miasma of excrement and urine that had dogged the column for several miles, leaving only a rich scent of soil and wet grass.

The rain drove on unabated, leaving men to drink their fill. I warned those around me not to drink too much or too quickly; such greed would only lead to further stomach pains. Many ignored this, gorging on whatever liquid they had managed to trap with their helmets, but some took heed, sipping carefully to sate, but not flood, their parched bodies.

Yet even the relieving rain soon turned cruel. The sky turned darker still as the storm grew harsher in its swirling gale. Men were shivering, and some tied their cloaks around their bodies in a pointless attempt to shield themselves from the chill air and the torrential downpour. Perenus clung to me all the more as the tempest brewed overhead, leaning his weight on a body near its own breaking point. Fighting the panic that rose in my body like bile, I willed myself to take one step, and then another, and then another. For a moment, I even considered the poisonous temptation of dropping Perenus into the muck, but the rain-soaked cross felt heavy against my chest, and I dispensed with my selfishness and hauled my friend onward.

Some men did collapse. Their friends and comrades picked them up and herded them farther down the path as best as they could, but our pace dropped to a crawl. Even Mundus was half carrying a recruit as I did Perenus, his face pinched with grim determination. No lordly centurion's pride showed in him; this was a man who knew what must be done and simply did it, obstacles be damned.

After hours upon hours of this lumbering and cursing and whipping ourselves forward, someone ahead bellowed notes of sheer joy. Others echoed him, and soon it was clear wherefrom such jubilant hope arose. Our feet, having pounded and pounded over long stretches of dirt and grass, now trod over orderly dressed stone. Mundus had guided us well; civilization was surely near. A man near me struck up an old Greek song of the Trojan War, his rich, full voice carrying his even notes throughout the ranks and across the countryside. Many began to sing along, and the gait of the march rose into a final, frenetic burst of our all-but-spent reserves of strength. Even I joined in, singing with my fellows of the Mycenaean Army as it marched from their homes toward the thousands of ships that sought to take them to the shores of Troy. I was not a Greek; my ancestors shared none of the glories of Agamemnon or Achilles. Yet the soaring notes were a welcome distraction from the throbbing pain in my heels and made hauling Perenus seem less burdensome.

We shivered and grunted yet pushed onward as the rain grew heavier. After some time, swiping thick droplets of water from my eyes with my free hand, I saw a glow in the distance. Though the encampment had only been my home for a day and offered little in the form of comfort, I hooted with blissful relief, tears mixing with the stinging raindrops that slapped my skin raw. The gate emerged into view, and the silhouettes of sentries stalked the battlements. Our journey was ended.

After drawing his column to a final halt, Mundus identified himself and demanded entry, and with a creaking of iron and wood, it was granted. Men filed into the training yard, many still singing in a show of stubborn defiance, and we gathered into the same ranks in which we began the day, standing at wobbling attention as officers surveyed what remained of us. Our uniforms were sopping wet and muck-strewn, stained from sweat and those other less-pleasant bodily humors that had been kicked and dribbled in the long miles from the Euxine Sea. Many, like Perenus, stood on tender, uncertain legs, yet every last man held his chest high.

Archelaus emerged from his tent, summoned by some unseen attendant, staggering on his feet. Ignorant of the rain, he stood bare from the waist up. Droplets sprayed a corded chest tattooed with a

Roman eagle, the design identical to the golden figurines that the age-distant legions once bore proudly into battle. But Archelaus' flesh was carved, too, with the more random marks bestowed by victory: divots from arrowheads and puckers of gashes healed decades ago, all evidence of dozens of battles under old Emperor Anastasius.

Even in the thrum of that downpour, I could hear Archelaus ask if ours was the first group back. "Yes, Lord," the attendant said, as though unsure if this would please or anger him.

With a nod, Archelaus summoned Mundus, who saluted and hurried to the excubitor's side. Mundus looked as shabby and soiled as the rest of us; even his centurion's plume sagged under the weight of incessant rain. Archelaus demanded a report, and how many of us Mundus had been forced to leave behind.

"All present, Lord." Mundus sounded proud, yet sullen. Archelaus considered, then nodded.

"Dismissed!" he bellowed in a deep, almost uncaring voice.

At long last relieved from their labors, the men fell out of formation, dropping bags and stripping off torn and ruined clothing for the attendants to clean or dispose of. Many, single-minded in their drive for rest, stripped naked, grabbed a waterskin and bread, and disappeared into the barracks. For my part, I helped Perenus unfasten his sandals, which fell to the mud, and aided him as he hobbled over to the healer's tent. His cut had spread and taken on a sickly yellow-green color, the sign of a swelling bruise that would cripple him in the days to come. I deposited him in the tent, retrieved food and water, and gave Perenus his share, then wandered over toward my own bunk.

Inside, I threw down my own tunic and cloak, did what I could to make myself dry, and garbed myself in clothing blissfully untouched by the cold and damp of the Thracian countryside. Half chewing on a loaf—my evening ration—I fell onto the straw mat, most likely asleep before coming to a full stop.

LORD OF THINGS GREAT AND SMALL

My dreamless sleep was interrupted with a soft nudge. My dulled limbs screamed resistance, begging for the restored vitality only slumber could bring me. Yet the thin hand would not be denied.

"Come, Varus. It is time for your morning prayers and lesson," came the voice, reassuring but firm. From its timbre, I knew at once it was the priest I had met the day before—a day that had felt as long as a week.

Groggy, I groped for consciousness, and for the cross that the old man had given me. It was still coiled around my neck, where beads of lukewarm rainwater had hidden within the silver chain and left a wet collar around my neck. I stifled a groan as I rubbed sore and blistered feet. The priest exited the barracks, and I slowly reached for a clean shirt and trousers. Though thin and soft, the linen fabric felt oddly heavy around my frame, further burdening strained muscles that protested the task before me. I resisted the temptation to return to sleep and gnawed at last night's crust of stale bread until I'd gathered the strength to walk past the rows of men who snored and stank of musk, mud, and sweat.

As he had the previous day, Father Petrus had prepared his lesson before dawn. Rain had ceased some hours ago, leaving a dark and starry night overhead with just a hint of the day's light to come. When I reached the open brazier where he waited, the priest handed me a candle and a leather-backed codex, and ordered me to read aloud the scripture he had chosen for the day.

The text was in Latin, the language of the Western Empire and the papacy, and one that a common soldier of the East would have had difficulty understanding, let alone reading from vellum. As Liberius had frequently noted in his lessons, the Eastern Empire's fondness for all things Greek left it with little to identify with the Empire of Caesar. True, even in my old age, knowledge of the Latin language remains a sign of education and noble breeding, yet then, for common purposes, Greek had claimed all elements of trade and general society. Samur and I were unusual for our knowledge in the ancient and hallowed language of the Romans, for as barbarians and slaves, we had no right nor reason to study it. However, our dominus insisted that we learn, and thus equipped, I read aloud the thin script that marched across the page.

I confess, I have never been a perfect follower of the Christian God. Of all my responsibilities in the palace, mass—truly, any formal act of devotion at all—received my absolute minimum effort, though I dared not ignore the rituals of faith entirely, as the Emperor Justin had been a pious adherent to the Latin Rite. I am no fool, for then as now, I believe in the power and forgiveness of Christ the Savior, but I would be speaking a grave falsehood if I denied that, in the weeks and years that followed this cold morning with Father Petrus, I would lie under oath, lie with unwed women, and take men's lives beyond what was required as a soldier of the Empire.

It seems easier to me that a person with no knowledge of the great cities of the Empire might adhere more closely to the teachings of Christ, which were by law the religion of the state and its people. However, even for slaves at the Palace, the proximity to senior Church leaders gave us an acute awareness of the many failings such holy men had sworn to avoid. Many priests were just as corrupt and venal as the courtiers and governors who interpreted and executed the Emperor's will, and used the message of Christ for financial or personal gain. It was harder still for an outsider like me to gain favor in the Church, where a Herulian was looked upon with distaste even by those who professed to love their enemies.

Yet there I stood, and Father Petrus patiently watched over me as I read a passage from the book of I Petrus. As I read, I remembered the many questions I had for this old man the day before, and itched for a chance to gain greater insight into who he was and why he was attached specifically to me. The old priest, however, looked silently on as I traced the prim Latin text, his expression startlingly grim for a figure who had been warm and inviting moments before.

Such stern sentiments were echoed in the passage chosen for my first lesson with the elderly man. At the end of my prescribed section was the large-script phrase *"Be sober, be vigilant; because your adversary the devil, as a roaring lion, walketh about, seeking whom he may devour."* When I finished the short exercise, the priest asked what I made of the passage.

I thought to my previous lessons with Justin's priests and gave what seemed to be the expected answer, assuming the old man would nod in affirmation and allow me to continue. I had loathed such tests of my biblical knowledge and understanding as far back as I could remember; the repetition was dull compared to Liberius' tales of Caesar's first voyage to Britain or the legendary journeys of Xenophon. And so, that morning, fool of a young man that I was, all I desired was to end this exercise and return to blessed slumber. My answer was accurate but uninspired.

"That we should be always mindful of our behavior," I recounted dutifully. "Sin is everywhere, and in all things of this world."

Father Petrus smiled and closed his eyes, relaxing. He stilled, the faint rising and falling of his chest the only movement. Many heartbeats passed as I waited for the priest's response, and I grew irritated, thinking the old man had fallen asleep, yet such impatient thoughts were soon swept away by a warning.

"There is a darkness coming, Varus, and it threatens to swallow us all," the priest said. "God is our last great candle in that darkness, yet a vast and hungry evil stalks the land, seeking to take all that it can in its gnashing jaws. I saw what happened to our brothers in the West when they turned their backs on God in favor of their own pride and vanity, and I fear that we are walking along that same dark road, a path favored by the Great Enemy."

"The West... Do you mean the Western Empire? You saw its collapse?" I studied the man more closely now, my curiosity ensnared.

Another silence. "Yes. A lifetime ago, and more, I saw Ravenna fall, and with it, Rome fell into a dark sleep that it cannot seem to wake from. We have so many enemies around us, Varus, even more than the Western emperors had! If we fall to these pale riders, these collectors of men, the last candle of the world's salvation shall be extinguished. All that will be left are men plotting against one another, merchants of death and sin with no hope of salvation."

With that, we fell back to silence and sat around the fire as the sky bled pink and wiped the stars from view. "You did well yesterday," the old man said at last. "The Emperor would be proud."

Now my questions surged. Why was this man here with me? Where did he come from? What were these gifts, and why should I receive them? Most importantly, what was I doing here?

He laughed, waving off my confusion and choosing which questions to answer—not enough for my satisfaction. All would come in time, he assured me, and we would have plenty of time indeed in the months ahead to address each concern in turn. This day, he answered but two.

First, he claimed to serve the Emperor, and had done so for a considerable time. He had known of me since I had arrived with my brother to Constantinople. As for why he was attending to me, well, that had already been answered the day before—it was the Emperor's will. A mere priest does not question the will of an emperor.

Second, he had come from Italy, long ago. He had been in Ravenna when Romulus Augustus, no older than sixteen years, had been forced to surrender the crown of Caesar to the conqueror Odoacer, thus ending the Empire of the West.

"And what happened to the Emperor? His subjects and soldiers?" I asked.

The priest frowned, rubbing his sunken eyes as he recollected. "The young emperor was allowed to live, but only he could say to where he left. He disappeared from history not long after Odoacer's own death." He looked pensive, then went on. "As for his followers? Most died at the hands of the Goths and Heruli. Some were allowed to live, but most were butchered in Ravenna and in Rome. Within a few decades, even those military commanders who held out against the growing darkness succumbed to illness or death in combat, fracturing Caesar's legacy into dozens of tribes who knew no religion but the sword."

I considered pressing for more information but thought better of it. We warmed ourselves by the fire as the officers' tents stirred with activity. The priest broke the silence one final time, thwarting the chance of any escape to the barracks for a last morsel of rest.

"As I said, you did well. Archelaus is a brute, but he will make you into a good fighter. Pay him and the others respect, but do not back down from a challenge. The army despises weakness and makes it impossible to recover from once witnessed." His final warning conveyed, he offered a parting grin and a hand upon my shoulder. "Godilas would be proud of you, too. You have already become a fine swordsman."

How did he know this, too? I demanded, politely, to hear how he knew the old general from the palace.

"Another day," the priest said. "You must prepare yourself for another morning of tribulation. Remember our lesson."

And so camp life went. I would be woken in the early morning for lessons, participate in drills from dawn until dusk, and spend what little time left to me gathering the strength for the next day. Though Father Petrus had been friendly enough, the mystery of his origins and the imposition upon my mornings made me question his intent to remain in our camp. Yet any such questions, no matter to whom I posed them, were met with a brusque response.

"Archelaus was paid half his weight in silver to keep the old man safe," Mundus grunted, chewing at a chicken bone during our midday meal. "Get used to him, because there is no way our komes will return those coins to the Emperor."

The camaraderie of the barracks, at least, offered a respite from my labors or studies. From that second day on, I was invited to meals with Perenus' small group of friends, all of whom were young recruits to the Emperor's Thracian Army. It was a fluid group, with many comings and goings; regulars included Cephalas, the harelipped and bearded man who was first to duel me, and Isaacius, a squat and dark-haired man who confided in us he was a Jew.

With his helmet off, Cephalas could even be described as handsome, if one only took in the top half of his face. He had been born slack-jawed, which gave the impression of dimwittedness to a casual observer. Though somewhat shy and reluctant to share much about his own past, Cephalas eventually revealed it was he who had begun the singing the evening before. I balked in surprise, for Cephalas' face was the last I had pictured offering up such poetry. I grew to know Cephalas as a devoted and competent man who, despite the accident of his birth, had always sought to make the best of things for himself and his friends.

With a bushy beard, heightened brow, and an overlarge mouth, Isaacius appeared uninviting to a casual observer, yet like Perenus was apt to smile at the slightest prompting. Jews were prohibited from serving in the Roman government and army, yet, as I learned, few lawgivers bothered enforcing such restrictions at the lowest ranks of the infantry. Isaacius was careful not to let his identity be too widely known—not even Mundus was aware of this legal quandary, let alone Archelaus. But us, he seemed to trust. Before Isaacius, the only Jews who had crossed my path were the merchants or artisans who weaved through Constantinople's vast population; any Jews who gained entry to the Emperor's government were dogged with vocal displeasure from the councilors. I confess that as a child I had grown wary of Jews, who would kidnap unsuspecting and misbehaving slaves as a sacrifice to their mystic arts; I assumed, as many did, that they were demons, cursed in the eyes of God. Yet Isaacius had neither the tail nor the horns of a demon, and shared our daily joys and sorrows with an unflagging trust. I found Isaacius impossible to dislike, and, eventually, knew him as the man one yearned to tell a joke or story at the end of a day's tedium. We kept his secrets well hidden, and he did ours.

The first morning after the march revealed how much the men had overtaxed their strength. Many required healing, and others, though uninjured, were too stiff or sore for the tasks set before us. Even still, Archelaus gave us no respite, and demanded further exertion that the centurions scurried throughout the ranks to extract of us. By the noonday sun, I learned of the plight of other detachments that were less lucky than ours: Some returned within an hour or two of us, while others did not reach the relative warmth and comfort of the fort until well into the night. Though all had reached Mundus' same conclusion upon reaching the sea—that, having been given no supplies, they should return—some did not do so right away. Some centurions were less lucky with their navigation through the shroud of rain, several of the detachments had abandoned men along their journey back, and riders had been sent to retrieve more than one sodden corpse.

After his murderous forced march, Archelaus had earned the enmity of most of the camp. Yet he scoffed as dead piled up—to him, these were men too soft for his concern, who did not deserve a place in his army, and who would only endanger those real soldiers that held the Empire's frontiers and met war bands and hordes alike in a pitched battle. Archelaus did not seem to care for our comfort, morale, or even survival, but instead sought to inflict pain and hardship both frequently and unpredictably.

"This is nothing compared to what real soldiers must endure!" he would cry. "If you think you are ready for a real enemy, you are dead wrong. When you're marching through the sands of Arabia for days on end with no water, no sleep, and an uncountable army of Persians ahead, you will all die in the first wave of combat. And it will be men like me who will count your bodies and plug the holes you left in our lines."

The following two weeks of training consisted only of physical exercises. Our bodies grew leaner, harder, and by the beginning of the second week, sickness and death yielded to discipline, leaving us a body of men ready to mold into a fighting force for the Emperor. It was not until each unit had sufficiently pleased Archelaus that it could proceed onto the next stage in training, and soon enough, our time had come. Mundus was granted approval to begin our education in combat.

Each day still began with physical exertions in strength and endurance training, yet we spent more time in the training yard with swords, spears, and a wide array of edged and blunt instruments. Other units had already achieved combat training status long before my arrival, while other recruits, like Cephalas, had been demoted and assigned to our unit to retrain after some poor showing or another.

Though I had apologized, Cephalas never blamed me for his defeat and ignominy. He would simply clap his hands and insist life goes on. In truth, he had never been much of a single combat fighter at all, but when placed into the massed ranks of spearmen or swordsmen, he was a man of indefatigable discipline. Roman soldiers were required to be skilled in both single combat and discipline in massed ranks, yet far greater emphasis was placed upon the capability of each solder to move in step with their leaders' commands and with one another. Cephalas did so naturally, easily, and never struggled with formations as he did with single combat.

Godilas had ensured that I had a thorough education in the weaponry of the Roman arsenal, to be sure. But he had also taught me the tactics and tools of the enemy: the many who had prevailed or had fallen under Rome's old legions as well as the newer ones arising in the Eastern portion of the Empire. My fellow recruits had some skill, yet most simply flailed their blades and spears loosely and wildly. At first, the centurions watched disapprovingly, interrupting frequently to demonstrate proper technique with and without shields in tow, even mocking our efforts from time to time.

I had taken to secretly training my comrades more directly. Several had asked outright, having seen my duel against Archelaus, while others approached when they heard I'd trained with a formal master-at-arms in the Imperial Palace. In my experience, men learned best not by drills or pointless exercises, but by plunging right into the situation where proficiency is lacking. For single combat, this meant constant practice in single combat. As we paired off as sparring partners during our daily drills, I took turns with each of my would-be pupils, striking them as they left themselves open to attack and instructing upon the proper defense as I had learned from Godilas and the palace soldiers. Some, like Perenus, possessed an innate dexterity; he took to the footwork and quickly shaped up into a passable swordsman and even better spearman. Others, like Cephalas or Isaacius, took longer to understand the lesson at hand, yet they too grew more competent with each training session. The consistency, the repetition, was what mattered. As the months passed, centurions began to note their approval at our progress. Even Archelaus, upon inspection of our work, grunted his own sort of approval; he could find no serious fault in our technique.

Winter gave way to a late spring. At a half year of service to the army, Mundus awarded me with a command of ten as a *dekarchos*. Though this was no formal commission—the command had only applied to recruits still in the army—it had given me some level of authority and control over the training of my ten, or *kontoubernion*. With a clap on the back, Mundus handed over the small plume that denoted my change in rank, and smiled as I accepted the charge. Giddy, I eagerly shared my appointment via a letter to Samur, who had dutifully sent his own missives each month since our parting. My brief and less frequent responses held a feeling of shame across my shoulders, my nightly weariness from training leading me to procrastinate with my brother. Yet in this instance, I detailed my new position under the centurion Mundus, spending a great portion of an evening scratching Latin letters onto a scroll.

Mundus held command over forty recruits at this point, though this was still far below the strength of a centurion's classic responsibilities from the days of Caesar or Trajan. No clear reason was ever given for this reduction; the nagging rumor told over campfires was that the Eastern Empire, despite its wealth, simply lacked the men to stock the ranks to their intended fighting strength. Emperor Justin's pronouncements had sought to swell the ranks, with some success, but the sheer need for spears and swords at all edges of the Empire remained voracious. Whatever the reason, Mundus did not complain, and set to task the need to train his four dekarchos as instruments of his will.

Father Petrus, despite his professed love of peace and abhorrence of violence, celebrated my military success with a dinner in his tent. Even now, still garbed in the same stained black robes belted at the waist with a length of common and fraying rope, he managed to purchase a small feast from the provisions quartermaster with a few silver coins. Father Petrus insisted that we extend the bounty to my new charges, which included Perenus, Cephalas, and Isaacius and several other men I befriended during our bouts in the training yard. Though Christian devotion was offered to all recruits, Father Petrus did not demand any proof of shared faith, simply offering genial greetings to the men sitting atop the worn wooden stools in his quarters. Instead, the old priest offered words of praise at my success, and rejoiced further still when I named Perenus my second. Perenus flashed a toothy grin at the promotion that, while yielding little increase in coin, charged him with executing my orders over our men, and required him to assume command should I fall on the battlefield.

Our bounty was a hearty cut of beef, its expertly roasted and tender flesh a delicacy we had not tasted during our months as new recruits. The old priest had even snuck in several wineskins which, though sour, were another delicacy frequently denied raw recruits who had not yet earned the right to drink as men around a campfire. We all joked and told stories, yet it was the priest who shone with the greatest joy. Though Father Petrus appeared somber and melancholy during our morning sessions, for this limited occasion, he seemed to forget his age and station as he partook of the companionship of young men whose futures lay firmly ahead.

Training was never easy, yet the banda never suffered the same measure of hardship as we had on my first day. Our bodies were always sore, and bruises common, yet the pain of the training yard grew less and less sharp, and Archelaus' fits of rage grew less common. My men grew more skillful with their weapons, and after a time, were among the most feared in the training yard. Mundus again voiced his approval, even going so far as to take meals with us at times, telling us stories of his previous years of service in Armenia and Persia. He had even fought the dreaded Huns when they still held their power near Dacia, though he humbly admitted that their force and fury had been diminished long ago at the Catalonian Fields near the Gaulish city of Troyes.

The Last Dying Light

Men still spoke reverently about that titanic clash of civilizations—the Huns and the dozens of conquered tribes that supported them under Attila, challenged by a shaky alliance of Western Romans and free barbarian tribes under Magister Militum Flavius Aetius. Western Rome had already fallen into a state of disrepair—vandals in Africa, Seuvei in Hispania, and Goths, Alans, Burgundians, and Franks taking slices of Gaul and Illyria that remained provinces of Rome in name only. Yet Aetius had patched together an army that stood against the overwhelming might of the Huns and held their ground. Legend had it that Attila had consulted a woods witch on the eve of battle, who told him that he would not emerge victorious and that a king would be slain in the fighting. Even so, this did not dissuade Attila, the Scourge of God, who left flaming ruin in his wake. Wilder rumors even claimed that where Attila's horse had trod, grass never grew again—although Father Petrus assured me that this was sacrilegious prattle.

Even in my advanced age, I hear that battle, and how Attila was repulsed from Roman Gaul, still retold in countless ways. However, few tell the story of what came next. I had only heard pieces of it until I joined the army, when Father Petrus had been coaxed into sharing with our small band of ten.

Though victorious, the battle had cost Aetius and his allies dearly. The Visigothic king lay dead, and dozens of minor tribes squabbled over scraps of land and spoils from Attila's camp. While Aetius attempted to reestablish order in Gaul, Attila regrouped his forces and invaded Italy with all the might of the Hunnic horde at his back.

Thousands were slaughtered, perhaps even tens of thousands. Aquileia, once a major city and seat of government and Church alike, was razed so thoroughly that no two stones remained stacked upon one another. As all northern Italy lay sundered, Attila came south to take Rome.

The Emperor of the West sent three emissaries to treat with Attila to gain his favor. The first promised great riches—more gold than the Hunnic warlord could even imagine. Attila scoffed at this offer, for he already had accumulated enough wealth to found a dynasty for a hundred generations. The second offered power and influence—recognition over all the dominions that Attila had conquered to this point for the rest of time. Attila again rejected that offer, for the Emperor had promised what Attila had already come into possession of. The last emissary, however, caught Attila's eye.

Pope Leo, walking alone with his pastoral staff and white robes, beckoned his enemy to a private meeting. The two entered Attila's tent for a time, and when the Hun emerged, he ordered his hordes to return over the Alps whence they had come. Few knew the contents of that conversation, and the only accepted facts are that Attila had departed empty-handed and stern.

He would never return to Italy again. Attila, the Dread of the World, died from a nosebleed on the night of his wedding to a particularly alluring Gothic girl named Ildico. The conqueror's sons attempted to claim their father's mantle, taking up his sword as the divine right to lead the Huns. Hunnic lore states that the sword was granted to Attila on the Scythian plain, the sword of Mars that granted him dominion over the whole world. The eldest died in battle against his former subjects the Gepids and Heruli, while the second son fell later against his father's prized companion and leader of the Ostrogoths, Valamir. The third son gathered what remaining forces he could and retreated to the plains until he, too, died years later against other unnamed peoples of the steppes. Attila's legacy evaporated in a matter of years, leaving behind a scattering of tribes who sold themselves as mercenaries to their former enemies.

When I entered Archelaus' camp, Attila had been dead seventy years, yet his memory still haunted the lands he had once trod. Even in the Eastern Empire, once-great cities sacked under Attila's gaze had not been rebuilt. Farmers plowed up skeletons in their fields. Attila may have failed in his life's desire to conquer Rome, yet in his wake, the great collection of slaves he had amassed had spread unto the provinces like gnats and ate away the crumbling power of the Western emperors. Some twenty summers after Attila perished, the Western Empire fell as its final boy emperor surrendered his crown to Odoacer, one of Attila's loyal servants. The East, more Greek than Roman as Liberius was so fond of arguing, was left to safeguard civilization with what few men it had.

By mid-spring, when farmers sowed the seeds that would feed the Empire for the next year, our training was complete. We swore our oath of fealty to the Emperor, and to Rome, and to our God, and promised ourselves to a lifetime of service under the Imperial Standard.

God help me, but I was hardly more than a child, and knew not what that decision would bring.

BEYOND THE EMPIRE'S LIMITS

THOUGH WE WERE BLESSED and cloaked into the Roman Army, we were still unbloodied, and thus, in Archelaus' eyes, contemptable. Soldiers who had never killed in combat could not be relied upon, he frequently argued, and were more likely to run than to defend their brothers in arms. When word came from the capital that Gepid war bands had begun raiding over the Ister River, Archelaus volunteered his men to patrol the area, and the frontier commander, already thin on soldiers, happily endorsed this request.

We sailed on barges past Dacia and into Moesia to the city of Singidunum. Calling it a city was generous—as it stood on the outer edge of the Empire, it had been viciously sacked by the Huns and frequently attacked by the Goths, and barely held down its own perimeter. It held an uneasy peace with the Ostrogoths to the west, who eyed the gateways to Eastern Rome for any signs of weakness. The Gepids, on the other hand, never left the Roman frontier at peace—frequently fording the great river to take a rich harvest or slaves for their pleasure.

The Gepids shared many traits with the Huns: a people who lived on horseback for whom value could only be measured in terms of strength and the capability for destruction. However, unlike the Huns, who were squat and dark-haired, the Gepids had thick white manes and skin pale enough to show the body's humors swirling underneath. They were famously resistant to the spread of Christianity in their lands and were rumored to sacrifice captive children to their dark god before departing for a battle.

Once valuable members of Attila's vast army, by the time of Justin's rule, the Gepids rarely presented a serious threat to massed formations of limitanei. Such guards were rarely skilled fighters, yet were plenty capable of holding off most assaults from barbarian foes until Imperial *comitatses* could be assembled for battle. Yet as we arrived at the ruins of Singidunum, with charred watch posts and churned earth at its outer expanse, it was clear that the limitanei had been bested by a determined body of Gepid raiders.

We cleared the boats as a limitanei commander saluted and identified himself to Archelaus as Narcissus. With a sideways nod of greeting, Archelaus requested a report on the situation in the area, his eyes narrowing on an outlying wooden building whose timbers had smoldered in the week prior.

Strewn with hills and mountains to the south, the Ister flowed into fertile plains of Dalmatia and Pannonia that the Gepids now called their home. As the Gepids were still somewhat nomadic, Narcissus could not tell us where the war band had arrived— only that they had crossed the border at night and had raided villages around Singidunum.

When asked how many were in the band, Narcissus sputtered, "A few thousand, at least. Likely the outriders of a larger army."

If such numbers were intended to give caution to Archelaus, the excubitor merely chuckled. Nodding absently, Archelaus turned away from the limitanei commander and barked orders for the men to further unpack the boats of our supplies. Incredulous, Narcissus asked when the additional soldiers would arrive from Rome, and how sizeable the force would be.

"We're all you'll receive." Archelaus chuckled. "The Emperor has more pressing concerns than a few sheep-molesting barbarian riders."

"One banda?" Narcissus cried. "I wrote the Imperial Court asking for a whole fucking army! What am I going to do with just two hundred men?"

Beside me, Perenus choked with laughter. Eyeing our banda commander from a safe distance, he elbowed Isaacius in the ribs.

"Keep quiet!" I hissed. I clutched my spear, silently gauging whether Archelaus heard our disruption.

"Sorry," Perenus mumbled.

"Can't be helped," Isaacius said gleefully. "That poor fool is about to be skinned alive."

Our disturbance unnoticed, I breathed a sigh of relief. Archelaus' wrath had fixed upon Narcissus, snaking veins along his neck pulsing a deep crimson. The excubitor glowered. "You will do nothing," Archelaus said shortly, "except stay at your post, and report to me if the situation changes from its present state."

Narcissus tried to interject, yet Archelaus raised a hand to silence any debate. Though grateful that Narcissus, and not my friends, was the recipient of such anger, I pitied the poor man, and gave up a silent prayer that he not goad Archelaus into a more violent outburst. And, with blessed swiftness, my prayers were answered; Narcissus stormed off to call his banda into lines and receive orders.

"The limitanei have one job: to stare across the river until something stares back. After that, they are useless," Archelaus said, his voice loud, mocking, and aimed at Narcissus' retreating figure. To us, he said, "Set up camp at the outskirts of this dung heap of a city, and bring the officers to my tent before sundown."

We set off to work building our camp as limitanei watched curiously, our crisp discipline foreign to their plump physique and overall laxity.

It was a piteous place indeed where we set our camp. Razed by Attila nearly a century prior, Singidunum remained in ruins, its stone roads marked by gaping holes and its once vast stone walls crumbling and patched with dry earth. Though Justinian had ordered Singidunum repaired on behalf of my former dominus, its barracks was rat-infested and generally uninhabitable. Therefore, Mundus instructed us instead to carve deep trenches and raise a tight square palisade wall that housed enough tents for the spearmen, servants, and messengers that had accompanied the banda to this far edge of the Empire. Many complained, yet I secretly enjoyed the honest labor, my mind fading far away as I fell into the repetition of jamming an iron shovel into rock-strewn soil and clay. Though such labor grew more punishing as I myself grew older, the simplicity of using my hands to create rather than to cleave limbs or take a life has always reassured me.

The old priest had accompanied us on our journey up the Ister, insisting he keep up my lessons per the Emperor's orders. Initially, I assumed Father Petrus would remain in the relative safety of Thrace, preferring a tranquil straw bed to the rocking discomfort of a river voyage into Moesia. Yet the priest declared he would not stay, leaving no room for argument.

"The Emperor's orders were quite clear." Father Petrus seemed to find even the suggestion of leaving him behind unbearably rude. "Besides, Lord Archelaus will be paid for any further expenses he deems necessary for me."

"I wouldn't give Archelaus that option," I retorted. "The Emperor will owe him an entire province by the time he balances the scales in his favor."

Whether by guilt at wishing the old man back in Thrace or from concern for his comfort, I ordered my band of ten to establish Father Petrus' household in our makeshift fort. We carefully raised and furnished his tent to take in cool river breezes against the humid night air, a luxury that he gratefully accepted with pats of his frail hands on our backs.

"It has been many years since I have been here." The priest chuckled. "And it might be difficult to believe this, but it hasn't gotten much worse."

Our task complete, I accompanied the priest as he explored the ruins of the inner city beneath the bleeding orange of the dying sun. Outside one building, he slowed, then shuffled inside as quietly as possible. The interior was dimly lit and had not been swept in some time, with leaves collecting in corners and cobwebs collecting along the periphery. At the center stood the statue: though the size of a child, it was bearded and wore the antiquarian tunic of an elder lawgiver. Despite the building's disrepair, it had once been a place of solemn beauty.

"This was a temple to Vulcan, the god of fire and metalworking," the priest said softly, his tone almost reverent.

It made me wonder. "Isn't it sinful to visit a pagan church, Father?"

The priest shook his head. "Our forebears did wonderful things with their talents. Great things come to those who have the vision to see it through," he murmured. "Of course, I wish that the sculptor had known the true God, and had never paid homage to any graven image, yet I will not disdain the beauty he wrought here."

We stood for a time, saying nothing. As the sun sank lower, we walked back to camp, and the priest went to take his rest. Before I left his side, however, he called me in his tent and produced the same oiled leather bag that he had carried that first morning in the barracks. It seemed like a lifetime ago, before the constant drills and toil that were now well-known to me. Gingerly, he unknotted the heavy bag and drew out an object wrapped in a black velvet cloth. He slid the cloth away, revealing a dagger the length of a man's forearm in an onyx sheath.

"Godilas gives you your second gift, which he wanted you to have before your first deployment. This is the dagger that Aetius wore at Chalons, which was passed to him through his family that had served on the West." As he handed me the dagger, I inspected it carefully. It was a beautiful weapon: whorls led to a "SPQR" that had been cut into the blade, the handgrip a supple wood stained pure white, the pommel and crossbar dyed black as its sheath, the thin blade ending in a wickedly sharp point, more deadly yet delicate than the broad-bodied poignards carried by most Roman soldiers. I held it up to the last dying light of the sun, its rays glinting off the steel in a way that magnified the dagger's lethal purpose.

"Father, I..." I could not find the right words to express my gratitude and incredulity. "I don't understand why I am being given this. It is priceless, and I have no claim to it."

The priest offered a weak smile. "As I explained before, you are my charge by the Emperor's word. Godilas is similarly charged with continuing his care over you, even if from afar. It is his gift to give... and his right to explain why it is now yours at his leisure. You will understand in time."

I wanted to press further, or at least learn how Aetius' dagger had come into the possession of my old master-at-arms, yet with the sun's final rays fading and my meeting with Archelaus only minutes away, I swallowed my curiosity and gave the priest my thanks. After aiding the old man into his cot, I passed the latrine, already stinking of dung, and arrived at Archelaus' command tent.

As a commander of ten, I had a right to attend the komes' officer briefings. Others gathered near the open fire outside the tent and walked in as its curtains were drawn open by Archelaus' servants. The centurions took their places in front; Mundus winked at me as I hovered at the tent doors. Archelaus sat at the head of a great map of Moesia, using his dagger to pick at the dirt that invariably accumulated under the fingernails of every Roman soldier. As the last officers took their places around the map, the tent flaps were closed, the only light within from a small hearth and a few short tapers that sent shadows dancing on the canvas like spies angling for Archelaus' plans.

"The Gepids are gone, and probably re-forded the Ister days ago," Archelaus said, tracing the map to indicate our best approximation of the Gepid Kingdom. "I also doubt it was larger than a small war band—maybe a few dozen horse riders stealing a few cattle or iron tools."

He tossed down his dagger and picked at his tunic, capturing a louse between two dirt-crusted fingers. He flicked it into the fire and scratched at his beard, the twin forks along his pointed jaw swaying. Few wore a similar look, preferring the smooth cheeks favored by aristocrats of the old Republic and even the Great Alexander before them. Others, particularly Greeks from the hills or tribesmen north of the Ister, preferred long mustaches or thick beards. For my part, I favored a light beard; many philosophers cautioned this sort of unkemptness, yet I was too eager to appear older than my years—and my ill-fitting dekarchos plume—to heed them.

"Well, there's nothing we can do here. I say we return the favor—we'll cross the river and cause a bit of havoc. What say you?" Archelaus shot a look of bemusement at his audience. Many of the other officers growled in assent and pounded the table with gnarled fists. With the decision made, I left with Mundus and prepared my men for the expedition that would begin at dawn.

Over a dinner of salted mutton and twice-baked bread, Perenus gawked over Aetius' knife as I explained what little I knew of its origin.

"If all I had to do to get such pretty gifts was to be a lazy palace slave, I wouldn't have been so excited to be a chariot driver," Perenus said, giving me a good-natured slap on the back.

We shared a half-drained wineskin as the others knocked off to as good a sleep as they could get on the hard earth. As the flames contracted and dimmed, Perenus asked me more of palace life: What were they like, those with power over the Empire's citizens, those who fulfilled the Emperor's will? I, in turn, asked of the traditions and customs of the Laz people, and learned they resided at the far eastern edge of the Euxine Sea along the Empire's perimeter. Perenus explained that though he was a prince of Lazica's noble family, he was not heir to the throne and had enjoyed no power or authority in his youth. Instead, he was seen as a liability to the ruling family, who conveniently sent him to Constantinople as a symbol of friendship between the Laz and the Empire.

"I wouldn't want to go back," Perenus said matter-of-factly. "My life has had many turns of fate, but I can't say that I haven't enjoyed it." He grinned a drunken grin, gulped the sour red, and wiped his mouth dry.

A tent flap flew open, allowing Isaacius to slip into the open air and back to the cookfire.

"Can't sleep with you women gabbing all night," Isaacius said, his tone friendlier than his words. "Is there any wine? And maybe some beef? I can't stand the mutton they make us eat. Too greasy."

"Can't sleep?" Perenus asked. Isaacius shook his head, staring into the flames. "That's fine, neither can we. Instead of sleeping before another suicidal march tomorrow, we're dreaming of all the wonderful things we could be doing instead of shitting in a trench and scratching at mites in our clothes. Oh, and Varus received Aetius' dagger. There's that, too."

Isaacius furrowed his brow and, seeing my unearned prize, held his hand out to inspect it. I did my best to explain, yet as with Perenus, I ended my story with more questions than answers.

Isaacius held the blade in two hands, spinning it from its point. "I always dreamed of being a great soldier," he murmured, gazing longingly at the thin blade. "My father always warned me that the Romans would never allow a Jew to rise high, yet when I was little it was the only thing I wanted in the world. We had this old wooden bucket—my father intended to break it into kindling, but I begged for it as a toy and used it as my legionnaire's helmet instead. I even cut eye and nose holes with my father's saw, and when I closed my eyes, I pretended that I was Caesar at Pharsalus. In my mind, no man could touch me."

I smiled at Isaacius, who was not usually one for such intimacy. I asked him if Archelaus or even the recruiters had known he was not a Christian, and he replied no.

"Maybe one day, when I make a name for myself, I'll tell them." Isaacius handed the blade back, a contented look settling on his features. We talked more of his family, who had moved from the old province of Judea to seek a better life in Constantinople, but were interrupted by one of Archelaus' servants, who warned us that his dominus had not yet fallen into a stupor, and his lack of rest would *surely* be our fault unless we quieted. We thanked the young man and doused the flame with water before retiring into our tents for a night of fitful sleep.

Father Petrus woke me before dawn, offering me God's blessing before venturing into the lands of the Gepids.

"Varus, don't get yourself killed in some foolish skirmish," the priest said sternly. "This is a vengeance raid, and the Lord abhors the pursuit of such folly. Only He shall judge the wicked and the just for their actions. You must perform your duty to Caesar, but not more than that."

As the priest touched my head in blessing, I shivered with a brief sensation of wrongness. Even as an old man, I struggle to understand how our priests can condemn violence yet justify war, rendering the difference between warrior and murderer so subtle as to be invisible. For me, a young man who was by no means a priest, it was only ever a passing conundrum, supplanted by my ravenous desire to earn soldierly glory and fulfill my promise to Justin, Liberius, and all others who had placed their hopes in an ill-fated Herulian slave. That morning, as I recited the Christian creed to Father Petrus, my doubts ebbed, and the thrill of the march ahead took over.

The camp arose in a frenzy of activity, and I fulfilled Mundus' command by ordering our tents to be repacked and weapons inspected for signs of rust or weakness. My own armor was cheap, a borrowed ringmail with a deep rent near the ribs that had been closed together with brittle pig iron. Thick leather ribbons curved over my shoulders, bronze greaves protected my shins from any spear thrusts beneath the shield wall, and my loose tawny trousers were belted at an iron ring that held my new dagger, a fine weapon, and a borrowed sword, weighted near its tip and poorly balanced. It kept its edge well, however, and had been spared any clumsy smithing that would cause it to crack in battle. Whoever had forged it had worked quickly but well.

The final armaments were a spear—half again taller than a man and tipped with a vicious point that could disembowel a horse with a well-placed thrust—and a rectangular iron-rimmed shield that bore the "Chi-Rho" of Constantine. Armored, chest puffed, and chin high, I threw my crimson cloak behind my shoulders and stood ready for the instruction of the komes.

My kit may have been less than enviable, but few men of the banda were better equipped, and several a great deal worse. Though soldiers of the Emperor's army were paid silver for each month of service, costs of food, supplies, and rental of any gear we required for combat were all deducted from our pay. Most men thus sought rich plunder to equip themselves with better armor—or wealth enough for wine and women—and hoped to live long enough to see retirement and the gift of land that Rome had granted its veterans since the days of the Republic.

By Justin's rule, it was rare for a modern Roman army to travel in full military gear, yet Archelaus insisted we do so. Wary of a surprise reprisal from Gepids angered by intruders, he quashed any grumbling with the cautionary tale of an infamous battle in Germania, when three full Roman legions were caught unawares and crushed by a swarm of angry barbarians. Though we were but a single banda, Archelaus would not permit his name to be tied in disgrace to those unprepared fools who left thousands of veteran legionnaires to their slaughter on foreign soil.

Spearmen gathered in marching columns, five abreast and forty lines deep. Mundus was given the honor of first centurion, placing my group in position as the column's spearhead. Anxious for further command, I tightened the straps of my helmet, which was little better than a soup pot with a russet horsehair plume to mark my rank of dekarchos. I glanced at my men, who were calm yet alert—true soldiers at the ready. As one, we stood at attention before the Ister.

Archelaus was the only officer on horseback, his excubitor's armor polished and glinting against the rising sun, his eyes fixed on the forests on the Ister's opposing bank. He paid several boatmen to ferry the banda to the shoreline that marked the end of Rome's territory, and signaled each dekarchos to lead their men and bring their supplies onto the squat wooden craft. Though this took a few hours, the sun had yet to reach its zenith as we reformed within Gepid territory, with Singidunum and its limitanei at our backs. Archelaus cantered toward the center of our formation and signaled the start of the march.

Mundus nodded. "Forward!" he bellowed. The banda banners, a collection of the Imperial insignia and Archelaus' own coiled viper, dipped forward, then lifted upright, and we advanced down a cart-beaten path into the Gepid woods.

Our plan was to remain near the forest, thereby veiling our column from potential enemy horsemen or stray arrows. Rather than moving due north, we followed a circuitous route ever eastward, making little sound along the way, again for fear of attracting a curious enemy. At sundown, we made camp, set sentries, and did our best to sleep without the luxury of fire or the safety of friendly territory.

An evening chill woke me well before dawn. My teeth chattered as I cursed all the discomforts that the early Moesian spring had wrought upon us. After brushing a thin layer of hoarfrost from the tents, we marched on, and repeated our encampment again in the evening.

It was not until early on the third day of our march that we found evidence of human habitation. A scout had discovered a discarded saddle, its leather straps torn from overuse. Archelaus inspected it carefully, running his hands over the worn material. "Riders came this way, which means that a village must be nearby." With that, we marched yet farther, now taking further pains to conceal ourselves, covering our scabbards with muffling cloth.

Not a while later, scouts returned again and reported a settlement at the edge of the forest just a half mile ahead: several dozen thatched huts, perhaps a few hundred Gepids. Most significantly, the village appeared undefended, emptied of its younger men with only boys, cripples, and old men to mount any resistance. There wasn't even a wall, just a shallow ditch that could be cleared by a few paces at full sprint. After sketching a crude map into the dirt, Archelaus summoned his officers and pondered his next order.

"Fan out in a half circle and enter on my signal," he ordered, nostrils flaring. "Once inside, the flanks should push hard to the other side, not stopping until they meet."

Archelaus gazed over his banda, then signaled to the handful of servants there to care for washing, cooking, and attending to the officers.

"Bring torches," he ordered them. "Light them in the cookfires and burn the village to the ground."

Mundus cleared his throat and asked permission to speak, and, when he received it, raised his eyes to Archelaus. The komes loomed a full head above Mundus' own helmeted form, but Mundus did not flinch.

"Lord, these are not warriors here," he said, "and they could not have participated in the attacks around Singidunum. Surely we should pass this village over?"

Archelaus glowered at Mundus, breathing slowly and grinding his fist into the wooden pommel of his sword. "If they didn't attack us, they shelter and support those that do. I make war on the Emperor's enemies, whatever shape they may take. But you would have a reason not to, wouldn't you, centurion?"

"No, Lord," Mundus replied, lowering his head.

I shot a confused look at Donus, who was another commander of ten under Mundus. He placed a callused finger to his lips and whispered close into my ear. "Mundus' mother was a Gepid, and his father was a Greek spearman," Donus whispered. "And you know what Archelaus thinks of any with barbarian blood."

Archelaus proceeded, ignorant of our exchange. "Hearing no questions, I order you to fan out and wait for my whistle. Kill any who resist. Do not hesitate in your duty to Rome."

The officers hurried back to their units and relayed instructions. Mundus stopped me as I went to my ten, his normally stoic face oddly pensive.

"Varus, I'm giving you the far-left flank and freedom of command," he ordered, voice tight as though straining against any greater emotion. "I will not be far if you need me, but do not act recklessly in the village—we do not know what we are getting ourselves into, and there is no sense getting our men killed or starting a larger war with these people."

I nodded and hurried back to my men, who offered light cheers when told of the honor of our place at the far left, normally reserved for the best-trained and most-reliable soldiers.

"Protect yourselves," I added, "but do not attack anyone without a direct command to do so, or unless you are already being attacked."

My men stamped their spear butts in acknowledgment. Perenus, my new second-in-command, offered further advice. "I've seen villages like this before in Lazica, and they have no predictable layout. Don't assume that the huts are arranged in any particular order." I nodded and signaled the group to move.

"Good luck, Varus," called Mundus as we broke away from the main group. The men that would take the right flank had begun similar maneuvers, and the body of the banda had followed our lead. We all but flew over the half mile, nevertheless taking care not to divulge our position by stumbling on hidden logs or jostling weapons.

As we crested a hill, we came into view of the village; smoke billowed from open firepits and young Gepid children ran along its forest line. At the sight of the children, sudden, rancid bile rose in my stomach, and I fought it down, determined not to retch in front of the men. Though the Christian faith condemned the slaying of children, there was little doubt that many who ran and played within that village would lay dead in but a few moments, victims of battle lust and poor fortune. I ardently wished it would not be so, yet all the years of my life have demonstrated a willingness to abandon mercy at the slightest provocation or hardship. Our training had repeatedly insisted upon discipline and restraint, yet neither a fear of God nor centuries of military doctrine would protect those Gepid children from Archelaus' banda that day.

Fifty paces out, we halted in the thickly wooded outskirts of the village. Birds sung atop the trees, which had already come into a rich bloom despite the recent grip of winter. The foliage provided additional cover to the men, yet any normal Roman city's sentries would have had little problem scouting us and sounding an alarm. Thankfully for us, the Gepids of this village were not so primed, although whether this was from a lack of concern of Roman attack or a lack of forces to maintain a defensive perimeter, it was impossible to know. All that I understood was, at the precipice of my first attack against a foreign people, I hefted my spear and shield and waited anxiously for a signal to begin. Soon enough, a piercing whistle rang out in the distance, and we leaped to respond.

We ran hard toward the village and cleared its ditch in under three paces. Some of the village children had seen us and had begun to run in the opposite direction, yet no adult resistance had formed. I touched the outmost building, then switched directions, running fast yet keeping a wary eye for any signs of ambush from the huts. It did not take long to complete Archelaus' circle, as we came up on our fellow red-cloaked banda members. The other dekarchos sprinted into the village, and we followed his example with our shields raised and spears lowered.

My first clear few of the interior of the village told a story of surprise, panic, and chaos. Buildings at the southern end of the village had been set ablaze, fires jumping from one thatched roof to another as they consumed the dry timber and straw. Red-cloaked soldiers slipped between the buildings, seeking enemies and any plunder among the huts.

We approached slowly, spreading among the nearest buildings. To my left, a group of men raised shouts and ran into view with scythes and crude iron blades as they charged at me. One ran ahead of the others, and I speared him full in the chest with one quick motion. As warm blood sprayed along my arms and face, the man's features gaped in an expression of shock. Crimson staining his matted white hair, the Gepid tried to pull my spear from his body, yet he buckled in pain and fell to the ground, mewing in pain as his body curled around my spear shaft. I dropped the spear and scanned for further enemies in the Gepid village. I thought so little at the time, yet even today I can see the pained look of surprise lining his age-weathered face, anger matched only by a desperation to pluck the iron spearhead that tore into his soft flesh and ripped at the guts underneath.

As I trained my attention on my enemies ahead, a crash sounded to my left as a huge Gepid man collided with my left shoulder. Unable to avoid the blow, he drove me to the ground, defenseless. He pinned my sword arm with a knee and drew a blade. He struck downward, which I blocked with my forearm. The blade skirted over my mailed chest, yet cut into my exposed forearm. He raised his dagger again, ready for the killing stroke that would send his hated enemy to the afterlife.

As he swung his arm, a spear buried itself in his torso, the sheer force of it forcing him to sit. He grasped at the spear shaft, choking in agony as the iron point dug further into his body. Coarse hands pulled the spear from the man, and his guts spilled over my trousers and onto the surrounding grass. Isaacius pulled me up and nodded at my arm, asking if I had been wounded.

The cut on my arm bled, yet did not seem too deep. "Just a scratch," I said. "Nothing to worry about." Isaacius nodded, and my men formed up around me as the other Gepids closed in.

With no choice but to watch their countrymen fall, some of our enemies fled, yet others charged at our flimsy formation, howling defiance. Far from undefended and unpopulated, the village teemed with stocky warriors—though no horsemen—and though there must have been three dozen that formed up outside of our makeshift wall, they came at us as an undisciplined rabble relying more on shock than on skill. Such a display might break inexperienced ranks, yet my men had trained too hard under Mundus and Archelaus to cower from such a mob.

"Shields up, high and tight!" I yelled. Shield edges overlapped into an impenetrable mass of wood, iron, and hardened muscle that faced down the onslaught of Gepid villagers.

The quicker ones were able to dodge our spear points, and their bodies clattered against our shields in an attempt to break the line. When they saw my plume, the Gepids bore down their wrath upon me, barging right into my shield boss. Cephalas dispatched the first, his knife impaling the man's arm. A second man swung a maul at my head, which I blocked with a raised shield. Perenus then severed the man's neck, and blood fountained from the gaping hole. The intestines and blood of the slain left the Gepids following their kinsmen, struggling to maintain their footing as they charged our line. Perenus echoed my previous warning, reminding the men to stay tight together and keep the shields up toward the enemy.

An older burly man, his arms thick with tribal markings and his neck adorned with various trinkets and amulets, roared a challenge and jogged forward. Many of the remaining men followed his example; presumably this older man was some war leader or chief. Unlike our initial assailants, the man understood the threat posed by the shield wall, and tried to pull our shields apart with a reaping scythe as his men piled into the gap in our lines. One of my men toppled over from the assault, yet Isaacius bashed the attacker's face with his shield boss, reknitting the wall and preserving our discipline. The man spat rotted teeth and blood on the ground as Isaacius levied a spear thrust.

Bodies piled before our shields, and the frenzy faded. Fewer warriors volunteered to climb the mound of flesh to attack our tired but intact wall. Other Roman soldiers had edged toward our fight and surrounded the remaining dozen Gepid warriors that occupied the northern corner of the village. The leader screamed curses at us in a language I did not understand, glaring at his adversaries. He found a discarded Roman shield, spat heavy yellow phlegm onto its face, and strode forward.

I could have resisted the invitation—Mundus had given me strict orders to not place myself at any great risk, and my men had edged closer to defeating the Gepids in pitched combat. Yet to avoid such a direct challenge would have inspired the Gepids and disheartened my spearmen, who placed as much faith in omens and symbols as they did their own wits and training. Thus I stepped forward, accepting the warrior's invitation to single combat. He grinned wolfishly, with a stream of Gepid words that were indecipherable in meaning but clear in intent.

I spat in his direction, called him a worm, a wretched relic, an insipid limp thing, and a variety of other insults that had spread around the camp during our training days. I called out to him in a variety of languages to see what caught his attention, from Latin and Greek to Heruli and even the coarse tongue of the Huns—a language that Justin had insisted that Samur and I learn in our studies. The last may have caught his attention—I cannot say for sure—but indeed, he stopped grinning and charged with an open-mouthed snarl.

He was large, muscular, and tall, a man who had probably overwhelmed dozens of opponents throughout his life through brute strength. Yet he seemed unused to fighting against those of a similar capability, and I had also been larger than most for much of my life, standing a head taller than most other Romans. I would also like to believe that the Gepid was intimidated by my outward sureness, though my scowl masked a pumping heart fluttering too quickly for calm work. Even so, Archelaus' grueling instruction had left me well-prepared for such an encounter, as he had insisted that any Roman officer should possess the unquestioning will and aptitude to slay an enemy champion in single combat. Such customs had even pervaded legal proceedings against those who had broken military law, where soldiers could request a trial by single combat to weigh their guilt or innocence. Justin disdained such practices, arguing that they were foreign to traditional Roman culture and allowed the wicked an opportunity to walk free of their crimes. Yet even as Emperor, he had limited capability to curtail it.

As I soon discovered, the Gepids shared none of Justin's misgivings. My opponent lashed out with a sword in one hand and his scythe in the other, searching for an opening in my defense as I led with my shield first. Splinters sprayed from the wood under his assault; it was only a matter of time until it broke into pieces.

I retreated a few paces and loosened the straps that locked the shield tight against my left forearm. As the Gepid warrior advanced, I threw my shield into the air, but the man knocked it aside with his sword arm. Still, in the moment he attended to my shield, I had drawn my dagger. I drove it into the warrior's heart.

He collapsed, his entire weight falling on me until I pulled Aetius' dagger free. The other, unhurt Gepid men threw down their weapons and were taken hostage by my men as we checked for any hidden blades or valuables. I left three to take the prisoners to our previous camp a half mile away, including one man who had taken minor injuries during the attack. My remaining men and I traipsed through the village, covered in gore and bruises, yet still in fighting shape.

Other corners of the village revealed similar scenes—piles of bodies from miniature battles, with several of our formations still defending against semi-organized attacks. Archelaus, dismounted amid a larger body of Roman spearmen, fought like a demon. He roared with hatred and ordered the banda to press, to kill, and to send these savages to whatever underworld would take their maggot-strewn corpses.

After sprinting through the village, we found Mundus, bleeding from a scalp wound and surrounded by his men.

"Bastard grazed me with an arrow," Mundus said, pointing to one of a dozen corpses that surrounded the shield formation, including one Roman. "Undefended, my ass. This place is crawling with warriors. Clear out the huts and let's start back for the tree line."

I nodded and ran with my men back to the northern edge of the village where we had begun our invasion. Uncontrollable fires spread toward the village center, and many Gepid women took children by the hand and ran toward the open fields. Despite Archelaus' order, I let them pass freely, and my men gave no indication of wishing to defy the instruction implicit in my doing so.

Screams echoed through the din of battle and crackling flames as men searched huts for plunder and slaves. As fewer Gepid men attacked the invading spearmen, our Roman discipline was cracking; men in groups of two or three ventured off on their own. There was little resistance at this point, yet the breakdown of command hindered any efforts to organize ranks or calm the bloodlust of battle. My men kept order, although some must have been tempted to join their comrades in search of gold, weapons, and slaves.

We walked through the northern edge of the village, its huts half standing from combat and emptied of inhabitants. Occasionally, we encountered other soldiers running toward the larger huts in the village center; this meant there were likely goods worth stealing.

Yet Archelaus showed no such predilection. He exited an outer building that was covered in chalk formed into strange figures and runes that I had not seen before, straightened his lamellar armor, and acknowledged my presence.

"Lord, Mundus requests an immediate evacuation of the village," I reported, saluting. "The fires are spreading too quickly for us to contain, and men risk being trapped in the inferno."

Archelaus scoffed. "And why are there no fires in this section, dekarchos? Was this not your sector to attack?"

He did not wait for an answer, but stormed off toward the village center, barking orders that all looting must cease and to return to formation at the original staging point.

Flames danced overhead. Though the conflagration had yet to spread beyond control, there was no telling how long the dry kindling of the thatched Gepid village would take to alight, trapping all who remained in an unforgiving inferno. I had begun orders for my remaining men to depart when I heard the faint yet urgent sounds of sobbing.

Leaving Perenus in charge, I followed the sound to its source—the rune-etched hut, which I entered with Isaacius. Within, bones, powders, and animal skins littered the space, the interior walls engraved with yet more runes. A lone figure huddled in the corner. We stumbled over the bodies of two others, a man and a woman, their throats slashed and their bodies still warm with life they no longer possessed. The figure sobbed heavily, its face covered in long white hair over a thin frame bedecked by an animal-hide jerkin. The figure drew closer, looked up at me, and shrieked louder. Even in the gloom, I could tell the figure was a younger woman, perhaps sixteen years. I gave my sword to Isaacius and asked him to leave, showing her my open palms.

With a glance at my blood-soaked mail, she screamed a litany of Gepid, a tongue I knew, but only enough to recognize it—a smattering of words at best. I raised my open palms higher and made a clumsy shushing noise, blushing at the absurdity of such a gesture given the circumstances. As her curses poured forth unabated, I attempted to communicate with her in the languages I had learned under Liberius' tutelage, finding a measure of success with my native Herulian.

"My men and I will not hurt you," I yelled above the din.

She ceased her sobbing and yelling. Her face slackened to confused astonishment. "You are Heruli?"

"Yes, but a Roman soldier," I replied softly.

This provoked fresh sobs, but she calmed faster this time, now eyeing me with curiosity.

"Why did your people have to come here and kill my family? What did we do to you to deserve this?" Anger rose in her wispy voice.

As heat rose from the burning thatch, I felt a bubbling irritation urging me to abandon this Gepid girl and follow Archelaus back across the Ister. The ten spearmen under my command were responsibility enough, and what of it if another of Rome's enemies went cold and hungry in Dacia? Or if they died? How many tens of thousands of the Empire had been butchered by a century of invaders, or survived similar pillage only to suffer the horrifying fates of famine or disease? More than the stars in the sky, and all of whom lay unavenged and forgotten in ruined villages or cities all the way to the Great Ocean.

Yet such thoughts were met by a piercing jab of shame. Father Petrus' cross burned against the skin above my heart, and the guilt saw me return the gaze of the tear-strewn Gepid before me. In that moment, I saw all the slave girls who served alongside me in the Imperial Palace, violated and tossed about by patricians and ministers who cared little for their fates and did not hear their screams in the night. Most of all, however, I heard the muffled cry from so many years ago, a sound of pain and terror at the genesis of my memory—and, indeed, of my life. My soul resolved, I unstrapped my helmet and faced her with sweat-strewn hair and grime-covered cheeks, forever altering my fate.

"You did nothing wrong, and I am truly sorry," I said, embarrassed at my clumsy speech, "but we do not have time to discuss this right now—we need to escape this village before the flames seal our exits. If you come with me, I promise you will come to no harm. Understand?"

Her bloodshot eyes locked on mine, suspicious, before her gaze dropped to my belt and Aetius' blade—the only remaining weapon I kept on my body.

An idea struck me. "If I let you borrow this"—I pointed to the dagger—"will you come with me?"

She considered a collapsed section of thatch at the far end of the hut, its structure weakened by the crawling flames. With little other choice, she nodded, and I handed her the sheathed blade and secured my helmet once more. Though I half expected her to stab and run, the dagger remained in its sheath, her grip firm on its pommel as she contemplated my outstretched hand.

Slowly, she took my arm, and we spirited into the outdoors. Still waiting outside, my men eagerly accepted my order to leave in haste. Isaacius returned my sword and gave a curious glance toward the woman on my arm.

"Later." Ash filled my throat, and we left the village for our encampment in the original half circle that we had begun with hours before.

As we passed beyond the outermost huts, the scent of burning flesh mixed with the heavy smoke of burning wood; I could only imagine the number of bodies left behind. A small trickle of Roman soldiers exited the last few standing buildings, some arms heavy with plunder, others leading newfound slaves at sword-point. Many buildings had begun to collapse, their weakened timber and thatch suddenly unable to bear the weight that had housed generations of Gepids. A good deal of the fires had merged into one great blaze, and its heat billowed out as it consumed our air, shooting a great pillar of black smoke into the sky.

The Gepid village had died before the noonday sun, and not a soul was left to occupy its ashes.

The Last Dying Light

ROSAMUND

In silence, we marched—my group of ten, myself, and my captive—toward our original staging ground. Others nearby were less taciturn, some cheering their newfound wealth while others groaned from injuries. Yet most noticeable of all was Archelaus, browbeating those scouts who had promised an easy conquest.

"Undefended? There was an entire fucking war band there!" Archelaus roared. "At least three hundred men, and twice as many women and children. I've got at least four men dead, another ten wounded, and God knows how many still missing."

Abruptly, Archelaus wheeled his anger onto a servant. "And where is the fucking update to my count? Are all of you blind, or just stupid?"

Perhaps four dozen Gepids stood in a haggard circle, guarded by sentries who kept at a spear's distance. Some men, yet mostly women and young children who had stayed out of the fighting but were not swift enough, or lucky enough, to escape. One older woman wailed, fat tears streaming down her face. Others tried to comfort her until a sentry stamped his spear butt and called for silence. The men reacted to little, dour looks on their faces as they prepared themselves for whatever indignity their captors had intended for them.

As I walked through the ranks, I found two red-cloaked Romans who had been disarmed and locked in thin iron chains. Though their faces were caked in soot and lined with sweat-strewn hair, I discovered one as Barda, among the first I had met—and fought—upon entering the camp. He looked upward, his baleful gaze a mixture of shame and fear as he stared beyond any of his onlookers.

"Cowardice, and attempted desertion," one of their jailors said, his voice empty of empathy or concern. Barda had a gash under an eye that was puckered and swelling, while his companion bore a split lip and winced as he stepped forward.

My Gepid companion looked with suspicion at the deserters and her captive kinsmen, her surprisingly steely fingers suddenly releasing my arm as she put a pace of distance between us. In doing so, she released pressure from my wounded forearm; its shallow cut was unlikely to require stitches, but it still throbbed. Yet I fought to ignore the pain as I kept my attention toward the girl, who still clutched Aetius' sheathed dagger, yet was careful to keep it hidden.

"We need to keep moving," I instructed in Heruli.

She glared. "And if I don't?"

"I swear to keep you safe," I told her, "and to speak more when there's time. But there are others that would have no misgivings about mistreating you."

"And that is supposed to make me grateful?" Her words stung like vinegar in a wound, her accent yet more clipped. "A docile lamb for the noble Roman?"

"Interpret it as you wish." A flicker of regret flared in my chest—I did not need a new ward, least of all one so contrary. "But understand that our danger is not over."

"*We* are not in danger," she said. "*I* am."

Yet despite her words, she kept close as I weaved through the ranks, placing distance between sounds of whooping spearmen drunk at the prospect of plunder and slaves. Against protocol, some had even discovered an overlarge wineskin, its crimson liquid sloshing and spilling against unkempt beards and filthy clothing and armor. Even more than the bombastic and unpredictable Archelaus, I feared them, these men whose wanton hedonism was identical to so many of Anastasius' Imperial Palace. Though I knew officers would soon restore order, I nevertheless steered my ward from the spoils of pillage, only now realizing that both of us reeked of smoke, as filthy as those we passed.

My cares loosened as I spied Mundus. He was hurriedly inspecting his men's injuries, restoring a semblance of order to his column. His forehead flashed an angry red stripe and a line of hasty stitches from the banda's *medicus* that had begun to redden and swell. Still, he bore his own pains no mind, and stopped only we he saw me arrive.

"Glad to see you made it out," Mundus said in Greek, wiping sweat from his eyes. "Any losses among your men?"

"Just a few bruises, but nothing to write poems about," I replied. "Although the komes implied that others were less fortunate."

"Aye, that's so." Mundus sighed. "We need to put some distance between us and the village before any roving Gepid war bands arrive. That fire will be a signal for any horseman within a half day's ride."

At that, my centurion's attention had already gone on to the next man, but before departing, Mundus motioned toward my Gepid companion. "You can put her with the rest. No one will claim her from you."

Here, he gave me a second opportunity to rid myself of a troublesome and likely costly responsibility. Temptation again rose to leave this Gepid girl to the fates. Yet my instincts stayed their present course, still hardened by memories of those whose sufferings I had been too young or fearful to abate. War is kind to no one, but its most imaginative horrors are reserved for women, especially those with the misfortune to survive. Even in those early days of my manhood, I knew all too well what could easily await my companion with a few words of dismissal from me.

I did not speak them.

"Respectfully, sir, I would like her to stay close to me." My voice was unsteady, as I was unwilling to countermand a superior.

"She can help carry some of my men's equipment, and fetch water when the time comes."

"Not the best idea, in my experience." Mundus grunted. "She's got a wild look about her."

"I'll keep her under close watch," I promised. "And Archelaus' guards already have too many Gepids to keep watch over."

"Likely true." Mundus nodded. "Very well. The girl is your responsibility, whether or not she behaves herself. But keep her out of eyeshot of Archelaus," he added. "You are within your rights to keep a slave on the march, but... you'll save yourself a confrontation by laying low about it."

Slave. No single word could ever lay so heavy around one's neck. It was at once a stark evaluation of a person's worth and a doom for any hopes of a lofty future. Yet I did not balk at Mundus' words, and offered a crisp salute in return for the centurion's permission and trust. Mundus saluted back and departed to inspect another portion of his men. Thus I was left to dictate the activities of ten trained spearmen and one Gepid girl.

The silence persisted another forty paces until we encountered our amassed supplies. Cephalas shot a curious glance at our new companion—who trailed never farther than a pace behind me as we sought smokeless air and distance from the stinking humanity by Archelaus—but a single nod quelled his curiosity. He firmly fixed his eyes upon our group's leather packs not far away.

There, abandoning decorum, several tore at their packs and withdrew their beloved waterskins. Groans of pleasure billowed outward as the lukewarm liquid slaked dried and ash-riddled throats. Isaacius even tipped a skin over his head, sending thick rivulets of dirt and ash to meander through hair and body and to puddle around his soiled boots. None spoke until Perenus broke our modicum of pleasure.

"That one big bastard almost had you there," Perenus said, his teasing interspersed with greedy gulps of water. "I didn't think we would reach you in time."

"If it wasn't for Isaacius, you probably would not have," I said solemnly.

Isaacius stood straighter at the comment, his chest rising as others joined in with praise of his heroics. Perenus gave a few more playful jabs before braving a question, one that many likely held yet none were willing to ask.

"Who's the girl?" Perenus nodded at my Gepid shadow. "Camp slave?"

The Gepid drew back as helmeted heads turned to take in her slight figure. I saw her reach into the folded cloth along her waist, her muscles tensing as she drew a half step closer.

"What are they saying?" she whispered in Herulian. "What do they want?"

"Nothing, they're just curious," I replied in the same tongue.

Perenus raised an eyebrow at the exchange, eyeing Isaacius for answers. Isaacius merely shrugged, and the rest peered even more attentively at the interloper.

"She is not a slave," I said. "And you're all under orders to make sure that no harm comes to her. She is our responsibility until we return to Singidunum."

"Is she someone important?" Perenus pressed. "Chieftain's daughter or something?"

"Something like that," I lied. "It matters little. Just keep watch, and find me if she starts talking. She'll help us with carrying and cleaning, once we put some distance away from the village."

"Thank God!" Perenus cried, never one to resist blasphemy. "My back is an absolute ruin, and my clothes are filthy."

"It's because you're duck-footed and don't bathe nearly often enough," Isaacius said.

Perenus gave his friend's shoulder a friendly smack, his curiosity of my captive temporarily forgotten. Instead, he regaled me with information gleaned from the other *dekarchoi* who fought to bring their men to order, resolving squabbles over disputed plunder, yelling orders to prepare for the march and other petty indignities.

"We think there were at least a few dozen warriors in the village," Perenus said. "One of Archelaus' dekarchoi was ambushed as we executed the raid, and at least a few Romans were killed."

"I can't believe how badly our scouts fucked up," Isaacius snarled. "From what we're hearing from the other centurions, the raid was more of a brawl than any pitched combat… small fights in tens and twenties than any organized attack."

My Gepid captive stirred behind me. I raised a hand—she needed to stay still, though just a few moments longer. Most of Perenus' or Isaacius' report was easily deduced from our time in the village, but one question needed to be asked, a question that drew from Mundus' initial reservations about this attack. Its answer was the crux of our exercise: Were the banda's actions an act of defense of the Empire, or an illegal foray into an otherwise peaceable forest village conducted without the approval of the Emperor or the provincial governor?

"Did we find any Roman prisoners from the Gepid raid?" I asked, insistent but calm. "Any evidence that the villagers were responsible for the attacks around Singidunum?"

"No," Perenus said. "But from what the other units are reporting, we fought off the village chief named Fastida, that old man you skewered."

Perenus winked, and I laughed as he offered a wineskin; I felt no real joy but did not wish to reject my friend's praise. Another glad tiding arrived as we learned one of the other centurions had captured a few dozen ponies, useful transport for supplies and the wounded.

"Five days, and it's back to the comforts of Singidunum," Isaacius said merrily. "What a cheerful place Moesia is."

A final detachment of soldiers filed into our temporary camp, their clothes scorched and faces blackened with soot. They had been ordered to retrieve the Roman dead, or, if retrieval was not possible, at least identify remains and tally our losses. We had also left supplies behind—spears stuck in corpses, blunted blades and daggers, discarded shields. This left many soldiers only partially equipped for any further fighting, their gear consigned to the white-hot destruction of the flames. Such uncertainty facing his men angered Archelaus, who vaulted onto his horse and ordered the banda to begin its journey out of the Gepid Kingdom.

As he rode past my ten, which now occupied the rearguard of the column, I urged the Gepid girl to hide from view. The komes took no notice of us, and as he passed, the Gepid whispered a flurry of questions regarding the identity of the Roman commander, his rank apparent from the richness of his armor as much as the careless confidence exhibited as he strode through the ranks. As we walked along the forested path, I finally took a moment to inspect her as I offered answers to her many questions.

Her long white hair reached her shoulders but was tangled with grime and forest debris, covering her face like a wild veil. Her head barely reached my chest, and her skin was radiant with the famed Gepid translucence. Her hands bore no callouses from a life of tilling soil or spinning wool, yet her jerkin and shift were smattered with blood and burns. Even in her withdrawn state, however, her narrow eyes were both firm and suffused with a raw violence any of Rome's spearmen would envy—green eyes ringed by a narrow band of yellow. She regarded me with a mix of loathing, curiosity, and unfathomable sadness.

"My name is Varus," I said in Heruli, careful to keep my voice low. "What is your name?"

"Rosamund," she replied in that airy, hollow voice, those sharp eyes fixed on the men marching before us. None were at our back — only the thickening forest, and the ever more distant pillar of smoke that fed into the heavens.

Rosamund answered each of my questions with equal abruptness for the rest of the half day's march; thus, I slowly pieced together her story. She said that she was sixteen years old, confirming my assumption. A daughter of the village shaman, Rosamund had helped him collect roots and herbs for the poultices and potions for to treat the sicknesses and injuries of the villagers, and to appease the many gods of the Gepid pantheon. When I asked if any of her relatives had died in the attack, she nodded, her pointed jaw quivering as tears welled in her eyes.

"You ask many questions," Rosamund observed. "But you give no answers. What do you intend to do with me?"

"I do not know," I confessed.

"Rape me? Enslave me?" she bayed. "That's what your kind do, anyways."

"Romans?"

"Warriors," Rosamund said simply. "You never make anything better, but everything worse."

I shook my head. "I've promised that no harm will come to you, and I intend to keep that promise."

Rosamund's fiery eyes went heavy. She bit her lower lip. "Why?" Her voice brimmed with rage, the word more command than question.

Still, I did not reply. No answer I could give would bring Rosamund to trust me, nor capture the visceral instinct that brought me to protect a foreigner who had been my sworn enemy just hours before. Instead, I silently submitted to the glowering scrutiny of Rosamund's gaze, and as I did, a profound sensation of wrongness pervaded my body—not from my newfound responsibility for this Gepid captive, but from the burgeoning worry that Archelaus' raid had been a thoroughly evil thing. That belief has remained with me to this day; Mundus' statement of the village's innocence echoes still, all the way from those days of my youth.

Archelaus kept a punishing pace, deaf to the complaints of the wounded and exhausted who trailed behind their leader's horse. My own men joined in the grumbling, and despite my remonstrations that they stay vigilant and quiet, I, too, privately wished for a chance to peel the ringmail from my chafed skin and scrub the grime from my body. At last, as the sun sank low, Archelaus had little choice but to capitulate to the bodily needs of his men. He ordered trenches dug and tents erected for the evening's encampment.

Not that such an order immediately granted our rest; the concerns of forming a defensive perimeter meant another hour of backbreaking labor for the two hundred spearmen within Archelaus' banda. Many unacquainted with the Roman army believe the soldier's duty is merely to fight in the shield wall, yet even the most unseasoned recruit understands the soldier more often wields a simple iron shovel than any blade. Some would dig deep trenches half the height of a man to frame the camp's square borders, while others with axes would fell trees and lash together rough logs to form our palisade wall.

Such duties were to be carried out each evening, and all defensive fortifications dismantled or torched the following morning. Those of elevated status like Archelaus were exempt, of course, but those of smaller titles, like Mundus and I, had little choice but to fall into the crushing rhythm of carving into the stone-wrought soil. That night, Rosamund eyed our labors curiously, never more than a few paces' distance away; she may have even smirked as Perenus' shovel accidentally fell upon his boot-covered foot, setting the Lazic princeling shouting and cursing.

Yet as the banda completed its defenses, men swarmed to their tents; many collapsed into sleep still armored. I handed my pack to Cephalas and dismissed my own men to their rest, ordering Isaacius to pass around the salted mutton and twice-baked bread that had been our staple. Isaacius, who cheerily compared the meal to sawdust and goat shit, gnawed greedily on the rations all the same. After leaving my men, I grabbed one of our ten's wineskins, dreading what I must do next.

"I need to leave you with the other Gepids for tonight," I explained in Heruli. "At first light, I will find you once more. You will be safe."

Rosamund's eyes widened, an unusual twinge of fear briefly interrupting her typical look of rage and betrayal. Her breathing quickening, she looked toward the large enclosed pen where the banda's captives had been herded.

"You lying bastard!" Rosamund hissed. Her slim fingers dropped to the dagger hidden at her belt. "Why take me this far just to abandon me now?"

"I'm not, I'm not," I answered clumsily, anxious at her growing noise. "I simply… there is simply no better place for you to sleep for now. Until I return, you may keep the dagger with you through the night."

Rosamund's eyebrows arched, the yellow edges of her eyes luminescent with anger. Despite her ferocity, fatigue had taken a visible toll on her body; her legs were lightly shaking and her head swaying. Thick tears formed amid her rage, her lip quivering yet defiant.

"Fine," she said bitterly. A tear streamed down her cheek.

Rosamund's resignation only unleashed a further bout of confusion and guilt. Truthfully, I longed for carefree sleep, an impossible dream given my need to rest with one eye open to

Rosamund's whereabouts. Still, it could not be denied that the looming slave tent was overstuffed with stinking bodies and weeping children and a generally revolting miasma with little security.

Yet still, I ordered the entrance opened, and the on-duty guards were more than happy to add another captive to the banda's haul. All heads turned to face the merciful breeze. Most of these men were younger and until recently had been in good health, yet now all were haggard from their assault and subsequent journey. Several of them raised hands, raining pleas in their foreign tongue.

"Please don't leave me here," Rosamund whispered in Heruli. "Please."

"These are your kinsmen, and I promise that I will return in a few hours." A lump had formed in my throat.

I waded through the press of bodies and found Rosamund a space to rest. While none would have described it as comfortable, her spot was near an opening in the tent that gave a fresh breeze. Provided it would not rain, I assumed it was her best possible choice… though it did give the Roman guardsman just a few steps' distance from her prone form.

"Just a few hours," I repeated, thankful that the darkness hid my reddening face.

Rosamund offered neither retort nor resistance. She merely raised her face one final time, her features as if etched in stone. With a sigh, Rosamund knelt and lifted her face to the slim opening.

"Hold on to the dagger." Perhaps I could leave her on a more hopeful standing.

Rosamund only faced the tent opening, silent. I muttered a brisk goodbye before slipping out of the pen and into the mercifully fresh air, finding a single spearman waiting on the other side. I nodded to the guard and drew a copper coin from a pouch on my belt, its front showing the face of the miserly Anastasius from my youth. Even on his currency, his pinched face showed the famed tightfistedness behind his ruinous taxes, enriching the palace at the expense of the provinces. The guard accepted the coin readily enough, his gaze unchanged as his hand remained outstretched in expectation. Smirking, I handed over the wineskin, and the guard nodded.

"Watch over the Gepid I came here with," I said. "Give her the chance for fresh air if she requests, and come find my men if something serious happens."

"Understood, dekarchos," the spearman replied, already unstopping the wineskin.

Head swimming, I left the Gepids without looking back. By that point, Archelaus had already ordered pickets set and sentries to patrol the perimeter of the camp, yet none questioned nor stopped me as I returned to my men. I stripped to the waist, walked into the tent, and found nine hard, tired bodies inside. Several had already fallen into a deep sleep, and Cephalas snored loudly despite still wearing full armor. Others did what they could to clean themselves and take in some nourishment; Perenus tossed pilfered loaves of bread and salted meat to those still awake. As the tent grew dark, Isaacius drew my attention and threw yet another half-full wineskin to my corner of our tent. I caught it and drank greedily, the rich fruity flavors flooding my throat. Even when barred from anything intoxicating, Roman soldiers always found wine to share, even when food and water had long fallen to rot, worms, or unchecked hunger.

"I owe you my life," I said after a time.

Isaacius smiled at the compliment, surprised as I was at the weight of my words. "I owe you my livelihood—I don't think I would have survived training without your help."

We clasped arms and finished the remaining wine in silence. His bushy beard covered with stubborn ash, Isaacius slept first, and I soon followed, my various bruises and cuts now viciously felt my whole body over.

That first night after the raid was plagued with haunted sleep. Evanescent dreams placed me again—I saw the man who slashed my arm and nearly ended my life, yet in my dream, his eyes and nose wept blackened blood as he held me down atop a burning pyre. Behind him were the men I had killed, watching with indifference as my attacker lowered his blade to my throat.

The nightmare was cut short; something had nudged me awake. My eyes darted from one direction to another, but I could see little in the night's blackness beyond a figure leaning above me. I shot up, my imagination rioting with the impossible horrors of my nightmare made real before me.

"Better come quickly." The Gepid guardsman sounded cross. "My watch is nearing an end, and your captive's kicking up a fuss."

"A what?" My voice was rough. I rubbed my groggy eyes.

"She won't stop crying, and it's bothering the others." The guardsman's Greek was thickly slurred. "Me most of all. A horribly grating noise."

Not bothering to don a shirt or armor, I rose and ventured out into the evening chill. Stiff legs groaned from incomplete rest, and I half stumbled several paces until proper balance was restored. The cold air prickled the hairs on my arms as the guardsman and I reached the Gepid tent, though its stench preceded it from over thirty paces distant.

Another guardsman had patrolled the main entryway. An ash spear in one hand and my wineskin in the other, he nodded as we approached, taking another deep swig before tossing the skin to his comrade.

"Finally," he said, and burped.

It did not take long to understand his irritation. Amongst the general weeping and groaning emanating from the tent, one young woman's voice rang out above the rest. The piercing rage of her cries was as insistent as the fear, and as she wept, she spoke, a litany of thickly accented Heruli interspersed with the unintelligible Gepid tongue.

"Your captive is disturbing the others," one of the guardsmen hiccupped in Greek, leaning upon his steadying spear. "She was fine for a few hours but started screaming her damn head off not long ago."

Frost slithered through my veins as I considered their words, laced with boredom. "Any thoughts on what the cause may be?"

"No idea," one said, belching into a closed fist.

"Who knows," the original recipient of my bribe added. "She's a tree-worshipping Gepid. They are all lunatics."

They chuckled, and I rolled my eyes. I grabbed a nearby torch and went to unknot the cord at the entrance, suppressing a gag as the crowded interior revealed itself.

Heat from dozens of bodies thickened the already pungent stink. Few of the white-haired Gepids slept as I slipped toward Rosamund, with many scurrying from my path. Along the tent's edge, I found her, her breathing ragged and face blotchy from weeping. I woke her, gently, and motioned for her to follow me out of the tent, which, to my surprise, she did with nary a question or complaint. Once outside, I forced myself to show a patient face as I set the torch back to its holster and sought answers from Rosamund.

"Please explain." My Heruli came out in a shudder as the crisp air billowed against my exposed skin.

"You told me I would be safe here." Rosamund gestured to the tent. "But your soldiers come, laugh, point to Gepid women or girls, and then carry them out into the night."

Frustration simmered in my veins. My anger was not with my captive but with myself; my own weak conviction had seen my ward placed in considerable—yet easily avoided—jeopardy.

"None took you?" I asked lightly.

Rosamund shook her head, her eyes dropping to the dagger concealed at her waist. By torchlight, she appeared thoroughly exhausted, her dagger hand trembling faintly as she held my gaze.

"Did your people not try to protect the women? Or you?" I spoke callously, wanting the blame to lie anywhere but with me.

Rosamund snorted. "Did they try to protect us? They're beaten, bloodied, and unarmed. And none would fight hard to save *me*."

"No?"

"I'm the shaman's daughter." Rosamund sighed. "Most fear the gods and seek their blessing from those who commune with them. Yet few ever seek the company of those with the gods' ear, for cruel endings await all who hold that mantle."

I shuddered, yet whether such reaction was from the rising chill or from Rosamund's invocation of her pagan deities, I do not know. As a war captive, she had no rights and few protections under Roman law, and as a soldier, I was under no obligation to believe any of her claims. Yet as Rosamund stood against the Dacian night, I found I did indeed believe her account, and all the implications that came with it.

"You will not allow any other soldiers to take liberties with the captives." My Greek was a hard growl at the two guardsmen at my back. "Once we reach Singidunum, their fates will be decided, but not before."

The first guard smirked. "And why is that?"

"Because it is against the law, and a violation of your oath to the army," I all but snarled at him. "Unless they show violence against a Roman soldier, they are not to be harmed."

Amusement gave way to hostility, and the second guardsman advanced with weapon in hand. Yet his companion signaled him to stop and nodded at me.

"As you wish, dekarchos," he muttered. He pointed to Rosamund. "But why should we let you leave with this one? Surely that is a breach of banda law?"

I drew closer, towering over the smaller man. "Because Centurion Mundus afforded me such privileges, and if you impede me further, I will explain to him that you were drunk while on sentry duty."

Upon reflection, only a little of what I said bore merit. Roman law did prohibit the unnecessary despoiling or assault of captives—thus preserving their bodies for sale at the slave markets—yet few soldiers were ever charged with such violations. Mundus did allow Rosamund to remain at my side, but he would have strongly disapproved of me allowing her any liberty at night, at least while we remained on Gepid territory. Here, she was the enemy. Nor did I even trust the guardsmen to keep their word, for once their watch concluded, the successors would likely continue trading in Gepid flesh to sate the depravity of Rome's spearmen. Only their fear of punishment for drunkenness on duty gave me leeway to ensure Rosamund was spared further torment, and though doing so placed me at odds with others from my banda, I had rarely felt more at peace with a decision before, or since.

"You do not have to return to the tent," I said, "but there are no empty tents, and no other women in our group other than the captive Gepids."

With a deep breath, Rosamund wiped tears from her cheeks, now raw from weeping and cold.

"Please don't leave me alone again." Her Heruli was curiously deferential where before it had been laced with disgust. "I could stay in your tent, even for one night."

Rosamund had few, if any, other options, I knew, yet her words still surprised me beyond any logic. But the more she pleaded, the more serious her intent became. Her teeth were chattering as she shuffled lightly for warmth, waiting.

"What makes you think you would be any safer with my men?" I asked at last, genuinely curious. "Or me?"

Fresh tears erupted from Rosamund's fatigue-lined face, yet still she scowled, frustration boiling. "If you were going to assault me, you would have already done so," she said bitterly. "That's more than I can say for your comrades in arms."

As wind gusted through the camp, I raised my hands in surrender. "For tonight only, you can stay with my men."

Relief washed over Rosamund's face. I motioned toward the tent that housed my spearmen. The girl followed close, clutching hard at her upper arms and rubbing the exposed skin in a feeble attempt for warmth. Her coarse linen shirt had been ripped and burned and could afford no real protection. Always a pace behind me, Rosamund observed warily as I ducked into my shared sleeping quarters, holding the tent flap open for her to follow.

"Trouble?" Perenus mumbled in Greek. Half asleep, he rose to meet his intruders but found only Rosamund in the doorway. "What's she doing here?"

"Other groups were taking the captives, so she's staying here tonight," I whispered. "Keep an eye open for any trouble."

"Trouble always seems to find me," Perenus remarked. "Wish it would go away, but it rarely does."

Amid the rumbling of snoring spearmen, Rosamund followed me to the corner of the tent that had previously been my berth. I offered my cloak, which, though just as ragged as her own clothing and suffused with sweat and smoke besides, she snatched greedily. Bundled into the thick crimson mantle, she fell to a seated position, where she scanned her surroundings and gripped the cloak with thin fingers, clenching her loaned dagger against her abdomen all the while.

"Thank you," she whispered grudgingly, and lay her head on the hard earth.

With the cloak yet tighter around her body, Rosamund turned to surveil the men under my command. I would like to recall her newfound surroundings as granting Rosamund the peace and security of sleep, yet the truth, as always, is not nearly as noble as I would hope to tell myself. Multiple times in that frigid Dacian night, I awoke to her muffled sobs. She faced the tent's interior, at first away from my prone form, yet eventually, her body nudged within a handbreadth of my own, her shivering yielding to not only the insulation from the cloak but also the heat of the tent's bodies.

I awoke well before dawn, a habit instilled from a lifetime of servitude under Justin as well as the insistent lessons of Father Petrus. Rosamund jumped at my sudden movement, but she stilled when I placed a finger over my mouth. She trailed me out of the tent, where stars flitted overtop the Moesian forest and a sharp breeze that lacked the chill of the earlier evening blew. I grabbed fresh clothing and enough biscuits and dried fruit for two, walked to the edge of camp, then motioned for Rosamund to follow.

"I'm heading to the nearby stream to bathe," I explained, holding out the smallest tunic and trousers that I could find. "If you'd like, you can change into clean clothes and eat something while I'm away."

"You're going alone?" she asked, and added, "Unarmed?"

"I don't plan on fighting any fish." I grinned. "I won't be long, and I'll tell the sentry to leave you to your privacy."

I placed the food and clothing into Rosamund's hand and offered a thin smile, surveying the thick woods along the camp's western edge. After passing another of my copper coins to the patrolling sentry on duty, I wormed my way between dense clusters of sycamore trees and followed the sound of flowing water just over a hundred paces distant. Though the sky was still dark, its slow gleaming to the deepest shades of violet helped illuminate my path once the thick brush obstructed the camp's torches.

Just beyond a small downhill clearing, I found it: the stream was swift, yet safe enough to keep a man from slipping and drowning within its deeper center. Perhaps thirty paces across, it fed into the much larger Ister, and had provided our camp with refilled waterskins for the following day's march. Its rustling water helped stifle any ambient noise from the camp, and provided a rhythmic sense of peace rarely found within the company of soldiers.

At the banks of the water, I placed the bundle of clothing and clean white cloths next to an overhanging tree. Though most of the Empire's merchants and patricians regularly visited baths that served most Imperial cities, many of the Emperor's soldiers refused to bathe but once or twice per year despite such supplies being issued to every centurion, claiming that bathing invited fevers or even a more serious illnesses. Liberius had scoffed at such talk as fool's prattle, and was known to eject pupils from his classroom when they grew too rank. Samur, who took great pains to avoid the Roman baths, was a frequent victim. Yet where Samur had the courage to defy Justin or Liberius, I acquiesced to their demands early in childhood, and thus for me, bathing was as regular of a habit as could be expected within the palace's slave quarters or, indeed, within an Imperial Army outpost.

I stripped from my charred and stained soldier's garb and dropped the filthy garments onto the ground before venturing toward the rushing waters. Though the breeze had grown warmer overnight, my skin still prickled at the chill, which only sharpened as the frigid water swirled over my ankles. At last, I surrendered to the momentary discomfort and waded toward the deepest center of water, rising well above my waist. I plunged into the ink-dark abyss only to shoot upright, wiping water from my eyes as the cold flooded me.

Those brief moments of solitude were nothing short of heavenly. I scrubbed at the caked-on soot and grime and washed away dried blood—some mine, but most Gepid. Streaks of dried gore, dirt, and ash fell away in the current, the frigid water more tenable after my initial bout of shivering. When I closed my eyes, the bruises and aches of my body felt more urgent, massaged by the flowing water in a delicious ache. I slowly submerged up to my neck, my eyes closed and breathing slow as I offered my own private thanks to God for allowing me to survive my first raid. It was only then that I even recognized it as such: I, a soldier, had fought and lived through a raid.

Senses blurred, I did not hear the approach of footsteps in the grass and leaves of the hillside. The swirl of wind and the gently rushing stream even dulled the interloper's movement as they reached the stream's embankments, a stone's throw from my position. My trance only broke when a light splashing shattered the harmony of the stream. I snapped to alertness, ready for ambush or enemy and cursing my lack of weapon.

Yet I found no enemy. Only Rosamund, wading in my direction.

"What are you doing here?" I cried. "How did you leave camp?"

Yet she did not reply. Still clad in her faded green tunic, Rosamund shivered as she entered the water, a hand behind her back as she navigated uncertain depths.

"Rosamund! This isn't proper!" I called out in more deliberate Heruli. "Please go back to shore and wait for me to dress."

Again, she gave no response. Long white hair glued together with blood, Rosamund sank deeper into the water, allowing it to rise above her waist and grow level at her chest. As she came closer, the lingering moon illuminated her pale face, still ravaged from heavy weeping. At just a few paces away, her eyes broke away from my own, intent on staying steady. Utterly exposed, I considered splashing toward the embankment and toward the safety of clothing, strongly preferring modesty than whatever predicament I now found myself. Yet the trees were much too far, and Rosamund too near to avoid such impropriety.

"Rosamund?" I asked one final time. Fear and concern bubbled in my chest as this strange creature waded into the frigid current—

could she even swim? Her body was slight enough to drift away like a leaf if she lost her balance.

She let out a single cry, though it was more a pout of resignation than a bleat of pain. Thinking she was injured, I waived concerns of immodesty and stepped forward, the flowing water reaching to the base of my ribcage. Whether dulled by prolonged cold or a pervasive bashfulness, I cannot be certain, though my instincts nearly failed me for what came next.

Rosamund snapped her arm forward, lifted the dagger above her matted hair, and plunged. The winding slash into my shoulder was slow and clumsy, yet still struck hard toward its target.

I grasped Rosamund's forearm, halting the dagger a finger length from my left shoulder. With a screech, Rosamund lashed at my body with a flurry of blows from her other arm, her closed fist smacking against my other shoulder. Though painful, her jabs inflicted no real damage, merely smacking against wet skin with a sting.

"No!" Rosamund screamed, one arm suspended in air and the other incapacitated.

"Give me the dagger!" I growled, straining against Rosamund's squirming and the gradual tug of the current.

Rosamund hissed and grunted as she struggled for freedom and yanked against my grip. Yet her ferocity quickly waned, heavy breathing interspersed with curses in frustration. She smacked my chest and shoulders again and again, even striking my jaw with an open palm. I would not strike back, but swiftly twisted Rosamund's arm across her body, spinning her until she faced away. She squirmed and hissed once more, yet as I dragged her deeper into the stream, her resistance waned at last.

Now held in my arms, she melted into wailing grief and convulsions. I relaxed my grip enough to slide one hand past her wrist and toward the priceless dagger, which slipped without resistance into my palm. Her head drooped toward the water, and the sudden fear that Rosamund's cries would be heard from the camp's sentries shot through me. I silently prayed that the clamor of stiff winds and the rustling stream would drown any of our human noise. For how long we stood there, I cannot say, for I held Rosamund still as she emanated a bottomless grief known only by those who have lost everything in life suddenly, unpredictably, and without reservation.

"They're all dead," she choked out. "My mother, my brother, anyone I've ever cared for."

"I'm so sorry," I said, though not without confusion at my own empathy for one who moments before had attempted to injure me.

Rosamund belted a laugh tainted with sarcasm. I motioned for her to face me and released my hold over her arms. Rosamund only shook her head.

"Why?" she demanded. "You've probably earned plenty of wealth on this raid, and our peoples were never friends. How can you be sorry for what your precious army has done?"

"Because you and I are much the same," I said. "When I was little more than a babe, my own village was burned to the ground, and my brother and I were taken as slaves for the Romans. I grew without knowing my mother or father, knowing only bondage to those who see me only as a savage."

Rosamund's features pinched as she wept once more and spilled a stream of ferocious anger and sadness in her native tongue. Her wrinkling hands rose above the water, and she buried her face in open palms, strands of sopping white hair screening her from view. Curiously, however, she bent her shrouded head forward until it brushed against my shoulder, once the very target of her attack. For several heartbeats, I remained motionless, flooded with confusion, wariness, and, indeed, bashfulness. Yet all I could do was wrap an arm carefully around her body, my hand still clinging tight to Aetius' dagger.

We remained there for a short while, our embrace only broken when the cold finally set Rosamund shivering once more and she lifted her head upright. Though it was still well before dawn, the deep purple of the heavens slowly brightened, heralding yet another day on the march.

With the layers of blood, ash, and dirt washed off Rosamund's form, I could see her features more clearly. Her skin lacked the scars and sores that plagued most Roman citizens, whether from illness or from injury sustained while toiling in the fields. She was thin but not sickly, and possessed firm muscles that ladies of the Roman Court would have disdained as unfeminine. Her face was, I could not deny, enrapturing, not only for its simple beauty unlike the soft-bodied patrician women who inhabited the Emperor's Court. Rosamund's face nevertheless bore flaws—eyes slightly too far apart, a sharply pointed nose, and a mouth just a mild degree too large for her face—yet such features were not unpleasant, at least not to me.

I locked onto Rosamund's eyes, ready to give my Gepid captive a choice that would forever change her fate.

"You are free to leave if you wish. I will not stop you," I said. "Nor will any other Roman in this band."

A flicker of surprise lined Rosamund's brow that immediately returned to one of skepticism and doubt.

"I am not your slave?"

"No," I said firmly. "Not long ago, I was a slave to Romans, along with my brother. I will not force others into that fate on my behalf."

The thought of Samur stung, releasing a deep-set shame that had haunted, but never overtaken, my every step in the army. He had written several letters as my months of service drew on, offering words of encouragement and requesting tales of life as a warrior far from the filth and noise of Constantinople. Sickeningly cheerful, Samur's writing further assured me that his own service in the palace had been relatively peaceful and unbothered. Yet my thoughts still lingered on the measures of revenge that Solomon or his followers might instill in my absence. In our exchanges, I repeated my promise to free Samur from bondage, a pledge that seemed no closer to fruition than the day I last saw my brother.

Of course, Rosamund knew none of this, yet she eyed me curiously all the same. Rosamund glanced at her surroundings, sighed and shrugged.

"Where would I go?" she asked bitterly. "How would I survive? All that I have ever loved is ashes and dust."

"As a free person, only you can make that decision," I said. "But if it is your wish to stay, you may remain on as my servant, at least until we return to Thrace."

"A servant?" she asked. "What do these servants even do within your armies?"

"Cooking, cleaning, sending messages... things that an army camp requires," I explained. "Most officers have a servant or two, either on campaign or while stationed in a barracks. The work is ceaseless, but offers payment for loyal service."

"But I will still be free?" The skeptical look did not leave her face. "And safe?"

"Yes, you will be free, and any mistreatment of a soldier's servant is met with a grave punishment." I offered a broad smile. "In my service, you will be given clothing, food, protection, and some coin for your own purposes. If you wish to leave, for any reason, you may do so."

Rosamund's shivering intensified to full shudders, yet she broke her silence only for one remaining question.

"Why? Why would you do this for someone you do not know? I could have killed you."

My smile faded into a grimace. In truth, there were only a few good reasons to take permanent responsibility over Rosamund, and a great many better ones to cast her aside. In less than the span of a day, she had been immensely troublesome, and would likely require many months of patient training to become any kind of decent camp servant. Further, she spoke neither Greek nor Latin, and was no kind of Christian whatsoever; Father Petrus could only disapprove.

However, my increased wages as a commander of ten did provide more than enough pay to afford a servant or two. Such was common and expected, even; the more senior officers, like Archelaus, commanded dozens of servants and slaves. It was not the nature of the expenditure, but what it would deprive me of — dispensing my earnings on a half-wild Gepid only set me further back from paying my brother's freedom. Yet, if I dismissed her to the forests, Rosamund would die; I held no doubts. Starvation, or illness, or an attack by some other roving band of warriors — she could not survive alone. And if I left another innocent to her death, I knew with certainty that those screams from distant memories would haunt my sleep for the rest of my days.

"Because it is the honorable choice," I replied. "I believe in fate, and it seems that ours are intertwined, for better or worse."

At that, Rosamund chuckled, her face brightening for perhaps the first time. "Fate," she muttered. "Very well, I accept your offer."

To seal our bond, I recited the servant's oath, its words burned into my mind from a lifetime of servitude to Justin. It seemed a lifetime ago that I had spoken the words as a child, yet where Rosamund came to them freely, mine were as one indentured to the Empire. I replied with an oath that I would not mistreat her, nor ask her to violate her own conscience, during which her eyes narrowed, yet she kept silent.

Though many nights have passed, I cannot imagine any single instance since that has wrought such sweeping changes upon my life, or, indeed, upon the lives of so many thousands within the Empire and beyond. Yet that tale must be told in its own time, with all its joys and crushing sorrows born from this genesis. For it is as

Liberius often noted: Order demands that everything find its proper place. From this moment forward, Rosamund's fate has far to go in this tale. As our pact was sealed, how could we, still so young, know the world would be forever altered?

"It is done," I said. "I'll leave you to wash, but turn around so I may leave."

Rosamund shrugged as I backed away. She dunked her head beneath the frigid water and gasped back to air, then tied her waterlogged hair into a thick knot atop her head.

"Turn around," I asked again, fearing to proceed to the shallower portions of that mighty stream.

"Why?" Rosamund cocked her head.

"Because… it is not proper for men and women to bathe at the same time." My face grew hot as I struggled to look away. I thought of the indolent nephews in the palace, their sloppy groping of hordes of women—men I never sought to imitate.

She stared at me with growing bemusement. "Do women in your country not bathe?"

I stammered for a response. "No, they—of course they do, maybe even more so than men." God help me, what was I saying? "It is just… not normal for both sexes to bathe together, you see?"

"Oh," was all she said, eyebrow arched. She neither acknowledged nor denied my professed taboo, but simply glided several paces away until the flowing water lapped atop her shoulders. She tugged the tunic over her head, pinching and rubbing at the material to remove smears of dirt and blood.

Gathering courage, I darted toward the bank of the stream and toward the pile of clothing near a sycamore whose twisted branches hung precariously over the water. Raw skin and deep bruises ached as I dried my body; a still-healing cut on my forearm even leaked a thin trail of blood. With a quick glimpse of my surroundings, I spied a second pile of clothing not ten paces distant, neatly folded and stacked atop a squat boulder.

My privacy was soon disrupted by a light splashing from the stream. Rosamund waded farther, toward the boulder of her discarded items, but halted when the water lowered to her waist.

"Varus, can you hand me a cloth for drying?" she called, shivering as the wind blew against her exposed skin.

It was not as though Rosamund was the first woman I had seen. We were soldiers, true, but we were still men. Though I myself had abstained, plenty of spearmen in my banda had spent their hard-earned stipend on prostitutes who traveled from the capitol for a stint at the barracks, and as a youth I shared pleasures with another of the palace slaves—an indiscretion that neither she nor I ever shared with our masters, or—for me, at least—with any confessor. Despite whatever libertine past I could lay claim to, I did not want to disgrace Rosamund; neither did I have any desire to hold her at my every beck and call as so many other officers had done with their female servants and slaves. I did not leave behind slavery myself only to chain others to the same kind of fate.

I scurried for my trousers, huffing in indignation at Rosamund's breach of modesty.

"Turn round and wait, by God!"

Rosamund rolled her eyes and groaned. Rather than obey, she darted from the water and toward her fresh clothing, wiping droplets from her skin and donning the overlarge tunic. The Gepids, I would soon discover, held wildly un-Christian notions of dignity and morality; their gods demanded no apparent shame for the human body. Fully attired, Rosamund walked toward me and tossed aside her previous garb, its burns and stains ruining the garment beyond repair.

"Show me your arm." She pointed at the stinging cut.

I hesitated. "What are you going to do?"

"You need to clean your wounds more thoroughly to keep the body from poisoning itself," she commanded again, her eyes concerned as she took in the damage.

I tried to stall. "How do you know this?"

Rosamund chuckled. "You are a poor listener. My father was the village shaman, always healing aches and pains. He made me learn his ways young, and I have seen enough cuts like this to understand what they will do if left alone."

Rosamund held my arm outwards, grabbed one of my washcloths, and scrubbed at the opening. I jerked away, wincing. Rosamund clicked her tongue.

"Stop fidgeting. You're making this more difficult than it needs to be."

I could feel her body heat as she drew close once more, her breathing as regular as if she were at rest. Her labors undeterred, Rosamund dunked the cloth into the stream and rubbed forcefully around the cut's edges. Hidden streaks of dirt flowed down my arm, mixing with occasional oozing droplets of blood.

"Finished," she declared at last. "Although you'll want to wrap the gash to help the skin knit back together."

As a thin ray of reddish-orange flitted along the horizon, our time at the stream drew to a close. The tunic and trousers hung loosely on Rosamund's frame, but she did not complain or perhaps even notice, for they shielded that near-translucent skin of hers from the cold. Without hesitation, I yielded the dagger into Rosamund's keeping once more, its blade and scabbard quickly hidden inside the folds of her clothing. Together, we walked toward the camp, my mind stirring at all that had transpired.

At our arrival, the duty sentry barked initial wariness that quickly morphed to bemusement as he surveyed us. Not wishing to contend with any lascivious jibes, I led Rosamund through the picket line. Though the first rays of sun had snuck along the skyline, no officers had awoken to prepare for the day's march. With no desire to rouse them myself, I opened the tent flap and crawled into my corner.

William Havelock

A warm body climbed in behind me. Re-wrapping the cloak around her prone frame, Rosamund shuddered several times as she fought for sleep, her chest heaving, though whether from cold or sadness, I still do not know to this day. Perhaps if I had deigned to ask, the years ahead would have turned out differently, yet in my ignorance and fatigue, I merely surrendered to my body's urges for sleep, leaving Rosamund behind as my world drew black.

The Last Dying Light

RETURN TO THRACE

Horns blared to order the breakup of camp; it was, I noticed, unusually late in the day for such a command. I rose to find a folded cloak where Rosamund's body once lay. I panicked; had she escaped in the night with Aetius' dagger? Thankfully, moments later, she appeared through the tent entrance, with Perenus close behind. The two bore considerable breakfast rations and heavy waterskins for the men, who accepted with a mixture of thanks and curiosity.

"Can't understand a thing she's saying!" Perenus noted cheerily. "A lot of pointing and grunting thus far. No matter, though; food is a language all its own."

While Perenus haphazardly tossed rations to the others, Rosamund handed out the twice-baked bread and dried fruit more carefully—even cautiously. She did not shrink at deformed Cephalas, extending him his food with a warm yet melancholy smile, hinting she felt, as I did, the upheaval of so much change in so little time. With the others satisfied, she took a portion for herself, gnawing at the meal, unbothered by the men's curious stares.

"This tastes terrible," she told me in Heruli. "It's going to break my teeth."

Grinning, I translated her words to the men, who hooted in laughter. If nothing else, the Gepid girl and the Roman soldiers shared a distaste for our pitiful food. Isaacius clapped as he nodded to our newfound companion.

"Will she be staying with us awhile, then?"

I nodded, raising my voice so the others would all hear. "Her name is Rosamund, and she is my household servant. Treat her with respect and patience, and she will assist you with camp needs."

My command acknowledged, the men ate in silence, sore from the previous day yet all alive, and, for the most part, hale. As they finished, they drew together clothing and armor and girded their limbs for a long march ahead. The men's attention now turned to equipment, Rosamund approached me with the half-full sack of remaining food.

I knew what she wanted. "To the Gepid tent," I confirmed in Heruli.

Beaming, Rosamund hurried off to her captive countrymen, and I set to my own preparations. When she returned, however, her sun-bright cheer had succumbed to another bout of tears and rage. "They called me a Roman whore!" she cried. "They took the food, all right, but still they hissed and shouted at me."

This was undoubtedly my fault. If I were an unlucky Gepid captive, I would see Rosamund's improved circumstances and conclude only the same thing. Men and women have done far worse for the sake of survival, yet the vanquished never see friendship with the enemy as anything but unforgiveable. And Rosamund, I recalled, was already something of an outcast. She of all Gepids was least likely to earn the understanding of her kinsmen.

But it did not deter her long. Rosamund wiped her eyes, packed her few belongings into a cloth bundle, and joined us outside the tent as we decamped. Mundus hailed me as we fell into formation; his face was purple from healing bruises, yet he looked happier than the day before.

"Still alive?" Mundus asked.

"Still alive."

Satisfied, Mundus remarked that my new servant had visited him early in the day — with Perenus as escort — and had re-stitched the sloppy sutures that Archelaus' camp healer had tugged through the flesh of his forehead.

"Can barely speak a word of Greek, but definitely a valuable friend to bring along," Mundus said, fingertips at his temple and admiration in his voice.

We shared knowledge of the status of the men, including those who were recovering from injuries, and who would need greater attention at Singidunum. After further idle talk, I changed the subject. "How long after a battle are you able to sleep normally again?"

"Without the nightmares, you mean?" Mundus said. "For me, it took a whole month. You are getting them?"

I nodded, but gave no details. Without prying, he offered me his advice. "I've spoken with several priests, who said I needed to do penance, but none of that helped."

"What did?" I couldn't help but pry.

"Time, lad. That is the only real cure," Mundus said. "I have seen men drink themselves into a dreamless sleep, yet that is no behavior for an officer. I have seen others that pray, but I can tell you that, for me, if God listened, He did not act. The only thing that made the nights more bearable was when I would go to the training yard and pretend a post was one of the men I had just killed in battle. I poured all of my anger into that face, telling them they could not attack me from death." Mundus considered. "Some nights, I would spend hours in the yard, hacking and slashing until the post sawed over or the sun came up. A month passed, and my dreams became my own again."

So we began our travel homeward. It took another four days until we reached the Ister and returned to Roman soil. Rosamund shared more of her life with me, and I explained more of Roman culture. She listened intently of stories about Constantinople and the Emperor, and asked if the capitol was as large as Singidunum, which she had glimpsed once as a young girl.

I laughed, hopefully not unkindly. "Many times larger. So vast that you can spend a lifetime walking its streets and never see all it has to offer."

I taught her a few phrases in Greek, the main language spoken in any Roman camp. She had a quick mind, and needed only a little repetition to memorize camp instructions, soldier ranks, and other choice words that a camp servant would find useful. Yet during one lesson, she paused, confused.

"Why do you call yourselves Romans? You live nowhere near Rome, and you speak Greek."

"What do your people call us?" I wondered.

"Greeks." She thought a moment. "Or Christians, depending upon what brought you to our villages."

In the end, I left her question unanswered. On the second day, as we neared the Ister, she balked, just barely, as we neared the edges of her peoples' lands.

"Why did you come to our village?" she asked me softly. "You and your war band?"

My soul teemed with excuses. I reasoned briefly that, at least according to Archelaus' explanation, any Gepid group was our enemy after the raids on Roman settlements. I thought better of it.

"I honestly do not know," I said. "We were ordered to do so, and we followed those orders."

Rosamund kept silent until the banks of the Ister came into view. Her jaw clenched, her onetime boiling resentment visibly simmering again. She held particular disdain for Archelaus, and always spat after he had passed—and made it a safe distance away, thank God—as a pagan ward against his evil. Still, she was savvy enough not to challenge a komes of the Roman army outright nor raise complaints to any but me. To do so would have meant her death, and mine.

At last, we concluded our expedition; the banda reached the Ister's banks on a warm spring morning. Archelaus trotted to the front and signaled the limitanei with our banda's flags; the boatmen came to ferry us to the other side.

Archelaus reported our progress to Singidunum's governor. His story, which we were oathbound to repeat and affirm, was that we had followed the Gepid raiders back to their village. They resisted our attempts to speak with the village leaders and launched a battle that cost six Romans their lives. The governor, representing the Emperor at this frontier province, commended Archelaus for his bravery and pursuit of justice in the lands of the barbarians. Shortly thereafter, the governor saluted our banda, and promised a written commendation to the Emperor detailing our noble deeds.

The Gepid captives were taken to the slave market; the bulk of the profits went to the men who claimed ownership by right of capture. All were sold—that is, none were taken on as a camp servant; our onetime foes simply could not be trusted to care for us who had sacked their homes without provocation. Mundus did question Rosamund's own trustworthiness, but I assured the centurion of her loyalty. Nevertheless, I did offer Rosamund the opportunity to leave, promising her enough money to buy a horse and provisions to find other Gepid villages.

She declined with little hesitation. "I have nothing left there, and nothing else to find. So unless you wish me to leave, I would like to stay." But this was not without a note of bitterness as the last of her Gepid countrymen were sent away from Singidunum.

After the profits from the slaves were distributed, Archelaus next assembled the men and servants to witness the discipline of the two deserters. Stripped of their cloaks, the unlucky men each wore only a stained white shift that left their legs bare and feet scraping the cragged stone ground of Singidunum's broken forum. A wooden stage had been erected for onetime Imperial decrees to be shouted to the city's masses, yet few enough remained within

Singidunum's walls other than the limitanei for such a luxury to continue.

With us, his banda, in formation, Archelaus dragged the two prisoners to the platform by a long iron chain. For cowardice, both men were given thirty lashes that reduced their backs to bloody ribbons. One cried out for his mother, blubbing fat tears as spittle ran down his chin and onto the platform. The other—Barda—bore his punishment silently, biting down hard on a wooden block as the whip bit deep into his flesh to muffle his cries to mere murmurs.

Rosamund watched with us, wincing and seething hatred at Archelaus. "He is an evil man," she said in muted Heruli.

A small mercy was that the men would not have to suffer the gashes long, or any inflamed illness in the wounds that led to a slow and painful death. For, as deserters, they were sent to the hangman.

Father Petrus offered to give both last rites, which Archelaus tried to brush away.

"Save God for those who don't piss their pants and run, Father," Archelaus growled, glaring at the two men as they rose to the gallows.

Father Petrus would not be denied, however, and gave the men their last hope at salvation for an afterlife they would soon meet. Nooses were fitted around their necks and stools kicked from under their feet. There, they choked, tongues lolling impossibly far from gaping mouths. Foam spread onto their chins, their bodies swinging as their souls departed at last. The regulations satisfied, Archelaus dismissed us, leaving the bodies to be disposed of by the city's gravediggers—no soldier's burial for them.

The next day, we took our leave of Singidunum, boarding the barges that would return us to our camp in Thrace. My men told stories and drank wine to pass the time, while Rosamund practiced her Greek. Father Petrus, still, disapproved of her presence.

"Gepids are unabashed pagans, Varus," Father Petrus admonished. "Some say that they sacrifice deformed babies to their dark gods, or send the elderly off to die when they are unable to gather food or fight in battles."

"They say the same about the Heruli, Father," I pointed out. "Surely mercy and the opportunity for redemption is preferable to banishment and death?"

Father Petrus relented with a tepid smile. "You may be right," he ventured, then hurried to add, "Yet only God knows such things. We mere sinners must be wary all the same."

Together, we left the Ister, and none dared look back to what remained in our wake. Yet our return to camp would be a brief one, for merely a month later, an Imperial summons came from Constantinople. Its messenger arrived in haste, carrying a hardened leather tube bearing the Imperial Eagle through the banda's wooden gates. After depositing his horse with a camp servant, the courier grabbed his bag and walked to the tent that marked Archelaus as the camp commander. The komes was soon joined by his centurions, and Mundus disappeared into the commander's pavilion for the better part of an afternoon. It was not until later that the rest of us learned the urgency of that missive, and the warning that it bore.

The Empire's northernmost province, Chersonesus, had been invaded by an unnamed tribe from the east. The act of aggression threatened to topple our critical outpost that straddled the northern coastline of the Euxine Sea. Our banda, as part of the larger army, had been summoned to the capitol for organization and dispatch by boat.

We were ordered to war.

The Last Dying Light

THE THRACIAN ARMY

And so, days later, the camp emptied of men and servants, leaving just a token force of new recruits, the wounded and crippled, and enough servants to sweep the buildings and destroy rat's nests. Archelaus insisted that our armor be polished and our weapons sharpened as we headed for the capitol, taking pains to personally inspect—and then punish—those who fell short.

Constantinople's deep ports along the Marmara allowed for easy dispatch of large numbers of men to all corners of the Empire, and thus was the Thracian Army commanded. We left at dawn, striving to arrive in Constantinople without once stopping for encampment.

Rosamund came too, walking in the long stream of camp stragglers and servants that followed the more orderly military column. I had purchased an old mare for her to ride, as much to ease her journey as to carry our growing number of household objects. Before leaving, she levied a barrage of questions about the city, its inhabitants, its rulers, its customs, and how she should behave. She kept my dagger hidden safely in the folds of new clothes that I had bought for a few copper coins. The trickling loss of what little wealth I had earned was my own private concern; Rosamund's blossoming cheer, as well as the prospect of recouping any losses in war, eased my worries.

Rosamund styled her clothes in the Gepid fashion: a dark leather jerkin over a white shirt, with tight breeches that met a pair of closed leather boots just around the knee. The clothes were simple yet still expensive for a young servant of a junior officer, and she cared for them diligently—since, no doubt, they enabled her to ride a horse, which she had taken up with a joy rarely seen since our first meeting in the forests of the Gepid Kingdom.

The Last Dying Light

At last, we neared the city. Its colossal walls came into view, and with it the thousands of banners—the Imperial Eagle, but also the personal sigils of dozens of other senior officers already arrived at the Imperial Barracks. Those looming stone fortifications prompted a longing to rush through the gates and find those I had left behind long ago. Yet, a curious sensation of disquiet anchored in my stomach when I considered their reactions at my progress, whether it be the Emperor's approval of my newfound rank or Samur's weary understanding that I did not yet have the coin to free him from bondage. We halted before one of the many gates into the outer wall as the head officer called for us to identify ourselves in the name of Emperor Justin.

On horseback, Archelaus trotted forward to answer the challenge and ritual required of any armed band that sought entry into the capitol. The officer satisfied, he commanded the gates to open, and the komes led us into the breach.

The noise and smell of the city hit me in a rush as we passed through the second layer of stone walls. Small knots of peasants gathered on each side of the street, which had been cleared by those palace guards permitted to carry weapons and police the city. Urchins dogged our steps, begging and begging for money, unknowing that we had earned little, if anything, in our limited deployment to Singidunum. To their eyes, we were soldiers, and soldiers had money. How long had it been since I was more like these dirty children than my fellows in the banda? It seemed so recent and yet almost a lifetime ago.

My thoughts were dashed as Mundus threw a handful of coppers onto the side of the road, scattering the children in a fight to claim a prize.

The palace guards escorted us to the Imperial Barracks—a huge building that could have fit at least ten bandae and their servants with ease. High ceilings opened to arcing windows, ensuring fresh air swept away the miasma of sweat and dung that accompanied any sizeable encampment of spearmen. Wooden dividers cordoned off each group of ten, leaving the men crammed in increasingly tiny spaces yet retaining close cohesion with their direct officers. Several sections were already occupied, yet we were led to a choice location that emptied out into a side alley diagonally facing the Hippodrome and the Imperial Palace. Our horses were led to the army's stables, and we took to stacking our weapons and armor in the bunks that had been assigned to us. More senior officers — Archelaus, but also Mundus and the centurions — had been provided separate quarters, but even we enlisted men were given small screens to create a luxurious sense of solitude unknown in a Thracian camp.

As the sun set over the Golden Horn, some men ventured into the city to spend coin on wine and women; Perenus and Isaacius led a particularly rowdy group, singing songs of Caesar's conquests of Pontus. Exhausted, I decided against it, set aside my armor, and selected a vacant bunk. After drawing the screen, the narrow quarters and wooden bunks claimed by my group became oddly peaceful, broken only by a breeze fluttering through a vaulted window and the light snores of men already collapsed from a day on the march.

I slept dreamlessly, and awoke late the following morning to a message nailed to the bunk. Leaving Rosamund still asleep in the adjoining bunk — a rare occurrence, as she preferred to awake first to begin the day — I unfurled the note. Spidery text spread across the paper.

Dekarchos Varus of the Herulians, your presence is requested in the Imperial Library as the sun reaches its zenith. You are excused from any other duties.

"Liberius." I smiled at the prospect of seeing my former teacher after a year apart.

I dressed in my tunic, trousers, and armor. Though I was expected to venture to the tiny apartment where Father Petrus lodged near the Forum of Constantine, the message's intent was clear, and Liberius had always hated delays. I scribbled a note of apology to the priest, to be delivered by another, and ventured outside. As I took my first steps into the sun on my brief journey to the Imperial Palace, a form rammed into my side. I stumbled and swung around, fists raised against the unseen attacker—I had no weapons, since Imperial rule forbade soldiers to wander the streets of the capitol with arms in hand. My eyes locked on the assailant as he lashed out once again... and locked my chest in a familiar squeeze.

"Varus!" Samur cried. "I've been waiting for hours, the guards would not let me in! And I hardly recognized you with that beard..."

My brother. I embraced him, surprised at how much taller he'd grown in my absence. He was still as thin as I had remembered, yet his attack of greeting demonstrated that same unassuming strength of his. He still wore the collar of a slave, but clearly still enjoyed the same freedom of movement around the city as I had in our service to the Emperor.

After I guided him back into the barracks, Samur unleashed an onslaught of questions, inquiring about my new life and all that had happened in the previous year. We sat down in one of the barracks' gathering rooms as I answered each in turn, as briefly as I could—our training, our barracks, my new comrades. Samur eyed my exposed arm and traced the long scar that had at last healed.

"How did this happen?" Samur asked, concern shining through his awe. So I told him of our raid against the Gepids, of Archelaus and the other officers, and finally narrated each of the hardships inflicted upon us in the months before deployment at length.

I had just arrived at the advent of Rosamund's presence in my life when, as if I had summoned her myself, Rosamund appeared, fully dressed and bearing rich fare of fresh fruit and honey. She set it before us as I introduced my brother, who leaped to his feet in a formal Greek greeting. Rosamund lifted an eyebrow, turning to me with an amused glance.

"He looks like you," she chided in Heruli. "What does he say?"

"He offers greetings as Varus' brother!" Samur answered excitedly, his words a crude mesh as his pace of speech quickened. "But who, may I ask, are you?"

Rosamund introduced herself, her speech measured yet curious at my blood relative. In turn, Samur's words of welcome spilled awkwardly from his lips, insisting that he would acquire anything that Rosamund might need in her service to me. Rosamund flashed her own smile at such a display, assuring my brother that such an offer would surely be taken advantage of. After a few further moments, I interjected into their conversation, noting my need to speak with my brother before rushing to the palace. Rosamund nodded and slipped from the barracks, heading out onto Constantinople's streets for her own morning of exploration.

"A servant, too? You and her…" A wicked grin spread across Samur's face.

"She is a member of my household, not a lover." I would not let him wander down that path. "And speak Heruli. That is all she can understand, at least until her Greek improves."

Samur shrugged and changed direction, telling me stories of the palace. "So much has changed, Varus, and not all of it for the better." He retook his seat on the barracks bench. Eyeing a stray apple, Samur stole the fruit and gorged at the juicy pulp, beginning his tale of all the changes that had occurred in our year apart.

So it was. Samur told me first of our dominus' continued decline. Lacking the vigor for governance, Justin now oversaw his authority and responsibilities carried out by the combination of Liberius, Basilius, Justinian, and Theodora, now Justinian's wife. Justinian and Theodora performed all the traditional court ceremonies in the Emperor's name, while Liberius and Basilius signed orders and executed new laws for the provinces and the army. Liberius, Samur noted with relish, was still the same wild character that he always had been, but Basilius had slowed with growing age, and Godilas had taken further to heavy drink. He still held the position of master-at-arms but had faded to a shadow of the legends told by army campfires.

Samur also shared news of our old classmates, many of whom had been sent to various corners of the Empire in service of the army or the Imperial government.

"Antonina, that cow, was married off to Justinian's pet general in Cappadocia," he told me, "yet *still* she skulks around the palace! She's always whispering in Theodora's ear. Poor lady."

That surprised me. I had thought that Antonina would decamp with her husband, Flavius Belisarius, when he took up his role of general of a new army in Cappadocia and Armenia. Still, it made its own kind of sense; in the capitol, Antonina enjoyed both protection from her father and, evidently, new favor as a leading lady of the court.

"What of Solomon?" I asked, though I regretted the question as soon as I voiced it.

Samur winced. Less than a year had passed since I left for training, but in that time, my brother's nose had been permanently bent out of shape, and his arms and face latticed with scrapes and scars. His broken limbs had fully healed, thank God, yet I found my rage still simmered at a host of fresher injuries along his body.

"He was just granted command of a new banda by Justinian," Samur spat. "All under the loving gaze of Senator Nepotian."

Though the Senate held little real power in the Eastern Empire, men such as Solomon's father possessed untold mounds of gold. In a wealth-starved Empire, such resources could stretch far and shepherd many patrician families into the Emperor's innermost circle. Without a day's training in a formal army, Solomon had been promoted above Mundus, and even equal to Archelaus himself.

"Do his idiot cronies still stalk you?" I had to know.

"Liberius does his best to intervene, but the Emperor does not have the stamina to stay directly involved in the lives of his slaves any further."

Samur gave no more direct an answer, simply narrowing his shoulders and rubbing at thick bruises that spotted over his arms. We had talked so long it was now nearly midday, so I left him in the company of Rosamund, and the two chattered excitedly in their shared Herulian tongue. I had to admit, it pleased me greatly to see them get on so well—for with Rosamund and Samur both, one could never know how a stranger might fare.

I left the barracks to attend my meeting with Liberius. I had traveled these streets adjoining the palace for years, yet they somehow seemed smaller as I strode in full armor, my hobnailed boots smacking proudly against the stones. As a soldier, I was not expected to scurry out of the way for a passing merchant or freeman; I could stay my head unbowed en route to the Emperor's sweeping residence. Yet it was not until I reached its gates that I felt the changes down to my core. From habit, or my own unbroken slave's timidity, I nearly went for the obscured servant's entrance rather than the grand main gateway. But no—now I had every right, with a letter to attest as much, even if I did not yet feel it in my soul. To the guard, I showed my missive, and the wax Imperial seal granted me entry to the building that, until recently, had been the only home I had ever known.

The palace was alive with activity, far more than in my boyhood under Anastasius. Dignitaries from a dozen nations flitted about, some with familiar, though foreign, manners and dress, and others whose tongues and sigils were utterly unknown even to one of Liberius' former pupils. Some were garbed in coarse fur and wool, others graceful in fine silks fit for the wardrobe of any emperor. I took it all in, and was headed for my old teacher's rooms when I was stopped by the last man I had wished to see.

"Varus!"

Solomon hailed me with a wide wave, his voice honeyed and familiar. A wolfish grin spread across his face as he greeted me as if I were an old friend, throwing an arm over my shoulder and asking about my year in the army. Spotting the plume on my helmet, he swatted at it with a chuckle.

"Dekarchos... Well, good for you, dear Varus." His tone was pure mockery, and I noticed he fidgeted with his own helmet under his arm, one that displayed the crest of a banda commander. "We both rise in fortunes, it seems. Have you taken a wife, too?"

I replied that I had not, though for a fleeting moment I thought to mention Rosamund. Solomon smirked like a well-fed cat.

"Pity. Father has secured me a marriage to a Ghassanid princess just this week. Doing my duty for the Empire just as soon as the expedition from Cherson is complete."

I resisted a bubbling urge to bash a fist into Solomon's aquiline nose. The Ghassanids had been a Roman ally for generations, a buffer between our rich Syrian provinces and the hungry Persians beyond. No doubt, Solomon's marriage was intended to further cement that alliance for yet another generation. My disdain must have shown, because my rival laughed.

"They say she's a rare beauty, this princess." Solomon's teeth flashed in a broad smile. "At least, as beautiful as an Arab sand-dweller could be. Though I won't disgrace Rome if she turns out to be a pox-riddled hag."

I dearly hoped she would be. But I bit my tongue, wishing him all happiness with his new bride—may God preserve the poor girl. Thankfully, we parted as quickly as we had joined, with Solomon making some excuse and leaving me seething.

Not wanting to give him the pleasure, I shook away my anger and fixed my attention on the flights of marble steps between me and the Emperor's private library. Liberius had always loved lounging in that room, stuffed with thousands of scrolls and richly decorated tomes that detailed thousands of years of human memory. I threw open its doors and found my old teacher, his gray hair and beard as wild as they always had been.

"Ah, Varus! Wonderful to see you!" Liberius proclaimed. "I was beginning to worry that you had forgotten your way around your old home."

With that, Liberius abandoned his thin pretext at decorum and placed two gnarled hands upon my shoulders. His robes smelled of incense and parchment, and ink stains blotched his hem and sleeves, as always.

"You've become a man," Liberius observed, happily rapping his knuckles against my armor. He gave me a little pat on my bearded face. "Tell me of your journeys."

We settled on a pair of benches as servants opened windows for fresh air. I sat awkwardly upon the cushion, now unaccustomed to anything kinder than a soft patch of earth. Nevertheless, I sat up straight and recounted my sojourn into the Emperor's army, from my first day of training through our return from Singidunum. Liberius sat unblinking, taking in each moment with a stern expression. As I finished, he congratulated me on rising to command of ten at such a young age, and chided me for saying so little about Rosamund.

"Such wild creatures, Gepids," Liberius said. "I've only befriended one in my time, and she had outrageous and indiscriminate appetites."

"I wouldn't know, Lord," I murmured.

Liberius laughed. "Of course you wouldn't. Father Petrus would rap you on the knuckles for such wanton behavior."

"Do you know Father Petrus well?" I said. "He claimed to be familiar with the Emperor."

"Varus, it is what I do not know that you should be asking," Liberius said. "Such answers are far more interesting, and far more important. But yes, I would say that I am the Father's oldest friend."

"But I've never seen him in the palace before."

Liberius' lips parted into yet another grin, his eyes twinkling in the torchlight. "That's because you weren't looking for him. Just another threadbare priest in the Emperor's care, at least as far as most others would know. But we can discuss the Father later, for our time together is sadly limited."

Indeed, we abandoned the topic, and Liberius updated me on the swelling activity and sense of purpose within the palace. Alliances were being forged, including, it seemed, Solomon's marriage.

"I never did like that insipid fool," Liberius said, "yet maybe his worthless father will be able to extract some measure of good from his precious son."

Liberius also told me of the ever-changing armies that were forming across the Empire.

"We're learning from our mistakes," Liberius declared, pulling several tomes from the library's shelves. "Godilas and Basilius have been adopting new tactics and units to better engage our enemies, and General Belisarius is implementing them in Armenia. Not all these strategies will be successful, of course, but some have already shown enough promise to share among our field armies. The most promising are the cataphracts, a type of armored horseman we've adopted from the Persians. You will see plenty of them in the capitol's training yard soon enough."

Not stopping to entertain questions or discussion, Liberius went about his business at a swift pace. I cannot know how many hours the wizened minister spent in that library; it was plain that Liberius was fully capable of plotting plans to carry out Justin's dreams in this rare cove of learning in our otherwise storm-tossed world. Liberius unfurled diagrams of new roads, transport plans for large armies, and even sketches of a huge domed church that he traced with loving fingers. "We need to replace the church that you and Theodora decided to burn down."

I marveled at the details of the building, expertly engineered to account for the scale and complexity of the design.

Liberius closed his books, returned to his bench, and leaned forward as though to deliver graver tidings.

"We have much to do, but first, I must go to Judea and Syria," Liberius said matter-of-factly. "You will receive a summons to appear in court in a few days. I am sure that Justin will wish to see you before you leave for Cherson."

Those areas were perilously close to the Persian border and frequently had flared up in a minor rebellion or from minor raids by rogue Arab war bands.

"Why there? Surely someone else can go for you?" I asked.

"In good time, I will reveal an answer to you," Liberius said. "But not this day. For now as you make sacrifices for the Emperor's army, so, too, must I place myself at risk."

"For what purpose?" I could not help a frustrated groan.

"For the only purpose that matters," Liberius answered firmly. "For the dream of Rome, and that we can return to what we once were."

Before my dismissal, Liberius offered a final note of wisdom, all mischief and sarcasm gone.

"You are doing exactly what is necessary to become a good man, and a good servant to the Empire," he said. "You have taken the first steps down a path that will take you to a greater destiny, to protect the last bastion of civilization in a shrinking world. Don't get distracted, don't stoop to the level of your enemies, and don't get killed. Father Petrus would also insist that you pray, and though I would rather put stock in men's actions, I cannot think that it would hurt to seek God's favor in your endeavors. Regardless, we shall see each other again, whether that hour comes soon or late." I nodded. My teacher embraced me one final time. "You are our hope, Varus."

The Last Dying Light

Despite myself, I sniffled heavily, fighting welling tears. I took my leave, the doors closed behind me, and I exited the palace with my chest out and head high.

By the time that I returned to the barracks, Samur had already departed, but he had left word that he would see me again on the morrow. Blissfully, Archelaus was nowhere nearby; he had remained with his old comrades in the excubitor's barracks closer to the palace. I did encounter Mundus, who noted that our banda had been among the first to answer the Emperor's call. We had at least another month before setting sail for the Tauris Peninsula, and would continue training as we awaited other portions of the reformed Thracian Army. Mundus distributed an extra stipend to each of his spearmen, warning all of us to employ such additional wealth constructively and to not dishonor the Roman Army. Perenus nodded; he had no intention of following Mundus' advice and immediately enlisted Isaacius and Cephalas to scheme a variety of ways to spend their unexpected fortune.

With no orders and no real oversight to enforce strict discipline, the men had taken to pursuing their own interests. We were required to maintain our regular drills each day, and the old priest still insisted upon my lessons each morning, though he thankfully allowed me to come to him rather than prodding me awake in the dead of night. Altogether, though, we soldiers found ourselves with the unusual freedom to marshal on our daylight hours to our liking.

Night fell upon our first full day in the city, and Perenus gathered our ten together with the ill intent to recruit companions for a foray into the city proper.

"Isaacius and I discovered where the good taverns are, so we won't waste time on cheap swill or watered-down wine," he assured us merrily.

Fearful of disappointing Mundus, I resisted at first, but then my men brought Rosamund to drag me to my feet; she was, to my surprise, eager to explore the Roman capitol with a group of overexcited spearmen.

Careful to leave our weapons stashed in our bunks, we ventured out into Constantinople. Rosamund gaped as she viewed the expanse of the city, from the palace to the vast Imperial dockyard. I did my best to explain all that I knew as we trotted along, roving from one tavern to the next. Perenus insisted upon making long and drawn-out toasts at each location, all of which cheered along "The glory of Rome!" As the hours passed, our words coarsened and speech slurred. Many of the men had set to teaching Rosamund various profanities in Greek and cheered when she came close in an attempt. She grinned and laughed with the rest of them, sipping horns of wine and clapping the backs of my men as though memories of her village were momentarily forgotten. Secretly, it pleased me that none sought anything more untoward from Rosamund than a good jibe; I gave a firm request in her first days with our small band that she was not to be a conquest for any of them, and they showed their understanding.

As Perenus concluded his final—and especially uproarious—toast to the glory of Rome for the night, Cephalas began to sing, a faint humming that soon swelled into a rich Greek melody. Deeper notes followed, and the tune turned somber as Cephalas belted out an old pagan song, one far older than even the old Republic.

"It is beautiful," Rosamund said. "What is he saying?"

"It's the Requiem for Iphigenia," I whispered back, recalling the Greek girl's name from a distant lesson with Liberius. "Thousands of years ago, the Greek King Agamemnon sought to invade Troy, an enemy city not far from where Constantinople sits today. However, as his boats lifted their sails, Agamemnon offended the gods, who blew harsh winds and stalled the fleet. To appease their wrath, Agamemnon sacrificed his most beloved daughter to appease the gods' wrath, and soon after, his ships found favorable winds once more."

Rosamund shook her head—it was, indeed, an odd story—and fell silent again to listen. As Cephalas concluded the melancholy song, the tavern dwellers broke out in cheering and applause, and his face lit in a broad smile. It was not until the moon hung high in the sky that we departed, Perenus and Isaacius singing wildly—and less elegantly than Cephalas—as they stumbled along the city thoroughfare, arms steadying one another.

By this time, the streets had emptied. Our boots slapped against the stones and rang out echoes in all directions. I was alert, as much as I could be; I thought that I heard other feet stalking us from a distance, or that I saw a blur of movement from one of Constantinople's myriad alleys, those known to house the city's urchins and beggars. Yet my vision was fogged with drink, and perhaps my other senses dazed as well, so I ignored the rising hairs on the back of my neck and rejoined the others in their jollity.

As we neared the Imperial Palace, we passed close to the Hippodrome, its long benches audience to nothing more than an empty racing track. Perenus regaled us with his past victories, and I heard more than a hint of longing in his voice; it must not have been easy to abandon the adoration of the crowd for a red cloak and marching boots. We stopped near one of the gates, and he gazed inside wistfully.

"Why don't we go in?" Isaacius suggested, to cheers and claps from Perenus and the rest.

I, however, protested—surely such trespass would invite Mundus' disapproval and Archelaus' discipline—yet I was alone in my objection. Even Rosamund goaded me on in her limited Greek. Defeated, I acquiesced, and one by one we lifted each other over the Hippodrome gate, the last scrambling up alone.

Taking us for hooligans, a guard ran to the gateway and demanded that we identify ourselves. The others refused, but I knew what the man was after and held out a silver *follis*. He stared hungrily at the coin—a month's wages for a lowly city guard, and likely much greater than the required bribe to gain entry—and he snagged it out of my hand. "One hour," he said, pocketing his windfall and drawing back into the shadows, where he could claim he saw no one and heard nothing. We did not inquire as to how the guard would keep the time, but in truth, it did not matter. We were drunk, and such details are for more responsible heads.

We walked inside, where the moon illuminated the stands and the outline of the track in silver. As only Perenus and I had even seen the Hippodrome before, the others marveled at its sheer immensity.

"They say the Colosseum in Rome is many times larger," I said, amused at their awe.

"No chance!" Cephalas shook his head. "Men should not even be able to build so high as *this*."

Perenus jogged far into the center of the track, where he raised his arms to the heavens in triumph, pumped his fists, and fixed his eyes on the Emperor's box. The moment passed, and he regarded us, the comparably smaller audience of a few friends. I could see tears staining his grime-ridden face as he shouted the immortal cheer of a victorious enemy or athlete alike.

"*Roma victrix! Nika! Nika!*" Perenus screamed, his voice straining to its loudest.

Isaacius repeated the cry, and soon we all did, a cacophony of cheers to the Goddess of Victory and the glory of Rome.

It was Cephalas who stopped cheering first. He pointed at the entrance, and as I followed his hand, dread set in: Solomon stood among a group of ten, all bedecked in army tunics that bore the Chi-Rho of Constantine. My old rival walked in front of his men, and as Perenus—the last—ceased his victory cheers, Solomon called out to me.

"You aren't hard to track down with all the racket that you make." Even at a distance I could see his smirk. "Shall I call the palace guards? They'll have you all locked in irons for sacrilege against the Emperor's peace."

Perenus started to bark some objection, but shut his mouth at Solomon's raised hand.

"Or," Solomon said, as though dangling a tempting gift, "I can repay you for your past kindnesses the last time we met on the sands, Varus."

At that, Perenus laughed, swaying. "Varus, *this* is that elephant's cunt you told us of? The one who shit himself after losing a practice fight?"

Solomon, who ordinarily prized any kind of widespread fame, did not care for this sort. He snarled, and several of his men dashed for us, insults flying fast as their feet. The first out pushed Cephalas, calling him a monster and an imp, and for it, took a wild blow to the jaw from Isaacius. Then, chaos: the Hippodrome sands exploded as men jumped upon one another, kicking and striking with bare fists and booted feet alike. Perenus had not lost any of his revelry, bellowing with laughter as he head-butted an adversary, keeping up his cry of *"Nika! Nika!"* as he pummeled his foe.

I, however, resisted the urge to charge in, for I could not leave Rosamund unprotected—or so I assumed until she smacked me on the back, yelling, "Go help your friends! I can see to myself."

Still, my urge was to resist such temptation—if trespassing risked our superiors' wrath, a nighttime brawl would ensure it—but then flashes of Samur's scarred and broken body emptied me of any restraint. Confident in Rosamund's safety, perhaps emboldened by wine, I grinned and launched myself to find Solomon amid the tangle of drunken curses and flailing limbs. Seizing Solomon, I threw my rival to the ground, driving my fist into his face. Dazed, Solomon managed to roll to his feet, a trickle of blood streaming down his lip. He swung angrily at me, and I found that, with the wine dulling my senses, I could not dodge his blows to my jaw and gut, but I could not feel them either. We sparred, trading shots; I stepped into the swing of his fist, yet managed to drive a knee into his groin. He doubled over, gasping for air and screaming curses as he gathered his feet once again. Solomon stumbled forward as he flailed his arms toward me, yet hesitated as a voice bellowed from the Emperor's box.

"In the name of the Emperor Justin," a guard roared, "cease this madness at once, and surrender yourselves to the Imperial Guards!"

The men scattered, with Isaacius aiming a final kick at his foe before bounding off to safety. Rosamund grabbed my hand and pulled me away as Solomon screamed my name; I turned enough to see him spit in the sand and depart after his own ten.

We hustled away from the stadium and back to the barracks, unaware that no one was, in fact, pursuing us. Perenus gave one jubilant hoot into the night sky, eliciting more laughs from his comrades and a smile from Rosamund. We snuck toward our barracks, bribed the duty guard to secrecy with a quarter-full wineskin, and fell inside. The others filed into our quarters, stripping bare of tunics thrown carelessly to the floor, followed by the thuds of shoes. I was following, last to enter, until I felt Rosamund clasp my hand tighter. I paused, and let her lead me down the cavernous barracks hallway.

Here, at a remove from our quarters, most of the rooms were still empty, their bandae scheduled to arrive in the capitol in a week or more. Rosamund guided me into an officer's quarters, where she jammed the door behind us with a wooden block. Though my head swam, I could see that the room had been prepared for its future occupant with a wooden writing desk and a long bench flanking the straw bed, yet it lacked the personal possessions of any centurion or komes. We were alone.

Rosamund twisted my body to meet hers and slammed me hard into the wooden walls. Before I could protest, she swung her hands behind my head and brought her lips to mine. She levied her strength to press my body into the paneling, its rough edges cutting through my tunic and leaving long welts on my skin. I let her control me for a moment until I gathered my senses.

"Rosamund, stop," I whispered. "You do not need to do this."

I gazed down at her face, and our eyes locked. Her pale hair, normally tied back or braided, fell straight back behind her shoulders, and her narrow eyes swirled green and yellow, unreadable. She emanated the sweetness from the many horns of wine we shared over the evening, but also a hint of an Oriental perfume that would have been familiar to any court of Persia. The scent infiltrated my wits; I wondered how she had come by such a luxury, then realized I cared little for the answer.

"I want you to," she replied faintly as her soft hands fell to my shoulders, her gaze unblinking.

Her chest smothered mine, and I felt her heart quicken. Her approach was slower, more deliberate now, and she filled me with her kiss while fumbling with the knots of her vest. As she guided me to the officer's cot, she let her jerkin and shirt fall to the floor, and slid her legs from the tight cotton breeches she had fashioned at the training camp. When I fell to the cot, she tore at my clothes too, her skin softer still in the pale moonlight streaming through the barracks window. She mounted me, fingers digging into my flesh, and leaned over me, mumbling all the while in the Gepid tongue, her lips brushing at my ear.

THE BETROTHAL

Nude, we lay in each other's arms, stretched together on the cot. I admitted my concern that she might conceive a child, but Rosamund dismissed me.

"It is not my fate to have children." Her voice was distant, eyes fixed on the dark ceiling of our borrowed hideaway.

"How do you know your fate?" I asked, especially curious since she had never spoken to me of childbearing at all, whether past or future.

Rosamund sighed, her chest rising in the moon's light. She had resisted revealing much of her past, yet of all my questions, this was the one she answered plainly and unreservedly.

"My grandfather was a great sorcerer, and the king of our people had even consulted his auguries before rebelling against Attila's sons so many years ago," she said. "He was very old and blind when I first met him as a young girl, and had a countless number of grandchildren spread across many villages, yet he told the fortunes of all who were brought before him."

I could not help but shudder. Now, as then, divination was a mortal sin. Father Petrus had lectured me on the evils of consulting oracles; knowledge of the future belonged to God and his Son alone, and any who played at soothsayer were blasphemers. Yet I said nothing to Rosamund, too curious to interrupt.

"I was brought into his hut, the last of the children of his bloodline, and he laid his hands over my face. He stank of decay and sickness, his mouth full of rotted teeth and sores. Yet I forced myself still has he chanted in the ancient tongue of our people."

Rosamund closed her eyes. "It has blurred with time. Forgive me. But his last pronouncement... that I can still hear clearly. I swear to you."

"He screamed in a voice that was not his own—the shrill voice of a woman, yet at the same time the deep voice of a man that had been many times larger than my grandfather. With my eyes shut tightly, the voices bade me to speak. I asked my future, whether I would be betrothed to the son of my village's chieftain as I already had been promised."

Rosamund rose gingerly to her feet, half fading into the trance of memory as she placed a hand along the stones of the exterior barracks wall.

"The voices screamed again and laughed with a cruelty that I had not known in my grandfather. I was prepared to run from the hut and escape far away, but those old hands clenched my head hard, and I was told of my future. They told me no children would come from my womb, nor would I marry. Yet I would lead a great lord to his destiny and command the countless to complete the unfinished work of our ancestors."

The old man's grip had slackened, she explained, and she escaped the shaman's hut for the freedom of the forest. The shaman died two nights later amid a thunderstorm, where many within Rosamund's village swore that his spirit left his body through a particularly violent thunderclap.

"What did your mother or father say?" I asked.

"I never told them."

Her father had received the old shaman's gift for healing, yet little of his ability to commune with the gods, no matter his desire or proffered sacrifices to hear their will. He took to drinking deeply from Roman wine; soon, too, did her mother. Rosamund had only ever spoken little of her family, and I did not press further. I chanced a question of the fate of her betrothed: He had died later in that harvest season, she reported. Plague.

We spoke softly all the while, as though reverent of this precious rarity of stillness, a moment of privacy never afforded to spearmen on the march or in camp.

At length, Rosamund offered her own question. "When you came to my village, why did you save me?" She spoke with her gaze still fixed on the ceiling, yet there was a distinct flutter to her words.

I paused to think on it. In truth, I had been sorely tempted to abandon Rosamund, and the explanation when she had posed this question our first day together was a hollow one. It was tempting to offer it again, but I found I could not, and relented.

"When I was a slave, even a young slave, I saw what happens to women—to girls—in bondage," I explained. "Things many happily ignore or shrug off. Slaves are property, and such was our fate. But…"

Rosamund placed a hand over my own, her eyes unblinking upon my face. Her soft skin felt chill against my own, as if she were carved from polished marble rather than built of blood and skin.

"Even as far back as I can remember, I hear the screaming of women." Tears rose in my eyes. "I think the screams are my mother's, though I never knew her. But I hear her cries of pain every night before I sleep… at least when my dreams are not stifled by exhaustion or excessive drink. I heard them in every slave woman I ever saw hurt. And when I saw you, I knew that I had to do all I could to prevent such brutality from befalling you, too."

Rosamund's arm threaded through mine as we lay motionless and wordless for a time. Noise from the streets echoed, muffled, into the barracks. The wine still held sway over my senses, and as the night drifted on, I knew neither the hour nor the truth of my heart. Though only a few months had passed, I had come to care deeply for Rosamund. Just that night, I had felt that instinctive urge to shield her from harm in the Hippodrome. Yet I did not feel it to be the ardor of love. Even now, I lack the words to describe what we shared, or how my sentiments might have fallen short of Rosamund's own; all I know is I lacked the courage to explain, preferring the security in leaving all unsaid.

The Last Dying Light

As we lay together, it was Rosamund who broke my reverie as her pointed chin grazed the tip of my shoulder. "You are a good man, Varus, and the Romans don't deserve you," she whispered.

She planted a delicate kiss on my cheek and sank back into her own wine-addled thoughts. Eventually, afraid to fall asleep in our stolen quarters, we dressed, shut the door gently to avoid detection, and slinked back to our assigned barracks.

However long afterward, our sleep gave way to a painful haze. A violent thud creaked the hinges on the barracks door. Mundus strode in, announcing himself and surveying the men who had formed the core of the first line of his banda.

"I was told that some soldiers got into a scuffle at the Hippodrome last night," Mundus growled. "That wouldn't be you lot, now would it?"

"Definitely not." Perenus smiled barely a moment before his face contorted and he vomited noisily into his bucket.

Others agreed; Isaacius went so far as to claim our group did not even venture into the city, let alone the Hippodrome, last night, which earned him exasperated glares from his bunkmates.

As explanations flew, Mundus' nose wrinkled at the sight—and smell—of our room.

"Very well. I will continue searching for the culprits." Mundus did not seem keen to linger, and made for the door. But there he stopped, shook his head, and smirked. "Well, you better have won, at least."

My head pounded. I gulped water, realizing that whatever the hour, I was late, and briskly set off for the priest's quarters near the Forum of Constantine. Father Petrus chastised my tardiness and poor appearance, of course, yet I thought I detected a small glow of amusement as we concluded. My lessons ended, I retreated from the heat of the day back to my bunk. The others had just begun to stir and, as I arrived, were accosted to their feet for the day's training. Though retching and moaning, my men nevertheless held their spears straight and sword arms true, to the appeasement of the Imperial officers who judged our fitness. An officer bobbed his head in approval as he passed Perenus, who promptly belched a fountain of red bile onto the sands at his feet. Isaacius cackled, and several other men cried, "*Nika! Nika!*"

When our training was completed, the men lazed throughout the remainder of the day, too lethargic for adventures or games. Even Rosamund lay in her bunk as though paralyzed, sipping a clay mug of cool water. I found myself wishing to speak of our evening together, yet lacking the words—or the heart—to do so, I abdicated my duty; in essence, I neglected one who was under my care. Still, though I would not broach any difficult conversations, I paid one of the barracks' servants to fetch us roasted beef and roots with a light yogurt that we nibbled slowly, stomachs churning from such fare as the previous evening's sour wine tore at our guts.

An Imperial summons arrived for me the following day. My presence was demanded at the Emperor's Court after the noonday sun. When she heard as much, Rosamund polished my armor, that loose-fitting and dented ringmail I had been assigned as a recruit, and did all she could to neaten my dekarchos' plume. Her efforts yielded a vast improvement, yet I knew I would still appear a mere peasant next to anyone aristocratic—like Solomon. Even so, I took pride in Rosamund's work, which left no signs of rust on any metal surface. Her labors complete, she helped me into my costume, and I returned to the palace to fulfill the demands of yet another official.

After gaining entry to the palace courtyard and presenting my request for attendance to the duty sentries, the palace doors creaked open with ponderous tugs by two grown warriors. I slipped inside, my nailed boots clicking against the marble floor as I maneuvered toward the Great Hall. Just outside that additional doorway, an excubitor demanded further confirmation of my right to be admitted into such an august presence, nodding grudgingly as his inspection of my papers was satisfied. Stepping into the hall, I joined a press of well-dressed citizens of the Empire, dozens of whom waited to present their petitions before the court.

However, the Emperor was not seated on the dais to receive his supplicants. Though my dominus still held all formal power, Justinian had taken up the duty of daily business in the Great Hall, reading dispatches and issuing rulings in the Emperor's name. The Emperor rarely emerged from his quarters, Samur said previously, except to venture onto the open balcony that provided a measure of warmth, the light of the sun, and a view of the city.

As I stood at the rear of the hall, I spotted Theodora, garbed in a dress of shimmering jade silk whose sweeping *V* of a neckline and fitted waist put the shapeless rough wool of the common Roman women to shame—and was, remarkably, somehow even more ostentatious than the fine silks of the proud patrician ladies of the Emperor's Court. Theodora smoothed over a thin crease along her waist and seated herself beside Justinian, where she listened attentively to the current supplicant from her bench. Her dress swished along the marble floor as she patted rhythmically upon one thigh, her long painted nails brushing the soft silk with a near-uncontrollable energy.

While a petitioner spoke their words before Justinian and Theodora, small cliques of wealthy men and women formed circles along the hall's expanse, whispering their gossip and plotting. Antonina, the schoolroom tormentor turned high-status bride, was huddled with several other court ladies, but did not seem to recognize me as I passed. I handed my wax-stamped orders to the round-bodied courtier designated by the Emperor to receive petitions and allow the worthy to address the court.

Though that courtier had not yet come to true fame or power, his name is one that would come to dominate the lips of millions, either in hatred or admiration. Portly and diminutive, Narses had none of a soldier's might, yet had secured his own kind of power through demonstrations of loyalty. He had not served the Emperor during my bondage, but arrived under the patronage of Basilius as an advisor to Theodora. I discovered later that Basilius had also secured Narses a position as the Emperor's spymaster, responsible for trading in rumors and spreading strategic discontent throughout the provinces. Since the Empire's founding, the spymaster had been equally loathed and feared as a cunning deceiver, and I would come to find that Narses was perhaps the most capable man to ever fill that role.

Having unfurled the document and peered over its contents, Narses slipped out of sight, only to reappear behind Theodora. I now noticed Solomon at the opposite corner, face swollen and eye blackened, feigning interest in the ongoing conversation with two older senators.

Similar to the law of the city streets, in the Emperor's presence—or that of his delegates—the palace guards lining the hall were the only men permitted to carry weapons. Next to their muscled breastplates and richly embroidered attire, I was sorely out of place in my rough soldier's gear and its hastily painted Imperial insignia, even after Rosamund's careful ministrations. I walked as close as I could to the ongoing discussion, uncertain in spite of my years of secretly viewing court proceedings through peepholes. Now, I came not as a palace slave, but as a soldier.

As I drew closer to Justinian and Theodora, I began to piece together their conversation with the older man who stood before their joint benches. The interlocutor was adorned in a crimson toga, an extravagant and antiquarian garb that denoted his status as a Roman provincial governor—those officials charged with filling the Emperor's needs for taxes, grain, men, and whatever other raw materials might shape an Empire.

"... the Gepids have been stalking the border for a month, probing for weaknesses and attacking our outposts far more than normal. I'll need at least a thousand men to protect the province from the larger attack when it comes—perhaps more." The governor declaimed his speech in Latin—which remained the court tongue even then, and even in the East—and I reattuned my attention so as not to miss a word.

Justinian wetted his lips and tugged at the hem of one of his sleeves. He lectured the governor: the Empire paid exorbitant costs to maintain its border defenses along the Ister, and the governor's waste of such largesse not only left his province unprepared but was an outright disgrace.

Justinian's vituperation was interrupted by Theodora.

"What my husband means to say," she put in, "is that we will find the soldiers that the governor requires for protecting the Roman people within a fortnight."

The governor bowed, thanking the gracious lady as Justinian sat, scowling. I failed to stifle a grin. Despite the intense stress and visibility of her role, Theodora bore the weight of governance with wit and grace, whereas Justinian seemed distracted and bored. The governor's audience came to an end as he left the court with a retinue of attendants.

The calm demeanor of the court began to hum with anticipation as petitioners jostled for a position to observe the next summons. The round-bodied courtier who had taken my summons motioned behind Theodora and whispered in her ear.

"Thank you, Narses," Theodora mouthed, smiling slowly.

Narses pointed in my direction, his unusually wide sleeves hanging loosely toward the floor. Theodora stood abruptly, sending the court's attendants to a deferent knee. I followed suit, my head bowed and helmet nestled in the crux of my shield arm. Theodora glided from the platform, though Justinian remained seated, visibly annoyed at the disruption. Theodora paid her husband no mind, floating on delicate steps, her fine dress trailing in a long arc.

"It cannot be you, Varus. How much you have changed!" The brightness of her voice cut through any whispered malaise and idle gossip lingering in the court. "Oh, do stand up, please. I am not the Emperor, after all."

Theodora's eyes sparkled as they met mine. For a moment, she reminded me of Rosamund, for green eyes had been rare enough in Constantinople. Yet while the Gepid girl's eyes blended green with a more ominous yellow, Theodora's eyes were a deep olive, reflecting her dress and lending an aura of nobility rather than suspicion. Now just a pace away, she leaned over and lightly kissed my cheek, launching muffled gasps and muttering from all corners of the court.

"This man saved me from a certain assault," Theodora announced, her voice carrying to the rafters. "Or worse. And for that, he shall always have a place of honor at this court."

She retreated to her bench, helped by a hand from her attendant Narses and various fluttering attentions from other aristocratic ladies. Antonina, for one, smoothed the folds of the silk at Theodora's feet, then looked up at me, a flicker of recognition in her eyes. His lady settled, Narses summoned me forward, and so I came, bowing before the Emperor's delegates. Theodora beckoned me nearer still as her attendants placed a wooden stool for me near her feet. Justinian, seeming to have lost interest in his wife's social call, chatted in hushed tones with two senior officials.

Theodora, too, ignored all distractions, and leaned close to demand of me every engrossing detail of my life since the day she had been married to Justinian. She held her hand over a gaping mouth as I told her of my initial march to the Euxine Sea and demanded to inspect my scarred arm as I retold the raid into Gepid territory. I left out several details, most especially by keeping my oath to Archelaus that the sack and burning of the Gepid village was warranted and no fault of our own. My tale complete, Theodora marveled and praised me on my rise through the ranks. "We will even have to find you a wife, soon!" she teased. I could only blush.

Yet she had not finished with me yet. At the wave of her hand, servants brought forth a dark wooden box.

"For your deft leadership in the lands beyond the Ister, and for your valor in victorious single combat against the Gepid Chieftain Fastida, we honor you," Theodora declared.

It was an honor indeed, yet my heart sank. Though I had consciously concealed them from the lady, I knew the true circumstances of our raid into the Gepid Kingdom. Now and before, I had kept that liar's oath to Archelaus. My guilt was not due to slaying Fastida; in battle, there can be no hesitation when facing an enemy, and our duel left no room for more than one survivor. No, my shame at Theodora's praise was born from that well-crafted, prodigious lie. Even as the governor of Moesia begged for soldiers to protect against further ambush, Archelaus allowed, even encouraged, tales of his own glory to be spread far beyond the court, tales that cast us as reluctant-but-noble combatants rather than reapers of death. Of all the questions that clouded my internal peace, from Justin's favor to the gifts from Father Petrus and Godilas alike, Theodora's pronouncement was the one that troubled me the most, for I knew it was wholly undeserved.

But I lacked the courage to amend the record myself, and in keeping silent, damned myself as no better than the arrogant komes. Theodora, oblivious to my inner turmoil, unknotted the box's straps and carefully drew out a newly forged officer's helmet. The plume was far taller and fuller than my own, and the headpiece was smartly crafted with deft hinges and reinforced padding within. It was unquestionably finer than the one I bore, yet it nearly repulsed me.

Theodora bade me kneel, and I obeyed.

"By the Grace of God, and in the name of Emperor Justin, I, Theodora, commission you, Varus of the Heruli, as a centurion of the Roman Army." She placed the helmet over my head clumsily, unused to handling armor.

Much of the room broke out into applause; several well-wishers even called my name. Off to the side, I could just see Solomon frowning, but his bitterness could not steal the joy of such a gift; if anything, his envy amplified it. Perhaps I was a liar, I reasoned, but as a centurion, perhaps I could do all the more good—just as Justinian's wife commissioned me.

"Thank you, Lady." I inclined my helmeted head as she beamed into the crowd.

As the applause died down, Justinian leaned toward his wife. "Dearest, can we move along? Tribonian has much to discuss regarding our new laws, and Paulus wishes to discuss the Imperial Treasury."

At the mention of the latter name, Theodora wrinkled her nose ever so slightly—only one as close as I would have noticed—but nevertheless, she concluded our audience with a smile and prayers of safety for my upcoming campaign. Dismissed, I fell to the back of the room, where a number of well-wishers greeted me—including my brother. Samur had slunk from his hiding space in the palace walls.

"You're a full officer now! A centurion!" Samur giggled.

I smiled too, but the sight of his slave collar dampened my happiness. "The first thing I will do with my money is free you." Samur only waved me off.

A pair of burly hands pulled me away—Mundus, whose face brightened as he caught my attention. He, too, had been promoted; he was to lead the banda, with Archelaus given command over an even larger collection of men.

"They need more officers for the new army headed to Cherson," Mundus remarked over the din, "and there's only so many men who deserve it."

"Do I deserve this?" I asked him, the twin bulls of guilt and jubilation locking their horns in my chest.

The Last Dying Light

Mundus was emphatic. "Absolutely. This is not just a victory for you, but for all the men under you. Don't forget that."

He clapped me on the shoulder and, spying a senior officer he wanted to speak with, left me to my brother's attentions. But Samur's joviality quickly heated to seething disgust as yet another interloper approached—not a well-wisher, but a purple-eyed, chest-puffed bully animated by the confidence only wealth and privilege can provide.

"Congratulations again on your good fortune." Solomon smirked. "Perhaps you will extend me the same courtesy soon enough."

My half-formed retort was silenced by movement on the dais. Justinian had called for attention, snapping his fingers as Narses drew away from his side. With my business completed, I could have departed unnoticed from the court, yet raw curiosity in Solomon's words brought me to stay a moment longer. Such curiosity was stoked further as Justinian rose to gather the attention of the room, his usual scowl replaced with beaming triumph.

"Before we go further, we will welcome our foreign guests." Justinian's voice filled every crevice of the hall. "Lord Marcellus, see them into the court."

One of the excubitores at Justinian's side leaped at his lord's command. Marcellus' armor was as grand—and surely as expensive—as Archelaus', yet where my commander was caustic and aggressive, Marcellus was calm to the point of silence as he carried out his duties over the lesser palace guards.

"By the grace and majesty of Justinian, heir to Caesar, enter, Jabalah ibn al-Harith, the fourth of that name, King of the Ghassanids in Arabia," the excubitor proclaimed.

The crowd presently hushed. Both doors swung open, giving way to what I could only assume was the extensive entourage of King Jabalah: dancers, flame eaters, and an impressive procession of women who swept in eagerly to mingle with their Greek and

Roman peers. Most had their bodies wrapped in colorful linen embroidered with all manner of flowers, with their hair adorned with loose-fitting scarves laced with rubies and other precious gems from the Orient. I saw Antonina frown as she instinctively raised a hand to her less richly adorned face, a small pout framing her lips as the Ghassanid procession continued.

A herald marched in next, alongside men bearing a huge golden cross; the Ghassanid tribe was, it appeared, faithful to the true God. Using an accented and formal Latin, the herald offered his own introduction of the illustrious and benevolent Jabalah, King of all Arabia, a true and dedicated friend to the Empire.

Next, two neat columns of thick-limbed, dark-skinned guards filed in, whom Solomon smugly noted as the elite guard of the Ghassanids, mercenaries from the distant kingdom of Aksum. Even unarmed, the Aksumites drew gasps of admiration from the crowd. King Jabalah—so Solomon insisted on telling us, as though such trivia might restore his dignity—and his father before him had selected each man one by one based upon their height and strength, always maintaining at least one hundred of the hardened spearmen in the Ghassanid army. Their tunics bore the image of a kneeling winged man, apparently a legendary figure that had adorned the lid of the Ark of the Covenant of God bequeathed to the Aksumites by their ancestor, none other than the Queen of Sheba herself.

At last came the king himself, astride the hump of a mighty camel. He rode into the court with his chest high and eyes distant, yet all others could only gape at the spectacle. Camels were not unheard of in Constantinople, true, but for many in the court—particularly the ladies, who were forbidden to use such beasts—it appeared a near mythical creature. The king guided the animal between the columns of his Aksumite guards, its legs bending at odd angles as it cantered forward. Jabalah's body was utterly covered in gold—rings, torques, chains, and even golden fabric that adorned his tunic and shoes. With every eye upon him, the

Ghassanid King came to a halt before the dais. There, Jabalah saluted Rome and its Imperial delegates, and just as he nodded to Justinian, reaffirming his friendship and cooperation with Rome, the camel dropped a steaming pile of dung onto the marble floors.

"Clean that up," Solomon snapped at Samur.

I balled my fists, yet Samur had already scurried along to attend to the muck, lacking the freedom to refuse a member of the aristocratic class. I seethed. In that moment, I would have traded my every success in the army for one more opportunity to break my fists against Solomon's face.

Politely ignoring any disruption, Justinian formally greeted King Jabalah as a friend and ally. The King dismounted, and after the two rulers clasped hands, Justinian made bold declarations to the court about the value of an unshakeable Ghassanid friend, a terror to the Lakhmids and a bulwark against the hated Sassanid Persian enemy.

At that name, much of the court hissed, and myself along with them. The Persians had been an ancestral enemy of Rome and even Greece before her, one thousand years ago. Their current Shahanshah, or "King of Kings," had sat on the Persian throne for decades and continuously chipped away at Roman territory in the East. Through his *Zhayedan*, or Immortals, Shahanshah Kavadh ruled vast lands that few Romans had visited and survived. Eastern army commanders had even told stories that Kavadh employed an innumerable army of Eastern Huns known as the Hephthalites, who took particular delight in brutal desolation of towns and cities that was rumored to culminate in human sacrifice and wholesale slaughter of surrendering women and children. Rumors had spread that the Zhayedan and their Hephthalite mercenaries were once again amassing near Nisibis on the Romano-Persian border, meaning that the true measure of Jabalah's friendship with our Empire would soon be put to the test.

"Through the mighty arm of King Jabalah, we shall vanquish Kavadh and his pagan hordes once and for all!" Justinian exclaimed, drawing tentative applause from the room. Persia had been unbeaten in the field for over a century, their armies vast and more consistently trained than our own. Even with Godilas leading such an effort, I admit feeling a fleeting sense of fear at Justinian's pronouncement, and the suggestion that we might be sent to die in the desert like tens of thousands of Roman soldiers who came before.

What followed was an exchange of elaborate gifts and further proclamations of unshakeable fraternity that ended only when King Jabalah summoned his servants for what he declared to be his final gift. "Now, to seal our alliance for another generation," the Ghassanid King began, eliciting a smile from Justinian and Theodora alike.

The doors to the court reopened, and through them came a young man plucking a lyre whose sweet melody all but entranced us. As the notes grew softer, any lingering side conversations ceased as men and women alike strained to hear. Even Justinian grew still, his eyes transfixed on the lyre as the man's fingers danced over its strings. I wondered at first if this man and his song were the gift, finding it a bit lackluster for so much fanfare. Yet I found I was mistaken. The gift was only now to come.

At first, all I noticed was Solomon's thuggish face as it brightened into a lascivious, triumphant grin. When I, too, saw what he saw, I hated him for it.

"The Princess Mariya bint Jabalah ibn al-Harith, the Desert Rose of Arabia," came the King's announcement.

They say that love is the most pleasant of all madnesses. In my experience, it is also the least biddable, turning young and old alike into servile fools willing to do anything at all to sate their hunger for even the faintest return in affection. In the early years of my youth, I was not immune to its cruel whispers of hope and futility, nor did I have the patience to make sense of what it meant. Though before that moment I knew nothing of Mariya, the world and all others who inhabited it faded away when I first laid eyes upon her.

Fragrant perfume breathed across the court as she passed, sweet rosewater and savory incense. Her feet seemed to glide across the floor with no sound, no indication whatsoever that she touched the ground. I was enraptured. Though most of her body was concealed in silks of deep crimson and gold, her slim almond-colored hands shone with jeweled rings and golden torques. When I dared look to her face, I saw a straight nose and soft red lips, yet most striking were the deep-set eyes that glowed a soft amber, made all the grander by the striking, deft line of kohl at her lashes. Hair as dark as pitch fell around her face, covered by a translucent red-and-black veil that nestled atop her head.

The pain of desire in my chest was near unbearable; each gasp from onlookers struck me like a sharpened knife. The princess had yet to say a single word, yet in that moment I would have charged against a thousand Zhayedan for just a moment with her. She was a woman to start wars over, to sail a thousand ships across the sea to take on all combatants. Her perfume inflamed my senses, drowning out the world and all its ills like a drug. I knew my own foolishness, and I knew, even as I felt it, that such ardor was entirely without reason, but love and lust rarely obey the cold logic of a stoic. All I could do to stare as she gracefully drew beside her father, a beaming Justinian, and an approving Theodora.

"Mariya," I whispered.

Fool. Fool that I was. The glimmer of Rosamund in my heart's imagination was extinguished and replaced by the flame of Mariya, a woman who, for all I knew, may have been as twisted and vile as—

Solomon elbowed me in the ribs. "The Desert Rose indeed. And she is all mine."

My longing seared away into fiery jealousy. Of course—she was to marry Solomon. I had known this, yet forgotten. Heat burned from my chest to my scalp.

King Jabalah took his daughter's hand in his and waited. Justinian dutifully called for Solomon, son of Senator Nepotian, to attend to his soon-to-be bride. Solomon practically bounded to the dais, and I was left alone.

Solomon was introduced first to his future father-in-law, and then to his betrothed. He gently took Mariya's hand, offering a light kiss as he professed his love. She glowed at his words, to all appearances genuinely happy as she stared into the eyes of her future husband. And why should she be anything but? She knew nothing of Solomon's many faults, and there was no argument that he was a handsome man who showed great promise at court. His father was among the wealthiest in the Empire, and Solomon was to inherit his vast fortune and influence.

As the court looked on, Solomon charmed Mariya, who brought a hand to her lips as she laughed at some witticism or another. Even King Jabalah appeared overjoyed at his daughter's happiness; whispers around me revealed that Jabalah deeply loved his only daughter, rarely taking the lash to her even for impudence.

To my horror, Mariya touched even his face, cooing over his bruised jaw and blackened eye. "Soldiers' injuries, my lady," Solomon said, loud enough for all to hear. "Roman officers train diligently for the many foes who would take what is ours."

It was all I could do not to snort. Mariya made him promise to keep safe from such harm, fearing for him in those far-flung plains of Chersonesus, where this curiously unnamed foe had, after sacking many Roman towns, apparently thrown a punch. One of Solomon's men joined in the fable, boasting of his commander's skill with the blade and assuring her that we would be back to feast at their wedding before Christmas. I would not begrudge Solomon this: His men seemed as loyal as mine, however sorely misguided their allegiance. Mariya smiled at this, and Justinian stood at the dais, affirming the betrothal of Mariya and Solomon before God, the Emperor, and the King of the Ghassanids. A raucous ovation rang out as well-wishers cheered the impending union of a pair that was, it could not be denied, a handsome match.

I may have landed the last blow, but Solomon had won. And without reason or sense, I hated him for it.

The proceedings drew to a close as the Ghassanid royalty were ushered to a private audience, yet the princess Mariya lingered, and began to bid each of us gathered her gratitude as we filed from the Imperial Hall. After the unfortunately timed camel dung, Samur had snuck off early, yet I found myself among the last to leave as a line of well-wishers queued to meet the Ghassanid princess. As at last my turn arrived, the princess looked into my eyes and offered me a graceful smile.

"You are a Roman officer?" Mariya asked in faintly accented Latin, inspecting my new centurion's helmet.

"I... am, my lady." I bowed, fumbling for even those few words.

As I rose, she stepped yet closer. Though I had seen the Ghassanids proclaim their Christianity only moments ago, I could not help but wonder if she bore in her some other enchantment, the gift of some alluring, forbidden goddess that resided deep within the Arabian desert.

"Then may God protect you and see my betrothed safely back to me."

I acknowledged her blessing and swiftly took my leave, feeling sick and wanting nothing more than to leave on the first boat that could take me across the sea to Cherson. I slunk away like a coward, yet still turned back to steal one last glance of her black hair as the doors closed between our worlds.

THE THIRD GIFT

THE NEXT DAYS WERE FILLED with preparation and drills. More bandae arrived and filled the Imperial Barracks, and thousands of wooden barrels, stuffed to their brims and requiring multiple men to bear, were stacked onto the fleet of ships that would carry us to Rome's northernmost province.

A second army was making similar preparations in Sinope, where the Cappadocian and Pontic Army under Belisarius was scheduled to depart soon after the main fleet from Constantinople. Stories spread throughout camp of their new weapons and armor, fascinating gossip for us who followed the same ever-orthodox construction of battle lines. A centurion from another banda even claimed that Belisarius had packed African elephants into his cargo hold, yet Mundus quickly dismissed such talk as nonsense.

Now promoted and given overall command of the banda, Mundus poured most of his into efforts tallying up the many supplies needed for the march. One new task was the creation of his own banda standard, for which he took the figure of a long-tusked boar that would rest alongside Archelaus' viper and the broader army's Imperial Eagle. Mundus gave me the honor of selecting officer replacements for my own soldiers, which, as a centurion, had risen to fifty Thracian spearmen. Rosamund prepared plumes for my new dekarchoi: I gave one to Perenus to oversee our old group of ten, and another to Isaacius to oversee the new unit. After naming Cephalas his second-in-command, Perenus called for another round of raucous celebration, while Isaacius greeted his fortunes with a giddy cheer.

"You are more than worthy of this," I said, averting his face, but not so quickly that I did not glimpse his watery eyes. I left Isaacius and Perenus to celebrate as I gathered my few possessions and navigated my way to Mundus' old quarters.

For her part, Rosamund took to her increased responsibilities as head of a centurion's household with alacrity. She urged me to bring on additional servants, and though my wages could now support several other attendants, with so little time before our departure, I promised her I would do so once we returned from Cherson. Accordingly, she made do with the borrowed help from other servants and slaves that were the lifeblood of a camp. Rosamund procured new boots and armor for me, replacing first my dented ringmail for new, tightly woven scales that covered my body neck to groin, and then receiving a bevy of other deliveries from blacksmiths and tanners and all manner of other craftsmen. With diligence and skill, she transformed me into a Roman officer in appearance, not just in name.

"I will not permit you to be hurt again." Rosamund tightened an armor strap, surveyed and approved the kit, then brushed her fingertips against my arm with a playful, knowing glance. I still felt the guilt of never quite telling her the truth, that I did not love her the way I worried she did me, but it was not a guilt so powerful as to move me to speak, nor was I a brave enough man to battle against my own discomfort. Thus I returned only a smile and left Rosamund to tend to her duties.

In the hours she was not carrying out her duties, Rosamund took to venturing into the city, where she was learning more of the Greek language and ways. Though I assumed barely any—if any at all—pagans resided within the capitol's walls, Rosamund had a way of drawing them to her, and had found for herself acquaintances of all manners of creeds, faiths, and superstitions. Rosamund told me she met with an ancient Egyptian man who claimed to be a priest of a deity called Thoth. She spent many hours in the man's small library, off in the section of the city home to peasants, foreigners, and dockworkers alike. There, she claimed to be improving her knowledge of healing—merely the ability to identify and treat sickness, she told me, yet I quickly spoke of other things whenever her reports delved too far into the pagan arts.

I did not at all begrudge her exploration; my only request was that she always take one of my men as protection. Fierce as she was, she was still a girl, visibly foreign, with boundless confidence, but limited vocabulary in Greek. Besides, the streets of Constantinople had grown restless from the taxes that Justinian and his Minister of Treasury Paulus had enacted across the Empire's cities. Open dissent remained rare, but it was shiningly clear that the taxes were seen as oppressive; each dawn saw more and more bodies turned up in gutters, and tradesmen from smiths to fishermen cried out against growing theft. In a meeting of the banda's officers, Mundus had warned us of criminal gangs that, as the life of most peasants grew bleak, had taken to hoarding food and weapons, and he cautioned us against attending any further races in the Hippodrome. The events of the previous year were enough to convince me, yet thankfully no major games were even planned until after the harvest season.

Meanwhile, with his own promotion, Archelaus had been given command of five bandae, well over a thousand spearmen that would form the core of the Thracian Army. We saw little of him in those days; he conferred with his officers only for brief updates on the men and our state of preparations. In one such meeting, another banda commander inquired about requisitioning additional spears, arrows, shields, and other supplies that an army exhausted on campaign. Archelaus concurred that these were needed, but he offered no way to secure the funds or authority to procure them.

"Go get an audience with Theodora. She's the only person making any real decisions right now," Archelaus said at last, almost petulant. As the meeting broke and I departed, I could feel the hard eyes of the freshly promoted tribune on my centurion's plume. Still, before all the world, he dealt with me in a mild manner that a dispassionate observer might mistake for respect.

It was true that I, Varus, held a small grain of power beyond what was conscribed to me as a centurion. My friendship with Theodora—though I would not be so bold to call it as much, that was how it was perceived—left me as the one to make such requests as Archelaus intimated, and my entreaties for supplies or coin only grew more frequent by late summer; harsh weather and rough seas would end the campaign season, and we had to set sail soon. Fortunately, alone or with her husband, Theodora always greeted me warmly, and commanded her courtier Narses to attend to my needs. In return, however, she demanded total obedience, even if it meant rushing to the palace in the darkest hours of night.

Such was the case of Theodora's decision to reinforce the Empire's Moesian border. Narses arrived at our barracks as the moon hung high overhead and demanded my presence in Theodora's chambers immediately. I dressed haphazardly, then followed the courtier toward the palace entrance, where we slipped inside past rows of guardsmen and excubitores alike, no stamped missive needed.

Within, we ascended to the palace's luxurious upper floor, where Narses led me to Theodora's private offices. Though her chambers were, compared to the gold and silver of the Emperor's own rooms, rather plain, Theodora had lavished decoration not with precious metal but with frescoes: leaping pagan gods frozen at play in stories of myth.

"Do you like them? I confess they are quite pleasing to my eye, although Justinian disapproves heartily," Theodora said, noticing my gawping. "If only our forebears had known God—think of the beauty they would have wrought for His glory."

Clean of her usual powders and face paints, Theodora appeared an entirely different person than the one I had met in public. Her black hair fell about her shoulders in disorderly waves, while gray shadows of fatigue laced her eyes. Yet in such a state, Theodora seemed far more human, the blemishes on her skin softening the austere figure she struck in court.

"I know it is late, Varus, but I have an important question to ask you."

"Anything, Lady."

My enthusiasm earned me a smile. "The Gepids," she asked. "Do you find them to be fierce warriors?"

"What the lady means to ask…" Narses had spoken up. His boyish voice, I now knew, was no accident of birth; he was a eunuch. "…is whether they might overrun our border defenses in Moesia."

Though the question was not a complete surprise, it still gave me pause, a vague shimmer of shame and guilt on my skin.

"It is impossible for me to say for certain, Lady," I said, equivocating. "We… only fought a war band, not an entire force."

"Even so." Theodora leaned forward in her chair and propped her hand on her chin. "What is your assessment? Is the Moesian governor correct, or is he borrowing trouble?"

I sighed, the dull ache of guilt at the dishonesty of my recent honors leaving me again forced to keep Archelaus' oath despite Theodora's insistence. "I would take such concern seriously. Our limitanei aren't capable of securing the riverfront, with our border guards overfed and undertrained and their officers content to take bribes for border crossings. As a result, the Gepids are far more mobile than our own forces in the region. Even if we can beat them in a pitched fight, the smarter Gepid leaders will just ride around to burn another village."

To my surprise, Theodora's eyes brightened, and she gave a chest-deep, self-assured laugh.

"I told you, Narses!" she exclaimed. "My personal bodyguard—a man who slew a Gepid chieftain in single combat, no less—agrees with me!"

"That doesn't make him correct," Narses grumbled, yet he did not argue the point with his mistress.

Theodora rose from her bench and sat opposite me on a simple wooden stool. At night, she had donned a simple *stola*, and its woolen fabric rippled to her ankles as she settled. Such common display only added to my curiosity of Theodora, a woman who held the Emperor's trust and authority during the day, but by night was contented with the garb and furniture of the humblest plebeian.

"Believe it or not, I prefer to dress simply." Theodora grinned as she caught my curious glance. "Silk leaves me feeling too exposed. Linen and wool were the garments of my youth."

"That we… have in common, Lady," I replied awkwardly.

Theodora laughed politely, her eyes remaining fixed upon mine. She leaned closer and placed a hand on the outside of my knuckles. The intimate act made me suddenly desperate to leave; if any should speak to Justinian of this impropriety, my torture and death were all but assured.

"I believe that I can trust you, Varus," Theodora whispered, withdrawing her touch. "Together, we can rise high and surpass these old Roman men and their tired beliefs. But I need to know if you would willingly pledge your loyalty to me in this… regard."

"Lady." I bowed my head and willed my covered hand not to tremble. "So long as I do not contravene my oaths to God and the Emperor, I will gladly swear you fealty."

"Excellent." Theodora flashed her wide set of teeth in a smile. "Just as Liberius promised that you would, the old rogue that he is. So, I will depend on you to report the true conditions of our army in Cherson, for I distrust our official scribes. As your first task, however, tell me—should I deploy additional soldiers against the Gepids?"

I sighed again, for now I dreaded to think from which companies such detachments would be drawn. "If you do not, Lady, Moesia will not stand on its own."

Theodora's eyes closed for several heartbeats. She bobbed her head. "So were I to siphon a thousand men from the expedition to Cherson… would that eliminate the Gepid threat?"

"Yes." I nodded, and added, "Although I cannot say how that might affect our expedition."

"Pray to God that such men won't be missed," she said. "Because it doesn't seem we have any other choice."

Indeed, neither did we, the Empire's soldiers. But, God forgive me, I wish I had not emboldened Theodora to reduce the Thracian Army's forces so drastically. Counting Belisarius' Cappadocians, the joint armies would be over ten thousand spears, cavalry, and archers, and even such seemingly bloated ranks might prove insubstantial against the shadowy invaders. Yet, as Theodora noted, I, too, doubted a different course of action was available. Archelaus' destruction along the Ister had stoked the flames of war, and hundreds of Romans would suffer and die as a consequence.

After that fateful meeting with Theodora, another week passed until, consistent with Liberius' warning, I was summoned to the palace for the final time. I was escorted into a gilded office where Godilas sat at a desk strewn with maps and scrolls. My old master-at-arms welcomed me, the sight of his thickly muscled trunk and scarred limbs a stark contrast to the more delicate forms of my two other mentors. Yet, like Liberius, Godilas beamed hearing of my advancement within the army, and commended my victory over Fastida with a note of pride in his voice. Again, perhaps more than ever, I was sorely tempted to confess the truth behind that raid, but our time together was limited, and Godilas was intent on his business with me.

"I have been given overall command of the expedition to Cherson, and will be leaving with the Thracian Army when it departs in three days." Godilas sounded morose, his eyes tight on a crude outline of the Tauris Peninsula of our northern province.

I voiced my congratulations, which elicited only a tight smile. His eyes went glassy a moment, as though he'd faded to another world.

"I wanted to offer you the chance to serve in my retinue," Godilas said at last. "It will get you out of the front lines, and more likely to return home unscathed."

Stunned, I drew back into my chair. I could not offend the general, but I certainly could not abandon my friends in the banda. The right words evaded me until, with a deep breath, I explained that were I to depart, I would seem less in the eyes of the men, and I would likely never rise further if I surrendered my spear for the easier life of a clerk.

"Perhaps," Godilas conceded. "But perhaps not. I will not force you, although I did hope to offer some protection against what we are up against. There is no shame in such a role, you know, especially given the enemy we are to face."

Godilas then told me what he knew of our adversary, and I listened intently, eager to delve beyond what mysterious little I knew. Nothing could be verified for certain, he made clear, yet what reports we had told of a certain nomadic tribe, known as the Avars and hailing from far beyond the distant Caspian Sea. Most definitive of these reports came from an emissary of the Göktürks, a people with a vast empire in the steppes whose khagan claimed rights of succession from the Ancient Scythians and even the Huns; their reach was said to be ever-expanding along the plains and wastes of the north.

Liberius had once told me of those faraway lands of Asia, lands upon which even Alexander himself had never trod. Their buildings were bedecked with jade, said my teacher, and wild panthers roamed their bejeweled city streets. Of those fantasies, I knew nothing for certain, but it was true that these lands produced the precious silks so clamored for in Constantinople; their traders hazarded long journeys, and our aristocrats gladly handed over fat bags of gold and silver coins. Many a Roman scholar remarked that the Huns were born from such lands, although where or when, no scholar could say. The Göktürks, eager to establish such trade routes as to make both Empires wealthy beyond imagining, had thus sent emissaries all the way to distant Constantinople.

What this Göktürk emissary had shared was spare, but useful. Such harsh and windswept steppe lands were dominated by vast packs of wolves that stalked humans as prey, and the Avars were like these wolves, riding from place to place in search of food and plunder at the expense of their conquered. All Avar men were warriors; they wore pelts and furs and chewed an herb before a battle that maddened them with anger. They worshipped only their great sky god Tengri, whose dictates taught no conventions of gentleness or restrictions of behavior. The Göktürk said he knew of no reason the Avars would migrate, yet, as Godilas recounted, he had seemed relieved that they might do so, and that such a threat had decamped from his own Empire's borders.

That was the extent of our intelligence; though the Emperor had dedicated significant resources to combat the Avar threat, we knew next to nothing of who the Avars were, or why they had pillaged Roman territory, and most of what we did know came from the word of a man who was, trade aside, himself a barbarian. Yet I believed in the wisdom of Godilas and other seasoned commanders, and so such unknowns did not worry me. The Empire had weathered dozens of barbarian invasions over the centuries, and none of our top commanders believed that a previously unknown tribe could seriously challenge a single Roman army, let alone two.

But I was naïve, and my superiors hubristic. God help me, but I was wrong. We all were.

The Last Dying Light

We did have a verifiable Roman account available, Godilas emphasized. A lone Roman centurion named Alypius, who had marched with several bandae against a threat that had reportedly crept down the Tauris Peninsula, sacking minor villages and leaving naught but ashes in its wake. The few survivors Alypius and the bandae came across warned that the beasts, all claws and teeth, would only attack under cover of mist or darkness. The centurion said his men had laughed—just superstitious village folk too far gone from the civilized world—and after that, Godilas told me, Alypius had been reluctant to continue.

Yet eventually, he told the rest of his story. The Roman war band, a mixture of the fixed garrison and local levies, marched from Kerkinitis, an outlying town of Cherson, toward the interior grasslands. After scouting for five days, they were beginning to suspect that the villagers had fabricated the story to justify a war on the coveted farmlands of their neighbors. Yet, as the Romans neared the town of Theodosia, a dense fog formed around them. Blinded, they had no choice but to halt and call out to one another in the thick silence. Then came the hoofbeats, dancing around their position, and then a comrade disappeared, and then another, always to the sounds of scraping and snarls. Alypius stole a pack horse and rode hard from the formation, not stopping until he reached the gates of Theodosia and his horse simply collapsed. He sold his weapons and armor and bought passage on a merchant ship that departed the town that very day, saving only his centurion's helmet, which he surrendered to the commander of the city watch when he was arrested for desertion and cowardice.

"And did the governor of Theodosia confirm his story?" I asked.

Godilas shook his head. "We have had no word to or from Theodosia since around the same time that this centurion arrived on the merchant cog. The captain and its crew dropped their cargo and dashed toward the Aegean, leaving only this poor Alypius behind. And, really, we cannot even be sure if he *was* a centurion, or just a man who stole a centurion's helmet to gain passage to the capitol."

That I did not believe, in all honesty. "Wouldn't such a thief be more cunning in concealing his bounty from the city guards?"

"Perhaps," Godilas said. "Regardless, it is the story we have. And yet it *still* leaves us with little to act upon, and the seas are getting rougher every day. We're losing time to send out war galleys." He paused, jotting small notes in Latin around his map. "You still wish to stand in the ranks?"

The question was abrupt and tinged with disappointment. "Yes, Lord," I answered immediately, though I could not help but imagine how my life would grow easier as Godilas' aide. Still, I was resolved in my soul, and Godilas did not force the issue.

"We leave in three days. Make sure to prepare your men for the voyage," he said. I saluted, ready to leave.

"Oh, one more thing," Godilas added. I froze. "The Emperor wishes to see you today. At your leisure."

"The Emperor?" I wondered after my old dominus, who had remained invisible in the weeks I had lodged in the capitol. Even Samur had no contact with the man, although he knew where the Emperor hid away throughout his days and nights.

"Yes. The hour matters little, but it is very important that you see him today, before you leave the palace. And as for me... you may go, Varus." Godilas dismissed me. "But keep yourself safe." He turned back to his maps.

I shut the door and was not two steps into the hallway when someone seized me.

"You need to see this," Samur said, cackling.

I tried—and failed—to shake my brother off, so I gave in and followed him into an old servant's passage that we had often patrolled as children. The usual small holes gave us a vantage point, and through these we glimpsed one of the antechambers to the Imperial Hall, hosting two men in aristocratic crimson robes.

As I squinted into the room, I realized it was Solomon and his aristocratic father, deep in a heated conversation. The old senator wore a look of disdain, even disgust, as he eyed his son, whose arms were thrown wide in exasperation. Though the words were muffled by the walls, I could make out fragments of their conversation—just in time for the senator to launch a fresh tirade at his son.

"I secure your position in the army and arrange your marriage to a rich young princess, and you do this?" He grabbed his son's face, which, though largely healed, still bore a blackened eye and a yellowed bruise over his cheekbones. "You continue to disappoint me. Sometimes I doubt you are even my own son—taking a beating from slaves like a little girl and fighting in the Hippodrome in some drunken brawl!"

I saw thick tears run down Solomon's face. His voice cracked as he spoke. "Father, please…"

Yet Senator Nepotian was unchanged, looming over his son with renewed disgust at the sight of the tears.

"By God, Solomon, if it were not for your mother, I would have already sent you to the Persian border for a proper man's education. I am more the fool for going soft on you. You will attend General Godilas, and I do not want to see you until you've returned from your campaign."

The senator brushed his son's hands away and gathered his robes as he exited the door, not looking back. Solomon collapsed in the room's center, weeping and drawing choked breaths.

Samur and I ran out into the hall, with my brother bubbling laughter as he mocked Solomon's pleas. As if on cue, the antechamber door burst open, and Solomon stormed out. He eyed my brother and me, visibly angry that there should be such *mirth* on a slave's face.

"Did... did you..." Solomon sputtered, splotches of crimson spreading across his face. His breathing grew more frantic, eyes wide as he snarled at Samur. "I'll kill you!"

He lunged. He had no weapon, as we were in the Emperor's residence, but he threw up gloved fists.

"No," a sonorous voice called out. "You will not."

Solomon stood down—or tried to, tripping over his fine silks and sprawling onto the marble floor. Samur failed to stifle another giggle as Solomon hurried to his feet and shot a dark look at the interloper.

He soon relented, seeing it was Basilius. The Emperor's longtime friend and advisor had aged, his hair thinning and gray, yet he retained the vim of a senior minister in his prime despite the agelessly skeletal frame that left children fearful to approach him. Solomon's posture slackened to one of deference.

"Centurion Varus, the Emperor has been waiting for you, and it is unwise to leave your monarch impatient," Basilius said, sounding dispassionate, almost bored.

"Lord?" I could only gape. "Did the Emperor send you for me?"

"Though many more pressing obligations fill my day, yes, he did." There was a distinct note of irritation in his voice. "If you have no further questions, I would prefer this duty of mine be fulfilled."

Whether from eagerness or fear, my stomach churned at this revelation. Men like Basilius did not run messages or fetch young Roman officers; they had legions of servants and slaves for such work. Yet Basilius stood before me in his regalia, the irksome nature of his task evident on his face. And my dominus, whom I had not seen in so many months, had not only requested my presence, but had also ensured that his three most trusted councilors executed his will.

Basilius turned and beckoned me to follow. Solomon looked on, dumbfounded, while Samur wisely disappeared into the palace's labyrinth of twisting hallways. As I followed Basilius and we ascended the marble steps, I found I was curiously close to weeping from the uncovered longing to see the man who had been my protector for so long. Above all else, I hoped that he would look upon me with pride, and that I would find some reassurance of his continued grace and love for me.

As we arrived at the topmost of the palace's floors, the buzz of activity faded to a smothering silence. Where hundreds of men and women filed along offices and court hallways, the Emperor's hallway was vacant, filled only with statues and a wealth of gold ornamentation that, were it melted to coin, could have supplied an army for a year. Basilius' footsteps echoed along the hall until they stopped before great golden doors. He pushed them open, and as I fell in after him, I found my dominus on a cushioned chair beside an open terrace screen.

"I have brought him," Basilius announced, then rushed on with his own concerns. "Yet we must talk soon. The gangs grow bolder in the streets, and I cannot hold off the Games much longer. And then these reports of corruption… the docks alone are reported to operate on their own barter economy. And you know Justinian needs to be reined in… his reforms will be ruinous to all we have started, and—"

"Yes, later." The Emperor waved, his words hoarse and lifeless.

He had been old when I last saw him, but now my dominus had grown dangerously thin. His hands were spotted and his skin was thin as parchment. As he sat facing the morning sun, his breathing was labored, no matter the warmth that must have been soaking into his exposed flesh. The endless cares of the state had worn my onetime master to a wretched condition: the former commander of excubitores was now too weak to stand unassisted. As he glanced at me, I discovered what hair remained to Justin hung lank, his eyes sunken and dark as any kohl. Basilius tried again to quarrel, yet, as the Emperor refused to entertain him, he at last stopped, bowed, and left us alone.

"Come sit, Varus." The Emperor pointed to a cushioned chair to his left.

In violation of ancient custom proscribing against any common man from taking a seat beside the Emperor, I obeyed my dominus and perched next to him. Tears swarmed my eyes that, despite my best attempts, I could not stop from streaming onto my bearded cheeks. Whether Justin noticed was impossible to say; he only sat silently, looking down upon Constantinople and enjoying the breezes that billowed across his face.

"Liberius was right. You have grown up." A smile lit up his face. He went to pick up a glass on a tray to his right but knocked over its neighboring pitcher, splashing wine onto the floor and the hem of his robes. By instinct, I shot up, grabbing a cloth to dab the fabric at his feet. At the same time, two other servants slipped into the room, one to clean the larger spill on the floor and the other to replace the glass and pitcher with a second one, filled with the same vintage.

"Varus, you do not need to do that anymore…" the Emperor said. "You never should have done that to begin with."

"Dominus, I—"

He interrupted me, more strength in his voice. "You are a centurion now, a leader of men. No man is your master but God, not even the Emperor."

Blushing, I bobbed deference to the Emperor, now ashamed that my instinct had been to scrape and clean. Still, the shame flattened under an oppressive sense of *wrongness*—a sense that I belonged at the feet of my dominus, that my failure to attend him was a deep failing. I was a centurion, yes, but for all my soldierly training, I had spent far more years learning to be a slave. My discomfort only grew as Justin filled two cups and offered one to me. My fingers trembled as I accepted the gift.

Justin's features softened, and he met my gaze before he spoke again. "Your banda commander told me of your exploits, and of your courage in combat. You have surpassed even my loftiest expectations."

Now came a new shame, a shame born from my servant's instincts, yet tempered by my soldier's exploits. It swelled within me at such praise granted for this same bitter lie. My tears flew freely by this point, my throat knotted as I struggled to express the pain and guilt that resided in my heart.

My body knew what my heart only now realized, and if anyone deserved the truth, it was Justin. Caring nothing for my fate, needing simply to unburden myself before my dominus and avoid the dishonor of a lie to him above all, I shattered my oath of secrecy to Archelaus.

"Highness, that expedition was not what it seemed... there was no glory in it." I could not even begin to find the words.

"There is no glory in war," Justin said, eyes gazing over the terrace and into the city. "Yet it is a necessity to protect the little that remains of this world."

"But Highness—" I sniffled, breathed out heavily. "Not like this. We weren't goaded into battle. We ventured into Gepid territory and torched the first village we could find. *We attacked.*"

Justin did not interrupt. I boiled into a frustrated rage in all my flesh: lip trembling, fists clenched, head bobbed, eyes tight on the ground.

"We slaughtered people who were guilty of nothing other than living!" I cried. "What justice is there in that?"

"None."

The Emperor set down his cup and stroked the crown of my head with a wrinkled hand. My chest heaved as I wept freely, thick tears and spittle falling to the floor, a pathetic display of my own wretchedness.

"Thank you for telling me the truth," Justin said gently. "But allow me to ask, in the skirmish, did you, Varus, harm anyone who did not attack you first?"

"No, Highness," I said softly, still facing the floor. "But I don't see how it makes a difference."

"It makes every difference," he said calmly. "And did you do everything in your power to protect your men, both from others, and from themselves?"

I nodded. "I think so, Highness."

"Then you are a better man than me, Varus," the Emperor said. "Far better."

Justin's hand remained fixed until I was able to compose myself, and, rising from my misery, I sat upright in the cushioned chair. The Emperor smiled as his eyes met mine once more, a faint glimmer of sadness flickering over his tired features.

"I have done terrible things, Varus," Justin said. "I have told myself they were for duty or a greater good, but in my twilight I understand that my actions were purely driven by greed and vainglory."

"No, Highness." My brow furrowed.

"Yes," Justin insisted. "And I lack the days to set my choices to rights. But I will make amends as best I can. Do you remember what I asked of you before you joined the army?"

I nodded again. "To restore the Empire. To take back what is ours."

"What is ours!" Justin agreed. "Constantinople is the great refuge of the Lord, a final candle against the darkness. That last dying light is flickering, but not yet out. We are all that stands in the way between the people and a great darkness, which shall never be lifted if it is allowed to blot out our Empire. We commit ourselves to war, in all of its horror and evil, to keep the darkness at bay."

I sat silent as he lectured me once more of his great vision—the return of the Romans to splendor and strength, united under God and filled with plenty for the masses. No famine, no strife, only a peace to last lifetimes for all of the Empire's people. He longed to return the Eternal City to the Empire's control, a light that would spread into Africa, Hispania, Gaul, and even beyond into lands that the Caesars never conquered. It was our heritage, he said, and our only chance to find the fortitude and faith to hold out against the immense pressures at our borders that would raze all into bones and dust.

"I will not live long, and will not see this dream come true," Justin said, now visibly gripped by melancholy. "Yet you may, Varus. You know what it means to live hard, go hungry, have no one to care for you. And so, like good steel, you have tempered into a fine edge that will not break under the strain of a blow."

Though sitting, I still bowed my head. The old man grew livelier as his convictions rang out, his voice as full and pure as I had remembered in my childhood. Yet as he gathered his breath, he began to weep, a slow but insistent trickle.

"I have failed your brother," Justin said bitterly. "I lacked the vigor, the *courage* to protect him from the worst of the world, and he has already been hammered brittle and raw from the experience. You must watch out for him, Varus. His faults are my failings more than anything else."

My tears returned, but I vowed to protect and defend my brother as the Emperor desired. I had promised so much and had fulfilled so little. Truthfully, I was little closer to providing relief to Samur now than when I had first joined the Thracian Army. Yet as my gaze fixed upon the Emperor, a flicker of recognition halted my breath from sheer disbelief. And I waited, with more anticipation than I have ever known, for the words that came next.

"I free Samur from bondage and into your care." Thus sworn, the Emperor grabbed a sealed scroll from his table and handed it to me. I tucked it carefully into the pouch at my belt, avoiding any creases or folds.

After that, we sat in silence. Then, as the sun grew greater in the sky, Justin told me more of his dream—of grand churches, rebuilt cities, and just laws that applied to the commoners and the aristocrats alike. But that was all it was, a dream, for such ambitions require more effort than a man is willing to give. Such impossible goals require unfathomable sacrifice, the ledger so weighted that it consumes a man's life and all whom he would love. I nodded through it all, but at such a young age, what did I truly understand of the personal cost that such dreams would require? Much, I believed. But little, I came to understand in the years that followed. Timeless glory rises from the seeds of sacrifice, yet grief follows closely behind. My own glory, and grief, had hardly yet begun.

And I had heard it all before, a thousand times. Yet the Emperor dreamed aloud, and I fed his hopes by listening attentively. My own thoughts had flown to Samur; I was desperate to rush to the palace entryway and shout my brother's freedom to all who would hear. *Samur—free!*

Yet there was one question that had haunted sleep for my entire life, and I could not leave until I knew. At a pause in our speaking, I was ready. I gathered the courage and spoke the question that had troubled me since the moment Father Petrus had first awoken me in Archelaus' camp.

"Highness," I began, "why do you show such favor to me? I was just a slave, one of thousands."

Justin's eyes watered again.

"You never should have been, Varus," he said. Heruli, not Latin. My heart ached at the sound of those words in his aging voice. "Neither you nor your brother should have been. But I needed you, and then I came to love you, and then I could not let you go." The Emperor sobbed to himself as his answer left more questions than answers. "But I will take a step toward correcting my many errors."

The Emperor struggled to his feet. I dashed to offer assistance, but Justin shrugged me away and shuffled toward a small platform that held the old excubitor's arms and armor. It boasted dozens of small personal touches—shoulder guards that bore the faces of lions, a muscled cuirass that was lined with crosses and Latin script, and a richly decorated and plumed helmet that included carvings of the Emperor's past victories in battle. Yet Justin ignored all that grandeur, reaching instead for the sheathed pommel that rested on its own stand. Standing before his armor, he drew his sword from its scabbard and held it over his head as it glinted from the afternoon sun.

The blade was lined with foreign runes and shone with a blue-green tinge unlike any steel I had seen in the Roman Army. In all my years as a slave, I had marveled at its edge. I had never known it to rust, even when it was not polished and oiled. Before he had become emperor, and even after, I bore witness as Justin turned to the blade in times of crisis, staring at its runes as he contemplated the future.

The Emperor faced me. "Kneel."

I obeyed, and dropped to my knees. He levied the blade at me, his face a visage of authority. The Emperor recited the charge asked of all the Empire's soldiers, the answers I had dutifully given to Mundus as I passed from recruit to spearman. Yet where that moment had been met with relief at passing Archelaus' tests, something different stirred within me as Justin repeated my oath to the people.

"Do you, Varus, swear to faithfully execute the Emperor's commands, to never desert your service, nor shrink from death in pursuit of the glory of Rome?"

I lowered my head. "I do."

"And do you, Varus, swear to defend the weak, to protect the innocent, and serve as the shield to the poor and the mighty alike?"

His words flowed over me, and I nodded again. "I do."

The Emperor coughed, then lowered the blade's point to my chest, offering the most difficult of the three commands. "And do you, Varus, swear to honor and love your God, to seek justice, and glorify those dreams that are greater than yourself?"

"I do," I whispered. My heart and soul were a swirl of unknowable feeling.

As I sealed the oath, a look of triumph flickered across the Emperor's face, which was replaced by a stern and stoic gaze.

"You will be what I could not—a good man in the service of good deeds," Justin said. "Forge your own path."

The Emperor took the blade in both hands and lowered it to me. I received it in my outstretched fingertips as if at prayer, holding this long-desired object for the first time.

"I offer this gift in hopes that you will use it to make a better world. Never forget who you are, and all you must do, to see our shared dream become reality."

With his last command, Justin sat back into his chair, his strength spent. I confess, my ears perked at the word *gift*, and as memories of the priest's bronze cross and Aetius' dagger drifted forth, more questions burned within me. With the sword in my grasp, I again marshaled my courage and asked it once again through the gnaw of doubt.

"Highness, again I do not understand, why are you giving me your sword?" I asked.

"It is my sword no longer," Justin proclaimed. "It is now with its rightful owner."

I simplified. "Highness, what I mean is, why me? The old priest's cross, Aetius' dagger, and now your sword? Each of these are valuable on their own and bordering on priceless altogether," I said. "Why are you giving these gifts to one who a year ago was a Herulian slave?"

Justin sighed and rubbed his fingers together. "You deserve to know, but I do not yet have the strength to tell you." His voice dropped to a murmur. Still I asked why, begging for answers. These were the questions that had plagued my sleep for many months, if not my entire life; this one unknown rested at the core of my soul—*why me?*

"Come back from Cherson, and I'll tell you everything. I promise," Justin conceded, voice weak. "Now, embrace me, and may God protect you on your journey north."

My audience at an end, I had no choice but to sheathe my sword and offer my goodbyes to the Emperor. He clasped me close as he gave his blessing. I offered a salute, which he returned, then left me to see myself out of the palace for a final time before my deployment.

At the ground level of the Imperial Hall, I ordered a servant to summon my brother. He bowed and darted off, and soon thereafter Samur trailed in to meet me. With Samur ignorant of my exchange with the Emperor, it took all the discipline I could muster not to grab him by the shoulders, shouting his freedom and the fulfillment of a lifelong dream.

Having dutifully asked after the health and wellbeing of his dominus the Emperor, he asked the real question. "Anything interesting?" I barely needed an answer, as my brother's eyes immediately grew wide as he found the scabbard at my side, its dragon pommel unmistakable; this was the former blade of the Emperor.

Rather than speak any further answer, I pulled the sealed scroll from my bag, handed the missive to Samur, and gave him a moment to unfurl and read its contents.

"You are a free man now, Samur. But if you like, you may join me at Cherson, and consider fighting in the army with me when we return."

Samur's mouth opened, his eyes broad circles as he absorbed this new knowledge for several heartbeats. Yet soon he yelped with joy, drawing disdainful shakes of the head from passing aristocrats who Samur gleefully ignored. As did I, my cheeks strained from my grin. For all my lies, I had kept at least this word to my brother:

I had secured his freedom. Samur tore off his slave collar, dropping the unhooked leather straps before throwing his arms around my shoulders, not caring of any patrician disgust at the raw jubilation. I embraced him back, gripping his plain tunic and lifting him clean off of his feet, and he squealed with unashamed glee. For a moment all questions left my mind, replaced only by a bottomless sensation of satisfaction and relief. By Justin's command, my brother and I were together again, and free.

"I'm coming with you," Samur cried as we embraced. And thus decided, we returned to the barracks together, in bondage to Rome no more.

The Last Dying Light

THE LABOR OF A FOOL

THE MORNING BEFORE OUR departure, I was tasked with acquiring the remaining supplies to last my men on their voyage and expedition to Cherson. Courtiers had flitted from the barracks to the dockyard, their signed papers requisitioning the wine, oil, salted beef, and twice-baked bread that, more than any weaponry, gave the army its full force. Other supplies were more mundane, yet no less vital, from barrels of nails to thousands of feet of knotted rope. Yet even with the vast fortune of Treasury gold spent supplying and equipping the army, there were always small things that soldiers wanted for their comfort or survival. It did not help that many in the lower ranks were grumbling, too, about the poor quality of the spears and armor rented to the ranks, with some muttering that Justinian and his Treasurer Paulus had deliberately shorted their soldiers of anything *too* costly.

Rosamund, as my servant, offered to make the supply run in my stead, but as her Greek remained basic at best, and she would almost certainly be cheated by an unscrupulous merchant or smith—even with one of my men close by—I took that task upon myself and charged Perenus and Isaacius with overseeing the morning drill. The training with weapons and shields had grown more strenuous in our final days before deployment; our exercises increased an additional hour. Such exertion not only honed the soldiers' skills, but wore away the growing worry that pervaded the banda, where many of my men could not help but anticipate this beastlike enemy we were rumored to face. Perenus would simply refute any such unease, insisting that he had never met a man that Mundus' banda could not butcher.

The Last Dying Light

"You buy the wine; I'll make sure the men are itching for a fight," Perenus joked as I made for the market, a daft joke that I still took seriously. Both tasks were, in their way, essential.

Dressed in my cleaned centurion's armor, I gathered the supply list from my men and ventured out into the heart of the capitol, wondering when I would walk these streets again. I darted between shops, and securing everything on the list consumed most of the morning as I bartered and haggled with shopkeepers who—not unreasonably, given the new slate of taxes—saw the army as an avenue for bloated profits and a small revenge for the Imperial tariffs. Stalls hung with all manner of silks, parchment, incense, spices, and iron and bronze instruments, and even included a swordsmith that was a popular destination for much of the army. No soldier on the march needed such goods with little utility but considerable heft, so instead I purchased only a new dagger for Perenus, a waterskin for Isaacius, and dozens of other small necessities that would be delivered by the shopkeeper's slaves back to the barracks.

I neared the end of my outing and started back for the barracks, but as I passed the street filled by purveyors of silver, gold, and precious gems, I came to an abrupt halt. For there was one I had not thought to see again.

Flanked by a retinue of a half dozen black-skinned Aksumite spearmen, the princess Mariya was engaging in a lively discussion with a goldsmith who waved his hands in a small frenzy as he addressed her. Whatever he'd offered, the princess politely shook her head and declined.

A rush of courage propelled me toward the goldsmith's stall, longing flooding my veins even as doubt snaked around my heart. This was, I could not forget, Solomon's betrothed. I came within earshot of their conversation, in time to catch the goldsmith making a final offer so generous, he claimed, that it would be ruinous for his business, yet a necessary sacrifice to join the piece with so lovely a princess.

"He's cheating you, you know," I called. "I would only agree to half of what he is offering to you now."

The Aksumite leader blocked my view and glowered with aggression, but the princess ordered him to stand down.

"Do not worry, Sembrouthes," Mariya said in her pleasant voice. "Let him approach."

The Aksumite leader bobbed his head slightly and grudgingly allowed me room—barely—to walk forward. The goldsmith leered at me, muttering that an uncouth soldier had no knowledge of the craftsmanship and cost of such fine wares. The princess raised a finger to silence the peddler, took the charm from his hand, and attached it to a thin golden chain that hung at her throat. Her finger skimmed the edge of the charm, tracing its whorls and points. "A dragon, or a hydra from the Greek fables. What is your opinion, soldier?"

Giddy that she had addressed me directly, a tumble of responses riled my thoughts, all of which were utterly ridiculous. For all my worldly doings, I was unfamiliar with infatuation, unused to this unseen pull of one who was by turns exotic and forbidden. Love makes blithering idiots of the inexperienced, and at that age I was its most novice of apprentices. Thus, through a miasma of both bravado and fear, I refused to answer Mariya's otherwise innocent question.

"I am just a simple soldier, Princess, and have no knowledge of these things," I replied.

Mariya's eyes dropped to my hip, and she frowned. "That fine sword says otherwise. May I see it?"

Too surprised to object, I nodded and pulled the blade free of its scabbard, each move slow and deliberate; I was not so blinded by love to draw a swift blade against a woman of such royalty, regardless of my innocent intent. Even so, the muscles on

The Last Dying Light

Sembrouthes' neck tensed as I drew closer, as though he was prepared to strike at the slightest provocation. Yet Mariya showed no fear, only awe, as her hands swept over its pommel, caressing the intricate dragon that coiled above the handgrip. Her fingers, soft and delicate against this vessel of violence, ran down the blade and its grooved runes.

"A beautiful weapon," she concluded. "A work of art as much an instrument for war."

Mariya returned the blade and looked into my eyes with a hint of recognition. "We have met before." It was not a question.

Obligingly, I unstrapped my centurion's helmet, giving her a clearer view of the face she had acknowledged at her betrothal. Next to a Ghassanid princess or her retinue of immaculately attired Aksumites, I likely appeared thoroughly grubby, a middling Roman officer covered in sweat and coarse leather after a morning shopping for supplies. Having grown up among patricians, I was perhaps unusually aware of the chasm between us, and it took considerable resolve to hold her gaze without shrinking away.

"Yes, Princess," I said. My stomach knotted and squeezed as I fought to keep my voice level.

My sword back in hand, I clothed its naked blade back into its holster, the crossguard smacking against the scabbard's iron-rimmed tip with a satisfying click. As I did, Sembrouthes and the Aksumite spearmen visibly relaxed, yet Mariya paid their concern little mind as she drew a memory from our initial encounter.

"Ah, from the betrothal. Theodora's centurion," she remarked. She withdrew a gold *solidus* from the folds of her dress and handed it to the goldsmith. "As the centurion advises, this is my final offer."

The merchant accepted, and he bade the princess good fortune, yet showed his teeth to me when her gaze drifted.

"It is a nice day. Why don't you walk back to the palace with me?" Mariya said, turning to me once again. "It is rare to gain the attentions of such a Roman officer."

My heart fluttered at the command and I moved to her side without hesitation. "Forgive me, my lady, but you are mistaken; your betrothed is another such officer—the commander of an entire banda," I reminded her.

"Of course." Mariya smiled. "Do you happen to know my future husband?"

"Yes, Highness," I said, unable to control my tone. "For… many years now."

Mariya's eyes widened into a look of hungering curiosity. Before, I may have been little more than a diversion, now Mariya inspected me more closely, as though I were, perhaps, a confidante.

"Tell me, what kind of man is he?" Her words were barely audible, even to me, let alone any others in the marketplace.

I struggled for an answer. Nothing would have given me greater satisfaction than to tell the princess that Solomon was a fiend who fed on the misfortune of others, whose every injury or misfortune was erased from public view by his father. Though such temptation burned in my breast, I knew it would have brought dishonor upon myself and the Emperor; I would be placing selfish aims above my oath of loyalty and service. Solomon may have been an aristocrat, but he was also my fellow soldier. And that knowledge—that we were brothers in arms—suppressed, at least for now, the noxious urge to speak ill of him to his soon-to-be wife.

"He will make sure you are well provided for, Highness," I answered. The truth—a piece of it, at least.

Mariya's lovely face flickered with not relief, but frustration.

"A gallant answer, and one that is undoubtedly true. Yet I have heard more disturbing rumors, and those interest me far more."

She was too clever for my evasive response. "Rumors and gossip are the weapons of the weak and the cowardly." I scowled, cursing myself inwardly for such blunt words.

"Even so, they are spoken widely enough to reach the ears of a foreigner to your lands," Mariya replied. "I fear becoming another man's possession, something to be displayed to friends and later locked away to be forgotten."

I nodded, my gaze on her softening as I pictured Solomon's treatment of his future bride. "Forgive me, Princess, but that fate may befall you even absent a union with Solomon."

Mariya's lips curved with a sudden laugh that she swiftly covered with a delicate hand. "Too true!" she agreed. "But one can always hope for a better future, or at least one with companions not prone to cruelty or control."

"Indeed. I know the truth in this all too well, Princess," I said. "For not long ago, I was a slave, and saw the difference between kindness and evil as one with no power and little influence over their future."

No sooner had I foolishly poured forth my own ignoble heritage than my heart sank. Princess Mariya knew the life of gilded opulence and privilege; my lineage would only lower me in her esteem. My regret only grew as Mariya's eyes fell to the ground and her arms enfolded her chest. Once more, the urge to spring away overwhelmed me, and I wished that time might reverse itself and undo the embarrassment that I had brought on myself.

Such urges evaporated at Mariya's next words. "But what you must have seen and accomplished to get to where you are!" she exclaimed. "How can one rise so far, and so quickly?"

I offered a silent word of praise for the shift in conversation and puffed my chest, recounting my time with the Emperor and rise in the army. A hot impulse struck me, a need to embellish the travails of survival under Archelaus, the challenges of subduing the Gepids, but I resisted, favoring honesty over boasting. Mariya grew curious at my descriptions of Theodora and inquired further about Basilius, and maintained this avid attention as we paced leisurely through the marketplace. Through it all, Mariya's Aksumite guards were never more than a few paces behind, their boots clicking a reminder as they surveyed for any sign of threat or violence from all directions.

"You are a brave man, Varus. A brave centurion who owns beautiful instruments," Mariya murmured again in her accented Latin touched with notes of her native Arabic. "Tell me, is this a rare trait in Romans? Do you find yourself compelled by beauty?"

I shrugged at her first question. "I have yet to meet a person that does not," I admitted.

Mariya's laughter was so delicate, I was sure none but I could hear it. "Is this a love you acquired in the palace?" she prodded.

"Far more recently than that," I answered, incredulous even as the words poured from my mouth.

My body burned with shame from such tactless talk as my heart ached from my own clumsiness of speech; I lacked the sweet words of a practiced flatterer. I dared not look directly at her, yet caught the outlines of a smile on her face I prayed was not my hopeful imagining.

"Do you think Solomon would make me happy, Varus?" Mariya asked, the question so sudden I could only think it had been plaguing her.

"No, Lady." It was the truth, and a great weight released from my chest as I said it.

She grimaced and did not press further. "Thank you for your honesty."

From there, we took an indirect route back to the palace, and the walk would have passed in silence had a loud crash not rang out from an alley. Mariya jumped, and the Aksumites darted eyes in all directions for the cause of our alarm. Whatever it was, it was everywhere and nowhere, discordant voices rising from seemingly all of the market's towering buildings. An Imperial banner had been thrown into a gutter, its golden eagle on a purple field growing stained with the urban muck.

"What is happening?" Mariya asked, fear in her voice.

"Riots," Sembrouthes growled in Latin, then switched to Aksumite to bark orders to his men, who surrounded the princess and guided her forward.

"I'm coming with you," I told Sembrouthes, who eyed my sword before nodding.

"Keep to the right side," he ordered coldly. "And let nothing come close."

I unsheathed the Emperor's blade, and we walked slowly onward as peasants flooded the streets. Few paid us any mind, with most seeking the more urgent plunder tumbling from the bakeries and fruit sellers that fed the city each day. One small boy wormed his way from between dozens of men and women, carrying a leg of mutton half as big as he was and slapping aside grasping hands. Some shopkeepers resisted but were bludgeoned with crude clubs and mallets if they refused the mob entry. Overwhelmed by the press of humanity, the few patrols of city guards retreated toward the Palace, offering no defense to those who begged for protection.

Ever alert, I saw one peasant man, grimy-faced and carrying a sack of grain, bump into one of Sembrouthes' men and get shoved hard to the stone-lined streets for the imposition. We pushed on; livid voices flew in our direction as we quickened our pace, the princess in the center as we marched in an elongated square. Several within the mob, hands empty of loot, charged at our tight formation, grasping for the gold shining at Mariya's throat and arms.

"Avoid bloodshed!" I yelled, shoving several back, even rapping a particularly determined older man about the head with the flat of my sword.

Sembrouthes sent me a skeptical glance.

"Death will only rile them up further," I explained.

Sembrouthes nodded and relayed the order to the others.

After we at last crested the hill that led to the Palace, we came upon a formation of armed spearmen that had gathered in the palace square. Recognizing Mariya's delegation amid the riotous crowd, the formation's officers ordered our passage through their lines, a gap that opened for only a few heartbeats. Among these warriors I spotted Marcellus, Justinian's excubitor, who nodded at me.

"We can handle the crowd from here," Marcellus yelled. "Head to the barracks, Varus. Your men will need you whole tomorrow."

Though perhaps only ten years my senior, Marcellus carried himself with a raw authority that dozens of other excubitores heeded, following every command and forming a wall of shields to resist the incoming surge. I went to leave, yet heard a voice cry out through the din.

"Varus, wait!" Mariya reemerged from the palace door even as Sembrouthes begged her to return inside.

I paused, foolishly daring to turn back to the palace doors as Marcellus' spearmen held a rising throng at bay not twenty paces distant. The rioters screamed for Justinian and Paulus, their chants strewn with hatred and baying for death. Some lobbed the rotten fruit that had been distributed to many poorer households, the pungent and overripe fruit splattering across the men's shields and staining their Chi-Rho emblems. His excubitor's armor thus marred with juice and pulp, Marcellus removed his helmet to give his men a clearer view of his face as he barked instructions: remain calm, and do not trade insults with the mob.

I rushed to Mariya's side near the open palace door. "Princess, you must go with your guard, it is not safe here."

She reached for the thin golden necklace that rested high over her heart, unclasped the dragon pendant, and placed it in my hand. Our fingers brushed together for a heartbeat as she stared into my eyes.

"I will be praying for your safe return." Mariya's voice was low—again, I knew, her words were for me alone.

The Last Dying Light

With that, she disappeared behind the palace door that Sembrouthes quickly closed after her, and I heard the locks swing shut on the inside. Still, amid the chaos, my soul soared within me; more than any pride from my superiors or even the favor of God himself, her words filled me with courage, courage that I could overcome these Avars or any other that stood in my path. My brief dream was interrupted by the rising energy of the crowd, and a spoiled tomato that smashed at my feet.

The crowd's fever was burning its fiercest now, as they were throwing objects and rushing the guards. The palace spearmen were not known to be particularly skilled, with only the few dozen excubitores present having known the shield wall, the overwhelm of enemy screams, and the cries of wounded comrades. Many palace spearmen looked uneasily down the line, with Marcellus keeping order through the steady notes of his voice.

When spoiled fruits and vegetables ran out, the stones came. I watched with horror as one unlucky projectile flew above the formation and struck Marcellus in the forehead. A deep gash rippled in his temple, and the commander collapsed, pawing feebly at the wound as his legs buckled. Two excubitores leaped to carry their commander to safety and banged for an entry to the palace that was granted just long enough to slip Marcellus' limp body inside. Though other officers sought to take Marcellus' place, the shock of the assault had eroded their discipline. One spearman, struck by a stone that left a deep rent in his shield, hurled a spear at the culprit, impaling the stone thrower.

"Go now, centurion!" one of the remaining excubitores screamed at me.

I saluted and ran behind the lines, seeking the labyrinth of hidden alleyways that would bear me back to the Imperial Barracks. Still, I could not resist, and spun for one final look at the courtyard as the mob's anger intensified. One man rushed the shield wall and momentarily broke through, only to be stabbed by a half dozen spearmen. But this only further whipped the frenzy, and the fullness of the crowd rushed the formation. All restraint was abandoned as spears and swords came down upon the peasants.

I could watch no longer. I navigated the maze of side streets and rushed into the barracks door. Several of the men within crowded me, worry on their faces, and begged for news of the violent noises echoing into their dormitories and training yard. "It is a good thing we are leaving tomorrow." That, and a vicious oath of frustration, were all I offered before retiring to my officer's quarters and resting the Emperor's blade upon a stand. Though the sun had not yet set, I lay on my mattress, staring at Mariya's golden dragon for hours until it came time for an evening meal with Rosamund and my men.

The next morning, I carried that charm with me to my morning training with the old priest, securing it within a small pouch on my belt that hung tight against my body. Though these devotions had filled most of my mornings in Constantinople, the day after my encounter with Mariya seemed particularly blessed, its sun warmer and streets somehow less infested with lice and foul odors. Father Petrus, however, disapproved of the pendant after I showed it to him, cautioning that dragons were one of many symbols of the fallen archangel Lucifer. I countered that such creatures also arose from the Greek myths, which, although pagan, were at least not fully demonic, to which he agreed halfheartedly. In the end, the priest did not order me to dispose of the emblem, and smiled when he saw his bronze cross still rested securely from my neck and had not been supplanted by fantasy.

After my lessons, I returned with haste. Abuzz with activity, the many bandae were collecting their belongings into the wooden trunks that would be placed aboard the transport vessels commissioned to ferry Godilas' army across the Euxine Sea. Most of the expedition's supplies had already been divided into ten hulks that would carry us to Cherson, and our horses and pack animals had begun boarding well before dawn. Samur arrived as my men were filing into the training yard; I had secured permission from Mundus for my brother to accompany the banda to the north, with the qualification that, in spite of his thorough training under Godilas in the palace, Samur should be restricted to small duties only until he, too, had undergone the grueling training camp required of a Roman spearman. At this, Samur had grumbled, arguing that he was being wasted by not being thrown into combat, yet he did not refuse Mundus' command.

Rosamund had seen to the final preparations of my men and possessions, ensuring that the Emperor's sword was never removed from her sight. She still carried Aetius' dagger anytime she left the barracks and indeed had it belted to her waist as she cleared out our quarters that morning. As the banda marched for the docks, Rosamund followed behind with the small nation of servants, slaves, clerks, and attendants that would accompany the campaign. Father Petrus also joined such a procession, offering prayers to Mundus' banda before boarding the ship, which bore a modest cabin for the priest's comfort.

Mundus' boar, Archelaus' viper, and the Imperial Eagle held aloft, we marched for the billowing white sails of our temporary homes. Piles of rotting food along the streets paid homage to the previous evening's violence, as did the more sinister streaks and pools of blood that collected along the walls of many shops. Our banda and followers boarded together and found their quarters for the next several days. My men had been prepared bunks and hammocks in shared quarters, while Rosamund and I had secured the cozy cabin reserved for a younger officer such as myself.

The men packed away, and already stealing into the wine and meat that they had hoarded for the trip, I climbed abovedeck to observe the final preparations before departure. A small procession snaked from the palace as Basilius, his daughter Antonina, and

Theodora led a delegation of well-wishers from the government. I squinted toward the Palace and thought I spied a tiny figure at the topmost floor of the Palace staring back at us, yet with the sun blazing into my eyes, I could not be sure. Mundus boarded our ship, yet Archelaus was nowhere to be found, and I thanked God that he had joined another of the ships. Godilas stood at the front of our neighboring ship, trailed by several clerks presumably giving him the final tally of men, servants, beasts, and supplies.

After a time, the general gave the order to disembark, and the ships loosened their ties to port and raised anchor. Brass corni rang out from the shore as we pushed off, away from the capitol and into the open sea; the craft rocked lightly as they separated from their moorings. Mundus grunted in approval as the stench and noise of Constantinople faded into the distance, and the army proceeded toward its shadowy enemy.

The Last Dying Light

WAR IN THE NORTH

THE VOYAGE TOOK A WEEK. On the morning of the second day, we were waylaid by storms, tempests that rolled our ship with such abandon that even the hardiest soldiers retched and moaned. Father Petrus' audience mass was conspicuously fuller as even those who professed no love for the Christian God, particularly within the Latin tongue, gathered to pray for mercy against the seas.

I rarely ventured out of my cabin. Though I'd spent several days aboard a river barge through the Ister, this journey was my first experience along open water and the unpredictable machinations of the sea. Yet in one of the lulls between gales, I was seized by a desire for fresh air and reprieve from the tepid hold of the transport ship. Though heavy gales still pulled the ship, the rain had subsided at least a moment, and the seas had calmed enough to where an unlucky passenger would not be easily swept overboard.

Abovedeck, I was greeted with nods from the sailors manning the various posts of the ship. Slaves powered her oars belowdecks, yet we saw little of them, as our holds were separated from theirs by a thick wooden platform. I walked to the stern, and from there I spotted, across the gently churning waves, one of our partner vessels trailing a mere hundred paces behind. Nothing in particular stood out from the ship, yet as I sharpened my gaze, I made out the form of Godilas, alone near the front. Motionless, he seemed covered in the freshly fallen rainwater, and did not stir even as the wind whipped at his face. I called out to him, yet he merely stared forward. With that, the rain picked up again, and with it, the winds, stirring tall waves that crested near the top of the ship. The boards beneath me swayed sickeningly, and my own footing faltered.

"Better go back down, sir," called one of the sailors near me.

The Last Dying Light

Nausea swirled in my stomach. I nodded to the sailor and gave one last look at Godilas. His ship rocked more violently than our own, yet he sat like a stone as his eyes remained fixed to the north.

Belowdecks again, I passed a game of dice but ignored calls to join in. Several of the men had fallen into affable drunkenness, all goaded by a wine-soaked Perenus. As the heaving ship shifted an ideal roll of the dice into a losing one, he howled with laughter, and hooted all more as Isaacius shot upright, cursing the sea for his rotten luck.

Meanwhile, Cephalas led some of the men in song, though most had become too drunk, too seasick, or both, to make an honest attempt. The reek of vomit clung to the deck's walls even after much scrubbing from the servants, and despite any temptation of wine, I felt no urge to add to it. I would fight at the head of their shield wall, and fight for them in the palace to ensure their needs were met, but on the ship, nothing could sway me to linger outside of my cabin. Reaching the door, I threw it open and fell inside, finding Rosamund sitting at the small desk, cleaning Aetius' knife. Aboard, she had spent each night with the dagger close at hand, still prepared to ward off an assault at any moment no matter how often I assured her safety. Though she had quickly befriended several within my banda, certainly after our night at the Hippodrome, it was Rosamund's nature to trust very few, least of all those who professed loyalty to Archelaus. She shuddered when his name was spoken aloud, always making her open-handed sign against evil and spitting upon the floor.

Nevertheless, Rosamund seemed unperturbed by a storm that was bringing seasoned soldiers to their knees. I found Rosamund muttering prayers in her native language, grinning at the sound of my men retching in the ship's hold.

"A storm like this means the gods are near," she stated.

"Your... *your* gods?" My queasiness suddenly surged as waves rocked our ship. "Why would this be a sign of favor?"

Rosamund scoffed. "*My* gods, pfft. *The* gods. They are here among us, watching this voyage. They will test your strength and reward you if you withstand. But if you prefer their help, I could beseech them for calmer seas."

I shuddered, as much from my roiling stomach as from the mention of her dark gods and their designs; even now, I could not fully abide their mention. Properly seasick, I retreated into my berth, my body unable to resist rocking to the motion of the waves. Rosamund blew out our lone candle and joined me, rubbing my shoulders as her soft voice found its way into my ear.

"We will not die here," Rosamund said softly. "I will not allow it. Rest easy, Varus."

So help me, but her reassuring touch did yield a sense of safety. Not from any credence in Rosamund's pagan faith—of which, I cannot say enough, I had no interest and little knowledge—but from faith in Rosamund herself. Even as her soft fingers trailed along my neck and arms, my skin ached more and more for their touch, as if Rosamund were drawing pain out of my body and into her grasp. My body steady enough to close my eyes without retching, I rested my head upon Rosamund's lap and let her rub my temples.

Since that journey, I have always hated ships. In my opinion, if God had intended men to journey the seas, He would have fashioned us with fins and gills. Our voyage to Cherson was never pleasant, or even bearable, yet just then, in the darkness of my cabin, I at least knew some peace as my arms reached around Rosamund's body and she mussed my hair. I felt curiously vulnerable, more than on any battlefield, yet I drank in each passing moment, the sweetly cool skin of her arms as she massaged my neck and face. This was not that infatuation that had seen me helplessly in Mariya's thrall in the days prior, yet whatever pervaded me, it held its own power. The poets sing of the singular bonding of souls between those who share in hardship, one born of respect and a willingness to sacrifice for the good of the other. Other than Samur, I forged such a bond not with Perenus, Isaacius, or Cephalas, but with Rosamund. And for that, perhaps, I loved her, in a way.

As I was ignorant of her own thoughts and too cowardly to inquire directly, I could only pray that Rosamund felt that same bond. We lay in silence as I drifted to sleep, while Rosamund lay motionless and alert, a guard against disruption.

The next day was a mild improvement. While the seas rocked our ship, we maintained enough stability to spend more time abovedeck. One of the centurions from an adjoining banda had begun to fraternize with our men and had even struck up some small games to occupy our time. Rather than crack down, Mundus encouraged such activity, arguing that it would bring greater camaraderie among the spearmen under his command.

This centurion had introduced himself as Troglita. He hailed from the deep hill fastnesses of Macedonia, claiming to be descended from Antipater, one of Alexander's generals.

"A bastard line, to be sure," Troglita joked; indeed, he showed no real sign of the wealth of a more directly noble lineage.

By the fourth day, the storm had passed, and Troglita and I began to hold sparring matches between our warriors. Many were eager to participate, a chance to shake off the curious restlessness born of inactivity. Troglita himself was no mean swordsman, and we two spent several hours dueling. By the end of the week, we had both inflicted bruises on the other, but it was a lesson more than any kind of defeat. Isaacius was particularly taken to the exercises and, when his usual sparring partners declined, attacked wooden posts to keep his skills sharp. He was rarely denied a proper match, however, as Samur enthusiastically pursued all chances to learn with our Jewish dekarchos. Frequently, I found my brother laughing as Isaacius demonstrated new tricks, which Samur was then eager to test out on me in the few times that we crossed wooden blades.

When each day settled to darkness, I would lay in my bunk and twirl Mariya's golden dragon, fixed on the intricate whorls that decorated its body. As I held it close, I swore I could detect a trace of Mariya's sweet perfume, and with it, the faint but lovely image of her face. That mad yearning from Constantinople had not diminished as I ventured hundreds of miles distant, replaying Mariya's final words to me before our parting.

"I will be praying for your safe return."

I recited her words a hundred times in my solitude, praying that their meaning was more than a friendly gesture, yet not daring to hope for anything more than polite friendship. I kept it tucked away in my belt during the day, occasionally reaching for its metallic outline as a sign of reassurance and comfort.

On the late morning of our seventh day, a watchman proclaimed a glimpse of land, sending cheers across the ship. Our boat was the first to dock in Cherson's harbor, with servants and spearmen jostling to return to blessedly firm and dry land. I mouthed a silent prayer as my boots brushed against the worn stones of Cherson's streets, faint nausea still gripping my guts as servants unpacked the cargo from our hold. Rosamund and Samur followed closely behind as they ferried supplies and provisions into Cherson, while Perenus and Isaacius took the first possible opportunity to purchase additional stores of wine to replenish their depleted stores.

The city was old, dating back to the days of Odysseus and the heroes of Troy. It had never grown beyond a few thousand inhabitants, yet it had remained an important trading port, receiving grain and slaves from the steppe beyond in return for Roman gold. Many traders from distant points of Asia had even begun to import their silks through Cherson; although for many months now, fearful of the ghostly enemy that preyed upon the Tauris Peninsula, no merchants had braved the route.

Searching for our senior officer, the city's garrison commander settled on and greeted Mundus. After guiding us to a squat stone building that served as the provincial garrison command, the garrison commander shared his knowledge of our foe. Unfortunately, he knew precious little beyond what Godilas had learned from the deserter, only reiterating that the enemy came in the darkness, or when mists and fog made them impossible to see. These Avars were not known to negotiate and were incorruptible to a bribe.

"Horsemen," Mundus observed, "to be able to arrive and attack so quickly without being seen. They must have learned from Attila how to fire a bow from a mounted position."

The garrison commander wrinkled his face at that name, yet agreed. "That would explain why we can't find any of their wounded. The few survivors we've interrogated after battle swear that they stuck men with spears and blades, yet our patrols never find any bodies. No man could carry that kind of weight on foot for long."

The commander then informed us of recent developments that had not yet reached Constantinople. Kerkinitis, the last sizeable Tauric town outside of Cherson, had been sacked and burned. Ships had been dispatched to investigate when scheduled merchants had not arrived a week behind schedule, and found the town's walls broken and its buildings cracked and scarred from flames. Most confoundingly, however, the town's treasury was untouched. It was not unharmed, for its gold coins and bars had melted into a shapeless mass in the heat of the fire, yet it remained for anyone to take.

At this news, Mundus sighed. "Show me what we know of the province."

The commander unpacked several scrolls and unfurled a map of Rome's activities in the Tauris Peninsula. His finger found Cherson and traced out the major outlying towns that had been razed. Mundus scratched his head as he reviewed the town names scribbled on the chart.

"Which villages remain in Cherson's control?" he asked.

The commander shook his head. "Precious few. We have several fishing villages to the east, and one major outpost on the northern side of the Peninsula."

His finger traced the name Kalos Limin, which he said was among the oldest villages in the region. Though well beyond Rome's formal territorial boundaries, Kalos Limin had remained an important staging post for trade and diplomatic missions to the various steppe lords in the northern wastes, and it retained a Greek character as well as Greek-speaking colonists.

Standing behind Mundus with the other centurions, I eyed the maps myself. I could not help but wonder at the survival of so small and unprotected a village, especially when all larger towns outside of Cherson had been thoroughly sacked. It simply made no sense. "So far northwest," I asked, "how were they not one of the first to be destroyed?"

The commander shrugged, explaining that it was not a rich target for raiding in its own right.

"We lost contact with the village three days ago," he added. "Normally, we would dispatch scouts from Kerkinitis, but as you know, such soldiers have disappeared." Then the commander frowned, his eyes blackened and heavy from a lack of sleep. "I was about to order the evacuation of Cherson until I heard of the Emperor's armies heading our way. Our defenses are better than the other towns and villages of the region... but not by much."

"We'll provide men to double the city's sentries," Mundus said. "For now, tell any who ask that all will be well, and that the Emperor's soldiers will ensure their safety."

His words were a visible relief to the garrison commander, yet in truth they were hollow ones. Though we remained confident that, once Belisarius' army arrived from Sinope, we could easily overpower our adversary, our numbers were far too low to safeguard the entire province even after General Belisarius' forces arrived. I whispered as much in Mundus' ear, but the new banda commander was already concerned.

"We need to keep the people calm," Mundus said. "Cherson will be safe from an outright assault for now, and we can contend with the rest later."

Mundus relayed this new information to Godilas and Archelaus as they arrived, and I left the more senior officers to discuss their intended strategy now that all ships had docked safely into port. By the end of our first day in Tauris, Godilas dispatched written orders to the banda commanders for our moves in the next days. Until then, several hundred spearmen would be housed in Cherson's barracks, with others forming a small tent encampment just beyond the city's stone walls. My detachment was among the unlucky mass ordered to the less comfortable field encampment, and it was there that Rosamund helped organize my presence in the region.

Though I have little doubt that Cherson was sizeable for this far-flung and underpopulated province, its entire expanse could have easily fit within Constantinople's dockyards. Cherson emanated with the similar yet less oppressive odor of dung as Constantine's city, yet also reeked of fish entrails as one approached the dockyard. Stone buildings mixed with wood and thatch, evidence of centuries of habitation by dozens of peoples and architectural preferences. Its environment was overcast and seemingly always threatening rain, contributing to a dreary outlook on what our life would be as we ventured inland. I have no doubt that Cherson was a more enjoyable place during times of relative peace and prosperity, but during my stay I found it to be quaint, yet dull.

True to Mundus' plan, one hundred spearmen would reinforce Cherson's garrison and patrol its walls: a unit of primarily lighter auxiliaries who normally marched at the front of the army's ranks to throw darts and create disruption in the enemy's ranks. Privately, I asked the general why only such a minimal force would be allocated for this task, eliciting barely veiled frustration from Godilas.

"One hundred is already more than I can spare," he said tersely. "And we will have little use for large formations of light infantry if our enemy truly does attack only when it cannot be seen."

Other scouting parties of twenty and thirty would be sent out to garrison villages that were known to be inhabited, with small contingents clearing and rebuilding the defenses of Kerkinitis and Theodosia. Cherson's city commander applauded this plan, telling us that the province was only defensible thanks to the tight network of towns and villages that formed a protective perimeter around the provincial capital. Lastly, one group of twenty would venture toward Kalos Limin and determine its fate. The bulk of the army would depart by smaller boats off the shores of the village, arriving on the western Tauric coastline to search for our Avar invaders.

Gathering his officers into the provincial governor's building, Godilas further outlined his plan. The army would conduct a massive scouting expedition, sweeping from Kalos Limin to Scythian Neapolis, a larger village two days' march from Cherson. At this, Archelaus grunted his approval.

"Take all the fodder and forage to draw our enemy out, hopefully on favorable terms," Archelaus said. "That will give them no choice but to attack us directly or run away hungry."

Godilas confirmed and gave the orders to make ready. And so, the day after our landing, several detachments departed, with the larger army to leave within a week. Mundus' banda would remain with the main body, awaiting Godilas' orders to advance into Tauris' plains to hunt for our enemy.

"And what about the army arriving from Sinope?" Mundus asked as he eyed the Tauric maps, presumably looking for weaknesses or roadblocks that would be useful in a pitched battle.

Godilas frowned. "There's been no word on their progress, and we can't be sure they've even left Sinope yet. If they caught storms similar to ours, it could be well into the autumn before their first detachments arrive."

Other officers argued that we should wait for reinforcements and dig in to Cherson, yet Archelaus rejected any such defensive posture. As a centurion, my task was merely to observe and obey, although I burned to question Godilas about why we could not simply wait a few more weeks for the Cappadocian Army to reinforce our position.

"Grab hold of your balls and be a man!" Archelaus roared, slamming a callused fist onto a table. "This city cannot support an army of our size for long, and we need to make the most of surprise if we're to catch these Avars off guard."

Again Godilas concurred with his second-in-command and ended the meeting with a prayer and orders to proceed.

The following morning, many of our servants and slaves, nimbler than the full ranks of our soldiers, were sent ahead to Scythian Neapolis to make ready for our arrival. With reluctance, Rosamund joined their number, but only when she learned Archelaus would allow no civilians to trail the army to Kalos Limin, and even then with clear exasperation. Before she left our temporary camp outside Cherson's walls, she returned Aetius' sheathed blade.

"I am giving this to you for now, but you will return it when you arrive safely to the village, understand?" Rosamund said in strained Heruli.

"There is no reason for concern. We will meet you again soon enough." I smiled. "Just a couple of weeks of hard marching and I'll be there to meet you in Scythian Neapolis. Perenus, Isaacius, Cephalas, and everyone else, too."

Rosamund shook her head. "You have no idea what's out there," she said. "Something evil happened here, and it won't hesitate to swallow your army either."

"Rosamund—"

"You're fools!" she cried. "Can't you ask to remain in the city?"

"*No.*" I neglected to mention Godilas' standing offer. "And even if I could, I wouldn't leave my men."

"You cannot save everyone, Varus. If it comes down to your safety or the army's needs, take your brother and run." Rosamund was almost begging. "I've told you before, Rome doesn't deserve you. I've seen your Empire's cities and wept at the filth and terror in which its people live, all so that stupid batch of plump nobles can stay refreshed and entertained."

"I will not run!" I insisted. "I made an oath, and I'll be damned if I break it."

"Then you are a fool as well." Rosamund sighed. "Oaths bind you to something that is rotten. You may not believe me now, but eventually you will. And on that day, we can leave this behind for something truly free."

I opened my mouth to retort, but stayed myself, remembering Godilas' long-ago chastisement of my rash temper, my need for a cool head, and steered myself back to a more prudent path. Rosamund's outburst was not surprising; I knew, and always had, that she loathed the Empire's senior leaders, since to her, their motives and behaviors were one and the same with those of Archelaus. Nor was I surprised by her willingness to seek a life elsewhere; she had no reason to be loyal to the Empire, and was only bound to its service in the interest of serving not an Empire, but a small circle of friends. Nevertheless, I felt sure that she would stay on with me regardless of the difficulties ahead.

"I don't wish to part in disharmony," I said. "We can discuss this when I return."

Rosamund gave me a resigned sigh. "There is no disharmony among us, ever. I just wish that you would allow me to protect you from yourself."

"I've always been stubborn." I grinned. "And I don't expect to change anytime soon."

Chuckling, Rosamund embraced me, then ran to join the baggage train that contained the belongings of my men. Against her jerkin, Rosamund's plaited white hair was a shock against the sea of black and brown heads, and she was easy to track as her column advanced toward the northeastern horizon.

Father Petrus, too, would soon join Rosamund with our carts and baggage, yet not before offering blessings to me and my men.

"No matter where you go, God is with you," Father Petrus assured us, sitting astride a small but sturdy pony as he stood outside Cherson's gates. "Regardless of how dark or desperate things become."

I bowed my head and clutched at the bronze cross that hung from my throat, asking God to grant the priest safe journey. With the servants and slaves and others departed, all that remained were the thousands of soldiers sworn to Godilas' service, eager, if a bit ill at ease at what might come, for the journey toward glorious battle. Despite my experience with the Gepids, despite what I should have known from any one of my mentors' teachings, I was fool enough to count myself in their number.

THE MISTS OF TAURIS

PER GODILAS' INSTRUCTIONS, a number of smaller craft were commissioned to transport the bulk of the Thracian Army toward Kalos Limin. When departure day arrived, many of the men grumbled at the thought of returning to such unsteady wooden craft. My own spearmen held no qualms about joining in such complaints.

"I enlisted as a soldier, not a sailor, and all I seem to do now is avoid drowning," Perenus griped.

Others insisted an urgency to head into combat, eager to take slaves and plunder even if such measures required another brief sailing along the Tauric coastline. With fair winds, a ship could skim over a distance ten times faster than an army on foot, to say nothing of sparing the men the endless blisters and aching limbs of such a march. Isaacius was one who bragged of his desire to rush to combat sooner, brushing aside as laughable any rumors that the Avars were not men, but horned beasts belched from some infernal underworld.

Fortunately, the voyage was a brief one, skirting the craggy Tauric coastline on our way to Kalos Limin. Sailors insisted they spied dark figures watching our voyage with curiosity, but when other eyewitnesses saw none, claimed they had been wild animals all along. Mundus, exasperated, assumed the outlandish rumors of Avars as some sort of agents of Satan had gotten to the sailors' heads. Troglita was more skeptical.

"Perhaps they do have spies," he reasoned. "And if they do, we have lost the element of surprise. And if we have, we should reconceive our strategy."

I wanted to argue that Troglita's concerns were unlikely, yet privately, the recurring sightings of dark-hooded figures in the distance made my sleep uneasy. I lay awake, wondering what, exactly, we were sailing toward. Within two days, we approached our target, an ominous sky and rising winds greeting us along Tauris' western coastline.

Anchored outside of Kalos Limin in the early morning, on the second day, smaller boats ferried groups of spearmen and horses ashore. Many took to their duties as the same ritual that army life had instilled in their limbs, but Samur, a novice to the work, was the one who noticed something amiss.

"Where are the lights?" he asked. "All of the fires?"

I took in the outline of Kalos Limin. He was right; it was dark, no glimmers of flame, no smoky plumes from its thatched roofs. Others soon joined Samur in his concern—why had none of the previous detachment ridden out to meet our army? Why were we greeted only by saltwater and thickening fog? Now a bit worried myself, I sent Perenus and Isaacius with their men to scout out the area while the army disembarked, and they soon returned with matching grim expressions.

"Something happened here." Perenus kept his voice strategically low. "And it was bad."

"There's nothing," Isaacius added. "No men, no women, no children, no animals… it is as though they all just vanished into the air."

I ventured into the village, simply for my own perusal. Isaacius had not been entirely correct. While no living soul lived to greet us to Kalos Limin, it was not wholly vanished, either: Its wooden palisades had been charred and broken, and deep rust-colored stains covered the surface of what few walls remained standing. Samur, accompanying me, inspected one larger formation, churning the markings into the dirt and grass that surrounded them with his fingers.

"Blood, and by the looks of it, a week old or longer," he said gruffly. "It's caked on all the stones and staining those buildings still standing."

We had assumed that Kalos Limin had been attacked, that its villagers would have likely suffered a similar fate as those of dozens of other villages in Tauris, yet when at last confronted with the evidence, the men were still rattled. Many crossed themselves as they walked through the village center, yet a large number instinctively spat to avert evil. As such, I wondered whether Rosamund's beliefs would be more welcome here than even our Imperial Christianity, especially considering the Avars' own religion was rumored to be driven by brute strength and merciless devotion.

As more of my men arrived to inspect the village, shouts rang out from its far gate. At the alarm, several spearmen formed a half circle around a burned and broken gate that had served as the village's primary entrance. I found Troglita leaning close to inspect the wood panels.

"This blood is more recent, only a day or two old," he noted, explaining that it differed from the rust and black stains that lined many of the ruined village huts and buildings.

I cautioned those men gathered around Troglita that such a sign meant little, reasoning that such markings could be from an animal or left for a reason unrelated to a struggle or fight by armed men. Yet my words did little to ease the worries of the spearmen, and truthfully I did not myself believe that such markings had been left by accident. The most likely scenario was that our detachment of spearmen had arrived to Kalos Limin a day or two prior, and fled, or fell to some adversary. As Roman soldiers were—and still are—loath to run from a fight, I believed the latter was more likely.

Godilas was even less sanguine, sure that the Avars had fought our scouts and carried off the living and the dead alike. After our transport ships unloaded the last of our men and supplies, they lifted their anchors with the speed of sailors deeply uneasy with a journey so far from Rome's shrinking domain. Godilas ordered a report on the state of the army and tasked Solomon with preparing it, and my boyhood rival happily jumped to this matter of perceived importance.

So, too, did the other men run to their assigned tasks, shivering at the evil omens of the changing weather, where the blowing winds and crackling thunder of our sea voyage had found us far north at the edge of Tauris. Creeping dark snaked into the foothills of Kalos Limin, layering a thick, damp warning of rain to come, over the ruins of the village. Waves crashed onto the rock-strewn shoreline, yet through the fog, only their thunder reached the army. Even the sky, already dimming along the horizon, darkened and hid from our scouts, giving the impression that night was approaching despite the sun not yet close to its midday zenith.

Before its sack, Kalos Limin had been well past her prime as a trading outpost, and her inhabitants had grown plump and uncaring in the relative peace of a Roman backwater. Others, now long dead, had given the area much greater attention and care, from the Greeks who founded the town to the Bosporan Kingdom that was born from their labors. In lieu of adventurers and pioneers who shared blood with the Argonauts or the Great Pontic King who supped on poison rather than meat, the town profited from slaves, and even contained quarters for those who had been banished or exiled from Constantinople.

Yet the town no longer held anything for the living; it surely did not for us. Godilas ordered the men to form columns, and we soon marched away from that dead village and whatever malignant spirits remained of its former residents. Even today, men talk of the walking dead of Kalos Limin, the northernmost village of the Eastern Empire that had been left derelict rather than rebuilt. I know nothing of such stories, only that we were the last real Roman military force to visit that village by the shore.

Many in our ranks voiced concerns at departing the town: The threat of poor weather, they protested, and the present lack of a clear vision of the surrounding area, had left the Thracian Army blind to its surroundings. To the former, Godilas reminded them that the village had no habitable buildings to house even a portion of our army, and that it was imperative to keep from becoming bogged down in an indefensible position by the sea. To the latter, Godilas dispatched small scouting parties in groups of five to survey the surrounding area, ordering them to report back to the army at regular intervals based upon our intended progress toward Scythian Neapolis. For the first two days, these reports arrived regularly. Yet, on the morning of the third day, only a few of the groups trickled into Godilas' tent. By afternoon on the third day, none had returned at the appointed hour. By the fourth, none still.

Godilas offered no explanation for such ominous signs, and the men began to conjure wild guesses at the fates that had befallen their comrades. Though I still believed in the success of our mission—due to Godilas' leadership and our overall strength in numbers—our exposed position on the Tauric coastline gave me pause. I fully believed that, to a man, our scouts had been ambushed and slaughtered.

On that fourth day, the officers' meetings in Godilas' tent became heated as arguments arose regarding our proper course of action, with a small number calling for withdrawal to Cherson. As a banda commander, Mundus was expected to offer opinion and soon joined those who called for a retreat. Not invited to provide an opinion, even I quietly supported my banda commander, believing it pointless and dangerous to proceed without understanding the path ahead. Godilas remained impassive until Archelaus added his voice, berating such arguments as defeatist and insisting the army make an immediate thrust to the interior and along our intended path toward Scythian Neapolis.

"Retreat," Archelaus insisted, "is against the Emperor's explicit orders to pacify the region. I will not rush back to Greece without having so much as drawn my blade against these Avars."

Then, in my youth, I disagreed with Godilas' choice, but now, as an older commander, I recognize Godilas had no real ability to undermine Archelaus. Retreat at this stage would be seen as the height of cowardice, antithetical to Roman virtues of courage and grit against unfavorable odds. Further, the scouting bands had been small, and there was no intelligence to suggest that our far larger formation was exposed to serious risk. As such, it was unsurprising that Godilas ordered the army to prepare for its march, plunging onward like a spear thrust through the Tauric countryside.

Supplies packed and orders distributed, the army marched away from Kalos Limin toward Scythian Neapolis. Our banners billowed against the wind. Other scouts were appointed to run ahead of the army's intended route, yet they rarely ventured out of our eyeline, which made them of limited use to Godilas or his officers.

Dark clouds followed our path, a chill rising at our backs that threatened a storm to come. Yet rain never arrived, and our progress was favorable with three days of unencumbered marching. The army passed by a dozen abandoned villages, which I had been ordered to investigate for any signs of those living or dead. My riders, however, found not so much as a dog or a rat in the ash of the collapsed huts, and my unease boiled over into outright fear. It was all I could do to resist the urge to believe that some ungodly, unnatural force prowled the plains.

I kept such concerns to myself. Our army was to all appearances still alone on the Tauric Peninsula. Some men grumbled of boredom and discomfort, the lack of action duller than what they'd expected on a mission abroad. I did not begrudge any of my men such complaints—idle complaints, yes, but ones that fostered camaraderie—but still I ordered at least one of my spearmen to keep watch every night, even if our banda was not appointed for evening sentry duty.

Then, on the fourth day of our march, a mist descended along the plain. It came first as a light veil, a vapored kiss that seemed almost refreshing to a horde of sweating soldiers continually marching onward. But soon the mist thickened to a shroud that coated leather and metal in a layer of moisture. My hair and beard grew slick and matted as my vision blurred, and the previous day's glimmer of fear rose afresh, Alypius' warning resonating in my heart.

"They came with the fog, and none survived."

I shivered, a deep sense of wrongness pervading my body. Even without laying eyes upon an enemy, I had seen enough to suspect our surroundings and to abandon any pretense of safety or superiority. For it was undeniable: we could not see beyond a few paces in any direction.

"Keep the column tight!" I shouted as the wide column trudged forward. "If you cannot see at least two others of our century, seek an officer to rectify this immediately."

At such a command, Perenus and Samur trotted toward the sound of my voice. "We should make camp," Perenus told me in a low voice. "Cut deep trenches and wait this out."

"Agreed," I said, "but you'll never convince Archelaus at this point."

"Well, of course not. It won't be Archelaus doing the dying," Perenus said crossly. "Let's hope this Godilas is as good a leader as you claim he is."

If Godilas had called upon me for advice, I would have echoed Perenus' sentiment. True, there were many advantages to forging onward; we could not be far from Scythian Neapolis, and adding a further night to our travails would admittedly do little to improve sinking morale. Yet, with God as my witness, if I had known what awaited me in that devil's fog, I would have begged Godilas to heed the wisdom of halting our advance and building a defensible camp until conditions improved.

But I did not speak up, and the army progressed onward. By midday, our column's pace slowed to a trickle, our vision so whited out that I ordered my men to hold fast to the cloak of the man to their front. We attempted to march for another hour, until at last stumbling and cursing men brought the march to a halt. Men and horses were bumping into one another, and there was no longer any cohesion within the ranks. A general halt was finally ordered, and runners distributed water and food to fill the tedium of the wait. Archelaus commanded additional scouts to serve as sentries around our perimeter, yet they, too, were reluctant to go more than twenty paces from the army column.

"Varus, what in the hell are we doing here?" Samur called in Heruli.

"I don't know," I called back, thoroughly honest. "But keep your weapons ready."

"Barking lunacy." The anger in Samur's voice bore a trace of fear.

Around me, men were muttering their own small fears. I still believed the tales of Kalos Limin and Theodosia to be exaggerated to the point of impossibility, yet even as I attempted to reassure my company, images of the dried blood and charred ruins of Kalos Limin flashed in my memory. I grasped at my cross, praying for divine protection in this evil land.

Archelaus grunted his disapproval at such chattering, sparking yells from the centurions for quiet in the ranks. Dutifully, I followed suit, threatening to lash any man who shattered Archelaus' call for silence. Yet, as the men's voices faded, a cascade of dull thunder rang out in the distance. It rolled along the grasslands, a slow crescendo of chaos getting louder and nearer moment by moment.

"Jesus Christ!" Cephalas blurted out.

"What is that? Where is it coming from?" Samur demanded.

I had no answer. With a shaking hand, I tucked the cross back under the safety of my armor and unlashed the shield at my back. The swell of noise had me looking in all directions, alert for any sign of what stalked Tauris, but I found nothing against the pressing fog.

"Form lines!" Archelaus roared.

Mundus echoed the command, and my men fell into two neat rows, backed by men from other bandae. Within moments our shields formed crude squares, our progress monitored by Godilas and other senior officers riding through the formation's center. Most of our cavalry, however, had dismounted to join the lines, while our small number of archers fitted their bows and stood in the innermost ranks of the formation. I found Troglita's men to the right of my own.

"See anything, Troglita?" I called out.

"Nothing," he called back.

We could not see, but we could feel, and the approaching thunder quaked the soil beneath our boots. We waited, unspeaking, as the chaos hurled closer, the deafening roar making spoken commands impossible. And so stood near four thousand men of Godilas' army in the shield wall, staring into the void whose din rose with each heartbeat.

Then, as if by the snap of a man's fingers, the plains stilled. The only sounds were officers calling for scouts that had not yet returned to the army and the low mumbling of tepid, uneasy laughter echoing along the shield wall. I stood in the second line as I stared out beyond my men's shields, eyesight blurred from the water matted in my lashes. One man even cried out a curse, but his officers swiftly silenced him, and we stood waiting, listening, for any sign of what had come—and then gone, perhaps—on these plains.

All that greeted us was silence.

Then a scream. A shriek, really, that no sooner than it began was cut off a short distance away, as if its owner had disappeared into nothingness.

"Oh Christ!" Cephalas swore. "Jesus Christ!"

"Shut your mouth and listen!" I cried.

The man in front of me jumped, and I laid a hand on his shoulder. All my men looked around, yet I cautioned them to keep formation and train their attention on whatever lay out in the mist. Some mumbled, but most obeyed, wordless in the lines.

A second scream rang out—closer. But the sound was the same: first a cry of surprise, then swift silence in the span of heartbeats.

"Varus, we *need* to leave!" Samur called again in Heruli. "There's something out in the mist!"

"It's too late," I replied, sure that none other than Samur would understand our Heruli. "Keep your shield up and the wall tight. That's all we can do now."

Yet my hand trembled still, disguised by the fog yet leaving my spear arm unsteady all the same. With a deep breath, I ordered a torch lit and handed over to me, a command quickly executed by the banda behind my own. With the torch in one hand, I handed my spear to the man on my left, then hurled the flame forward as far as I could. It arced high in the air, its flames congealing into a glowing mass as layers of mist veiled its light. It reached its zenith, then fell to the ground about thirty paces distant, where its faint and shrouded yellow orb bounced atop the grass. It lingered there for a few pulses, a symbol of reassurance, the flames dull but still luminescent in the moisture of the air.

And then, the light rose from the ground. It hovered at eye level, then was somehow extinguished.

We were not alone.

"Shields up! Now!" I screamed, the command immediately echoed by Perenus and Isaacius across the line.

Troglita, too, ordered his men, and around us clacked the din of wooden shields smacking into one another as the wall held firm. The senior officers, Archelaus and Godilas and all their company, either remained silent or could not be heard over the din of an army preparing for an engagement.

Then, from the mist, a spear hurtled through the air and connected against the shield of one of my men. He cried out and tried to pull out the iron-tipped head from his shield's upper half, but as his shield mates darted in to help, the man flew into the mist, leaving behind a gap in the line where he had once stood.

"Glycas!" Perenus shouted.

"Quiet!" I hissed. "At attention!"

Dozens of loud thuds rang out from all directions. Another man—one of Troglita's command—took a spear to the shoulder, its iron point punching through shield and armor into flesh and bone. His squeals of pain rose throughout the lines until he, too, was dragged away from the formation and out into the mist.

Several of his comrades ran forward to rescue him, their comrade's name fast upon their lips, but Troglita stayed them.

"Keep in formation!" Troglita commanded. "The wall is our survival!"

But the noxious fumes of fear and confusion can dissolve the firmest discipline. Another man hit by a spear struggled fearfully and cut at his shield's straps, the iron-rimmed bulwark sliding from his grasp into the fog, and it was then that I spied, dimly, the thin rope or chain at the spear butt, but I could not see how far out the weapon reached into the distance.

Man after man was dragged away from the formation by that unseen enemy. The line thinned, gaps sagged open, as the dekarchoi fought to keep the line in place.

Then, as suddenly as it began, the murderous volley of spears ceased. In the relative silence, amid the cries of the wounded, a specter of fear shuddered through the Thracian Army. With no orders coming from Godilas, each of the centurions was left alone in his strategy, yet each of us lacked the vision to see whether our square still held strong fully down the line. Though I forced assurance to my face when Isaacius and Perenus turned to me for guidance, I already knew that we had lost. And, for the first time as a soldier, I feared that my own life was at its end. And for but a heartbeat, I thought of Mariya, our paths never to cross again if I perished in this godforsaken place.

"They're not men!" screamed one of my soldiers.

"Shut it!" Isaacius barked. "Eyes front!"

Oddly, though death haunted the mists just paces before my eyes, curiosity pulled my gaze onward. I could hear nothing over the moans rising from the square, and any sign of movement was masked by the thick sheet of gray. Many around me mumbled prayers, and while I briefly clutched at my bronze cross, my attention remained fixed on the world around me, held firm by a sensation that somehow, impossibly, I was being watched.

Then, in an instant, something bright, a glowing sphere, hurtled through the fog. Then three others, and then a dozen more. Before long, the dull light stretched across the distance, a volley of flame rising in the air and growing larger with each passing heartbeat.

"Up! Shields high!" I cried.

The shields rose, and not a moment too soon as a torrent of flaming bolts pelted against their wooden panels. However, whether by fear or confusion, our massed bulwark was woefully imperfect, crooked and gaping, and men across the ranks were open to the flaming arrows that pounded against our position. Men grunted and cursed as we cowered under our decaying protection, my own shield hoisted above the head of the men. For a moment, my responsibilities were blotted out in a wash of mortal fear; too quickly for words, I begged God to fortify my men against this unseen enemy.

Men bleated for help, smoldering arrowheads jutting from their bodies. Blood sprayed over our heads and pooled at the front of the ranks like a macabre moat. Mercilessly, more and more arrows followed, feathering our shields with spent shafts.

After uncounted volleys, I heard Archelaus, bellowing fury, call for return fire. Our men obeyed; Roman arrows sailed overhead, reassuring in their precision, yet their targets were unfixed, unknown, and perhaps unknowable. As the hail of weapons pierced the mist, I could hear no wails from the enemy, yet somehow the bolts found *our* spearmen, and it was their familiar shrieks of pain that echoed from all sides. A pained braying came as the arrows stuck our Roman horses. Such was the hellish song that filled this forlorn expanse of Tauris—our men dying at our hands. All we could do was cower behind shields, our survival dependent upon the wall. Even that was further strained as the flying spears returned, finding vulnerable targets along our lines and dragging men away from the formation, screaming in terror. Thus fell the spearman before me, and I gasped, as much for his lost life as for my lost layer of protection.

Then, with no audible signal or warning, the arrows and spears stopped. A rising cacophony of pain and grief bubbled from the ranks, our enemy curiously silent. I stepped forward into the front rank, girding my courage yet ashamed at remaining silent while under attack.

"Recover!" I yelled. "Count the dead and reform!"

Perenus and Isaacius repeated the command, shoving men into line as our eyes remained fixed upon the mist. My new neighbor took his sword and cut away at least a half dozen arrows that jutted out from his shield, handily snapping their shafts in half. Fresh shields were passed up the ranks from the interior of our square, their new owners hurriedly strapping the iron-rimmed guards onto their arms.

"See anything, Varus?" It was Mundus, dismounted and yelling nearby.

"Just arrows and flying spears!" I called back.

"They're definitely on horseback," Mundus shouted. "Keep watch for a sudden charge!"

We did not have to wait long. A great cry rang out from the mist, a chorus of deep hoots and cheers approaching our position. Our spearmen, ragged from the wounded and the dying, braced together as they knitted the wall into the most contiguous line they could. The rippling thunder resumed, the howls growing ever closer with each heartbeat.

"Brace!" I screamed.

No sooner did I let fly my command than the Avars appeared. A mere five paces before the lines, they spilled into view: Some were mounted, others on foot, but all rushing forward in savage disarray. I saw some Roman *spathae* and spears in their hands, likely looted from our dead. But I did not look long. One rushed ahead of his comrades and drove a curved dagger into my neighbor's exposed neck. He lunged, and his charred and blackened shield clamored against mine, his mouth a flash of jagged decay, his eyes bright with surety. This Avar, stinking sweetly of wine and sweat, knew his victory was at hand. With a defiant roar, I drove my spear into his gullet. He reared backward in pain, the victory mine, yet it could not save my shield neighbor, who buckled, blood gushing from his neck, and fell away from our lines.

With that, the Avar masses collided. They unleashed a force that boomed across the plains, crashing into our shield wall. Rider and spearman alike were covered in thick furs, pelts slicked with grease and hanging lank around their bodies. They threw short spears before hitting our shields, carving gaps into the Roman wall to weaken it for a final charge. Several furred Avars thronged toward the break in my own lines—they would drive a wedge, shatter Godilas' square, and leave my men as easy meat for their butchery. One neared me: I launched my spear, then thrust forward the Emperor's sword to puncture the furs until the tip protruded from his back. Cephalas downed a second man with a spear to the neck. Blood sprayed both our helmets.

I took quick stock: Down the wall, Perenus fought two or three who had breached his lines. Isaacius, clearly prepared, had ordered the breach sealed, and as I watched, his wedge shoved aside enough fur-clad Avars to relieve pressure on Perenus. But Avars bore down on Troglita and his men, the centurion crying demands for reinforcements.

But I could not aid him. No sooner had I pulled free my sword than another Avar, larger than his countrymen and bedecked in gold and silver torques, rushed at me with frenzied eyes. My shield barely stopped the swing of his huge axe, which rent a deep gash in the paneling. I dropped low, throwing two quick cuts along calves, tearing the muscles keeping my enemy upright. A further stroke—a spearman at my left—sliced the Avar's windpipe, but my new comrade fell as swiftly as he'd come to my aid, an Avar spear flung into his gut.

Others stepped forward to take my neighbor's place, yet as I glanced backward I found our reserves running pitifully thin. Samur, not yet permitted to take part in the fighting despite wearing ill-fitting ringmail, was carrying the wounded away from the front to be treated by the few stretcher-bearers available at the center of the square. One man grabbed Samur's arm and begged for a mercy strike, groaning in agony as silvery guts slipped from a thin gash along his side. Samur half dragged him to relative safety, shoving the viscera back into the man's stomach as they left the shield wall.

Spirits were failing as much as bodies. I barked to the rearward ranks to come forward. My own limbs were heavy with fatigue, and I sheathed my sword and drew rest within our reserves, joining others within my century who panted for air and swiped sticky blood from their faces. The fog had now thinned somewhat, and I looked to the interior of our square, hoping for a semblance of reassurance or order—what exactly, I did not know. Instead, I saw Solomon rushing toward our position, finding Mundus pacing just behind our shield wall. I ordered Perenus to guard our lines and hurried to my commander. Troglita also converged upon Mundus, he, too, in need of answers, of any way to recover from this hopeless situation.

Such a naïve fool that I was. Solomon eyed me warily, yet did not hesitate to relay his orders to Mundus, his voice straining to be heard over the clash of wood and metal.

"General Godilas greets you, komes," Solomon said, throwing a brief salute toward Mundus. "He commands you advance your lines and relieve pressure elsewhere."

"Christ and the apostles, how am I supposed to do that?" Mundus shouted, veins popping under the skin of his neck. "There could be ten thousand men out there, and we'd never know!"

Solomon's eyes fell to the ground, his brow furrowed. "I... the order stands, komes."

Mundus cocked his head at Solomon, yet appeared resigned, no matter how senseless the command from his general. But I myself could not be so resigned; I rushed forward, seeing in Solomon no general but only one whom I loathed, one who would send my friends and family to needless deaths.

"Pick up a spear and join the fight if you want us to charge in," I spat. "By the look of that immaculate clothing, I'd say you're fresh enough for battle."

Solomon snarled and reached for his scabbarded sword. "Are you threatening a superior, centurion?"

"Varus only means to procure additional reinforcements," Troglita said firmly, stepping between us. "And Mundus is correct.

We need more men to push forward, and I ask that you seek the general's assistance in this task."

Solomon opened his mouth, no doubt eager to stoke tempers further, but said nothing; in fact, at the sight of the blood-soaked Troglita, his face and hands and cloak and armor caked in gore, Solomon shrank back, and, as a new surge of Avars threatened Mundus' defense, he saluted and returned to the center of the square, leaving our banda in an uneasy peace.

Though the square retained its defensive perimeter, the ranks were slowly collapsing inward. A fresh onslaught of force crashed into our position, and our officers scrambled to fill more and more gaps as more and more men fell, dead or wounded. Other parts of the line, even if intact, had been pushed backward by the sheer weight of the Avar advance, leaving a pile of corpses and sheets of blood and dung slicking the grass. Men with one leg, one arm, any manner of ragged stump, screamed to the heavens for God to grant them respite as there was none remaining for them on earth.

"Thousands," Troglita yelled, wincing as he took a step toward me. "Thousands of them, easily!"

"Tens of thousands." I groaned as I rejoined my men along the line, standing just behind our foremost ranks.

"Hold on!" Mundus bellowed. "Varus, go, go and brief Godilas and see that he understands our need. I'll take charge of your lines."

With a final glance at Samur and my men, I had little desire to abandon my men and even less to leave Samur exposed to such danger, and considered defying that order. Another option was to take Samur with me, using an excuse that Godilas knew Samur well and would assist with my task. Yet the first action would dishonor myself and the second would humiliate Samur before the men. Instead, I decided to wordlessly obey, reasoning that I would only be parted from my charges for a few brief moments as I pleaded our situation to the general.

The Last Dying Light

I nodded back and followed Solomon toward the square's center. Between lines of battered bodies, rows of firing bowmen, I darted to the square's command center. As I ran, I was sure I would find Godilas at work, busily constructing a defense that would see the Thracian Army safely away from this godforsaken battle.

Instead, all I found was a mirror of the chaos facing our spearmen. As I drew closer to the mass of army banners, I could make out Godilas, his voice incoherent, with Solomon and a half dozen other officers seeking his attention. Archelaus, though, was most insistent of all, roaring and railing at the one responsible for our fate in the Tauric plains.

"*Strategos*, we need to make a breakout now, while we can move in good order." Archelaus' voice boomed out the Greek honorific to his general. "To the south is our best bet."

Godilas did not respond. I glanced at my old master-at-arms and saw the same stony face I had once seen in his office and on our ship voyage toward Cherson. His eyes were glassy, peering far through the mist many miles away. Godilas was either suddenly deaf to Archelaus' pleas or unwilling to answer.

"*Strategos?*" Archelaus repeated, drawing yet closer.

Yet still the general did not respond, his eyes unblinking over the shield wall.

Archelaus lost his patience. "Godilas! We need to move now!" He slammed his gloved hands together. "*Now!*"

When Godilas did not respond a third time, Archelaus ordered Solomon to guard the general for the remainder of the battle. The other officers, he ordered, were to distribute *his* orders, and none other, from then on.

A stray arrow sailed within a few paces of his boots, and Archelaus cursed.

Yet before he could relay his commands to the lines, a great shout rang out along the western edge of the square. I could not see why—a sea of horses and bodies blocked my view—yet I did not need to see to know: The shout meant the Avars had pushed past our reserve lines and into the square. With bile in my throat, I abandoned Mundus' order and rushed back toward Samur and the men I had left in the care of others.

Samur and the others were alive and orderly, albeit mired in ceaseless combat, and I indulged myself a shudder of relief. Avars swarmed along our lines where, even as one black-shielded warrior was cut down, three others took his place. As our lines shuffled inward, a trail of Roman dead were left to the enemy's mercy, leaving many Avars to rip at the corpses of our men for weapons and scraps of armor. I drew my sword and rushed toward my men, locking my shield alongside that of my brother.

"Varus…" Samur called, his eyes darting for possible routes of escape.

"Archelaus is in charge now," I yelled across the lines. "Be prepared for a breakout to the south!"

Such obvious signs of defeat would have shamed Roman armies of centuries past, but Godilas' men only called in relief that their hoped-for avenue to survival had opened. Gone was any illusion that our superior arms and tactics would sweep aside these plains riders, who whooped and cheered with each spray of blood and slain Roman. At my words, Mundus ordered the lines to continue their backward crawl, and he frequently turned toward Archelaus, looking for signs of retreat.

From my place at the rearward lines, I saw the fullness of the gruesome toll the Avars had wrought, our survivors flailing desperately to retain discipline as they slipped in their comrades' blood, and could only gape. Just paces away, I saw Perenus, his sword stuck in an Avar rib cage, forced to draw a dagger to fend off another enemy that thundered his horse toward our formation. Perenus jammed the dagger into the Avar's thigh, and from the rear, Cephalas struck his chest with a discarded Avar spear. My own shield hopelessly splintered and arrow-marked, I cut it loose and yanked up another, only to find a man's arm still hanging loosely from its leather holster. Recoiling, I tore the arm away and inserted my own, praying for the dead man's soul as his blood ran down to my elbow.

Archelaus had sent a small detachment of cavalry to plug the growing hole through which the countless Avars streamed, but it was fruitless. Thinking back, I doubt that Archelaus ever believed that he could salvage the utter debacle we faced, for in truth, there was little he, or any man, could have done. In less than the span of a single hour, the Thracian Army had been butchered beyond recovery; how could he or any senior officer salvage the bloody pulp of us into a victorious force?

To this day, when songs retell these next actions of proud Archelaus, men will spit in disgust. The self-serving dishonor, even within the safe confines of a tavern or a theater, are still unthinkable. Now, I will always join my voice to such blame, but then, in the final moments of battle, all I felt was a desperate urge to flee, to lead my brother and my men to salvation in Cherson and onto the first boat that would see us safely back to Constantinople.

"Northern and eastern lines, fall back! Push south, wedge formation!"

Archelaus yelled the command, even though the frontmost of our ranks were fighting, actively, fruitlessly, to push back this surging tide of riders and spearmen. Mundus ordered our archers to engage in volley fire, giving our front lines precious moments of relief as they backed their footing in good order. Together, Troglita and I led our lines slowly backward and toward Mundus' objective toward the south, stopping only for a coordinated thrust of swords and spears against those Avars who continued to press and slash against the collapsing Roman lines.

It was likely that Archelaus had chosen his route of retreat early in battle, for the southern route led directly to Scythian Neapolis. A small contingent of light cavalry had been allowed by Archelaus to gallop through a small hole in our southern lines, and they chopped away at the thin waves of Avars that blocked our path southward. With the path cleared, horns sounded the Thracian Army's retreat, and hundreds of men rushed, in as clean a file as they could, through the breach.

"Follow south, in good order!" Mundus croaked. "Hold the wall or we die!"

As he shouted orders, Mundus gripped his shoulder, fingers wrapped around what I now saw was a fire-hardened Avar arrow. With a grunt, he pulled hard and tossed the spent missile to the ground, sending blood leaking from its place. I had seen blood—here, now, elsewhere—yet from this wound, Mundus' wound, I found I could not tear my gaze away.

"It looks worse than it is," Mundus said stiffly, noticing my staring. "At attention, Varus, and get our men out of here!"

I barked back that I would, yet, as we retreated, Archelaus' steed trotted across our path. Archelaus was painted in the carnage of his victims; thin rivulets of blood flowed between his eyes and into his open mouth. He ordered the nearby hundreds of soldiers still capable of riding to mount a horse and follow in our retreat, essentially abandoning those hundreds of men still clashing at the northern edge to their fate. Before joining in the retreat and departing the dying shield wall, however, Archelaus issued a final order.

"You, dekarchos." He pointed the stained tip of his sword at Isaacius. "Take your men and retrieve our standards."

At his words, I looked to the standards. They rested a good ways off, stationed near the northern edge of Godilas' square, the Imperial Eagle lifted a head higher than the dozen minor emblems of the senior officers. Some must have toppled to the ground; the remainder wavered as Avars slowly encroached, our proudest symbols now ragged and gory.

"Lord, that's impossible!" I shouted at Archelaus. "There's no way in. Retrieving them is suicide!"

Nostrils flaring, Archelaus used his knees to nudge his horse a pace closer. His bloodshot eyes loomed over me, his blade lowered but his fist still tightly clenching the hilt.

"This is an order, centurion. Command your dekarchos to obey." Archelaus' teeth were bared.

"Lord, allow me to take the entire century," I said, all but begging. "I will lead the assault myself."

And I would have. Foolishly, pointlessly, and unquestioningly. All I knew was that without such an intervention, Isaacius would die—a man who had risked his life to save my own in our foray against the Gepids. I was determined to do the same, for friends such as Isaacius are worth sacrificing for. In my naivety, I believed that Archelaus would concur with such a mad rush.

I was wrong. Unfathomably wrong.

"Are you defying me, Varus?" Archelaus vaulted from horseback.

Even over rusting blood and muck, the sour scent of stale wine reeked as Archelaus stepped toward me. His sword arm quivered slightly, though he made no motion to attack. Instead, he lowered his face to within a handbreadth of my own, letting his forked beard brush against my armor, close enough that I saw thick veins pulsing at his neck.

Yet, before I could speak, Isaacius stepped forward.

"Yes, Lord!" my friend shouted. "I will do as you command." His voice was formal and stern.

Archelaus' rage-filled face softened to a sly grin. "Good," he said in a voice so low that even I, close as I was, strained to hear. "You're obedient enough, for a Jew."

Alarmed, I opened my mouth, yet Archelaus had no mind for a response. He swung atop his horse once more, gazing upon Isaacius as the Avars pressed forward. Just a few dozen paces distant, our remaining shield wall buckled, with whoops and jeers from our attackers rising near the banners of the Thracian Army. I wanted to scream at Isaacius to refuse, or simply to wait a few moments further, to do anything but obey Archelaus' insane order. Yet I lacked the courage, dual sensations of rage and shame burning under my skin as I did nothing further to prevent Isaacius from rushing northward toward the enemy. There was little doubt that Archelaus would punish insubordination with torturous death, and that knowledge brought me to pause.

Isaacius offered Archelaus a small bow and me a weak smile. In a heartbeat, he unsheathed his sword for the final time.

"On me, men! For Rome!" Isaacius shouted, thrusting his sword to the heavens.

His men roared and ran toward their dekarchos. Isaacius rushed along blood-slicked grass toward the banners, swinging an arcing gash against a nearby Avar, while others threw spears at the fur-clad barbarians that crowded the standard-bearer. The Imperial Eagle drew upright once more, although Isaacius' men were unable to escape to safety.

Amid the struggle for the banners, Archelaus ordered the horns blown to officially signal retreat, abandoning any too wounded or embattled to the Avars as our remaining rabble scurried southward. Those who were able relocated to the southern corridor, our forces forming a temporary wedge that allowed for free passage. Archelaus trotted his horse in the direction of his escape, but I sprinted toward the commander, pleading for his permission to relieve Isaacius.

"But, Lord, if we leave now, the standards will not be retrieved in time," I said.

Archelaus shook his head. "We are leaving *now*, centurion. Make it known to your men. I expect you to follow, immediately."

I felt utterly helpless. Every instinct burned to rush to rescue Isaacius, to drive my blade into the sea of Avars that enveloped the hundred or so men who remained to guard and retrieve the banners. Isaacius' men pierced deep into the Avar lines, yet I could still make out his dekarchos' plume amid a wash of fog, torches, and bleeding men. Several of Isaacius' spearmen had fallen around him, a blade thrust to their flanks as more Avars rushed to chop down the Roman sigils. The western lines finally broke and spilled Avars into the center of our square, the dead and dying sacrificed so that we might flee.

Though I had always disliked Archelaus, it was not until this moment that I understood Rosamund's loathing. This was a man who traded in lives with little thought or consequence. I wanted to scream, and the urge to draw my dagger and bury its steel into Archelaus' neck grew into a senseless fever. Yet I still made one final attempt to reason with the commander, believing him capable of seeing reason and the senselessness of leaving Isaacius to be butchered for no discernible gain.

"Lord, I ask again," I said. "Permit me to retrieve the standards with Isaacius."

"Denied, centurion!" Archelaus bellowed. "Fall into formation immediately."

Fury boiled in my blood as I approached Archelaus. Though his horse's gait made for a difficult angle of attack, his back was turned to me, leaving a painfully easy target. God help me, but I thought of it. I weighed an attack against Archelaus even as my spearmen looked on, wobbling yet awaiting instructions as the Roman square collapsed.

If it were not for Mundus, I may have followed through. But it was then that the banda commander returned to assure my escape. He pulled on my cloak, leaning toward me, and ordered me to leave.

"Think of the rest of your men," he said, his voice hoarse. "There is nothing we can do for any others."

William Havelock

I took one last look toward Isaacius, and saw no plume where he once stood. The last standard toppled, sending an eager roar from nearby Avars. As our men burst southward, the last of our western lines were solidly outflanked, encircled, the survivors so few that they were fighting back to back. Other groups toward the north and east were embattled and broken, unlucky enough to be denied retreat with the remaining bulk of the Thracian Army's spearmen and horses. Under Archelaus' gaze, we ran through the widening gap in the south, and the Avars in that area seemed to allow us a passage, leaving only our own cowardice to pursue us.

And I ran in a maelstrom of emotions. Shame at abandoning my friend, humiliation from defeat, and blinding rage against the architect of it all. I did not feel the fatigue of my bones, nor the pain that doubtlessly pervaded my overtaxed feet. My mind was awash in both the relief of escaping the Avars' trap and the urge to rush back into the fray, killing as many of the black-shielded savages in some impossible hope that I could rescue my friend. Yet curiously, I did not weep at the certainty of Isaacius' death, a numbness falling over me as we jogged away from the battlefield. A lone comfort was the relative safety of Samur, yet somehow his bearing witness to such total dishonor sharpened the shame burrowing in my soul. As a young man, I lacked the faculties to harness such raw feeling or even make sense of it, yet as I grew older, the maelstrom became a familiar enemy. Above all things, I later understood such emotions as the sting of grief, when a piece of the soul dies and leaves a shriven being behind. I would never be the same.

The Last Dying Light

THE SACK OF SCYTHIAN NEAPOLIS

We rode away, leaving the Avar horde to grow small along the horizon. After a safe distance, we took in the extent of our hideous losses, learning of dozens who had been left dead or missing in the ruins of Godilas' square. Each of Mundus' officers reported their tally, running forward all the while, discipline unaffected by the somber duty. It was only then, as we made the count, that Perenus realized who was missing. He rushed toward Mundus and me, followed closely behind by Samur and Cephalas.

"Where's Isaacius?" Perenus asked, panting between paces. "He was with us just before we left!"

I looked over my friend. The Lazic dekarchos was covered in no fewer than a half dozen shallow cuts, rivulets of blood staining his skin and raiment. His armor was in an equally poor state, the cheap pig iron dented near his hip and beneath an armpit. Blessedly, however, Perenus had not taken a serious wound, and like me seemed to ignore his own hurts as we ran onward.

"It was Archelaus," I blurted out. "He commanded Isaacius to retrieve the banners just before the horns sounded for retreat."

Perenus' eyes widened. He clenched his jaw, flushing the skin around his beard a fierce crimson. "That rank bastard!" Perenus cried. "I'll cut his throat, I swear to God!"

"No, you won't." Mundus was all but wheezing, draping his uninjured arm around Samur's neck. "Any vengeance you take now will only see you dead, and several of your men with you."

"I don't fucking care!" Perenus said, though his voice had lowered from his previous outburst. "Why would Archelaus send Isaacius to die for nothing?"

"Because he knew." At last, a tear welled in my eye. "He knew Isaacius was a Jew. I don't know how, but... Archelaus made that clear as he gave the order."

The truth was out. Perenus wailed, burying his gore-soaked face in his filthy hands as he ran. All I could do was place a hand on Perenus' shoulder, as did Cephalas, drawing to his other side. Wordlessly, Perenus threw an arm around each of our necks, and thus we shared his grief as we moved ever southward.

We kept a brisk pace for the remainder of the day and throughout the night. Many men fell as the army streamed ever southward through the thinning mist, bleeding from all manner of wounds and pleading for water. Few stopped, however; such charity would leave the savior exposed to any Avar forerunners eager to prey on stragglers. For most of the journey, Samur held Mundus over one shoulder, the banda commander pale from blood loss yet stubbornly refusing to slow his pace.

The numbers of our surviving army were pitiful. Many were on horseback; it was the more heavily armored infantrymen who were absent. As I ran astride my fellows, I saw one spearman who had sustained a ragged cut to his calf. He limped for several hours as he kept up our desperate march to Scythian Neapolis, whimpering with each step along the rolling hills, until at last his strength gave out and he collapsed. Again, none stopped to assist; for this luckless soul especially, little could be done. Foolishly, I made eye contact with the man as I passed by, globs of spittle forming along the corners of my mouth as the physical toll of our march began to strain my body.

"Don't leave me!" the soldier begged. "I don't want to die here!"

I could still hear his wailing as we crested over a low hill. I could hear as his pleas called for his mother, and I could hear his piteous cries lose any words at all and grow weak as we trudged onward. When they silenced, I could not tell if it was the distance or his inevitable death. It may well have been both.

As the darkness of the evening gleamed with the coming morning, Archelaus and his attendants galloped to the rear, toward Mundus' soldiers. Though fatigue weighed on every fiber of my body, at the bark of my name, my limbs found the vigor to jolt in surprise.

"Varus. You were among the last near the general," Archelaus said, trotting beside me. "Did you see what became of him?"

Godilas. With all that had transpired, I had forgotten about Godilas. The teacher who had raised me on tales of Alexander and Caesar, who had placed the first wooden dagger in my hand and educated me in the mortal arts of the warrior. The loss of Isaacius was painful, a throbbing ache, but it was the sudden knowledge of Godilas' disappearance that nearly brought me to vomit. In fact, I could barely comprehend what Archelaus had said, perhaps hoping against hope that he misspoke, that I was wrong.

"*Well?*" Archelaus insisted.

"I-I didn't know he was missing, Lord," I choked.

A second horse trotted alongside Archelaus, its rider stiff in the saddle.

"As I said, Lord, he's dead." Solomon eyed me from his mount. "I saw the Avars cut him down before I left him."

"Dead? It was your duty to protect him!" Archelaus roared, snapping to Solomon, his interest in me evaporated.

"I know, Lord," Solomon said hurriedly, "and I apologize, but you see, Godilas was deaf to my words, like some spell had trapped his mind. There was nothing to be done."

"Limp coward," I muttered, drawing an irritated glance from Solomon.

Seemingly satisfied, Archelaus grunted. He kicked his horse back to the front, and Solomon followed, leaving Godilas' fate at once unknown and almost certainly an ignominious, painful death among the wretched Avars. Godilas died alone and forgotten by his men, a man who should have enjoyed the peace of retirement and rest of an aged body.

At last, we approached Scythian Neapolis. In many ways, it held similarities to Cherson, with its grubby and worn stone wall and a multitude of building styles and materials lining its expanse. Yet it was smaller still than the provincial capitol, capable of housing only one or two thousand souls and the gaggle of animals that provided meat, milk, and labor to help till the soil. Thankfully, however, it did not reek of decaying fish, the swift inland winds of Tauris leaving the air surprisingly fresh to the nose.

As our column stumbled and heaved forward, its gates swung open to allow us passage. Archelaus trotted in first and watched over his army as it entered the village forum. Roman villagers peeked their heads from behind low buildings, curious to the commotion and eager for news of the enemy that had destroyed so much of the province. Many of our servants clamored forth eagerly, and among them I saw Rosamund and Father Petrus, their faces desperate as they peered down the ragged column of soldiers for anyone familiar. Rosamund's eyes eventually connected with mine, and she let out a sigh of unmitigated joy as she sprinted forward to greet us.

As more of the column of survivors spilled into Scythian Neapolis' forum, one dekarchos pointed at a villager and demanded food and water. Others joined, a chorus of need from exhausted, wounded, and angry soldiers that went broadly unheeded. Archelaus dismounted his horse and walked into a larger stone building that I soon discovered to be the possession of the village magistrate. The new commander of the Thracian Army was followed closely behind by Solomon and other senior officers of Godilas' retinue.

"Where's General Godilas?" Father Petrus asked.

With a knot clogging my throat a second time, again I gave voice to the swirling grief for Isaacius and for Godilas. "Taken in the battle," I replied. "Reports from Solomon say he was killed."

At that, the priest wailed. His wrinkled hands clawed at his thinning hair, and he crumpled to a heap. I fell to his side and put a hand to his shoulder, but he would not be comforted; thick sobs left the priest's face a dripping mess as he rose to his feet once more and rushed toward wherever his private quarters were here. I ordered a spearman to guard the priest's home; as much as I ached to console the man further, I knew I could not abandon Mundus as the sole senior commander remaining in the forum. My body desired nothing more than to collapse, my chafed and sore body spent as much as my sleep-deprived mind, yet such luxuries would have to wait awhile yet.

Absent their leaders to enforce discipline, many men were falling out of formation. At first, we centurions sought to keep order and hold us all in wait for Archelaus' command, yet soon the warriors spilled into the village in an overwhelming tide that the remaining handful of officers could not stop.

Mundus' banda remained standing in the forum, and was joined by a disheveled rabble under Troglita's, whose banda commander had been dragged away from the Roman lines and out into the mist. Leaning heavily upon Samur, Mundus shook his head.

"Do what you can to protect the villagers, but don't break up into groups of less than five," Mundus ordered. "Perenus, lead your men to take control of the northern gate and keep watch for an Avar attack. Varus, take the rest of our men and try to instill some semblance of peace in the city."

"And if our brothers resist?" I asked.

"Do what you must," Mundus rasped, "but avoid bloodshed or risk. We're a rabble now, and we've ceased to be an army of men."

The Last Dying Light

Without a reply, Perenus stormed away, leading his men to seize the gate that controlled the town's means of entry to the Tauric interior. As Troglita and I gathered our forces to reestablish peace and order, Rosamund rushed again to my side and threw her arms around my neck.

"You're hurt!" she exclaimed in Heruli, pulling away to a mass of congealed blood on her wool tunic. "What happened?"

"The blood isn't mine," I said. "Mundus took an arrow to the shoulder, and will need to close his wound quickly."

"Complete chaos," Samur put in, a third Heruli voice foreign to all other Romans present. "The Avars destroyed half of the army, with the other half devouring itself in this sty."

Rosamund bit her lower lip, her eyes fixed upon mine. "I told you, Varus. There is only evil here. I saw the look on Archelaus' face when he entered the town... it was the same as when I saw him in my village. There's no honor or reason within him, only lust and carnage."

"Then I'll go stop him," I promised. "I won't let that happen again."

"You won't," Rosamund said. "This town is dead, and there is nothing here for us but suffering. We should leave for Cherson."

"She has a point," Samur added, drinking from a waterskin as he checked his weapons for the task ahead.

I sighed. "Even if Scythian Neapolis is to be sacked, I have to try. Take Samur as your guard, Rosamund, and do what you can to save Mundus' arm."

Rosamund closed her eyes, shook her head, and returned my gaze once more. "As you wish."

She slipped from my grasp, her soft translucent skin grazing my own like a feather. I yearned to return to her clutches once more; again, the security of her embrace drew all the poisonous worry and weariness from my bones. Indeed, I wanted little to do with the roving bands that had already begun to sack a Roman town, too tempted by the prospect of sleep and the comfort of loved ones. All that this expedition had left to me were memories of butchery and chaos, and the knowledge that I had left behind two men that I had come to love. The world had gone mad, and I was powerless to do much more than allow the illness to run its course.

Yet the cross at my neck and the blades at my hip would not allow it to be so. Godilas' legacy deserved far more than rape and plunder, and the Emperor's words tugged at my conscience. And so, as Rosamund gathered bandages and stitching for Mundus' wound, I set about on a foolish task.

Absent Perenus' men, I reorganized those spearmen who remained loyal and orderly into teams of five. Troglita lent his survivors to our cause, and before long we swept through Scythian Neapolis, rooting out signs of lawlessness and mayhem along the town's perimeter and offering protection to those villagers who suffered the thorough sacking of their homes.

As I looked across the forum, and the cacophony of screams and breaking jars rang out from all directions, it appeared impossible to secure the entire town with the few loyal men remaining to me. One spearman hauled a burly sack of grain over his shoulder, harangued at every step by an older woman who demanded that the grain be returned. Finally fed up, the spearman spun and jabbed a knife into her throat. He wiped the blade on her shirt, sheathed it back into his belt, and walked toward his comrades, disappearing into the scrum before my men could act.

Not all the villagers or buildings could be saved, nor even most. The panic and lust that consumed the Thracian Army left we disciplined few hideously outnumbered, forcing us to prioritize those threats deemed to be of immediate hazard to the town and its citizens. Most pressing was the ever-present threat of fire, and I dispatched ten men to quench a conflagration that sparked near the thatched granaries. Simple looting went unpunished; the rampant violence inflicted by our armed soldiers was the intent of our attention on the Tauric outpost.

When a young woman's voice cried out in fear from a nearby hut, I dispatched Cephalas with a group of five to prevent what could only be a rape in progress. Two spearmen were thrown out of the building, their jaws running crimson from wine that had been stolen from the hut's owner, and ran off into the village as I lacked the force to securely guard such men while continuing to send teams to patrol the town's streets. Cephalas and other spearmen posted a guard outside of the hut, yet that remained a lone moment of optimism in a village that had descended into madness and hedonism.

Our men disbursed and put to task, I left Troglita in command of our ragged relief effort and walked toward the magistrate's building, simultaneously seeking knowledge of our senior officers' intentions while privately hoping for a confrontation with Archelaus. The building was no great feat of engineering—just a two-floor stone structure that was bedecked with the Imperial insignia—yet it remained one of the more regal buildings in Scythian Neapolis. I threw the doors open and walked inside. What I saw overwhelmed the senses.

Several jugs of wine had been discovered, and several of the senior officers gulped greedily at the rich red liquid. One, whom I recognized as a fellow centurion, had taken an expensively dressed woman onto a low bench, both clawing at the other's clothing. In a corner, I found Solomon with a desperate look on his face, sipping from a bronze cup.

"Where is Archelaus?" I snarled. Solomon shook his head and looked into my exhausted eyes.

"I couldn't stop the sack, Varus. There's nothing we can do," Solomon said, his eyes heavy.

His armor was largely clean of the muck and gore of battle, yet his forearm had been tightly wrapped in linen.

I pointed to Solomon's injury and wrapped my fists on Solomon's shoulders to shake the man from his stupor.

"I didn't see you in the fighting, so how did you earn this wound? Falling down as you ran away?"

Hurt creased Solomon's face, yet he did not rise to my challenge. And if he would not rise to it, I would pull him up. I slapped the cup from his hand, spilling its contents onto the wooden floor.

"*Where is Archelaus?*" I hissed, my face a handbreadth from his own.

Reluctantly, Solomon pointed to a door at the rear of the building. Leaving him cowering in his corner, I marched toward Archelaus' rooms and threw open the door.

The room was a simple one—wooden benches and a vast table, with walls covered with Imperial sigils and a crude map of the surrounding region. It was here that I found Archelaus leaning over the prone form of another young woman, who sobbed as she looked toward me, the latest intrusion into her life. Her garb had been torn asunder as her flesh pressed against the wooden table, rough welts hinting at her recent pain. A flash of gold at her throat was the only indication of her previously wealthy life, and I wondered whether she had been the offspring of the town magistrate, believing that remaining in her father's building would lend a measure of protection from rape and pillage. Given Archelaus' presence, she had been incorrect in such beliefs.

Archelaus, too, faced me, deep stains of sweat and wine lining his tunic all the way to his waist. His armor had been neatly stacked in the corner, yet he still held a thin dagger that belied his danger and authority.

"What do you want, centurion?" Archelaus wiped spittle from his mouth with his arm and sheathed his dagger, bloodshot eyes gazing into mine. Though he had been separated from the Thracian Army for less than an hour, he had already begun to sway and held out a hand to steady himself. An onlooker would have thought us half-dead ghouls, two men beyond the limits of their strength and caked in all manner of sour sweat and filth.

I drew closer, holding his gaze and searching for any sign of aggression. A pungent odor wafted from his clothing, the sweat-stained linen sticking to his skin. Deep circles shadowed his eyes, the irises wild from too much drink and perilously little rest. All that was apparent was that Archelaus had no intention of conversing with me, nor did he care about the evil that consumed Scythian Neapolis.

I wanted nothing more than to take the Emperor's sword and plunge it deep into his shriveled traitor's heart. The other spearmen would have butchered me soon thereafter, but the sight of Archelaus' soul leaving its body would have restored the sense of peace first robbed from us on our journey to the Gepid Kingdom, and forbidden us ever since by Archelaus' sins of wrath, falsehood, and wanton murder. Yet again, I did not strike at him. Perhaps it was a lingering sense of duty, perhaps a morbid need to know why Archelaus had condemned my friend to an inglorious and wasteful death. I nearly kept to proper decorum, yet surrendered to my passions as Archelaus offered a snort in derision as he began to turn away from me.

"Why did you send Isaacius to get the banners?" I screamed, drawing close to his matted beard. "They were already lost, any fool could have seen that. You cost him his life for no reason!"

Archelaus stiffened, his instincts sharpening from my verbal attack. Squaring his shoulders, he surged closer, baring crooked teeth as he looked down upon me.

"You *never* abandon the banners if they can be retrieved. What do you understand about being a Roman soldier?" Spittle flecked his lips as his face reddened. "I gave that Christ-killer a chance to do honor to Rome. He didn't balk or complain, so why do you bleat like some pox-riddled whore?"

At that, I abandoned any lingering restraint. I yelled another curse and reached for the hilt of my sword, thinking of nothing other than bloody vengeance. Archelaus backed away as he searched for his own weapon, a disdainful smirk lining his wine-darkened lips as he shoved the young woman to the ground and away from our confrontation. Yet before I could proceed further, a hand pulled at my shoulder, leaving me off balance and unable to attack.

"Not now, Varus," Solomon whispered. "Leave him be."

"He's a gutless, hateful bastard!" I was seething. "And so are you for defending him!"

"Be that as it may, he's the general now," Solomon said.

Spitting oaths, I backed from the room, all too aware of the spearmen's eyes, watching carefully for any sign of further violence. Archelaus' smirk broke into a wide smile, and his throaty laughter filled the building to its rafters. Solomon shoved me to the door, leaving me little option but to return to the havoc of the streets.

Despite the efforts of my men, small fires had broken out across Scythian Neapolis—though, blessedly, none had blazed beyond control. After rejoining several of Troglita's men, we patrolled the streets, frequently returning to the town's walls. Even with distractions from below, our sentries kept watch for any sign of messengers from Cherson, or more ominous signs from the Avar horde. We commandeered the town's barracks, allowing rotating shifts of men to peel away their filthy garments and steal what rest would come.

I slept poorly that night. However strange it was, all that gave me comfort was the dragon pendant, which I held to my lips before surrendering to the few hours of sleep allowed to me. In such moments, my mind wandered to Mariya's parting words, and I wondered whether I would survive this hell to see the Ghassanid princess once more.

"I will be praying for your safe return."

Rosamund had brought clean water for me to bathe away the greasy filth from the battle, and Samur had gathered news about the army's state of affairs. Even Father Petrus' prayers offered little consolation, their strength hollowed by the priest's own grieving for Godilas. I attempted to question the extent of their friendship, yet the priest merely shrugged such inquiries aside.

"One day, I will tell you," Father Petrus mumbled. "But Godilas meant a great deal to me. Just as you meant a great deal to him."

By the afternoon of our second day in Scythian Neapolis, officers could only account for two thousand men, many of whom bore wounds that limited their ability to fight in a wall, ride a horse, or shoot a bow. Several bandae, mine and a few others, had tried to maintain order, but the majority of our men had sacked Scythian Neapolis as thoroughly as any Avar raid.

Surprisingly, accounts of murder were limited; the rampaging soldiers seemed to prefer tossing aside a building's inhabitants to slaying them outright. However, such mercy did not extend to the town's women, and I could only assume the already staggering number of reported rapes was a pitiful underestimate. For most cases, all we could do was collect the survivors and offer a modicum of protection as Rosamund heard their cries and tended their wounds. Mundus swore that he would cut Archelaus' throat for such barbarism, yet with his injured shoulder, he remained far too weak to make good on any threats.

The Thracian Army camped at Scythian Neapolis for another day and night, with Archelaus ordering no scouts, no action at all against the Avars. He did send messengers to Cherson, yet none of our messengers returned with any news of rescue or support. The senior officers remain quartered in the magistrate's quarters, their only visitors a small number of spearmen who carried barrels of wine and cuts of meat and bread.

On the morning of the third day, sentries sounded the village's horn. A warning: riders in the distance. Several hundred paces away, fur-clad horsemen were spotted riding toward Scythian Neapolis, which appeared to be the vanguard of a larger mounted force. I learned of such grim tidings in the town barracks, and ordered Mundus' men to don their armor once more.

The news soon reached Archelaus, who donned his armor and ordered his army into formation. It took an hour, for many of the soldiers had dug themselves into drunken holes in the various huts and buildings that circled the village, yet soon near two thousand armored men lined the forum. Archelaus stood atop the battlements, surveilling the swelling Avar army. It seemed smaller than the horde that overwhelmed Godilas' square, yet still outnumbered our own forces by at least three or four to one. They seemed to eschew building any camp, their forces instead forming into battle arrays well beyond bowshot of the town walls.

Archelaus climbed down from the battlements and called his remaining officers forward, including those under the command of Mundus and Troglita. He explained that to remain in the village was to guarantee a slow death by starvation; its granaries and herdsmen had already given up much of their stores when the Thracian Army arrived days prior. Instead, the army's best chance at survival was to form up outside of the village walls, make a breakout to the west, and retreat in an orderly fashion toward Cherson. There, we could commandeer ships and sail away from this godforsaken land, leaving the Cherson Province to the consumption of the Avar hordes. Few offered suggestions to the de facto general, with most remaining silent as they pondered whether they would live to see Constantinople or Thrace ever again.

Archelaus mounted his horse and ordered the army forward, and we marched through the village gates onto the plains. No crowds greeted or cheered us as we left, though some old women shouted obscenities as the Imperial Army departed their homes.

The Last Dying Light

Our servants trailed us on horseback, ready to gallop westward to Cherson as soon as the Avars engaged the Roman shield wall. The old priest cantered up our lines, offering blessings and forgiveness for our many sins as we marched forward, and he stopped before me to make the sign of the cross.

"Keep your men safe, Varus," Father Petrus said, and left to administer his religious rite to the other bandae. "God knows that most of the rest deserve no mercy from what is to come."

Rosamund called out my name, but I could not see her over the mass of helmets and spears. Only Samur came with the men, donning the arms and armor of a Roman spearman who had recently died from his wounds.

"If I'm going to die, I'm going to do it with a weapon in my hands," Samur declared, a hint of mischief still present in his voice.

I kept him in our banda's reserve lines and warned him to not expose himself to unnecessary risk. We embraced, and then Archelaus and the banda commanders called for order. I took my place at the front next to Perenus and Cephalas.

Our more heavily armored spearmen took the center of the lines, backed by lighter-armored infantry and archers. Both flanks were guarded by our remaining bandae of light horsemen, yet I doubted that these warriors would fight in such an unbalanced struggle when their route of escape to the west would leave them in Cherson after two days of hard riding.

Only two hundred paces distant, many of the Avars dismounted and formed their own lines, stalking ours. They stretched their lines wide along a low and treeless knoll, yet had more than enough men to ensure a solid mass that would punch through our own shield wall and encircle the army. From the center of the Avar mass, two Avar men rode forward, dragging behind another two figures that bore black hoods over their heads.

They rode within fifty paces of our lines, surveilling us. The first man was younger, his dark hair hanging long beyond his shoulders and a thin beard lining his mouth and chin. Where many of the other Avars were covered in grease and filth, this man's furs shone pristine white, and his scaled armor was decorated with a number of ornate fantastical creatures that doubtlessly were prominent to the Avars' myths. The other man was far older, his scarred face betraying no emotion as he held the leashes of his two prisoners. Like the younger man, his furs and armor were far more lavish and richer than the mass of men at his back.

Taking one of the leashes into his possession, the younger man yanked his prisoner upright and lifted the hood: a Roman woman whose dark hair had been cut short and her tunic stained with mud. She would have been unremarkable, had her arms not been severed at the elbows.

The curved stumps had not fully healed, with only thick layers of scabs and layers of burned skin knitting the wounds closed. As the leash at her throat tugged violently, the woman stumbled, aimless as she faced the Roman lines. As she drew nearer, I saw her blackened feet were bare as she stepped between earth churned by the feet of thousands of Avar men and horses. As she walked, the woman's chin never left her chest, hiding her face with her layers of grease-matted hair. Still, incredibly, she held the stumps of her arms as if in greeting to us, but not a greeting of friendship—a portent of what awaited any who stood against the dark riders.

The younger Avar bared his teeth at the Roman lines in a grin. He shouted at us, his voice oddly high-pitched given his dark and looming appearance. When he concluded, he tugged on the woman's leash, and she stepped forward to address our soldiers in more familiar Greek.

Full of fear, her voice rang out toward our formation and over the walls of Scythian Neapolis.

"He introduces himself as Shaush, the son of Kazrig, Lord of Grass and Sky, Khagan of the Avars, and Ruler of These Lands," she screamed, her voice cracking as she spoke each of the foreign-sounding names and titles. "The man accompanying Shaush is Tzul, chief warlord of Kazrig, who with his own blade has felled a thousand men and has led the horde to victory in a hundred battles. The Avars greet you, Romans, on the morning that you will be damned by the Great God Tengri."

Shaush spoke again, his beard shaking, and spat in our direction. Each movement was tense with aggression, his arms thrusting in crude gestures at our shield wall. After Shaush finished, he tugged once more at the leash for a rough translation.

"In his mercy, Lord Shaush declares that you Romans may yet live, if you only slay your leaders and prostrate yourselves at his feet. He will take you as slaves, but none will die by his hand."

As the woman quieted, the warlord Tzul handed the other leash to Shaush. The figure slunk forward obediently, putting up no resistance at such ill treatment. Shaush spoke briefly again, laying his hand over the hood of the figure.

The woman translated Shaush's final proclamation. "As a sign of the Great God Tengri's favor of the Avars, Lord Shaush will demonstrate to you why Rome's domination over these lands has ended."

On cue, Shaush removed the hood. The figure was Godilas.

Though stone-faced, Godilas still bore signs of his three days in captivity. His clothing was torn and crusted in dirt, and even from such a distance, he appeared thinner, sunken cheeks and sallow skin suggesting an illness had taken root within his body. Godilas did not move as the Avars yanked at his leash or spat on his head, now stripped of all the ornaments and arms of a Roman general. As they paraded Godilas before our army, other Avars produced our various banners to the center of their formation, chanting in their outlandish tongue that none in our ranks could understand.

"Shit-eating bastards," Perenus said, fresh anger in his voice.

I glanced at Solomon, who shrank back from Shaush and Tzul's introduction. Archelaus, however, left no opportunity for the men to fight or argue to rescue their general.

"Tell your masters they can suck my cock!" Archelaus bellowed.

The outburst took only moments to relay to Shaush, and it seemed nothing was lost in translation. Unspeaking, Shaush drew the blade at his waist and rested its curved edge along Godilas' neck, holding it still enough for the wind to blow gently through the general's hair.

"Godilas!" I lunged forward, but someone held me back, grasping my arms and shoulders as I struggled for freedom.

"There's nothing we can do now, Varus," Cephalas said quietly. "All we can do is honor Godilas with our witness."

Tales abound of Roman stoicism. A Roman citizen is unenslaved to fickle emotion, and he receives each triumph or disaster with equal disinterest, knowing all can and will pass. This was an example I had never mastered, for despite my tireless work to conform to Justin's will, I was not truly a Roman at all. And, despite Godilas' remonstrations against surrendering to emotion, it was not until my onetime master-at-arms was unceremoniously thrown to his knees that I was consumed once more by grief at what was to come.

With a sudden, violent thrust, Shaush lifted the blade, its tip pointed to the heavens. Godilas' face did not change, frozen in its odd expression of peace.

"Tengri!" Shaush roared.

The blade slashed into Godilas' exposed neck, cleanly severing his spine with one merciful cut, and I screamed. The balding pate tumbled into the grass, the general's lifeblood spurting from its open stump and onto the captive Roman woman. Several of the men howled with indignation, yet the officers kept discipline and order across the lines.

Shaush grinned, stepping forward for a final pronouncement. His translator echoed his words, fear rising in her voice.

"If you will not accept his mercy, Lord Shaush will kill you all, just as he butchered your elderly father," she said. "Your bodies will be given to Tengri, and none will find any trace that you once came to the lands of the Avars."

A mere heartbeat after her final word, Shaush swung his blade in a high arc, and the woman's head tumbled to join Godilas' on the grass. A roar rose across the Avar lines, and many beat spears against crude wooden shields in a rough percussion. Tzul raised a gloved fist, and the Avars charged.

We were ready, as much as could be hoped. Our archers fired a volley as the first Avar lines closed in and downed a few dozen furred and armored spearmen. But other, eager Avars took their place, jostling to be first to reach the Roman shield wall. Our further volleys of arrows struck true, and thinned other points along the Avar advance, but we could not flatten them all. We simply had too few bowmen and no *ballistae* to sweep out their howling attack.

Archelaus' strategy had been to fend off an Avar assault long enough to allow for an orderly breakout of the Thracian Army back to Cherson. As the Avar advance continued, Archelaus attempted to slide his forces west to avoid being flanked, yet the ferocity of the Avar assault prevented any movement of our infantry in favor of defending in place.

My shield layered over that of Perenus and Cephalas as we withstood the mass of sprinting Avars. Their disorderly and uncoordinated charge flouted our training and would have been thoroughly condemned by any decent Roman tactician, for disorder along the shield wall quickly dissipated into rout if one's opponent stood firm. But we were too few to prevent an encirclement, and I doubted whether the men had the confidence or morale to stand against thousands of screaming barbarians. My own men stood firm, yet without any of the confidence or energy expected of a thoroughly trained and prepared Roman fighting force.

Yet as the swiftest Avars drew close, Samur shouted behind me, and he shoved his body forward to meet his enemy.

"Godilas!" With this battle cry, Samur thrust his spearpoint into an Avar's chest and drew his sword to slash at another.

"Samur, get back!" I cried.

Fear all but stifled me. I shuffled from my place at the shield wall, snatched Samur's cloak with my shield arm, and dragged him back to our lines. All the while, his blade was a flurry of movement, not slowing until he slipped behind me and the Roman lines. I gritted my teeth and centered myself. More Avars rushed us, slamming hard against wood and iron that drove our men a pace backward. Samur stabbed over my shield, felling whoever was pushing me backward, then patted me on the shoulder and ran back to the third line, cleaning his blade as he went.

Our wall held firm, yet losses were mounting as the Avars snaked toward our flanks. Archelaus had positioned our cavalry in a bent formation to prevent the Avar riders or spearmen from encircling our position, yet these positions remained perilously thin and buckled inward. As our flanks curled and Archelaus' orders grew more frantic, great drums sounded in the distance, and the Avars ran back toward their lines.

Not thirty paces distant, I glanced at the warlord Tzul arguing with Shaush, gesturing toward our lines as if to insist the attack continue, but Shaush ignored the older man and instead stood before his lines. He grabbed a spear, mounted Godilas' head at its tip, and hoisted it to the sky with a roar. I screamed in pain and hatred, yet my voice was easily overpowered by cheering Avars who chanted the name of their prince in a hellish chorus. Panting, Perenus looked toward me, his face awash in blood that seeped into his eyes and mouth.

"Injured?" He gestured at my gore-crusted armor and helmet.

I shook my head. "No, you?"

Perenus grimaced. "The gods don't seem to want me yet."

Samur clapped my armor for attention and asked if I needed a break, but I refused.

"Listen," I said, "at this next charge, take Rosamund and Father Petrus and leave. Three on horseback can make for Cherson faster than any Avar army, and you can tell the Emperor what happened here."

But Samur refused. "I'm staying with you, no matter what happens," he said. "You are all I have in this world."

I embraced my brother for what I thought would be the last time. By now there was little point resisting Samur, for even if he immediately parted from the army and gathered my companions, they would have little chance of outpacing Avar riders. Instead I relented, allowing Samur in his poorly fitting ringmail to remain, and hoping that Rosamund and Father Petrus might survive behind the town's walls long enough for Cherson to send rescue.

"As you wish," I said. "If I fall, take my sword and fight as long as you can."

The drums ceased. We parted and reassumed our places in the lines. Shaush seemed hurried now, barking orders and shoving his men into place in order to finish the attack. Of our original number leaving Scythian Neapolis, perhaps another five hundred had been killed or grievously wounded, and our lines no longer held any notable reserves to patch further losses.

"This is it," said Cephalas, nodding to me. "God be with you."

"And with you." I hoisted a new spear and tested the strength of my shield.

Shaush hefted his macabre standard into the sky one final time, the head gruesome on the spear tip, and fresh Avars renewed their pounding assault against our shields. With the fury of the Avars closing in on our lines, my heart's imagination surprised me. I saw Mariya, her lovely form, and how I would break my word to return safely from Cherson. For that selfish moment, I wished that God would lift me from this place and back to Constantinople, granting me my heart's desire instead of a slow and torturous death at the hand of an Avar rider. But I knew I could not. I shrugged off such thoughts and attuned my gaze to the fur-clad warriors, whose swords, axes, and spears were eager to taste Roman blood once again.

As they neared fifty paces from our lines, a strange horn rang out over the expanse, one long deep note. At the sound, Tzul turned his gaze with furrowed concern, and Shaush rushed forward all the faster, yet some Avar lines had slowed or even halted, as though the horn was a balm to their frenzy.

Several Avars struck our lines again, flinging their weapons as though to cut our remaining units to ribbons. Yet, after a few moments, their shields moved away from our wall, releasing pressure that drove Archelaus' spearmen several paces backward from our initial line. I speared a man through his leg, pinning him to the ground, and looked into the distance to see what new arrival had been summoned to the Tauric plain outside of Scythian Neapolis.

Hundreds of horsemen crested a low hill, each rider and horse encased in thick iron scales. Even in the rush, I could make out a half dozen weapons attached to their saddles—bows, lances, swords, and even crude maces I knew would drive into a man's skull as though it were melting butter. With long shields guarding the bulk of the rider's body, each horseman tightened to his neighbor, forming a wedge, and together they lowered their lances forward. A trailing white plume marked one as leader, with his armor decorated with his previous successes in various corners of the Empire.

The wedge of horsemen collided with the Avar spearmen at full gallop. Shaush broke from our formation and shouted orders that formed a crude Avar shield wall, but his Avars were skittish, unwilling to stare down the thundering mass of horse, rider, and armor. The riders drove forward and forward and forward until at last, they collided. The barbarian lines blew apart like chaff, leaving much of their army encircled between our position and that of the interloping cavalry.

The Cappadocian Army had arrived, and we were saved.

As the last Avars fled, a great cheer rang from our ranks, with some men even dropping to their knees in supplication. Perenus hugged me, battle fatigue forgotten and replaced with a face-splitting grin. From what I could see, something like half the Avar army had escaped the Cappadocians' trap and retreated north with all haste, following Tzul. Other Cappadocian reinforcements spilled from the eastern horizon, surrounding most of Shaush's army and goring hundreds with iron-tipped lances held by each Cappadocian rider.

As I think back to that day so many years ago, it is plain that Shaush and Tzul must have known that a second Roman Army had arrived on the Tauric Peninsula. Indeed, the old priest, showing a thoroughly unexpected military prowess, later raised the idea that Tzul had wanted to attack each of our armies separately, and thus make us riper for conquest. Yet it was Shaush, in his youthful arrogance and swollen pride, who delayed just long enough to leave his forces open to destruction.

Even as the Cappadocian hoofbeats slowed, and the Avars were clearly outflanked, few barbarians surrendered. Most swung their swords until the very last, until cut down by spearmen and riders alike. Yet a small number remained circled around Shaush, not attacking, but eyeing their Roman enemies warily. Alongside my men, I witnessed all this from the remnants of the Thracian wall, not thirty paces from where Shaush's flagging resistance looked onward at their conquerors.

While Roman spearmen paced throughout the splayed bodies and cut the throats of any Avars they found still breathing, the white-plumed leader of the Roman cavalry dismounted and walked toward the Avar circle. Several of the Avars raised their spears at the intruder, but dropped them when Shaush yelled a blunt command. Roman soldiers filed behind the white-plumed commander, though they gave the Avar spears a wide berth.

Their leader entered the gathered Avars peaceably, his gaze fixed on Shaush. He removed his helmet, and sweat poured from his clean-shaven face as he wiped his brow. His square jaw and close-cropped black hair seemed oddly familiar, and I squinted for a better look at our savior.

Against the furred Avar prince, the Roman commander was a figure of Imperial order, a rich set of close-knit lamellar armor encasing his legs and body. He drew a knife from his belt, and with it cut away a piece of cloth from the Avar's chest. Shaush's spearmen leaped to defend their prince, yet Shaush silenced them with a growl.

The Roman spoke first. "You don't understand me, but hear me all the same: I will let you live," he shouted in Latin. "For the rest of your days, you will tell all you meet that you fought a Roman army in battle, and lost. Go, and tell that to your leader."

With that, the Roman dug his knife into Shaush's skin, swift and skillful enough to draw a line of blood, but not wound.

"This is a reminder of your defeat, in case you should ever forget."

His task complete, the Roman sheathed his knife and faced his horsemen, showing his back to Shaush. He ordered the ranks to open and allow Shaush and all but two of his small cohort to leave unmolested. Initially, Shaush appeared suspicious of such behavior and refused to move, yet when the surrounding Romans gestured toward the Tauric plains to the north, he obeyed. Many Cappadocians hooted at the sight of the running Avars; most from the Thracian Army, however, remained silent. Shaush had nearly seen the end of all of us, and I, like my fellows, found little cause for gloating even after being saved by our comrades from the east.

The Cappadocian Army's horsemen gathered around their leader, cheering his name wildly. Now, I could see that many of the Cappadocians bore the darker skin of the Empire's far-flung provinces, Armenia and Mesopotamia, bitterly contested against the Persians.

Atop his horse, the man trotted to our lines, sunlight glinting from his armor. He saluted us, and the thousand battered and bleeding men before him responded in kind.

"I am Flavius Belisarius, *magister militum* of the Cappadocian Army," he called. "Where is General Godilas?"

All eyes fell to the ground. Hot shame crept up my neck. Our general's head and butchered body lay just a few dozen paces from our lines, lolling beside the corpse of the doomed armless woman.

At the center of the Thracian shield wall, Archelaus stepped forward and saluted the Cappadocian general.

"Tribune Archelaus, excubitor, second-in-command to Strategos Godilas," Archelaus introduced himself. "General Godilas was captured and decapitated in a previous engagement, and his body lies on the field before us."

Belisarius nodded and called for white cloths to wrap the heads and bodies of Godilas and the translator alike so that they might be carried back to the town with dignity.

"We will treat our wounded and pay respect to our dead with their desired rituals, pagan or Christian," Belisarius said in Latin, repeating the order soon thereafter in more familiar Greek. The Thracians murmured surprise at such leniency, for it was common practice to disregard any faith outside of the rigidly defined Christianity accepted by the Emperor. Archelaus himself was testament to such brutal indifference. Yet the Cappadocian soldiers snapped to their assigned task, neither surprised nor revolted by Belisarius' attempt to honor the Roman dead. Though Rosamund's paganism always left me with an uneasy sensation, I silently approved of such generous behavior, wishing that I could extend such measures to the remains of Isaacius far to the north.

As the de facto commander of the expedition after Godilas' death, Belisarius summoned Archelaus to give a proper report, and ordered his men to establish a fortified camp on the outskirts of Scythian Neapolis. Our army, so pitifully small, did whatever we could to assist the Cappadocians in digging trenches and raising palisades as the peasants from the nearby village watched on with equal suspicion and curiosity. By the end of the day, camp had been raised and set with reasonable defenses, and foragers were sent to gather food and water from the surrounding region.

As the sun sank to the horizon, nearly all soldiers within the combined forces assembled at a large square that was laid out at the center of the camp. Belisarius and other senior officers stood near a makeshift wooden stage, and the magister militum rose to address the combined forces.

As he ascended the steps, Belisarius' senior officers roared for Rome's soldiers to stand at attention. A great clattering of spears, shields, and boots rang out over the palisade walls as the men stood straight, eventually giving way to a solemn silence that paid respect to their commander. Belisarius gave a short, deliberate wave and began his address.

"Tonight, we mourn our dead. May they find comfort in the afterlife, and freedom from the toils of this world," Belisarius boomed.

At this signal, dozens of fires were lit along the plains outside of Scythian Neapolis, their pyres containing the hundreds of dead Roman soldiers that fell in the battle. Godilas' body had been carried from the village to the center of our encampment, his filthy rags removed and a suit of armor carefully secured along his torso. Belisarius grabbed a torch and walked toward Godilas' pyre, the head and body resting upon a bed of hewn logs that had been stacked close to Belisarius' position. He spoke a few words that none but he could hear and placed the torch onto the kindling below Godilas' body.

The blaze spread about Godilas' mangled body, the first embers lighting a cloak lent to the fallen general to be the last he would ever wear. I made the sign of the cross; Samur sobbed beside me, a forearm over his mouth. I grabbed him about the shoulders for a tight embrace.

"I can't believe he's gone." Samur sniffled. "They cut his head off in front of thousands of people, and there was nothing we could do."

"We'll make it right," I whispered. "The bastards will pay for what they've done to Isaacius, and Godilas."

"I know," Samur said darkly. "I'll kill all of them myself if I have to. The men, the women, and the children."

In my grief, I did not pay mind to such troubling words. Perhaps I should have. But after so much loss, such carnage, I simply lacked the strength to rebuke my brother, too wrapped in my own grief at the double loss of a friend and a lifelong mentor. For Samur, however, Godilas was by far the favorite teacher, the man who taught Samur that any may bear power in arms given proper training and technique. Though Justin and Liberius had both given Samur luxuries unknown to any other slave to the Empire, he did not feel the intimacy with those men that I did, and reserved his fondest affections for Godilas. Now, surrendering to his agony, Samur pounded on my armor as he wailed Godilas' name, eyes tight so he might be spared the body withering and crackling in the inferno. I whispered a prayer for Godilas and Isaacius, and heard similar words from Perenus and Cephalas close by.

Having walked back to the center of camp, Belisarius returned to the stage as the fires glowed in the foreboding night sky. Their orange flames flickered from the interlocking layers of his iron armor, reflecting light to the gathered armies. With a final glance at the dozens of pyres throughout the battlefield, Belisarius, the sole general remaining of the Empire's expedition to Tauris, faced us, his men.

"We have bloodied the Avars but have only defeated a small part of their horde. If we allow them to leave intact, they will return as soon as we are gone, and will rape and pillage their way across Tauris." Belisarius took a deep breath, surveying his forces.

"I will not allow that!" he yelled, shaking a fist. At his pronouncement, the soldiers beat their spears against their shields, and he allowed the clamor for a few moments until he raised his hand. "Rome is a dream that is not dead, but sleeping. And today is the day that it awakens! We will take back this world from its encroaching darkness, and fulfill the vision of so many men and women who have long passed into history."

The cheering arose again, louder this time as men's voices raised in volume. Samur's reddened face peeled away from my chest, curious to survey the young general whose words offered distraction from the grief of the evening. Belisarius raised his hand one final time, then drew his sword from its scabbard and thrust its tip into the air.

"When I was made into a soldier of Rome, I recited a creed that bound me in service to a vision greater than myself. Its words are burned into my mind, offering comfort when the days become more than I can bear. Given the enormity of the challenge facing us in the days ahead, I recommit myself to you, and promise that together we shall not fail.

"I swear to faithfully execute the Emperor's commands, to never desert my service, nor shrink from Death in pursuit of the glory of Rome," Belisarius called out, and a cacophony of voices echoed him.

"I swear to defend the weak, to protect the innocent, and serve as the shield to the poor and the mighty alike," Belisarius recited again, and the men, following suit, grew more spirited in their response.

"I swear to honor and love my God, to seek justice, and glorify those dreams that are greater than myself."

The fervor of the men grew ever louder as they followed the lead of their young commander—though some, doubtlessly, replaced *God* with *gods*. Belisarius raised his right arm out in broad recognition of the men.

"I swear this oath before God and of the Roman people, who shall never falter."

His creed concluded, Belisarius lowered his arm, and an outpouring of celebration and joy the likes of which I had not seen in many a month flooded forth from the men. Even Perenus, still heavy with grief over the loss of our friend, joined in the cheering, while Samur merely nodded, his face resolved, hard with purpose now that he'd sworn his oath. Noise rang through the plains, and I am sure that, if the Avars in their distant camps heard us, they must have trembled.

THE WICKED AND THE JUST

Though Belisarius' victory had brought the death of over a thousand Avar warriors, celebration was muted due to an understanding of the vastly larger and more seasoned fighters that the Avar warlord khagan could call to bear. To improve our anticipation of Avar movements, Belisarius implemented a new scouting technique: Scouts checked in with one another at regular and short intervals to prevent one from being ambushed and killed by Avar outriders. Our intelligence of the Avar armies' positions along the plains was still far from complete, but much improved.

On the morning of the day following the funeral pyres, Belisarius' officers flew through the camp, hounding us for detailed reports of the status of the Thracian Army, our provisions, and our numbers, before dispatching orders to Cherson for refitting and resupply. Several contingents of the Cappadocian Army even entered Scythian Neapolis to patch its walls and repair the profound damage to many of its buildings—a task that threatened to consume multiple days. Belisarius himself stripped to the waist and led an effort to haul away the charred timbers of the village gates, which were soon replaced with freshly cut lumber and masonry ferried by Cappadocian horses from Cherson. The remnants of our banda were assigned to him for this task, and so we temporarily traded in our spears and shields for hammers and squares.

"It appears we trade swords for ploughshares, Father." I smiled at Father Petrus.

"For now," he replied, eyes narrowing at my sarcasm. "If only such measures were permanent, and universal."

We were, perhaps, poor workers; Perenus swore viciously whenever he smacked his hand with a charred board, yet remained in high spirits as he joined Samur and Cephalas.

Belisarius had asked that I shadow him throughout this rebuilding process. He explained that he remembered me from the Hippodrome, and had orders from Theodora to watch over me on our northern campaign.

"Theodora? Why would she ask this of you?"

Belisarius shrugged. "Theodora is one who commands and receives respect. She did not explain her wishes, only that you are worthy of trust."

The young general was fascinated by the story that linked Justinian's bride to me and nodded in approval when he heard of my oath to the Emperor as I received my new sword.

"The Emperor was the one who gave me my oath, nearly a decade ago," Belisarius said.

He told me of his times with Justin, Godilas, and Justinian, even how he had rescued the latter two as the Huns ambushed their position beyond the Ister River. When he moved on to stories of Godilas, his gaze fell.

"He was a good man, and did not deserve this end," Belisarius said. "But at least he has escaped the pains of this life."

Belisarius told me of his more recent past, and how the rescue of Godilas and Justinian had propelled his fortunes in Rome's military. Justin had supplied Belisarius with the gold and power to form his own *bucellarii*, a bodyguard of heavy cavalry that had melded tactics from the Persians, Goths, and Huns into a more innovative cavalry unit—what Liberius had called the cataphracts. Belisarius paid the ruinous sums needed to equip and maintain each of the five hundred under his command, and then paid again to sustain the multiple servants required to clean, maintain, and mend the horses and armor for each rider.

In his earliest years in command, other men flocked to Belisarius' banner, which took the form of a black wolf's head on a gray field. Belisarius personally inspected each man before they joined his army, ensuring their character as much as their fitness as a representative of Rome's martial prowess.

When we met, the general was still a young man, only four or five years older than my near twenty, yet he carried himself an authority that saw much older men seeking his approval. Many concerns pressed on his time, yet he offered his own hands for the labor of rebuilding the village. He took time to learn each of my men's names, to know why each enlisted; he shared their mirth and heard their grievances about poor equipment, rotten food, and delayed pay.

Yet he was not without troubles himself. On a private walk outside of the town's walls, we spoke further of the Emperor and his grand designs, and once out of earshot of the sentries, the general confided his concerns in hushed tones.

"The Imperial messengers have spread the story of Archelaus' victory over the Gepids, the first such adventure into those lands in a generation," he said. "Yet I have heard darker whispers of what transpired in the Gepid forests, and those rumors are consistent with the rise in the recent attacks along our Moesian border."

"Lord, I..." I stopped, corrected myself. "I am bound by oath to keep my old banda commander's secrets."

Belisarius nodded. "I understand, and I would not want you to violate your conscience. It is a precious thing, and in the end it is all a man truly possesses in this life." He hesitated. "But if a complaint were levied, and I were to sit in judgment, should I give these rumors consideration, Varus? Or dismiss them as the gossip that they are?"

Eyes downcast, I felt my thoughts drift to my confession to Justin, when the overwhelming guilt led me to violate my oath of secrecy and unburden my soul to my onetime dominus. Though I yearned to assist Belisarius, he was still a stranger to me, and so I crafted an indirect answer that might still assist his search for the truth.

"All knowledge is worth pursuing, and this situation is no different," I said.

Belisarius nodded. "Good. As you say, all information makes for better decisions." He gave me a smile.

Belisarius also thanked me for the assistance of Rosamund, who had by now healed dozens of the gashes and broken bones left in the aftermath of battle. I had until then underestimated her healing abilities, perhaps despite my scoffing that she learned from assisting her parents with the aches and pains of a small village. Yet now, several in both armies owed life or limb to Rosamund, and when I saw her bask in their praise and thanksgiving, I grew curiously giddy.

Over the following two days, Belisarius and I spoke at length about how he shared the Emperor's vision for the Eastern Empire, and how he had molded his own personal army for that purpose. Where the Thracian Army had been simple in its structure and composition, Belisarius' forces comprised a diversity of soldiers that allowed him to respond with tailored forces to each enemy and terrain. Beyond his personal cataphracts, Belisarius also commanded light auxiliaries that threw javelins and shot bolts before the crash of the shield wall, as well as heavy-armored line infantry whose shields were thicker and larger than was common for Rome's spearmen. His officers even maintained a contingent of ballistae, whose bolts could impale three men before their iron points buried into the turf.

Most curious of all among his forces was a contingent of horseback archers that marched alongside his armored cataphracts. Such men were Huns, remnants of Attila's horde that kept to the Hunnic ways of fighting from horseback with lances and bows. Led by the brothers Sunicas and Simmas, some six hundred Hunnic riders had invested their trust in Belisarius, who returned it with complete loyalty.

"There are no better scouts, and they have incredible luck for sensing the turning point in a battle," Belisarius said of his Hunnic soldiers. "We treat them as foederati, as a distinct military unit that is allowed to retain its cultural character and fighting style. In return, the unit is assigned Roman officers for command. For the case of the Huns, Sunicas and Simmas were granted Roman citizenship outright, for no man can lead the Huns but one of their own, and I tell you, the brothers' loyalty is beyond reproach."

I doubted it. Samur's curiosity saw him join our conversation as we hauled lumber to a granary with a burnt roof. "Why not? What makes the Huns unique, when so many other tribes work within the Empire already?" Samur asked, ignoring the wide gulf that separated a newly freed slave from an Imperial general.

Yet Belisarius ignored such slights with a laugh. "They are a proud people, and believe that only one of their countrymen has the strength and right to lead the horde," he said. "They remember Attila and wonder what could have been."

Though many Romans were reluctant to invoke the great warlord's name, Belisarius shrugged such fears away. "Attila was the darkness that came within a breath of consuming everything we hold precious, yet was stopped by a few good men and women. We can't be afraid of the memory of such an enemy."

After two days of constant and grueling labor, Scythian Neapolis was restored, and many of the villagers had resumed their labors in the fields or to their crafts. I paid a blacksmith to forge Samur a better-fitting hauberk of ringmail, which my brother eyed lustfully as its light links folded between his fingers, their quality unquestionable. When I sought to replace my men's spears and shields, Belisarius added his coin to my own and promised that future replacements of arms would be carried from Cherson.

The Last Dying Light

Toward the end of the day, Belisarius assembled the combined armies in the repaired forum, our rows straight and banners crisp. The most senior officers gathered behind him, including, for the Thracian Army, Archelaus. A new second-in-command of our diminutive force was named, a younger cousin of Justinian named Germanus. I knew little of him, but the men who knew him gave their grunted approval; it seemed the man served honorably and shared none of Justinian's avarice and vainglory.

On the Cappadocian side, Belisarius was flanked by a collection of his commanders: one of the Huns, and a half dozen others—their skin light or swarthy, their eyes dark or fair, but their skill in battle universally fearsome. Father Petrus informed me later that the men had all served with Belisarius in other endeavors and had earned the right to act independently of any command. At Belisarius' right flank was one man who stood out from the rest. With russet skin and thinning hair despite his youthful features, the man was an Armenian called John, and he accompanied Belisarius in all things military or religious. More sinister gossip hinted at a kind of carnal friendship, but their behavior affirmed nothing of such slander; the love and trust shared between Belisarius and John was obvious to me even then, confirmed when I later learned that they had grown up together like brothers since earliest childhood.

As before, the standard bearers slammed the butts of their wooden poles to the earth, and officers called for silence in the ranks. Neat lines of spearmen stood with their chests out as Belisarius walked forward, his face unhidden so all could see who he was.

"Soldiers of Rome, in three days we depart here to take our fight to the Avars. We cannot let them leave only to return in a few years' time. I will consult with the officers regarding your assignments. Yet until then, I ask that you treat our hosts of Neapolis gracefully, and return nightly to our established encampment beyond the village's walls." Belisarius' voice boomed over our lines.

But before he could speak another word, a lighter voice screamed over the ranks.

"Your men already raped my daughter and stole my silver!" it cried. "No use in being gentle now!"

A man, clad in ripped robes that once would have distinguished him as a magistrate, stepped forward. Two soldiers at the edge of the formation moved to silence the man, but stopped at a swift swipe of Belisarius' hand.

Another voice called from the growing crowd of villagers. "Lord, you have spent days repairing our town. We would like to think you can give us justice for all the wrongs that were done to us by our own soldiers!" A woman now, who stirred shouts of agreement from the dozens of other villagers at the edges of the army.

Belisarius again raised a hand for quiet. "Citizens, I hear you. If it is within my power, I will try to ease your pain from this grievous wrong. But you say that this was the work of Rome's men—is the fault not due to the Avars?" he said in a slow, steady voice.

The crowd riled with anger, shouts flying from every direction. Men of the Thracian Army grew sullen, and I could see Solomon shrink away as Archelaus sauntered down the lines.

Above all the voices, the magistrate's alone carried. "Lord, we were attacked by our own army fleeing from defeat," he said brokenly. "We opened our gates, and they marched in to burn and pillage."

The magistrate waited as the crowd muted itself, hanging on his words. He wiped his eyes and pointed one long, crooked finger toward Archelaus.

"And it was he who caused it!" the magistrate said.

Archelaus roared in protest, and the village forum boiled as Archelaus' men faced down the growing mob that had formed from most of the village citizens. A horn blew, deafening all arguments, as Belisarius sought the floor again.

"Lord Archelaus, a grave accusation has been levied against you. What do you have to say in your defense?" Belisarius' face was fixed in concern.

Archelaus threw his hands into the air. "I say they lie. I am a soldier of Rome, and a leader of men. My word as tribune makes these villagers dissemblers, and cheats! And," he added, "my record is impeccable, and none can besmirch my honor as a Roman or a Christian."

Jeers rang throughout the crowd of villagers, yet none drew closer to the arrayed spearmen, and many even shuffled back toward half-rebuilt homes and shops rather than press an argument against Archelaus. Temptation nearly drew me to echo the magistrate's complaints, yet even such a release of guilt and resentment could not bring such impulses to bear, and I wavered in the opportunity. But soon a woman's familiar voice pierced the din, flailing accusations at my oath-sworn lord, and I knew in that instant that my life would be forever changed.

"I say you lie!" Rosamund shrieked, her Greek improved by months of practice yet still marked by a thick accent. "You came to my village for no reason, killed my mother and father, and burned my village to the ground with me inside."

I shot a look at Rosamund, begging for her silence, as I was sure that Archelaus would command the death of one who was a barbarian, a pagan, and a direct threat to his authority over the Thracian Army. Rosamund's eyes met mine for barely a heartbeat, but I needed no longer to see the loathing and rage simmering within. Seeing me did not see her soften, either; rather, her face contorted in a mixture of fury and sadness that she unleashed upon Archelaus.

"You are a liar, a rapist, and a murderer!" Rosamund cried. "You can send your men to cut my throat and silence my words, but the stain upon your maggot-riddled soul will last forever, and you will never know peace!"

Archelaus stared down his new accuser, his bearded cheeks reddening, and dropped his leather-gloved hand to his scabbard. To my surprise, contrary to all I had known since my time as a recruit, Archelaus spoke with restraint, his murderous look melting away into cruel laughter.

"My girl, I've never seen you in my life," Archelaus said. "And as I have said, everything I have done is in service to Rome. I've hardened my men to fight Rome's enemies, and I have killed those who the Emperor commanded me to do so. I can only decry you as a liar and have you whipped bloody for your insolence—little good though it will do for your barbarian soul."

At Archelaus' order, Thracian spearmen formed a square around the crowd, further angering the gathered villagers as other voices sought to join Rosamund's accusations against the tribune.

Yet Rosamund had not finished. "You are right; I am no citizen here, and have no power but my will to speak at an evil that I have borne in silence for too long. You crossed the Ister to attack the Gepids, and raped and burned your way through a peaceful trading village. How many orphans did you make that day, you and all your *brave soldiers?*"

Belisarius again signaled for the army's horn to blow, diverting the crowd's attention. Archelaus made as though to speak another pronouncement, yet Belisarius silenced him with a swipe of his arm.

"Lord Archelaus stands accused of waging war on Roman citizens, of violating Roman peace, and of the rape and murder of the innocent," Belisarius said. "However, he is correct: as a tribune, it is his right to be charged only in Constantinople, unless the purported crime is a serious infraction against Roman military law."

Archelaus sneered. Indeed, many senior commanders in Rome's past had avoided such charges by never returning to the capitol, thus retaining their military authority and escaping justice they so richly deserved.

The crowd bellowed, some even weeping at the injustice of their accused being able to escape condemnation for the similarly destructive deeds paid to Scythian Neapolis. As spearmen cordoned the crowd into sections in an attempt to pacify the worst of their anger, Mundus limped forward. His voice was hoarse and barely audible over the din but, leaning on his spear, he bellowed with all the strength remaining to him.

"I have served Lord Archelaus for years. He is a skilled soldier, perhaps one of the best Rome has ever produced," Mundus croaked. "But I have watched his talents slide in service of drunkenness and wrath. I, Mundus, a komes of the Imperial Army, accuse him of abuse of authority and dereliction of duty by knowingly sending his subordinates on pointless, suicidal errands."

Archelaus' face grew red, veins pulsing along his throat. Yet he said nothing as Belisarius' men circled around the tribune, waiting for instructions. No others spoke, and the duty to respond to the latest provocation fell to Belisarius.

"Lord Archelaus has been accused of a capital crime by a senior officer, yet no others have taken up this accusation. By Roman law, I cannot act unless other officers can testify to the direct knowledge of these claims." As he finished, the general's eyes found me in the crowd, unblinking.

The crowd grew silent. Archelaus' pulsing rage faded into a cruel sneer as he peered throughout the ranks, daring anyone to be foolish enough to question the excubitor. As men shuffled in place, my gaze broke away from Belisarius and landed on Rosamund. She bit her lip as she returned my stare, breathing heavily and ignoring the spearmen that crowded around her. For a few heartbeats, I remained motionless. She shut her eyes tightly, gritting her teeth as she shook her head in frustration. Overcome, she masked her face with slim fingers and turned away from the square, showing her back to Archelaus and me alike. With that, my heart tugged with a need to bring her some measure of comfort, this girl who had unquestioningly accompanied me to the northern reaches of an empire that had slaughtered her people and left her utterly vulnerable to the violent lusts of foreign men. As my hand grazed the dragon-headed hilt of my sword, I heard the Emperor's voice in my head once more.

"Take this gift from me in hopes that you will use it to make a better world. Never forget who you are and all you must do, to see our shared dream become reality."

And so, for love of a friend and out of duty to my father, I bet my future on a single throw of the soldiers' dice, leaving my fate to live or die in the hands of God. As I spoke the first of those long-delayed words, I knew I had chosen properly.

"I, Varus of the Heruli, a centurion of the Imperial Army, accuse Lord Archelaus of abuse of authority and dereliction of duty. His wrath led to the death of hundreds in the Gepid lands, the sack of the Roman village of Scythian Neapolis, and the senseless death of dekarchos Isaacius, a Jew and a hero of the Roman Empire," I proclaimed. Outside of his close friends and Archelaus, most likely did not know of Isaacius' hidden faith, yet it mattered little by that time. Isaacius was dead, and beyond the reach of even the cruelest minds that inhabited the Empire's army.

At the sound of my voice, Rosamund faced me from across the forum, eyes widened and face flushed of color even as she nodded. Perenus and Cephalas slapped their spears into their shields, and others within Mundus' banda soon echoed. Even Belisarius nodded, then whispered a message to John.

But most remarkable was when another accusation joined my own, sealing Archelaus' charge.

"And I, Troglita, a son of Rome and centurion of its armies, also accuse Lord Archelaus of the crimes that Mundus and Varus have already described. It is a black stain on the memory of the Caesars, and must be cleansed." The stamp of a spear sealed the statement.

An uproar flooded over the villagers and the formation, and Archelaus bounded toward the edge of the stage. His blazing eyes were ready to kill. Teeth bared at me, he pointed in my direction but said nothing.

But Belisarius would not be stopped. "It is done. As the acting strategos of this expedition, I place Lord Archelaus under arrest, to await trial in Cherson for his crimes against the people of Rome."

At this pronouncement, many cheered, while others looked worriedly around, unsure of what was going to happen next. The Thracian Army had already lost its first commander, and despite Archelaus' many flaws, he was a competent leader who had a rare, solid history of victory against Rome's enemies. Archelaus himself only narrowed his eyes at his three accusers, then went for Belisarius. With a melodramatic shake of his head, he shouted once more for the attentions of Scythian Neapolis.

"I do not recognize the authority of these men to judge me. I demand my right to a trial by single combat, and leave it for God to be my judge," he yelled, eliciting a wave of excited whispers among the crowd.

In all my years of war and slaughter, single combat has always been the most savage, the most desperate, and the least likely to yield a just outcome. It lacked the trust and camaraderie of the shield wall or the logistics of a siege, preferring instead to pit the brute strength and raw guile of one warrior against another under the pretense of justice and honor. Though single combat had been long beloved in Roman battles, it had not become a custom in military justice until Anastasius' time, influenced by the thousands of tribesmen who took the Emperor's gold in return for service in battle. I have rarely seen such a duel end with both combatants alive and whole, though custom dictated that the victor's righteousness was determined by the blood of the vanquished.

These duels were yet another cruel defilement of the old Empire, and now would allow Archelaus the ability to escape punishment for his many sins. And, for the life of me, I have seen few men better suited for single combat than the komes, a towering figure of strength and experience that relished the killing stroke to his enemies.

Bound by law, Belisarius nodded. "Very well. The trial shall be conducted after dawn tomorrow. The accusers must select their champion, as must Lord Archelaus."

Archelaus guffawed. "I choose myself, and I will break all three of these traitorous catamites if need be."

All eyes in the forum fell upon we three accusers, with few in the crowd dissipating as we met to decide who would face Archelaus. In hushed tones, Mundus spoke first. "I'm the eldest and the most experienced. I'll skewer this bastard and be done with it. Nobody knows Archelaus as well as I." He spoke with confidence, yet winced as he shifted his weight onto his spear.

Troglita disagreed. "You are too wounded to fight, and Varus has others that rely upon him for their livelihoods. I will fight Archelaus." He eyed both of us for consent.

Somehow, Samur had snuck in behind us, as always, unwilling to sit back and watch the proceedings. "Archelaus has never seen me fight, and I have no rank or future of note. I have nothing to lose, and I want this bastard dead," he said, the viciousness in his voice surprising.

"No," I said simply. All eyes were back upon me. "It has to be me."

As I spoke, my thoughts drifted to so many who'd shaped my life, from the Emperor and Liberius, to Godilas and Isaacius, to the old priest, and even the fiery mysticism of Rosamund and my senseless longing for Mariya. Though I held no assurance to win a fight against a man like Archelaus, an unbreakable pride swelled within me; I was determined that I would never again run from the man who had caused so much harm to those dear to my heart. Mundus, Samur, and Troglita all drew closer, muttering responses of surprise and reluctance.

"For Rosamund, for Isaacius… this is my fight. I alone have the right to finish it."

Samur protested, and Mundus wheezed as he sought to argue, yet Troglita spoke above both. "Don't be a fool, Varus. You have so many who depend upon you. If you perish, they will all fall into destitution and ruin."

Yet my mind was fixed. "Thank you, friend, but no. I swore an oath to obey God, protect the weak, and to live my life with honor, and I have let that promise abate for too long. I will fight Archelaus tomorrow morning. But I would not say no to your prayers and support, both for my soul, and for those I may leave behind."

Our meeting was disrupted by Archelaus. "Any one of you will do, just pick. But I cannot wait all day for an answer." He chuckled, and low, forced laughter trickled from his officers.

"I will fight you," I called out, though with less boldness than I would have liked.

Archelaus smirked but offered no retort. The legal rituals satisfied, with no objections or irregularities, Belisarius set the trial and dismissed the formation, which marched out of the village gates and toward our encampment.

"All I wanted you to do was support me, not to fight him!" Rosamund seized upon me. "Don't be a fool! Let one of the others fight that monster."

I smiled with a confidence I did not quite feel. "If I decline Archelaus' challenge, I'll never be able to look upon you with respect again," I said, "nor any of the many others who have had their lives ruined by that man."

Rosamund sighed. "What is it with you men? Better to live free than die an honorable corpse. The winds blow the ashes of the cruel and the holy with equal indifference."

"True," I said. "Nevertheless, it is what I want, and I will do it regardless. Still, I would prefer to part with your blessing."

Rosamund bounded forward, wrapped her arms around my neck, and planted a kiss on my cheek in an abrupt shift from her previous frustration. Her lips grazed my ear as she mumbled in our shared Heruli tongue.

"If you must, kill this bastard tomorrow for both of us," she whispered. "Don't leave me alone in this world."

"Never," I promised.

And so we parted, Rosamund remaining in the town while I ventured back to the camp outside its walls. In those brief moments of peace, I imagined the years to come with Rosamund at my side, leaving behind Archelaus and this foolish duel in favor of companionship and freedom along the plains. In such fantasies, Samur, Perenus, and Cephalas were never far away, members of our tiny camp as we trailed herds of game. And yet whenever I looked closely upon Rosamund in this imagined life, I saw only Mariya, a woman I had no right to desire, a woman who likely saw me as no more than an opportunity for diverting conversation. I know: I was a fool, desiring the impossible and declining the attainable, yet I was never quite able to master my heart.

Though the thought of freedom and the company of friends were lovely notions, in that moment, they were born of pure fear as the realization of my choices came to bear. And as I reentered my tent, it occurred to me that this might be my last evening in this world, and there was no promised Heaven sweet enough to stem my fear.

The excubitor was placed under guard and not allowed to leave the camp nor approach within twenty paces of my position. Belisarius similarly ordered guards to shadow my movements, but my own men insisted upon taking that responsibility for themselves. Perenus and Cephalas each embraced me in turn, insisting that I would take down the old tyrant and avenge Isaacius' memory. Perenus offered me wine, for which Samur scolded him. "Varus needs his wits tomorrow, all right? Make sure none disturb his sleep," said my brother.

It was Samur who kept a close watch on me that evening, and at one occasion even begged me to let him take my place. I refused again, and he accepted the answer glumly. Finally, I collapsed onto my straw mat, awoken hours later by the old priest, who I tried to shrug off and preserve the last remaining hours of rest available to me. Yet the old man was not deterred, until I finally shot up and looked him in the face.

"Prayer can wait," I said sullenly. "I need to rest. I am to fight Archelaus."

"Do you know the story of David and Goliath?" the priest continued, knowing full well I did.

I yawned, nodded, and rubbed my eyes. A wave of melancholy broke over me. I wanted nothing more than to leave the tent, grab the first horse I could find, and ride to the sea.

Unperturbed, he went on. "Yes, as do most. Goliath was a great beast of a Philistine, and would have looked upon David only with mockery and scorn. By any measure of his day, David was a mere boy and not entitled to any great future, but still God chose him to strike down the enemies of Israel and prove himself king above all—"

"Father," I interrupted, "I take your meaning. But Archelaus truly is a beast, and God has not spoken to me as he did David. Archelaus has even defeated me once before!"

The priest placed his soft and frail hands atop my own. "Varus, if you cannot look into your past and see God's hand lifting you up, then your eyes are shut to the truth. You made a bold decision yesterday, yet now comes the hour where you must stand for what is righteous."

To the priest's surprise, and perhaps my own, I fell to my knees and pressed his weathered knuckles to my forehead. As the priest lay his other hand along my scalp, I confessed to him. "Father, I'm afraid." A single tear ran down my face.

The truth of the words was a shock, where yesterday I had little time to reflect upon my actions. Archelaus was greater than any Goliath—he was the enemy that had bullied all my loved ones into silence in his drive to serve Rome.

The priest spoke in a low voice, his outstretched hand still as his voice rolled in soothing and familiar tones. "I know, my son. All who face such trials are. Yet what defines our heroes is their courage to act in the face of their fears. God does not shield us from darkness but grants us the fortitude to see ourselves through it." The priest guided me back to my feet before patting me lightly on the cheek.

The priest administered the sacrament, and soon thereafter a horn blared through the camp, signaling the break of dawn and for camp life to continue for another day. As the priest left my tent, he faced me one final time.

"I am proud of you, Varus. And Godilas would be, too."

Thick storm clouds gathered overhead, and a light sprinkle of rain fell to the grass and dust along the Tauric plain. Rain was a welcome sight to an area desperately in need of water, yet I could not watch the sky with anything but fear that a downpour would interfere with my duel with Archelaus—to my disadvantage.

Perenus, Cephalas, and Samur greeted me outside of my tent, offering food and water in preparation for the day. Feeling nauseous, I declined the meal and drank sparingly of the waterskin. Samur helped me into my armor, and once equipped, I nodded my readiness to head into the village. My men formed their own small column around me, joined by Troglita's soldiers as we marched out of the encampment. Too weak to walk, Mundus rode on a horse at the head of the column, and we entered Scythian Neapolis with a salute to the sentries watching our approach.

The Last Dying Light

The forum had been declared the site of the duel and was already lined with villagers jostling for the best viewing angles of the clearing. Makeshift platforms had been assembled for some, while others leaned from the magistrate's building for an overhead view of the square. Belisarius had already arrived and busied himself with preparations for the day, including the commission of a clerk from Cherson named Procopius who would detail the case and its outcome.

At my arrival, Belisarius walked to my position, parting the ranks of my retinue. He drew close, gruffly told me he prayed for my victory, and clasped his arm around mine. Our brief exchange ended, he returned to his dais, awaiting Archelaus' arrival. Unarmed, I took my place near the center of the forum, unsure of what formalities to observe next. As I faded into my thoughts, a low thumping sounded along the edge of the forum, and I found Perenus slamming the butt of his spear into the ground. Others of my retinue joined in, augmenting a deep thunder of noise that echoed over the village square.

A low chant arose from Samur, which also spread throughout the formation like wildfire. I struggled to make out their words, but when the citizens of Scythian Neapolis picked up the call, it was unmistakable.

"Varus! Varus! Varus!" they cried, hundreds of voices filling the forum. Some also called words of encouragement, and a rare few demanded I butcher that bastard Archelaus. Through it all, I nodded, swaying lightly to the sound of my name.

The cheering ground to a slow halt as Archelaus emerged from a squat stone building that had served as his headquarters, followed by Solomon and a dozen of the Thracian Army's veteran officers. He wore all the finery of a veteran of many wars and a senior leader of Roman soldiers, his excubitor's armor a thick cage of steel around much of his body, and his tribune's helm making him appear far taller.

Archelaus stalked to the center of the forum a scant dozen paces from me. He inspected my appearance and smirked. Rain began to fall, the light trickle swiftly giving way to a heavier shower that did not impair vision but left a chill. Father Petrus arrived and gave a blessing onto both men and disappeared back into the crowd. The Christian rituals observed, Belisarius signaled for quiet. Archelaus and I both faced the dais and saluted.

"Lord Archelaus, excubitor, tribune of Rome, you stand accused of wrath, of dereliction of military office, and of the wanton rape and slaughter of Roman citizens. You have voided your right to a military tribunal in Cherson for a trial by single combat. Your opponent is Varus, a centurion of Rome, champion of your accusers."

Archelaus grunted in assent. Several villagers cheered at the sound of my name, yet fell silent as they hung upon Belisarius' words. He explained that we were each allowed one set of arms — instructions that had been offered to us the evening before. Archelaus chose a massive two-handed sword that was permitted only to the excubitores, its blade nearly the length of a man and marked by deep channels that ran from the blade's tip up to its hilt. He tested the blade, swinging it with ease as gusts of air flew from its wake.

Samur brought me my weapons — the simple wooden shield of a spearman and the Emperor's blade, cleaned and sharpened for this occasion. We embraced, and he handed me the sword, removed it from its sheath, and returned to the crowd. Rosamund held onto my dagger, which had been returned to her after we reunited at Scythian Neapolis days prior. Her face was a mask of grief, yet she smiled weakly as I caught her gaze.

I ran a hand over the sword's runes, and gripped tightly that dragon pommel I had stared at for hours as a child. I instinctively felt for my bronze cross, which hung beside Mariya's golden dragon at my neck. I lowered my centurion's helmet onto my head, secured its straps, and faced Archelaus for the final time.

Belisarius gave the instructions for the bout.

"This is a fight to the death, with victory signaling the truth behind these accusations. The decision of this duel is final, and there will be no appeal. May God grant favor upon those who fight on the side of truth."

He stilled for a moment. And then, amid falling rain and the roar of the crowd, Belisarius dropped his arm. The duel began.

On cue, Archelaus darted toward me, droplets splashing from his armor. His monstrous blade swung a wide arc at my torso, and I blocked it, barely, with the iron rim of my shield, sparks flying into the air. He drew back, a large dent marring the shield's edge as he tugged the blade free. Swiftly, before I could regroup, Archelaus jabbed his blade at either side of my head. All I could do was parry.

I saw his grin behind the clash of our swords. He was pressing me back with his weight.

"Jews, Gepids, and backwater northerners… quality company you keep," he shouted, throwing an elbow into my gut. The blow was soft, no real danger, yet it sobered me all the same.

His massive blade always held me two paces away. I could never get within striking distance of his flanks, let alone his chest; whenever I attempted to move closer, Archelaus would bring his sword down hard enough to cut droplets of rain in half as they fell. Somehow, he always had his blade ready for a downward strike, never wasting a moment hefting the hunk of iron for a killing blow.

I backed away from another slash, but my right foot slipped in a growing puddle of mud and rainwater, forcing me to drop me to a knee. Archelaus swung his blade down like a scythe, faster than my instincts could rebuff. I clumsily hoisted my shield and caught Archelaus' blade on its topmost rim. The blade sliced into the shield a full handbreadth and sliced a gash into my shoulder. I cried out as blood bubbled from under the torn steel, and Archelaus merely laughed. He tore his blade from my shield and cut down again with enough force to fell a sapling.

I dodged, thank God, rolling off to the side and covering my body with my splintering shield. Slick with rainwater, I arranged my feet and did my best to ignore the pulsing pain in my arm and the draining strength in my shield hand. Archelaus grunted and approached me in all his anger, sending a flurry of swift thrusts toward my face and chest.

We traded blows, yet Archelaus never lost control of the dance as he drove me ever backward. I forced my attention on my breathing, fighting back a continual sense of panic and the desire to find a way out of the fight. I needed to end this. A quick conclusion, before my strength gave out or Archelaus' sheer skill overcame my own. I thought of the slight limp on his sword leg, the one that had given me some small advantage in our first bout. As he transferred weight from one leg to another, I timed the rhythm of Archelaus' blows.

Archelaus mocked me, insulting my friends, calling me a traitorous cunt. Near exhaustion, I conserved my energy as Archelaus landed continuous blows upon my shield and sword, and waited for the exact moment when he shifted weight onto the damaged leg. I launched from my own sword leg, directing my shield at Archelaus' chin, landing within his blade's reach.

Archelaus grabbed my shield with a free hand, laughing as his breath flooded my nostrils.

"Can't fool me with that trick again, you fucking savage," he jeered, chopping his sword at my shield.

I tore away, but not before he carved away a third of the shield's outer edge, rendering it useless. I loosened its straps and let it fall away from my arm. Free from its weight, I saw a triumphant look dawn on Archelaus' face.

Undiminished in strength, he ran at me with incredible speed for a man of his size. Though I had always been bigger than most others, I was diminutive next to Archelaus. His sheer bulk gave him an edge over any enemy. I could raise my sword against his blows, yet the weight of his blade threatened to press down into my flesh even if it was parried.

And so it was as Archelaus swung a dangerously low arc toward my hips. I blocked it, but the momentum of the massive blade carried its honed edge into my hip nonetheless, where it cut through mail and leather and bit skin. I pushed away, yet could feel the strength leaving my left leg. I fought to remain upright, blood flowing freely down my leg and pooling into my boot.

Archelaus paused, to my surprise. "That Gepid witch," he said with oily satisfaction, "I think I will have a go with her when I am done with you. She can warm my bed, and then I will pass her around to my men. What do you think?"

I growled at my enemy and charged with a vigor and resolve that I no longer really possessed. The excubitor knocked the blows away harmlessly, laughing all the while. I fell back as his jabs and arcs rained down, leaving me no room for any further attacks.

As his blows threatened to cave the rest of my armor, I stumbled into a growing puddle, sloshing mud and water around my ankles. I slipped again, dropping to a knee as blood poured from my shoulder and hip.

Archelaus roared in victory and swung his sword down on my defenseless form. As his blade passed eye level, I lunged forward with all of my remaining strength for my one and only time of the match. His eyes bulged, his speech interrupted mid-taunt, his sword dropping from his mailed hands.

My final trick had worked; the Emperor's sword jutted clean through Archelaus' body and out of his armor just below the ribs.

Blood burbled from Archelaus' mouth as he choked for air. He dropped to his knees, mud and water surging onto him. I jerked his helmet free as his head torqued toward mine, his face a grotesque mask between hatred and sadness. Quivering lips tried to speak, but he coughed up another gob of blood and kept silent.

I leaned close to ensure he could hear me and stared into his eyes.

"This is for Isaacius, a Roman hero," I said, drawing the blade from Archelaus' body.

Archelaus let out a long, tortured gasp as the blade cut from flesh and bone, yet still he fought to sit straight as I raised my blade over my head. He shot me one final look, a look absent his famed malice and scorn in the training yard, a kind of calm pain—acceptance.

In one smooth motion, I swept my sword down and severed the excubitor's head from his body.

The crowd roared in approval, and I raised my sword to the blackened sky. Yet I soon collapsed to the ground myself, all strength drained. My senses dimmed as I lost consciousness, my arm and leg bloodlessly numb.

The Last Dying Light

THE ARMY OF FLAVIUS BELISARIUS

I DID NOT WAKE UNTIL early the next morning, my head pounding and throat parched. I gathered my senses and tried to sit up, only to be resisted by the cooing of Rosamund, who sat over my body.

"No, Varus, you must be still!" Her tone was firm, but her hands were gentle as she guided me back to the mat.

I had been stripped from the waist up, and could feel a burning and scratching from the wounds that scoured my hip and shoulder. Rosamund applied a salve that cooled and calmed me, and I lay prostrate as she fed me small sips of water from a silver cup. She tore off small pieces of bread, and I ate greedily even as I fought an aching soreness rippling from my chest toward my stomach.

She sat silently over me as I ate, her brow creased with worry but her lips curved with satisfaction. The cut along my hip itched terribly, but when I went to scratch, Rosamund smacked my hand away from the thin rows of stitching forcing the flesh together. Satisfied that I would not struggle and reopen my wounds, she lay next to me, an arm gently draped across my chest.

"Thank you, Varus," she whispered. "Thank you."

Ignoring the din of the camp outside, we lay there for some indeterminate length of time. Dazed in every possible sense, I still did not fully comprehend Archelaus' death, and I was lost in a dreamlike state from either some pagan elixir that Rosamund had brewed me or from a simple loss of blood. Nevertheless, lying prone in recovery, my thoughts drifted to Rosamund's denouncement of Archelaus, and the look on her face when she met my gaze. Her anger, her despair, her disappointment... I had to wonder if she still harbored resentment against the Empire itself, resentment beyond just Archelaus. Perhaps, even, against me. But as I lacked the vigor (or, indeed, the courage) to interrupt my rest with such concerns, I convinced myself that any lingering bitterness had been washed clean with the excubitor's blood.

Our tranquility was soon disrupted by prying eyes from the camp. As the sun faded, my tent flap was pushed open, and Samur's head poked through the gap.

"Varus!" The joy was palpable in his words. He rushed in and kneeled at my side, chattering a happy stream that I knew concealed a graver worry.

Samur's voice soon drew others, and Perenus and Cephalas joined in to wish me well. Even Troglita stopped in, momentarily ignoring his duties as the acting commander of his banda. With all my friends and fellows thus gathered, my tent grew hot and crowded, and Rosamund eventually gave the crowd a light smack and ordered them to leave.

"He must rest!" Rosamund exclaimed in heavily accented Greek. "You will make him hurt himself!"

But I did not wish to rest, and I patted her on the hand and asked for help to my feet. Rosamund scowled, but carefully took one of my shoulders under her body and motioned for Samur to hold the other. Together, they hoisted me upright. Unable to dress due to the bruises and cuts that lined my body, I walked into the camp's training ground shirtless, the sun stinging my eyes.

Several spearmen had already risen to practice in the training yard, their wooden swords thudding together in an organized barrage. Several stopped and stared at me as I walk from my tent, and a slow applause grew throughout the camp. Many swarmed my position, clapping me on the back and shouting dozens of questions before Rosamund shooed them back, fearful of the stitches on my shoulder and hip. As the cheering subsided, many still circled around me, narrating the fight as they experienced it from their vantage point. Even Mundus, hobbling in my direction, smiled, and at last clasped my hand with respect.

"That was a brave thing you did, and a noble one. I am only sorry that I couldn't take that burden on myself."

Some officers, despite the praise, were conspicuously silent in their acclaim. Solomon was one, and he avoided my gaze to busy himself with his reports. My rival had lost the patronage first of Godilas and later Archelaus, and his future position in the Thracian Army was uncertain as a new officer rose to command. Archelaus clearly bore little respect for unblooded sycophants, yet ultimately was amenable to Solomon's silver tongue and willingness to enforce the tribune's orders. In the weeks, even months, to come, many would praise my stand against Archelaus, but low grumbling and disdain never seemed far behind.

My wounds left me in no condition to train, so Belisarius granted me a week's reprieve from the rigors of camp life. He assured me I could take all the time needed to heal, but—as he told me—assumed that I would quickly tire of the tedium of lying on mats and submitting to healers. I smiled as he took my arm within his—gently—and thanked me. My place and safety in his army, he assured me, was secure.

Two weeks passed, and my skin mended its deep gashes. Training with swords and spears was an agony in those initial days of recovery, and I tired far quicker than I was used to. But Rosamund's care ensured my gradual improvement, while Samur executed my orders and assisted with my training while I was at half strength.

My brother had, in my absence, even grown close to the Hunnic leader Sunicas, who had been giving him opportunities to ride with his horse archers. In the second week of my recovery, I found Samur sitting around the Hunnic campfire, his face enraptured by the soldiers' tales of Bleda, Ellac, and Attila, his old favorite, most of all. Bemused in the solitude of my tent, I at last questioned such changes in Samur's bearing.

The Last Dying Light

"The Huns do not turn their noses to Heruli as the Greeks do," Samur chirped. "And Sunicas has need of a rider who can read and write, so I'm useful to them!"

"Indeed, but are you sure this is a path that's wise to follow?"

"Varus, I will never be a famous spearman," Samur said. "I'm not burly enough for the shield wall, and these Romans will not treat my advancement as anything more than an appeasement of you."

"Samur—"

"Varus, you *know* it to be true. The Huns have none of the Roman jealousy or hypocrisy, and Sunicas thinks I'm a born archer."

I nodded. "I suppose… if you are sure, Samur. And as long as you will be safe."

"Absolutely certain, especially as we'll be fighting together." Samur nodded back. "And after Godilas… this is an opportunity to make something different of myself, more than a freed barbarian slave."

I worried still at my brother's training, but I soon came to see Sunicas as an honest and honorable a man as I had ever met. And even if he were a fiend, it quickly became obvious that, as he hardened Samur's body for the saddle and rejoiced as his expertise as a mounted archer grew, Sunicas enjoyed Samur's company, and that, at least, he and I would always share. I never failed to start at the sight of Samur's Hunnic furs, but Samur was content in his company, and after a life of so much disappointment, his contentment was all I desired for him.

Though Sunicas' dark complexion and wrinkled nose gave him a permanent expression of anger that warded off many of our fellows, I found him to be a joyful and black-humored rogue whose jokes were often levied at the expense of Rome. Alongside Samur, Sunicas assisted my rehabilitation by offering training with a Hunnic bow, which recurved in a manner that could drive a hardened arrow a handbreadth deep into even the firmest tree trunk. Sunicas and I came to share many meals in our weeks together near Scythian Neapolis, accompanied often by the Hunnic commander's shadow—my brother.

While I mended, Belisarius' men grew busy preparing for the upcoming expedition. Fresh supplies had arrived from Constantinople, although Justinian had sent few of the promised reinforcements that the Thracian Army desperately needed. Nevertheless, Belisarius sought to pacify the southern coast of Tauris, even taking measures to resettle Kerkinitis and Theodosia as outer bulwarks of Cherson.

Samur and Perenus took turns bringing news to my tent. I learned that the Avars had regrouped under the warlord Tzul along the Boristhenis River far to the north and turned their might back to the Tauric Peninsula. Avar riders scoured the plains and disrupted supply caravans, yet fewer scouts were killed as Belisarius' relay strategy bore fruit. Detachments of Roman spearmen or riders were under strict orders to avoid making open camp in undefended areas of Tauris' interior, and to never halt their progress in the presence of fog or storms. Belisarius occupied most of the Tauric coastline, going so far as to briefly reoccupy Kalos Limin and even Tanais at the far end of Lake Maeotis.

Yet the Avars still held the bulk of the interior land, leaving few opportunities for tilling the soil or harvesting crops for the winter. Supplies from the capitol sustained the army, but pressure mounted upon Belisarius to act, retake the fields, and forestall the famine that threatened the province's citizens.

Germanus, the new interim commander of the Thracian Army, was set to task to fill all vacancies, whether from battle or from the deaths of his predecessors. For his second, he chose Mundus, who accepted the position with the same even temperament as always. Yet I was taken aback when Germanus named me the temporary commander of our banda, and tasked me with getting a number of the recruits, newly arrived from Constantinople, into shape. In turn, I tasked Perenus with their training as I healed, handing him a centurion's plume as proof of his newfound authority. He drilled our banda from dawn until dusk each day, leaving the men too weary to move or venture into the village for wine and women each evening.

As Germanus gained familiarity with command of the Thracian Army, Belisarius' calls for meetings among the senior leaders of the expedition grew more frequent. The most important of these was called the day after my promotion and had been inspired by the latest of the growing Avar attacks upon Roman settlements and even upon the hinterlands of Scythian Neapolis itself.

As I entered Belisarius' tent, I found a number of older commanders deep in conversation with the general. Troglita congratulated me on my newfound, albeit temporary, position. We stood together as Belisarius rapped the meeting to order and pinned a vellum map to a large circular table at the center of his tent.

Where Archelaus had dominated these meetings through the sheer force of his presence, Belisarius took pains to listen to the ideas of his subordinates, even if his meetings ran late into the night. His second, John of Armenia, read a number of scouting reports that detailed the movements of our foe.

"Even if we discount the more skittish spies, we can conservatively number the Avars at some thirty thousand fighting men at minimum, and maybe more. Our reports say that Khagan Kazrig has entered the peninsula with their entire horde, taking personal command of its movements," John said, flipping through vellum scrolls dotted with ink of our scouting reports and maps of the region.

"And how many men do we now have under arms?" Germanus asked. "How badly do they outnumber us?"

"Discounting those who are guarding other towns and villages along the coast, the sick, and those too wounded to ride or fight, we have a bit over six thousand men ready to fight, one third of them on horseback," John answered, only a slight waver in his voice. The Avars, as he numbered it, stood five to one against our army.

Silence settled over the officers. Though I shared their worry, such unbalanced odds did not surprise me, for, even weeks after Godilas' battle in the mist, I could still hear the screams of Romans dragged away from the wall, and the howls of black-shielded tribesmen swarming over our lines. As Germanus paled, I wondered not whether our victory was possible, but whether God would allow me to survive yet another stand against the horde.

"Can we just wait for them to ride away?" asked Baduarius, a Gothic tribune of Belisarius' spearmen. "If they have no siege weapons, they must eventually leave when winter arrives. It would be the only way to continue to feed so many men and horses."

Baduarius was one who seemed chiseled from the boulders that lined the hills of Greece. His arms and chest rippled with muscle, but his skin was marked with scars from a lifetime of war against Rome's enemies. Still, rugged appearance aside, he had been nothing but friendly since our initial meeting, where he'd offered a throaty laugh and a painful smack across my shoulders in commendation for my skill against Archelaus. In the meeting, I silently urged Belisarius to heed Baduarius' notion, sparing the army a further battle against a vast foe.

Yet Baduarius' ideas were soon cast aside by a darker-skinned cavalry officer. Where Baduarius was sociable to the point of gregariousness, the Armenian Bessas' taciturn nature left him a stranger to me. I would come to know him to be as forthright and dedicated as Belisarius' other officers, yet in that initial gathering of the officers, I only saw one of Belisarius' fabled cataphracts, those thickly armored horsemen who fought with lance and bow alike and had little need to be loquacious.

Bessas raised his hand. "The Avars don't think like most civilized men," he said. "I've ridden the plains and tracked their movements. We've wounded Kazrig's pride by shaming his son; we have made him look weak. If he does not turn back to annihilate us now, his rule will be in jeopardy by the year's end."

"That was the Hunnic way," Sunicas added, and his brother Simmas grunted in assent. "Power above all things, that's how we measure our leaders."

Low rumbling grew across the table as smaller conversations took root. Solomon cleared his throat, catching the attention of most in the room. "But if they invade, what option do we have but to sit back behind trenches and walls? Five to one against the Avars in pitched combat… you saw what they did to Godilas' forces."

"We'll learn from previous mistakes." I all but snarled the words at Solomon, wanting more to shame my longtime rival than to force a battle. "We won't be surprised when we meet the Avars again."

"Certainly," Bessas put in. "But be wary, all we faced was a sliver of the Avar forces, and Kazrig will bring the entire horde to bear against us. Bloodied riders and veterans of innumerable skirmishes on the eastern plains."

John rapped on the table. "Yes, but you didn't have Belisarius then. That's worth ten thousand screaming riders alone!"

Though many of Belisarius' longstanding officers slapped the table in a rolling drum of assent, Solomon would not be denied his voice against further action.

"Yes, but we *did* have Godilas!" Solomon said, visibly exasperated. "The Empire's most seasoned general. If we couldn't defeat the smaller portion of the Avar outriders, how can we expect to do any better, Belisarius or no?"

Many eyes fell to Belisarius, who sat at the table's head, his eyes entranced upon the map of Tauris. Lingering side conversations dwindled as the meeting's attention settled upon the general, who patiently waited to see if any others might offer an opinion on the matter. After several heartbeats of silence, however, Belisarius finally rose from his chair, leaning over the map as he pronounced his will.

"We'll attack them directly," Belisarius said flatly.

"Lord?" Germanus sounded concerned.

Belisarius, however, was unfazed. "We will march out to engage battle, and will encircle them on an open plain."

Loud outbursts filled the tent, the loudest voices of dissent largely rising from the remaining Thracian officers. Above them all was Solomon, his chin held high and brow furrowed in distaste for such perceived foolishness.

"General, a small force as ours cannot keep and hold a ring around such a large force as the Avars, even if they were less-capable fighters. Such a thing is impossible."

But it was not. Improbable, certainly. Unfavorable, absolutely. But from Liberius' lessons to Godilas' stories, one tale struck a mixture of awe and dread in many a Roman's heart, a battle that seemed half myth even as a youth uncorrupted by the grinding disappointment and loss that comes with age.

"Cannae." I spoke softly, yet I caught Belisarius' attention all the same.

"Precisely," he said. "Hannibal proved to us that such a thing not only could be done, but how to execute it."

All men and women delude themselves into believing that their deeds will live for eternity. In my twilight, such naivety seems laughable, yet even I, too, once entertained such desires. Of those whose names shall live forever, however, Hannibal is one that shall live beyond when my bones are turned to dust, for he achieved a feat that all felt must be impossible. Even as a young boy, I gaped in awe at the seven-hundred-year-old tale, when Hannibal led a few thousand exhausted, sickly, and battered Carthaginian soldiers to the fields of Apulia and into battle against a fresh and vastly larger Roman foe. Yet, through guile and tactics alone, Hannibal goaded his enemy from one mistake to the next until the Roman infantry was encircled, their superior numbers becoming a rank disadvantage in the suffocating crush of bodies. Of the eighty thousand, only a handful survived to escape back to Rome, with the rest pressed and butchered from all sides.

With his officers sitting in rapt attention, Belisarius laid out his proposal for how he would make use of Hannibal's strategy to save a Roman province so many generations later.

"The Cappadocian Army will approach from the south, holding the center position. The Thracians"—Belisarius nodded at Germanus—"will be divided along either flank."

Belisarius nudged wooden pieces around the map, repositioning his armies around a mass of black figures that faced the Cappadocians. The Cappadocians were positioned ahead of their flanks, closer to the Avar army.

"Baduarius will command the Cappadocian spears, and will bait the Avars to charge at his position. Ascum will lead the archers and Baduarius' reserves."

Germanus raised an eyebrow, while his second raised a question. "How are you going to goad the Avars into battle?" Mundus cried. "We can't even speak their language!"

Baduarius chuckled. "Leave that to me. We've learned a lot from our two captives. The Avars are vicious but headstrong. Prideful."

Belisarius nodded. "On my signal, the Thracians will move in a crescent away from and around the Avars, pushing hard toward their other side. Sunicas and Simmas will each protect one side, but their only objective is to keep the Avars penned in." As he spoke, Belisarius slid pieces around the rear of the Avars, with a smaller Roman army guarding the northern route from their barbarian foe.

As Belisarius' plan unfolded, I was stunned at its sophistication, desperate to hope that it might come to pass. Yet I also grew wary at Belisarius' insistence that the Thracian spearmen would form an impenetrable wall against the Avars' rearguard, knowing full well that such a maneuver was as difficult to execute as it was exhausting even to attempt. Even at a dead sprint, the weight of weapons and armor would leave us pitiably slow to close Belisarius' circle, giving the Avars more than enough time to counterattack.

My concerns were given voice by another Gothic officer named Dagisthaeus, who I had learned was brother to Baduarius. Though swarthy and looming as his kin, Dagisthaeus lacked the overwhelming bulk that shaped Baduarius as a born brawler. Further, where Baduarius fought on foot, Dagisthaeus preferred the swift combat of horseback, where he led large segments of Belisarius' forces on sweeping motions—such as was proposed here.

"Even if they run quickly, in full armor, the Avars are too swift to be penned in by Roman soldiers marching by foot," Dagisthaeus said. "After all, even Hannibal did not have to face many mounted enemies."

"Some good tidings for a change," Bessas said, "but I have more than enough horses for every man in the expedition. We can position ponies on each flank, and the Thracians can mount and gallop off. The Huns will be swifter, and can clear any resistance with their bows."

Sunicas grinned, his long thin beard swaying as he nodded. "The Avars are a steppe people, and will retreat and regroup if they feel that they are losing their edge… it is what I would do. For this to work, Baduarius will need to draw the bulk of the Avar force far south, bending his lines without breaking."

"Damned right I won't break!" Baduarius cracked merrily. Surprised by his coarseness, I failed to stifle a chuckle, which in turn drew a wink from the burly spearman.

"The two halves of the crescent will meet on the north end of the circle, with Germanus and Mundus commanding the left and right halves, respectively," Belisarius said, facing his fellow general. "Your job is not to engage, but to keep any of the Avar spearmen or riders from escaping north." He looked about and found me in his ring of officers. "Varus shall be the first spear, and will command the center banda that holds the northern lines together."

"Well deserved!" Baduarius roared.

"Indeed," added John. "But be wary, Varus. Though you'll have easy going as the battle starts, you must keep any Avars from breaking through your lines. If they do, and we become encircled, none of us will live to see the morrow."

"Cheerful," Dagisthaeus deadpanned. "Varus won't break, will you?"

The conversation would have been overwhelming even if I had been prepared for it. Archelaus had been unpopular, but I'd doubted that I would be rewarded for his slaying. And, as Belisarius smiled his approval, my elation faded into crippling worry, not only that I might fail the expectations of so many hardened veterans, but also that their lives rested in my hands. I had little choice in the matter, however; to abandon such opportunity would see me forever labeled as one who shrank from duty, my victory in the duel notwithstanding. For a Roman, there was no greater dishonor, then or now.

"We'll hold the northern lines, no matter what," I promised.

"I have no doubt," John added with a note of finality. "But how will we bring Varus and the Thracians into position?"

"When the Thracians are in position, John will extend the Cappadocian right flank forward, and Dagisthaeus the left with a larger force," Belisarius said. "I will ride with Bessas and the cataphracts, and close the trap between John and Baduarius." Belisarius pushed more figures forward to complete a circle around the Avars. "Then Sunicas and Simmas will ride around our armies, filling gaps and firing at any attempt of an Avar breakout."

Sunicas chortled. "It will be hard riding, I'll probably kill my horse underneath me."

His brother Simmas shrugged. "Such is life."

With that, the matter was in Belisarius' hands. The group loomed over the map, imagining their place in the grand design.

"I don't need to tell you that any breaks in the line means the death of us all, not merely on the northern front," he said. "The Avars will give us one chance to defeat their whole army, and we must take it to stop them from raiding and burning their way through Tauris for the rest of our lifetimes."

Troglita frowned and traced a finger along the northern edge of the circle. "Lord, the northern lines will be light, especially given the diminished size of the Thracian Army. What if the Avars send a large breakout to the north early, before they are bloodied?"

Belisarius smiled feebly. "Kazrig will attack our Cappadocian lines first. As Bessas said, he needs to attack and defeat us in the field, or forfeit his kingship. It is likely that any breakout will be concerned with the main assault, which will be facing toward our southern lines." He took a moment to survey the assembly. "If the north is under threat, Dagisthaeus will shift his reserves northward to Germanus. I will take whatever cataphracts I can to reinforce the Thracian center, but you must hold your lines, no matter what happens."

Germanus and Mundus nodded sternly. The room was awash with hope and concern at once. The scale of the operation was considerable, yet, as Belisarius said, this was likely the one and only chance that a Roman army had to quell the Avar threat, and if we did not, we faced the overwhelming likelihood of abandoning Cherson to the horde.

"We have much to do, but we need to ride out to meet the Avars before they spread across the peninsula. Practice your maneuvers and prepare to decamp and move out in a week," Belisarius said, and thus drew the meeting to a close.

The officers filed out, with several congratulating me again for my latest honor. I waited behind the rest and asked to speak privately with General Belisarius. He nodded and dismissed his guards, who departed into the night.

Alone, Belisarius sank into a wooden chair and asked of my concerns. His tent fire had burned low, leaving only a dim light to illuminate the tent's interior.

"Lord, I am grateful for the opportunities you have given me... I am just unsure of whether I deserve them."

Internally, I asked a far more pointed question. *Why me? A question for Theodora, Justin, Liberius, Father Petrus... and now Belisarius.*

Belisarius beamed to allay my concerns. "You are no senator's son, Varus, it is true. But opportunities for soldiers like us are not granted; they are earned."

"Yes, of course, but these honors... all for slaying my former commander? Why do so many of the men cheer for such an act?" I asked.

Belisarius sighed. "Archelaus was a peerless soldier, but a terrible man. I do not fault him that—he is what fate and circumstances have made him. Give me a thousand trained soldiers, and I can win you any battle, but give me a dozen good men, and I can build you an empire."

"Why do you trust me with this responsibility?" I prodded.

Belisarius gave another warm smile. "I have been dishonest with you, Varus. Godilas wrote to me of your honor and abilities, and your duel with Archelaus has only confirmed such words. I owe much in life to Godilas, and I have more than enough reason to trust his word."

I considered his words in silence for several heartbeats. As I did, Belisarius poured water into two wooden cups and handed me one.

"Some within the Thracian Army will not forgive you, although your actions against Archelaus were more than just. They will not bother you now. But as soon as we return to Constantinople, they will slap you in chains and drag you through a dozen trials in the Imperial Courts."

My eyes grew wide as I sat back.

"You won't be convicted or condemned," Belisarius said, "but your career, your freedom… will be all but over."

I sat, dejected. What would the Emperor think of me then? Or Liberius? To become a nothing, a disgraced former officer haunted by rumors of slaying his leader… such was the fate of many a beggar that skulked along Constantinople's various gates. The tent walls closed around as fear sapped the strength from my legs.

"After this expedition is over, you and your men may join my army," Belisarius said. "If you would like, that is. We receive few favors from the Emperor, yet we serve Rome as best as we can."

I let out a sigh of relief. "Yes, Lord, of course!" I beamed, and Belisarius let out a light laugh.

"Good!" he said. "Now, you must rest, for your banda will need to practice your horsemanship if we are to defeat the Avars."

I saluted the general and exited, my every fiber alive with eagerness and wonder. I nearly even forgot of the battle ahead, nor that all Belisarius' promises would be for naught if Kazrig's horde broke our bodies in worship of the Avars' dark god.

The Last Dying Light

THE SHIELD WALL

Our remaining days outside of Scythian Neapolis were dedicated to training for Belisarius' battle plan. With horses donated by Bessas, the Thracian Army drilled along the low rolling hills, mounting and dismounting a horse, first from a standing position and later while running. All of this was conducted in full armor, for Belisarius insisted that we train in as realistic a setting as possible.

Sunicas and Bessas oversaw our training. Our first day was largely a disaster, with men leaping up and over their mount and largely unable to move faster than a trot when they succeeded. The Armenian galloped across our lines, indicating the proper manner to mount the saddle and keep formation. Sunicas guffawed at each of our mistakes and chided us as footsore spearmen with no love for the plains.

"I was riding when I was still sucking at my mother's teats," Sunicas said proudly, his bowed legs a testament to his life in the saddle. "Let the horse work for you, not the other way around."

Though I had learned some horsemanship in my youth, Godilas had never given the technique more than half a day at a time, and I struggled alongside my men as I struggled to maintain balance on my horse. Once we were all astride, Sunicas and Bessas led separate sections of the army on extended rides throughout the surrounding area, not returning to camp until well after the sun's setting. I dismounted, my legs crumpling as I rubbed my chafed thighs.

Samur was one of the few who delighted in the training. A born rider, Samur had always loved horses, and regularly cantered ahead of his struggling brethren in the Thracian Army. Though not formally recognized as a trained spearman, Samur was, with Mundus' permission, permitted to join our reduced ranks, having proved his prowess in our previous engagement with the Avars. By the end of the week, Mundus and Germanus administered the soldier's oath to him, which he gave with Perenus, Cephalas, Sunicas, and myself present. I could tell Samur's voice lacked passion when he declared his allegiance to Rome, yet he embraced us with a grin after he joined our brotherhood. Sunicas in particular celebrated Samur's achievement and took my brother riding with the rest of the Huns in their own private exercises.

We would not become accomplished riders in such a short period—and we were told as much by our tutors—yet as the week wore on, fewer mistakes were made, and the pace of our rides increased. The pain and soreness at the end of each day grew less as my legs and back grew accustomed to the saddle, and Rosamund's salves helped ease sore muscles for the next day's exercises. By the end of the sixth day of training, Bessas and Sunicas were content enough with our progress, and reported to Belisarius that we were ready.

As the Thracian Army drilled relentlessly with Bessas' horses, John had moved between the various units and ensured the army's provisions were ready for the march. Additional horses and oxen had been acquired to carry replacement spears and armor for each man, as well as the vast barrels and crates of food, water, and wine that subsided an army on the march. John had even commissioned ox drivers to drag Belisarius' ballistae alongside the army, to say nothing of their complex springs and triggers that required three men to operate.

Our date of departure arrived, and the armies dismantled their sprawling camp outside of Scythian Neapolis. As my banda dismantled their tents and prepared for the march, I was summoned by Belisarius for one final meeting. Camp servants had already begun to deconstruct and pack Belisarius' tent into a cart, yet the general still busied himself by issuing instructions to officers that surged around him.

At my approach, Belisarius called for a servant to fetch a leather bag, from which he procured a new helmet more ornate than those of a common spearman or lower officer. Its red plume stood thick and high, and its interior was lined with a soft leather that padded my skull from the polished iron above. Alongside the helmet was a set of rich scales, the shimmering iron bordered by deep crimson cloth and leather straps. It was a gift that any young spearman would salivate over, the layers of boiled hide, mail, and scaled armor rendering its wearer immune to all but the most vicious of cuts.

"Congratulations, Komes Varus," Belisarius said, his eyes brightening as he spoke.

Though the honor was a temporary one, and would be surrendered if I returned to Constantinople, I took it happily nonetheless. Troglita hailed me as I came back to my men, having received a similar honor earlier that morning, and we exchanged commendations.

As we were not permitted to bring slaves or servants on the expedition, Father Petrus again blessed the joint armies, and Rosamund threw her arms around my shoulders in a tight embrace. They instead would remain in Scythian Neapolis, awaiting our return and assisting the local villagers in rebuilding their broken lives.

"Just come *back*," she said sadly, handing me Aetius' dagger. "You have nothing else to prove, Varus."

Close by, Father Petrus hailed for my attention, and chastised me for not seeking him out far earlier. He laid a finger upon the cross at my throat before offering a blessing, praying that the Lord would see me safely home.

"Never forget that you are loved," the priest said, "and that wherever you go, God is with you, always."

Farewells completed, I rejoined my men, the komes' plume rustling against the low breeze. With Belisarius and Germanus in front, we departed, and I offered final salutes as Rosamund and Petrus faded from view.

The weather held fair as we crossed the boundary marking the outer edge of Scythian Neapolis' territory. Belisarius had divided the armies into three columns for the march, with two smaller columns of the Thracian Army on either flank. Germanus had been charged with leading the right, with Solomon as his deputy trailing behind. Mundus and I led the left, freed from the baleful influence of Archelaus' friends and sycophants. Squeezed in between, the central column was deeper and wider than its flanks, containing the core of Belisarius' spears and horsemen.

Though Samur spent his days marching with our column, his spare moments were occupied at the fires of Sunicas and the Huns. I felt a pang of jealousy at their mirth, yet mostly I was pleased for my brother's newfound happiness and belonging. Sunicas had even given him permission to join his foederati if we survived against the Avars, leaving him close to me given Belisarius' offer to transfer to his army.

The Tauric Peninsula was small compared to the Empire's other provinces, yet the soft earth and occasional rain slowed our progress to a crawl. Even without the hindrance of servants and camp followers, the small horde of wagons and oxen that carried the armies' supplies kept a slow pace over the grasslands and rolling hills of Tauris' interior. Dew glistened on each blade of grass in the sunlight, a pleasant aroma of damp soil filling the vast open expanse of the plains. As before, we passed occasional collections of ruined and half-burned huts, their inhabitants long departed from the area, yet the ominous gray of Godilas' march had avoided Belisarius' sojourn northward.

Not that such good fortune left the senior officers with an illusion of safety. Fearing a raid by a smaller Avar war band, Belisarius had prohibited the main army from venturing too far ahead from the wagon train, tying our pace to the slowest ox that

John had commandeered. Men grumbled at the drudgery, yet we Thracian survivors appreciated the care taken with securing the armies' advance.

Even with the slow pace, morale was markedly higher than Godilas' initial march from Kalos Limin. Belisarius' outriders kept a tight perimeter around the columns, and the fair yet cooling weather was a welcome reprieve from the black skies and heavy fog of my initial foray into the center of Tauris. Some chatted idly to pass our slow procession, while others sang songs and shared bawdy stories to captive audiences.

As a senior officer of the expedition, I was granted the right to move throughout the army with a freedom that most of the spearmen could not. Belisarius had even encouraged this, hoping that his commanders would gain familiarity with one another in ways that would translate to better communication in battle. I grabbed a horse, trotted along the Cappadocian column, and was hailed by Baduarius.

Baduarius and his brother Dagisthaeus were both Goths from Italy, yet bore no love for the Gothic Kingdom that dominated Rome, Mediolanum, and Ravenna. As Baduarius passed a wineskin that had been diluted with several cups of water, he and Dagisthaeus shared tales of their childhood, born within an Italy that had once been home to the Roman people.

Their father had been a wool merchant who scratched a fair living from his herds. Keeping to a litany of pagan gods instead of the heretical form of Christianity the Gothic tribes adopted when they migrated west to escape from Attila, their father held little favor in the Ostrogothic Court. As King Theodoric stamped out any perceived opposition to his rule by stealing gold and goods from his pagan subjects, a band of armed thugs stole everything that the boys' father owned, and broke what would not be easily carried off for sale. Unable to feed his children, their father sold Baduarius and Dagisthaeus to a Greek slaver for ten silver *folles* each, and they were placed in a cargo ship bound for Constantinople. Yet their ship had wrecked near the Hellespont, and the boys survived by paddling on small wooden boards until they reached the shores of Ancient Troy.

"But how did you end up in the army?" I pressed.

Dagisthaeus was the one to answer. "We stole a donkey from a camp of herders and rode south to Pergamon. Not speaking any Greek, a Roman magistrate threw us in a cell as bandits and spies, yet a recruiter gave us the choice to fight in Anastasius' army."

Baduarius butted in, chuckling. "We did the things that boys normally do in the army—fetch water, carry bodies, make food, and slowly learn Greek. After a few years, I was old enough to join as a spearman, and Dagisthaeus a year after me."

I shook my head, marveling. "And how did you come into Belisarius' service?"

"Our army was dispatched to protect a province on the Ister, but we were ambushed. Most of our banda ran, yet we stayed to fight along the wall. Belisarius charged in with his cavalry, and later asked us to join him," Dagisthaeus said, delighting in the macabre humor of their story.

That story jarred my memory. *They served with Godilas and Justinian,* I thought, piecing the links together that connected so many of the Roman Court.

"And why did you stay?" I asked, curious of my soon-to-be lord.

Dagisthaeus met my eyes, the twinkle of humor replaced with a firm stare. "In a world that punishes you for who you are, Belisarius gave us the opportunity to rise high." As he spoke, Baduarius nodded in agreement.

I soon found that the brothers tended to make light of all situations, regardless of how desperate or dark they may be. A day later, I asked Baduarius about this odd habit, and he replied that he had seen too much sadness in life to be melancholy, preferring the black humor of veteran soldiers. Yet whenever I questioned the brothers of their loyalty to Belisarius, their expressions grew serious and deferential.

Just as Samur spent his evenings with the Huns, I shared stories with the Gothic brothers. They patiently taught me Gothic, joking with one another as their language fell clumsily from my tongue. Yet as I improved, we held simple conversations in that Germanic language that had supplanted Latin in the spiritual home of the Roman Empire.

The brothers had a particular appetite for stories of battle and recounted their various exploits with Belisarius with relish. I had a few of my own now, too: the minor engagement in the Gepid Kingdom as well as the doomed chevauchee with Godilas. They indulged me with curiosity as I told stories of the Imperial Palace and laughed heartily when I told of how Justin was named Anastasius' successor.

This attracted the other senior officers, leading Ascum and John to join our makeshift circle on the march. Ascum was a squat man who hailed from the Alans, another tribe that fled from the Huns and found a home near the Caspian Sea. John was of mixed lineage of Rome and Armenia alike, and was rumored to be descended from one of the old patrician families that had dominated the days of Scipio, Marius, and Caesar himself. While John generally maintained a calm demeanor, Ascum only goaded the Gothic brothers further, their laughter drawing glances from the marching spearmen of Belisarius' army.

Perhaps the only topic more beloved than battles past was women. Baduarius boasted of dozens of women he had bedded throughout the Empire and was only too happy to tell of each, in gratuitous detail.

"And how many of those did you not have to pay?" Ascum chortled, earning a light smack from the wooden edge of Baduarius' spear.

The Last Dying Light

"I've never paid gold for a prostitute in my life!" Baduarius exclaimed, feigning indignity.

"Aye, 'gold' being the key word there," said Dagisthaeus. "Silver is cheaper, and far easier to find." Even John chuckled at that remark, leaving Baduarius to defend his honor with renewed enthusiasm.

I remained silent through most of this, which drew the attention of the others more than any loud boasting.

"And what of you, Varus? What women?" Dagisthaeus was nothing if not cheeky.

Blushing, I muttered that this was not a subject that I cared to discuss, although my mind betrayed me as it conjured the ephemeral image of Mariya.

"That's a yes," Ascum declared. "That Gepid girl that follows you around, maybe?"

John grunted. "The healer? No, much too pretty for Varus."

I sank back in the saddle as the others giggled and agreed. Mercifully, they had many of their own stories still to relate, and we parted ways to prepare the overnight camp as the sun fell from the sky.

Though I spent many days getting to know Belisarius' officers, I made sure to sup with my men every evening. Perenus held his chest out as he walked, barking discipline into the new recruits of our makeshift banda, while Cephalas and Samur ended each evening with practice bouts of swordplay and grappling. Troglita's men often joined ours, and we gathered kindling and brush to build a great fire to accommodate so many of the Thracian Army. Germanus and Mundus even shared a skin of wine with us early in the march, learning the names of the newer recruits and listening to the men's fears and aspirations for the days ahead.

Over a full week of grinding march, we found only hints of the Avars: some small outlying villages burned, or a discarded saddle painted black lying in the grass. Yet we found no bodies, living or dead, throughout the entire week. Our scouts nearly missed the battle site of Godilas' initial engagement with the Avars, the only evidence being a number of broken arrowheads, snapped flaxen rope, and a splintered shield whose Chi-Rho had been faded by rain and sunlight. Belisarius stopped the army for prayer, swearing an oath of vengeance against the hordes that had inflicted so much pain on the province of Chersonesus.

Yet, as the armies neared the isthmus of Tauris, Roman riders spotted the first evidence of our black-cloaked enemy.

At first, they stalked from a distance, well outside of earshot yet barely visible on the horizon. Black riders appeared on all sides of the Roman formation, which still proceeded northward, albeit in a more careful and deliberate fashion. Shields and armor had been distributed to the men from the army's wagons, including dozens of heavy rectangular shields that had long iron spikes attached to one of their narrow ends.

Baduarius hefted one onto his shoulder and patted its rim. "That will do nicely," he said to the quartermaster, slinging it across his back.

"New weapons?" I asked, gesturing at the heavy shields.

Baduarius shook his head. "Don't worry. We're getting standard shields, too. You'll see!"

I did, for we did not have to wait long. As we neared the isthmus on the late morning of the eighth day, a sea of black blanketed the land before us, tattered black banners fluttering in the wind. Each banner was topped by a human skull, the spearpoint breaking through the bone roof of its head.

"Sweet Jesus," murmured Perenus as the Avar force came into view. A great tenor of drums rang out, followed by deep chants that swirled across the Avar ranks. An older man walked before the rows of blackened shields, clad in the furs of a dozen animals and draped in the skulls of a dozen foxes. Some sort of Avar shaman, it seemed, he threw dark powders into the air and pointed a spindly wooden staff in our direction, prompting further cheers from the Avar warriors.

I trotted toward the generals, who had already issued orders for the columns to unfurl into lines. "Thirty, maybe even forty thousand, and at least a quarter mounted." Germanus' voice was full of awe as he recounted the Avar warriors before us. "This isn't an army, it's an entire people on the move."

Belisarius nodded. "This is our one chance to defeat them. Their entire army is here, for once not scattered across the plains or hiding in darkness. End them now, and we will be free of them for our lifetimes."

The other officers roared in approval, although some looked back toward the Avar lines with flickering gazes. Solomon trotted off to his lines with Germanus, his features tight with unease.

Belisarius grabbed my attention before we departed. "Varus, you are the keystone to our plan. Your banda must close the circle as quickly as possible. If you fail, or if the Avars break through, we will all die here."

His eyes flared with a grim determination that I had not known within that otherwise soft and welcoming face. In response, I saluted.

"I will come with help as soon as I can, but you must hold," Belisarius said. "Let Mundus and Germanus command the lines, but do everything you can to seal the northern exit to the isthmus."

I nodded, and he stretched out an arm. I took it in my own, and he drew me close and patted me on the back.

"God be with you, Varus," he said in a low voice.

"And you, Lord."

We parted, revealing lines that had already been fashioned according to Belisarius' strategy. John galloped between the lines with messages from the general, yet he, too, fell into the right of the Cappadocians at his appointed position. The twin Thracian flanks held back, well away from the Cappadocian ranks. Baduarius held the northernmost point of the Cappadocian crescent, his own banners portraying a broken ship flapping alongside the Emperor's eagle and Belisarius' wolf.

The Avars neared our lines and reached two hundred paces away from Baduarius' position. Dark riders galloped up and down their lines, drawing shouts and jeers from the Avar horde as they beat their spears into pitch-blackened shields. Amidst the black and brown furs, three at the center of the Avars' ragged line stood out from the rest. One was adorned in the snow-white fur of an albino wolf, outlining the man who killed my master-at-arms.

"That's Shaush," I pointed, gathering Perenus' attention.

"And next to him is Tzul," he said. "But who is the big bastard in the center?"

"Must be their king. Kazrig." I sneered toward the thick-armed man, who was covered with a spotless fur cloak.

Kazrig's head was crowned with a thin iron circlet, and his long dark hair was streaked with the first hints of gray. Kazrig appeared as an older version of his son, who too was tall and broad chested, his hair grizzled and long as it flapped in the wind. Of the three, Tzul alone remained emotionless, staring back at his Roman enemy as he considered the battlefield ahead of him.

The Avars held a slight advantage of terrain, being able to attack downhill at the Roman spearmen. John had indicated that this would turn into the Thracian Army's strength as we formed the northern terminus of Belisarius' circle of death, yet that advantage remained outside of our grasp until the strategy was in action. As the Avar cheering filled the horizon, Ascum ordered the distribution of sheaves of arrows to the Cappadocian archers, while John signaled for the loading of ballistae that had already begun assembly as soon as the armies came to a halt.

The armies stood still for only a moment, waiting for Belisarius' nod to move toward the second stage of our plan. At his signal, Bessas' centurions led two herds of horses to each of the Thracian flanks, followed by the Hunnic riders that galloped even farther toward the formation's flanks. Samur nodded at Sunicas as he passed our position and leaned to my ear.

"Stay safe, brother," Samur whispered in Heruli, briefly wrapping an arm around my neck.

"You're not staying with the Huns?" I asked. "Our task is risky."

"I spoke with Sunicas," Samur said. "I can't just leave you on your own right now. You'll get yourself injured without me!"

"If you insist," I said. Surrender was most expedient. "But keep your head down, and stay in the rear ranks."

"You wish." Samur grinned and jostled to my right in the front line.

I considered ordering him to the reserves; the sight of thousands of dancing Avars did little to ease my worries. Yet I resisted such urges, for Samur was unlikely to leave willingly, and such commotion would only distract the men from the impending attack. With no choice but to appease my brother's insane request, I pulled my komes' helmet over my head, knotted its leather straps, and allowed Samur and Cephalas to fix my cloak and armor one final time.

A great roar rose above the Avars with a singular voice, and I pulled out the chain that hung from my neck. I kissed its cross and dragon and tucked them safely back under the leather and iron scales that covered my body. With one final check, I cinched my belt, dragging my hands over Aetius' dagger and the Emperor's sword that rested along opposite sides of my hips. Samur handed me my shield and spear, and I motioned for silence as we waited for Belisarius' command.

It was not long in coming. Belisarius dropped a hand, and one of Bessas' men raised a violet flag toward Baduarius at the front lines.

The Goth raised a fist, and a great cry rang out from the Roman ranks as they howled and drowned out the Avar din. Baduarius' front ranks carried their rectangular shields forward three paces and jammed the iron spikes deep into the earth so that the bulwark was left standing on its own.

Baduarius stepped forward from the Roman lines, his body covered in the mail and lamellar armor that marked him as a warlord and a veteran of battle. He also made himself a rich target for younger Avar warriors, eager to prove themselves in battle and to claim a prize that would enrich themselves and their families for years to come. Twenty paces from his spearmen, Baduarius lifted his mail, dropped his trousers, and pissed toward the Avars and their leaders.

As he refixed his armor, Baduarius unleashed a litany in a savage tongue that I could not understand. Samur leaned to me, shouting over the din.

"Sunicas and Baduarius forced the Avar captives to teach them curses and insults in their own tongue," Samur said, his lips stretched in a broad grin. I stifled a laugh as Baduarius continued, shouting until he was red in the face.

An Avar rider answered his call. He galloped toward the Roman position and dismounted twenty paces from Baduarius in the clearing between the Avar and Roman armies. His thick furs and well-wrought steel sword marked him as a champion and a lord among the Avars, who otherwise fought with stolen weapons and cheap iron found in the vast wastelands of the northern plains. The Avar champion pointed his sword at Baduarius, shouted his challenge, and walked forward to initiate a duel along the plains.

Baduarius did not return the man's gesture but unslung a javelin that was hidden inside the second shield at his back. In a single motion, Baduarius lifted the javelin to eye level and thrust it through the air.

Taken aback, the Avar champion tried to pivot, but the spear pierced his armor, furs, and dug itself into his ribcage. He then tried to pull the iron head out of his body, yet sank to the ground in pain at the effort. Baduarius drew a dagger and drove it into the Avar's throat, ending his life in a mercifully fast stroke.

Baduarius wiped his blade on the man's furs and looked up at the Avar ranks, which riled at the dishonor their champion had been paid. The Goth then burst out with laughter, which echoed through much of the Cappadocian spearmen lining the plains, a shield wall eight rows deep.

Kazrig barked a command, and at least a thousand Avar riders galloped away from their lines toward Baduarius. The Goth ran back to rejoin his men, who unhooked their second shields and formed a wall of wood and iron.

The Avar riders swept parallel to our lines, and individually dove close to Baduarius' shield wall. They threw short yet thick spears, their ends knotted with a rope that had been tied to the rider's saddle. Though several spears bit into our Roman shields, most clattered harmlessly against the row of spiked shields that guarded the Cappadocian ranks.

Our men looked on as the Avar riders kept trying their maneuver, yet without the cover of fog, it had lost its surprise, and few were able to connect with the armored spearmen in the front rows of Baduarius' ranks. The few spearmen unlucky enough to be hooked by a flying Avar spear were saved by their neighbors in the shield wall, who had been instructed to sever the connecting rope rather than hang on to the man's arms or body for support.

Belisarius raised another signal, gathering John's attention.

"Archers!" the Armenian shouted, loud enough for the Thracians on the left flank to hear.

Ascum ordered his men to draw and unleash a volley that rained iron down upon the Avar riders. Most escaped, but dozens fell, quilled like great beasts. Another volley followed, and the Avar riders fled back to Kazrig and Tzul.

As his depleted outriders returned to the ranks, Tzul galloped before the Avar lines, waving his sword in a frenzy. His blade dropped from the heavens to point toward the Roman center, and a writhing mass of fur, spears, and shields surged forward. As they closed the gap between the armies, I counted at least two-thirds of the Avar force moving with Tzul toward our center, with the remainder straggling behind.

"Not yet." At Samur's confusion, I explained. "We can't charge in until they all move forward." Satisfied, my brother nodded and gripped his spear tight as sweat pooled down his face.

As the Avars drew within bowshot range, Ascum ordered another volley from his archers. They fired in good order, able to launch a second volley while the first had just begun to crest in the air above. Most arrows had no effect, dulled as the Avars raised their shields overhead, yet enough found an exposed limb or even flank of a horse that the ragged Avar lines staggered further still.

John then ordered the firing of the ballistae. Where Ascum's archers took few casualties, the great bolt throwers impaled multiple warriors at a time. Their force drove men clean off their horses as the bolt dug into the soil, hoisting their bodies in the air like some macabre banner in the heart of battle.

The first Avars collided with Baduarius' forward lines, filling the plains with the sounds of colliding shields and searing metal. Though their initial force was muted due to their need to knock over the spiked shields that had protected the Roman spearmen from the Avars' outriders, the swelling press of men drove Baduarius and his men ever backward. I spotted Tzul urging his men forward, directing masses of Avars at perceived weaknesses in the bending Roman lines. For a moment, the Cappadocian lines straightened, yet Baduarius' center was falling steadily backward under the onslaught of the Avars, although the Cappadocian retreat had begun to slow.

Spotting his opportunity, Kazrig signaled his remaining riders forward, taking personal command alongside his son, Shaush. They rioted forth with sudden frenetic energy, the Avar banners flying behind their khagan as they sought to apply a death stroke against the buckling Roman center.

Several Avar detachments were now swinging out toward our flanks, more eager to attack their enemy than stand stuck behind a mass of men. Sunicas' Huns, meanwhile, whirled behind us, firing arrows from horseback that drove the Avars back toward their main body.

As Kazrig's spearmen entered the melee, one great purple banner rose in the distance, leading to a great shout from Mundus.

"For Isaacius," Perenus growled, clenching his jaw.

"For all of us," I said, holding Perenus' gaze for just a moment.

Our lines broke, and we ran back to the Huns. Shaush pointed and laughed, yet the Hunnic horse archers kept the Avars from taking advantage of the disintegrating left flank of the Roman lines. Dagisthaeus' spears slid from the Roman center to cover the gap on the Cappadocian left, while John took command of a smaller group of spearmen toward the Cappadocian right.

"Faster!" Sunicas shouted as we ran behind the Hunnic ranks.

We grabbed horses that had been herded for us and formed ourselves into crude ranks as we prepared for our next move. I called for reports, and my centurions confirmed their readiness. I saw Troglita do the same with his banda.

"Ready!" I shouted at Sunicas, who nodded and galloped ahead, clearing our path of stray Avars seeking to outflank our lines.

Though we lacked the swiftness of the Huns, we galloped farther west and north and put two hundred paces between us and the Avar mass. Dagisthaeus saluted me as we bolted by, which I did my best to return while rocking back and forth in the saddle. Dagisthaeus' own lines had begun to curl in a similar direction, forming a bowl shape that would absorb the brunt of the Avar attack alongside the forces of Baduarius and John.

Sunicas' riders fired with abandon, while Ascum's own archers targeted the Avar flanks to grant us cover. Unable to launch their bolts with such speed or regularity, the ballistae fired new volleys every hundred heartbeats, cutting bloody ribbons into their unlucky targets. The pressure was rising along Baduarius' front, and Ascum ordered the ballista operators to train their missiles on those areas that threatened to break the Roman lines, and thereby offer a small measure of temporary relief to the embattled spearmen.

"Come on, move faster!" Sunicas urged, leading us ever farther along the outer edge of the battle. We swept eastward, and I saw Germanus' Thracian spearmen galloping hard in our direction. Like his brother, Simmas led his own detachment of Huns that fired arrows with deadly accuracy at Avar spears or riders who sought to bar our path.

Several of the Avar leaders were charging now, and we met growing resistance as the Thracian pincers closed together. Yet as Mundus saluted Germanus, panting from the exertion of the ride, our lines finally met. We dismounted and goaded the horses northward, away from the battleground.

Resistance struck almost immediately as Avar riders hit. Sunicas and Simmas defused some of their fury, yet most of the Avars reached the Thracian ranks unscathed by Hunnic arrows. I did not even have time to unsling my shield from my back as one Avar charged down on me, his javelin high in his hand. Samur gutted him easily with his spear, knocking the Avar from his horse just as Cephalas cut down onto the man's head. My rich plume caught the eye of many attackers, and other riders closed in on my position with abandon. I dispatched one with a spear through his groin, leaving him screaming and bleeding onto the grass. A man from my second rank threw his spear at another, cutting into the man's throat so forcefully that his head bobbed at an odd angle. Sword drawn, I dispatched with my downed foes, then found Perenus ordering the men into a sturdier shield wall.

Soon, the Avar interlude slowed to a trickle. Our attackers had been stragglers from the main Avar body—young boys and older men who were given no honors in leading the charge of their horde. In the brief respite, I ordered waterskins handed throughout the ranks, and unslung my shield and strapped it securely onto my forearm.

Samur handed me my spear, which was bloodied but unbroken. Even in that open area of the field, the air stank of dung and offal, with rotting furs and sweat choking beneath. I was thankful for each breath of crisp air that blew across the plains, keeping us from suffocating in a chasm of blood, flesh, and excrement from men and horses alike.

Sunicas interrupted my thoughts with a shout. "We're headed to the flanks, but I will return. You are the anchor—hold this position at all costs!" His horse's mouth was flecked with foam, yet the grinning Hun drove it ever forward toward Dagisthaeus' buckling lines.

Though the thousands that comprised the Avar horde were preoccupied with Baduarius' lines, others turned around, finding Romans covering every route of escape. Kazrig remained fixed on cutting into our still-bending center, yet Shaush and Tzul had formed their own bands that tested the outer flanks of the Roman resistance.

The Avar warlord commanded a large section of the rearmost Avar ranks to form lines. With their general's finger pointed at my banda, the Avars marched right for us. These men were not like the warriors we had faced before; they were almost soldierly, charging in straight lines with shields overlapping. These, then, were the hardened veterans of Kazrig's horde.

Small numbers of men from both sides exchanged a volley of spears, which clattered against shields and fell to the ground. Ten paces from our shield wall, the Avar commander cried out, sending the Avar lines into a feverish run toward their Roman enemy until they collided with our shields, the force enough to knock many a pace or more backward.

Though Belisarius' strategy was unfolding as planned, its weakest point lay to the northern edge. The reasons were many: the reduced strength of the Thracian Army in general, the need to bulk Baduarius' ranks for the initial assault against the combined might of the Avar horde. Yet another reason was a practical one: It was too difficult to relocate additional spearmen around the considerable distance of the ring. Sunicas and Simmas' Huns lobbed occasional repelling fire, but they were primarily attending to the eastern and western edges, where Dagisthaeus and John sought to funnel the Avars into ever tighter and more constricting ranks. Belisarius and Bessas had further reinforced the Cappadocian center and right flank; their armored cataphracts were not mobile enough to navigate the Roman ring as could the lighter-armored Huns.

This left me in a dilemma—with little chance of reinforcements, my task was to hold the center of the northern lines at all cost. Mundus and Germanus maintained order across the outstretched Thracian lines, yet this had left my small cornerstone of the formation an independent command. With my ranks a painfully thin four spearmen deep, we struggled to absorb the shock of the Avar charge.

Again, my plume caught the attention of any Avars seeking glory for slaying a Roman commander—which was most within that ravenous horde. As I reasoned, Samur's shield slid in front of my unprotected sword arm. An Avar spear that would have taken me high in the chest thudded against it. A man behind Samur gutted the Avar with his own spear, his intestines sliding out of a bloody gash that stained his furs. Another Avar ducked low to swipe his sword at my legs, and Cephalas gouged at the man's head, puncturing his skull with his iron point.

The force of the initial charge abated but gave way to a shoving match as the competing shield walls sought an advantage over one another. I tried to thrust forward with my spear, but it was grabbed by an Avar rider and pulled violently from my grasp. I drew my sword and cut at the Avar. His breath stank of wine as he cursed me over his shield, and he parried my jabs as his shield pushed ever forward. He took a step forward but slipped, his foot caught on the guts of one of his fallen allies. I lunged. My sword found his exposed neck, and I killed him instantly as I severed his spine. Jerking, his body collapsed, leaving a small hole in the Avar lines.

This small victory was short-lived, as another Avar spearman took the slain man's place, stepping over the body to seal the breach in their lines with his shield. The push resumed, broken only by an occasional clash of sword strokes that clattered against steel bosses and wooden shield panels. Any shield wall quickly lost force in the tight press of men, and both of our lines slowed in their intensity as men gasped for tepid air. My sword arm grew heavy, and I did my best to ignore its protestations. Blade flying, I stuck my sword into another Avar, below his armpit. Squealing, the man sank low, and was dragged away by his friends. Yet once again, fresh Avars filled these gaps, leaving no respite as my men struggled onward.

Though outnumbered, our lines held firm for much of the fight, yielding only slight ground and levying heavy casualties for each Roman who fell wounded or slain. Yet after a time, a roar echoed a few paces down the Avar lines, their black shields surging forward with renewed vigor.

"Cephalas, you have command. Do not let them break our lines!" I yelled over the din.

Cephalas nodded as I slipped behind our ranks and trotted toward the new Avar attack, which had formed a wedge and threatened to break our front wall. I slid between my men, where I found the cause behind the break in our lines. I screamed.

Perenus' plume shone out above the iron helmets of his men, yet his head rolled listlessly atop his shoulders as he fought to stay standing. As I pushed frantically to reach his side, I found that he had taken a spear to the shoulder, the wooden shaft broken just below its iron head. Perenus tried to lift his shield, yet visibly lacked the strength, leaving him exposed to the dozens of Avars incensed by the sight of his blood.

Perenus' neighbors shielded their centurion, and at last I dragged him away from the lines. A man from my banda took his body from me, and promised to watch over the Lazic prince. I wanted nothing more than to stay by Perenus' side, yet was called back to the lines that had struggled to repel the Avar wedge.

My sword's edge had been dulled by this moment in the battle, yet its point still cut through the thick furs of many of the Avar spearmen. I barreled my way to the front ranks and jabbed forward at the nearest body, a lanky man whose filth-stained beard hung down to his belt. My blade entered his gullet, and he gasped and choked. I pulled the sword loose, but its edge caught in the man's flesh and rotting furs. Swiftly, I released the sword, drew my dagger, and slammed its point into the underside of the nearest Avar's jaw.

Perenus' men grabbed my cloak, pulling me back into line and behind the shield wall. As I fell, I grabbed an axe that rested next to a black-clad Avar commander and joined the wall. Unlike many of the Avar weapons, the axe was quality steel, its handle decorated with runes and mythical creatures foreign to Greece. Its cutting edge ran long, at least the size of a man's hand, yet its reverse edge held a blunted spike that gave it the look of a savage war hammer. Though heavy and unbalanced, the blade held true as I cut down at the Avar to my right, its blade cutting cleanly through his metal cap and exposing pink brains underneath.

My shoulder and forearm screamed in agony as yet more Avar spearmen struck my shield, yet I dared not drop my guard for a moment. My neighbors were caked in blood and gore, many panting as their arms hung low.

"Hold! Shields up!" I cried, and the nearby dekarchos repeated my call. The front lines raised their wall once again and pressed hard at the Avar wedge that buckled our outer ranks.

Men called out to each other in support, yet even a growing mound of Avar dead did little to dissuade their rearward ranks to join the fray. Many in our front lines fell, stuck with spears or unlucky arrows that rang out from the distant center mass of the Avar horde. Our lines wavered and thinned, and even our limited reinforcements were unable to stop the growing pressure of the Avars.

A horn blew behind me, proclaiming a few dozen Roman spearmen who patched the gaps in my line. Troglita snaked his way toward my front rank, bloodied but rested.

"We killed all of ours, and I thought you could use a hand!" He grinned behind his shield.

Troglita's men halted their progress as my banda rose with renewed confidence. I nodded to Troglita and signaled for our next move.

"Now! Push now! Charge them!" I yelled, seizing on the brief moment of uncertainty across the Avar ranks as well as the limited burst of force from my own men.

Troglita pushed our ranks forward as we cut down on the Avar ranks, flanking their wedge and closing the gap in our lines. A dozen Avar spearmen were caught in our encirclement, fighting back to back as they fought to cut a hole toward their brethren. Troglita gored two down with his spear, and other Roman soldiers cut opportunistically at exposed arms and legs until the Avars lay in a writhing mass of blood and moans.

The Avar lines broke and ran toward the center of the circle, leaving our banners flying alone in the wind. A wall of bodies paid tribute to the press of the shield walls, black-cloaked Avars mixed with mailed Romans. Our men cheered at their victory, yet it could not be denied that the losses along our lines left us perilously weak in the face of another Avar attack.

I nodded my thanks to Troglita and ran toward the rear of our lines, where I found Perenus lying in the grass with two of his men. Blood streamed down his chest, yet he smiled as he saw me throw off my helmet and kneel at his side.

"V-Varus," Perenus choked. "I-I'm sorry."

I shook my head, using a forearm to wipe away stray tears. "You have nothing to be sorry for, you old bastard."

Perenus chuckled at my words and insisted that he would live. The man squatting near Perenus' head nodded, indicating that the bleeding had stopped and the wound sealed.

A look of relief washed over the Lazic prince's face as he faced me once again, his smile ghoulish but playful. "Do you think I'll still get a bonus?"

I leaned down, my head close to his, and clenched his bloodied hand in mine.

"I do not give you permission to die, do you understand?" I said, my voice serious. "You are not allowed to leave me alone in this godforsaken place."

Perenus nodded, clutching the back of my sweat-soaked head. He promised me, again, that he would survive, and ordered me back to my men. Perenus' battle that day had come to an end.

Horsemen trotted manically along our rear, with Sunicas hailing me from the saddle of a different horse than the one he'd ridden earlier in the day. He dismounted and took account of our condition, his features like stone as he gazed down the lines.

The Last Dying Light

Sunicas' report was a grim one. Though pressure had eased considerably from Baduarius' spearmen as the Avars spread throughout the great ring, other sections of the Roman encirclement were hit by formations of men and riders that sought to puncture our lines and curl around the rear of our formation for easy kills.

"The west is a bloody ruin, but still holding. Still look better than you lot, though," Sunicas said, glancing about at my men.

"Any chance of reinforcements?" I asked, panting and leaning upon my shield for support.

Sunicas frowned. "Belisarius and Bessas need every cataphract to shore up Baduarius and John, and my brother is as thinly stretched as I am."

"In other words, no," Samur added, drawing a wink from Sunicas.

"Kazrig has the bulk of the Avars still fighting southward, but be ready for another wave up here soon. I can leave you with ten of my horse archers, but I need to bring the rest back to Dagisthaeus in the west." Sunicas spat onto the ground, his face pure fury and death. "I am sorry, Varus, but you will need to make do on your own."

I leaned in close, muttering words that only Sunicas could hear. "I don't know that we can stand against another Avar wall. Half of my men are wounded or dead, and the others are exhausted."

Sunicas sighed. "You *must* hold," he said, "just for a while longer, and we will begin to close the circle. Do whatever you can to survive until then, and we will come for you."

I wiped blood from my face and nodded, resigned. Sunicas barked orders in Hunnic, commanding a small detachment of riders to sit at the back of our lines. Troglita hailed me down as I returned to the lines, holding my sword in his hands.

"Thought you would want this back," Troglita said, tracing its runes and edge as he handed it over. I slid my new axe into my belt and took the sword, sharpening it against a whetstone that had been handed to me by one of Troglita's men.

I took my place near Cephalas and Samur and surveyed my lines. Many sat in formation, settling in for whatever rest was possible as they watched the Avar lines crash into Roman spearmen far to the south. Others drank greedily from waterskins, few heeding my warning that they slow lest they cramp or vomit.

I even glimpsed Belisarius, his tall plume swaying in the wind atop his armored horse. They fought desperately against an Avar breakout attempt, using the weight of the horses to push the Roman shield wall forward. Yet with every movement forward, Belisarius' men were driven back soon thereafter, crushed by the press of Avar shields and wild horsemen.

I sat near Samur, who touched his shoulder and winced—a gash along his arm, iron rings split in a neat row.

"It's nothing," he said, noticing my concern. "Just an arrow that grazed too close."

I tried to inspect it closer, yet Samur refused any attention, let alone bandaging. His face shone with a stony pride, never betraying the fatigue and soreness that he doubtlessly felt.

Troglita found me again and saluted formally. "Mundus sends his regards and offers what's left of my banda to help you hold the center."

I smiled and thanked him. "Any word from Germanus?"

Troglita shrugged. "They were hit hard about the same time as us. Even with more spearmen under their command, they may not be in a position to help."

"May not, or will not?"

"Will not," Troglita said. "None else are coming."

"So much for Roman honor," Samur spat. "Leaving us on our own!"

"They have no choice," I reminded him, exhausted.

"There's *always* a choice!" Samur cried.

"True," Troglita said. "But I am still here with you, fighting along your wall with my men. Take that for what you will."

Samur raised his hands in surrender, asking Troglita's forgiveness for such an outburst. Gracefully, Troglita waved it aside as the frustrated words of a hurt and overtaxed body. Rather, Troglita urged that we commit to improving our defense, providing what protection was possible against the inevitable future attack.

With Troglita's help, I ordered the men to stack Avar bodies in a low wall before our position. We carried our dead Roman brothers behind our lines, leaving a low mound of black-cloaked corpses that reached to the men's knees throughout the length of the line.

"That won't stop them for long," Samur observed, cleaning his hands of the grim work. He upended one of the waterskins over his head, creating small streams of muck and guts that puddled around his boots.

"It doesn't need to, but it will slow them down," I said, reviewing the line of bodies that had already begun to stink in the noonday sun.

Lazy clouds blew overhead as the air grew colder, yet mercifully no rain or fog had come to the plains. Our idyll was disrupted by the pounding of a deep drum and the concomitant howling of Avar formations in the distance.

"Form up." I hefted my shield and walked to the wall.

A mass of Avars trotted north toward our position, lifting their spears to the sky as their officers built them into a frenzy. At their front, a shaman screeched to the sky and unfurled a torn Roman banner. He poured a mysterious powder over the Imperial Eagle, and the cloth snapped into flame. I shuddered at the sorcery and longed for Father Petrus, needing his protection and blessing in this desolate land.

As the shaman finished his ritual, two men walked before the Avar mass that grew steadily in strength. One remained clad in his white wolf's pelt, while the other trailed behind, yelling commands to the Avar lords to widen and straighten their lines.

"Shaush and Tzul," Samur said, grinding his teeth as the Avar leaders came into view.

Though the bulk of the Avar army remained with Kazrig, a swelling mass that dwarfed the remaining Thracian forces swarmed ever closer, stopping fifty paces from our forward lines.

"How many?" asked Samur, his hand shaking again as it curled around the shaft of his spear.

"A thousand, maybe two," I lied, as Shaush's horde chanted and jeered.

Though it is difficult to tally enemy forces on the battlefield, my guess was at least five thousand men, more than enough to slay the Roman center many times over. Shaush raised his arms, silencing the Avar ranks. The mass of bodies muffled the din of Kazrig's own attacks to the south of the ring, and a sense of ominousness saw us all stare at Shaush's grin. Shaush drew his sword and lifted it to the sky as he called for his god's blessing, then slowly lowered it until it pointed toward our center.

The Avars roared and charged in a ragged flood of men. The first dozen Avar spearmen, barely more than boys, reached the low wall of bodies first and hurdled over the impediment, some tripping over stray limbs or slick intestines as they landed. My men surged forward as well, jamming spears into their fur-covered bodies.

Yet still more Avars came, knocking over the corpse barrier as they collided with our shield wall. One mounted Avar guided his horse through the onslaught and threw his spear into the Roman ranks, knocking down one of my warriors with a blow to the chest. A Hunnic rider downed the man with a well-placed arrow to the eye, leaving a riderless horse trotting back to the center of the ring.

The Last Dying Light

The first wave of black-cloaked warriors now lay butchered, their wall malformed and open to attack from the disciplined Roman ranks. Yet as more formed up, their assault grew more orderly, smashing their pitch-covered shields against ours in a kind of unison.

I spotted Tzul in the fray of Avar attackers, directing his men and cutting his way toward a Roman banner carrier. I tried to push to him, but I was pinned at the front of the wall and lacked the strength to carve a path. Tzul fell into the front ranks, slaying two Romans as the Avars spilled into the gap.

Troglita's men hastened to shore up the lines, using our makeshift reserves to keep the northern lines knitted together despite the rush of veteran Avar spearmen. Hunnic riders rained arrows where the pressure was fiercest and struck many Avars in exposed arms or faces.

As I held my position, a giant of an Avar, easily another head taller than me and considerably wider, swung for me. Unlike the others, the giant bore a huge maul, its clublike shaft holding a heavy stone at its end. Unable to lift my shield, I watched helplessly as the man hoisted his weapon and swung it into the side of my helmet.

My memory darkened then. As a palace slave, I imagined war to be a glorious struggle where those of an unbreakable will can push beyond human limits of strength and pain. So many poets and philosophers make battle into a noble and even a desirable affair, a rite of passage that molds heroes and legends. Yet, as that battle dragged on, I knew I could only ever see war as nothing more than a test of the darkest parts of the soul, the willingness to shatter bones and shear flesh without pity or remorse. Rather than glory, the shield wall relies on the randomness of luck, and that late hour of our fight against the Avars found such luck in short supply. In fairness, I have always seen the purpose of battle, and the constant need for loyal and hardened soldiers, yet it was not until this moment, as my senses slowly returned, that I saw war for what it truly was: endless and all-consuming.

"Varus, can you hear me?" Samur screamed in my face, his eyes frantic with worry.

I nodded, my forehead throbbing and sore. "Water." At my croaking, he handed me a skin.

My senses trickled back at the crash of wood and metal just a few paces away. I shook my head and ran my mailed fingers through my hair as I asked for my helmet. Samur handed it to me, its left ear caved in and spotted with blood. I touched the left side of my head and recoiled at the sting, crimson staining my fingers. I tested the helmet and found it to be intact despite the ugly dent and retied its straps under my chin.

"Varus, just stay behind the lines," Samur yelled over the clang of battle. "You can't take another hit like that!"

I shook my head and knotted my shield back onto my arm.

"Let's go," I said grimly, and headed for the front before my brother could argue.

We pushed our way alongside Cephalas, who had plugged the gaps in our line with several of the newer recruits. The men protested as we pulled them back into the second rank, yet others cheered as their banda commander assumed his place at the front. I drew my axe and drove it deep into the neck of one Avar, then pushed forward to seek new foes. Another Avar advanced, swinging his sword in great arcs toward my shoulder. I parried with the iron rim of my shield and drove Aetius' dagger into his lungs, stabbing again and again as the man shuddered, dead before hitting the earth.

Samur spotted the Avar giant as the bodies piled before us. I wanted nothing more than to gut that bastard, but Cephalas was quicker and hurled a spear at the unsuspecting man. It drove deep into the man's shoulder, and he screamed as he pulled the spearhead from his body. Gore squirted from the gash in rhythm with the giant's heartbeat. He collapsed.

Samur and I roared. I didn't see the arrow overhead. It fluttered at my edge of vision, and then I felt it: piercing armor, catching me high in the shoulder, driving me off balance as the men behind pushed me upright with their shields. I caught a glimpse of Shaush, the bow dropping from his hands as he unsheathed his sword.

I fell back from the lines again, yielding command to Samur as I flitted between the ranks. He yelled angrily, trying to follow, yet I ordered him to stay and pushed into open air. Pain shot through my arm as my fingers grazed the shaft. The arrowhead did not sink far, slowed by my armor, yet the crude iron left an angry gash as I pulled it from my flesh.

A soldier ran toward me, seeking orders.

"Wine," I grunted. He handed me a half-full skin, and I drank a heavy gulp.

My mouth wet, I poured the liquid onto my exposed arm, growling as it stung the open wound. I handed the skin back to the soldier and swung my sword in wide arcs, testing the strength of my arm. It hurt viciously, but it was strong enough for my satisfaction. I ordered the soldier to find me a patch of leather, which he fetched from a pile of supply kits that had been stacked behind the lines. I took a square of leather, cut it into strips, and tied it around the wound for some minor protection against the press of shields.

I darted back to Samur's side as the pushing match between the armies ground to a standstill. The Avars' superior numbers gave them a considerable advantage, but the floor of corpses tripped and slowed their rush. After a time, a great drum sounded toward the rear of their ranks, drawing the Avars to fall back in good order. Each man dragged a corpse behind him as he left the melee, leaving rust-colored stains streaking the grass.

The Avars fell back one hundred paces, giving our lines a slight respite from the carnage of the battle. In the distance, Belisarius' horn blared, and we saw the east and west flanks push inward, driving Kazrig's horde into ever tighter constriction.

Clearly sensing danger, Shaush mounted a horse, taking a spear to organize his smaller horde into a new formation. The thousands of fresh Avar warriors formed a giant wedge, their jagged point aimed at Samur and me.

"They're coming for a breakout," Samur said. "Any ideas?"

Panting, I shook my head, sending another pulsing throb to my wounded shoulder. I stepped forward and looked down our lines, and found myself stunned at the horror of the scene. Every shield was painted with a thick coat of blood, and many men had soiled bandages wrapped around their arms and faces. Several still held spears, yet others were reduced to blunted swords and seized Avar blades. Every man sucked air into overtaxed lungs, and many were praying.

Shaush busied his ranks, in no hurry to force the charge that would end the battle. Tzul had taken his place at the tip of the wedge, yelling for his prince to order the charge, yet Shaush delayed as he packed more men into his lines.

Troglita walked to my side, his armor splashed in dark blood and panting heavily. "This is it, then," he said glumly.

I gazed at the fur-clad spearmen and shook my head. "Not yet," I said. "Grab as many bows as you can find from our gear and distribute them to the rearward lines."

Deep in thought, I pieced together a last desperate strategy to hold the arch of Belisarius' tightening circle. Farther away, Kazrig's men cheered as they exploited a gap in the western lines, driving Sunicas to fend off the Avar king's breakthrough. I shook myself to attention at the enemy before me, doing all I could to drown out the sounds of thousands of men to the south.

"Take command of the rearward ranks. On my signal, rain Hell down upon them," I said.

Breathing heavily, Troglita merely nodded and cracked stiff-sounding knuckles. We saluted one another as he ran back toward the line, ordering bows and quivers distributed throughout the ranks.

Mundus and Germanus were engaged on my flanks; no further help was likely. I looked around at the few hundred men left to me, remnants of several butchered bandae that were all that stood between the Avar horde and the open plain.

Stepping forward and turning to face my battered shield wall, I nodded to Cephalas, who yelled for the men's attention. Despite their exhaustion, and despite their countless wounds and aches, the Thracian shield wall slammed upright and saluted.

"Soldiers of the Thracian Army," I proclaimed, watching as their chests puffed out with pride, "I could not have asked for better men to stand beside me at the mouth of Hell."

My men hooted back, pounding their spears against broken shields and blood-soaked earth. Several called out my name, but most remained silent, as though to gather all their strength for the final assault.

"Before us is not a horde of men, but Death itself. He is hungering not only for us, but for our friends, our brothers, and our lovers scattered throughout these strange lands. Yet we have this chance, this one chance, to tell Death no! That we will not allow him to ravage our lands and slaughter our people any longer," I said, a determined anger in my voice.

The cheering stopped as men heeded my words. I paced across the wall, meeting the eyes of the remaining spearmen who had formed into three loose, under-manned lines. They panted and leaned on their shields and spears, yet stood upright all the same.

"I know you are tired, and I know you are hurting, but I need you to stand for one last effort and send these Avars back to Hell where they belong!"

Samur pounded his spear into the ground, summoning a ragged cheer from the men.

"When they come, I will stand against that darkness. Death will not claim me today." I let my words soak into the men as they eyed the Avar masses.

"Not this day! We stop them here, and now!"

At the ending note, the men raised their blades to the air with a deep cheer that belied their limited numbers.

As I walked back into the lines, Troglita nodded at me and ordered our horn to sound. Our banners flew high in the breeze, defiantly facing the skull-topped poles of the Avars. Amid the cheering, Cephalas raised his voice in song, his rich tenor sailing over the ranks. His words told of a somber march, the story of Leonidas' last stand against the Persians at Thermopylae. The other Greeks joined in, their voices amplifying the slow notes of the threnody. It was hypnotic; even Tzul looked up at his battered Roman enemies, brow knit.

Avar drums boomed again, adding an ominous undertone to Cephalas' lament. Shaush at last ordered his wedge forward, and they advanced in a slow yet determined procession. As they reached fifty paces from our lines, my few Hunnic riders launched their remaining arrows, dropping a dozen men from the outer edge of the Avar formation. Yet still they came, a mass of shields and furs ready to shatter our lines and envelop the Roman armies.

At thirty paces, I ordered the front ranks to kneel and raised my sword toward Troglita. The officer yelled a command, and a hundred bows fired into the massed formation. Even for untrained bowmen, the great mass of Avars were an unmissable target. Troglita's men launched a second volley, and then a third, raining arrows in a direct line toward the Avar front. The Avars' shields did little; the sheer velocity of the arrows traveling such a short distance punched easily through wooden barriers and dug into the bodies of men and horses alike.

Dozens fell on impact, while many others shrunk farther behind their shields. Tzul bellowed for order, yet the hard point of the wedge blunted as many of the black-cloaked spearmen fell backward away from the murderous volley.

"Now!" I shouted as the third volley connected. "Charge them!" I ran onward from the lines, with Samur close behind.

Our banners leaned forward as the Thracian center surged toward the Avars, closing the distance between the forces and flooding through the ragged gaps in the Avar wedge. I heaved my spear at Tzul, but it sailed just over his shoulder and struck another man behind him. Others at my back threw their remaining spears, which flew with Troglita's final volley of arrows like a hail of iron and wood. We drew our swords on the run, and a few paces before the Avar lines, we fell to the shield wall.

We drove into the Avar ranks, knocking their spearmen to the ground to be stabbed and butchered by men of our second rank. Many cried out in their savage tongue, but we showed no mercy. Crying Isaacius' name, I chopped down at limbs and severed heads as we drove the Avar wedge farther back.

At last, my shield clattered against Tzul's. We exchanged blows, but in the swirling press of men, neither could deliver a truly forceful stroke. He spat at me and cursed in the Avar language, pressing his weight forward and preventing me from lifting my exhausted arm to an attack. His eyes darted to either side, seeing only his men falling or retreating from our onslaught. Tzul backed away and slipped between the ranks of his men.

Like Tzul, the Avar spearmen tried to turn and run from our onslaught, but they were too tightly packed to retreat; our spears, swords, and axes impaled them. Many of my men had abandoned their own weapons, too blunted against shields and bones over the course of the morning. While Avar iron cracked and sheared easily, it still inflicted a fatal blow against lightly armored bodies. One of Troglita's men, his bow abandoned, picked up an Avar axe and flung it toward the dark mass of the horde. It connected with a man's face, splitting his nose in two and leaving its victim with a dumbfounded expression.

A few paces away, Samur fought like a demon, abandoning a shattered shield for a second short sword. He dodged in and out of our ranks, cutting at the exposed legs and arms of his enemy as crimson spattered his face like paint.

We advanced still, but our desperate charge faltered as enough Avars formed a cohesive wall. At the point of our furthest progress, our banners were fully upright and fluttered at the crux of the Roman and Avar lines.

Suddenly, one of the banners tipped forward. An unlucky axe strike had disemboweled its holder. Several of my men jostled to reclaim it, but the Avars continued to press their advantage against our flagging position. The Imperial banner fell again and did not rise in the fray.

Cephalas growled and darted toward the banners' last location. I tried to stop my friend, yet he could not hear me over the din of combat. I yelled for Samur to assume command and pushed my way to Cephalas and my diminishing lines.

Stuck in the press of my lines, I struggled forward and saw Cephalas reach the banners as he cut down two Avar adversaries. One of his Roman neighbors stopped to lift the banners up only to be cut by an Avar spear in the center of his back. As the man reached back in a desperate attempt to remove the spear, he tripped on his cloak and drove the spear farther into his body.

Alone, Cephalas shielded himself as he lifted the banners high. The Imperial Eagle and Mundus' boar were shredded from arrow strikes and stained red by the blood of the fallen. Cephalas shuffled backward, unable to strike out with his sword and left only with his shield to defend his body. I struggled to reach him, my progress agonizingly slow and leaving me helpless as another line of Avars advanced on him.

It was then that Shaush revealed himself. His white wolf pelt hanging from his helmet down to his calves, Shaush took his place at the head of his lines and roared his countrymen forward.

As Cephalas retreated back to the safety of the Roman lines, he was rushed by Shaush, who all but drove the Greek from his feet with a savage blow to Cephalas' splintered shield. Other Roman soldiers struck forward, but Shaush dodged their blows and slashed his sword across Cephalas' shield. Cephalas braced his shoulder behind his shield and bulled his way forward, toppling Shaush, who yelped in fear. Swiftly, another Avar lunged at Cephalas and plunged a sword cleanly through his upper arm.

"No!" I screamed, pushing my men out of the way as I ran to his side. I stabbed at the Avar's face, my sword cutting through the man's jaw and leaving his mouth a red ruin.

Cephalas winced, tears running down from his eyes as blood flowed freely down his arm and into his gloves. His shield hung limply as I pulled the sword clean of his arm, coaxing forth another fountain of blood. I struck forward to cover Cephalas' retreat as he was dragged through the thinning Roman lines, and caught one last glimpse of the man as he left, our twin banners still flying tall in the air.

Back on his feet, Shaush rushed me with his teeth bared in a sinister smirk as he jabbed with his blade. Roman and Avar spearmen alike tightened their shield walls around us, yet we still traded blows in a desperate frenzy. He managed to sneak his blade around my guard, grazing my already wounded arm and leaving a long cut in the process. I fell back a pace as Shaush rushed forward hungrily, the power behind his attacks contrasting against my own diminishing strength. His shield slammed against mine, jostling my head backward as he tried to push me over.

As he lifted his blade level with his chest, his eyes flew to the ground. I squared my feet and watched his shoulders twitch. He swung his blade underneath my shield, a stroke to sever the precious tendons in my legs that held me standing, but I slammed the rim of my shield downward, stopping his blade short of my ankle and crushing his forearm with its blunted iron cover. Shaush yelped and jumped to standing, trying fruitlessly to lift his sword arm for another blow.

I jammed my sword into Shaush's chest. He gasped, eyes wide with bewilderment and surprise, and spat blood onto my shield with a shudder. Avar spearmen grabbed his arms and dragged Shaush toward the Avar interior, his eyes rolling back into his head. My voice thundered in an incomprehensible shout of fury; I could tell the Avar lines were breaking, and I lunged forward at the Avar prince in one last attempt to extinguish my enemy's will to fight.

Something swung for me—a studded mace, which thudded off my armor just below my heart. The wind rushed from my lungs, and I gasped for air, finding none.

The attacking Avar raised his mace for a final strike against my helmet, but he did not land it. He fell, gored by Troglita, as my men surrounded my position. Both the Avar and Roman lines retreated, leaving one hundred paces between the bloodied lines that were littered with corpses of men and horses.

"Breathe, Varus! Breathe!" Troglita yelled as I struggled to bring my chest to rise and fall.

I spat a thick gob of blood, sending piercing pain through my ribs. Troglita threw my arm around his neck as he kept me upright, and blood poured from my gaping mouth and nose. Samur ran to my side and dropped to the ground, his breathing heavy as he helped me to a seated position.

"Get him out of here, now!" Samur called angrily. Troglita nodded and grabbed another soldier to carry me from the battlefield.

"No," I sputtered, coughing from the effort of the single word.

Samur drew close. "Varus, please! I can have you on a horse heading south immediately."

My breathing still pained, but less desperate, I shook my head. "No, Samur. My place is here. I will hold the line until my post is relieved."

"You stubborn ass!" Samur screamed, a tear cutting through the gore that covered his face.

Troglita sat me down below the banners, and I spied Cephalas, a tight bandage wrapped around his arm. The Greek nodded at me, but I could see he was not able to move his mutilated arm. His lower lip quivered, but he kept a stony face to the world. Faintly, I could hear that he sang to himself, his voice breaking up every few heartbeats.

"Pick me up," I ordered two of my men, who gathered my mangled arms over their shoulders and lifted me to my feet. I choked and spat from the pain in my chest, yet looked around at the surrounding horror.

The Avars were regrouping, their panic subsiding as they saw Tzul at the head of the army. A series of horns rang out in the distance, and deep Avar drums pounded.

Wincing, I regarded my lines. Nearly all my men nursed injuries, and many held no working weapons as they sat listlessly. My line of wounded snaked along our rear, a greater tally than those still capable of lifting a sword. As Tzul reformed the Avar wedge, I shook my head in anger.

"Back into lines, boys," I yelled, laughing involuntarily. "I will not give up this position!"

Despite being covered with swelling bruises and open wounds, my men clambered back to the line, squaring their shields for one final engagement. I did not have enough men to stack the shield wall, but by that point, even a hundred fresh reinforcements would have made little difference.

"Varus, this is it. No more tricks this time," Samur said, fear audible in his voice.

Samur grabbed a new shield, dented yet otherwise in serviceable condition. He threw his arms around my neck, and I squeezed him tight, ignoring the pain in my ribs and taste of copper in my mouth.

At Tzul's signal, the Avar procession revived, slowly but gradually gaining traction. Some still stumbled over small mounds of bodies, yet Tzul rushed headlong toward the flimsy wall that barred him from the open fields beyond.

Troglita shouldered his way to my side as my men gazed on silently. He rested a hand on the back of my helmet and checked the straps of his shield, then cleared his throat and yelled out toward our lines.

Our neighbors looked over at my fellow banda commander as he stepped forward from the lines.

"I swear to faithfully execute the Emperor's commands, to never desert my service, nor shrink from Death in pursuit of the glory of Rome," Troglita roared, drawing his sword and leveling it at the approaching Avar hordes. Many echoed his chant in ragged order, their voices rising in strength as others joined in.

"I swear to defend the weak, to protect the innocent, and serve as the shield to the poor and the mighty alike," Troglita called again.

"Hold these lines, boys!" I yelled out as Troglita gathered the will to continue.

"I swear to honor and love my God, to seek justice, and glorify those dreams that are greater than myself," Troglita said, and all followed in unison.

"Hold!" I screamed again, the Avars a mere twenty paces away.

"I swear this oath before God and the Roman people, who shall never falter," Troglita finished. He took his place in the line, and the men slammed their fists into their shields in the last great thunder of our battle.

"Hold!" I called frantically as Tzul pointed his sword at my head with a guttural growl. With that, the Avars lowered their spears and charged, closing the final distance between us.

"Now! For Rome!" I bellowed. The haggard lines took up my cry, and the Avar wedge collided between Samur and me as we fought to keep our shields locked.

"Fucking die!" Samur screamed, cutting and jabbing at Tzul as the warlord cursed his men forward. Tzul slashed his sword between Samur's guard, catching him high in the chest and unsealing my brother's shield from my own.

"Samur!" I screamed, fear and rage overpowering my tattered body.

Ignoring the pain, I cut forward, trying to carve a path to Samur. Troglita attempted to hold me back with a hand along my cloak, yet I brushed aside the commander's caution as I stuck my blade into an Avar spearman's hip. I drew my axe and hacked away at Tzul's shield, yet the warlord had begun to push into our second ranks and flew beyond my reach.

Our lines breaking, I slashed wildly at the enemy, downing one by severing his arm and stopping another as my axe blade jammed into the man's exposed neck. I drew Aetius' dagger and jabbed forward with my final weapon, but I was bashed backward when my lines could no longer resist the overwhelming pressure of thousands of Avar shields. All the while, Samur grew more separated from the protection of our flagging wall, fending off blows from three attackers at a time. Until, amid an Avar surge, Samur fell.

"Damn you!" I roared. "Samur!"

As I struggled toward the last location I'd seen my brother, the press of allies and Avars alike grew oppressive, choking me. Troglita and a half dozen other spearmen somehow formed a ring around me even as Avars flooded into our second line. Troglita's men faltered as Avar riders galloped through unfillable gaps in the lines. Few of my men ran, slashing with any blades that had been discarded in the crumpled grass and throwing fists when none could be found.

I caught a glimpse of Samur's limp body as I dove outside of our makeshift ring, cutting my way to his figure. With Aetius' dagger as my only available weapon, I cut and stabbed at the exposed limbs of my swirling enemies, dragging Samur back to Troglita's lines with one arm.

"Samur, get up!" I yelled. "Get up!"

Inside our collapsing wall, Samur choked and spat, swallowing fetid gore as he struggled in the muck. With a shriek of joy, I lifted Samur to his feet, and he moaned and stumbled as his legs struggled to hold his weight. Yet, though his eyes were unfixed and his torso wavered, he remained upright.

"I want to go home," Samur muttered. "Varus, can we go home?"

"Soon." I gripped him with one arm and stabbed at approaching enemies with the other. A familiar sensation of shame and regret filled my chest at an inability to fulfill the promise I made to Belisarius. Such despair was made worse in that my actions would lead not only to my own death, but more importantly to Samur's as well.

We stood back to back as the first Avar riders turned on the outer perimeter of the Roman ring of death, followed by small detachments of quicker footmen that ran with their black cloaks trailing behind in the autumn wind. Spotting the plumes of two komes, many Avars threw javelins toward our tiny ring, but our frenzy of cuts and jabs repelled them. When a man to my left was caught in the chest by an Avar sword, I picked up the fallen soldier's blade and cut down his killer. Through it all, I bellowed in frustration, desperate for a solution to bring Samur to safety yet

The Last Dying Light

finding no path forward. We had lost, and I had failed to hold Belisarius' lines, and the cost of such defeat would mean Samur's life, and all others of my men.

Horns blared behind the Avar lines as I caught one last glimpse of Tzul. The warlord's head jerked back as he yelled and formed the Avar lines for another charge against the remnants of my men from outside of the ring. Hundreds of Avars formed into a black-shielded wall and rushed toward our position, their screams echoing across the low slope. Sighing heavily, Troglita cursed our approaching death on the plains of Tauris.

As we braced for impact, Belisarius' horn boomed a dozen paces from our position as armored horses galloped around us, driving dozens of Avars to the ground as they were crushed by hooves and maces. Belisarius' plume rose at the front of the formation as the cataphracts formed a great wedge of iron and horseflesh, bearing at full gallop toward Tzul's men. Belisarius drove a lance through the warlord's shield and into his heart, sending Tzul's body tumbling aside in a spray of bone and blood. Belisarius' horse tore through the Avar ranks, which buckled under the force of the charge.

Bessas led a detachment to ride down any lingering Avar resistance, joined soon thereafter by Germanus' spearmen. Sunicas' Huns quickly rode down those few who managed to escape from Belisarius' stranglehold, letting none run toward the Tauric Isthmus and into the steppe wastelands beyond.

The final skull-topped black banners fell to the grass, and our great battle with the Avar horde came to a close.

Belisarius gave Bessas command of the remaining attack against the Avar holdouts and galloped toward my tiny ring of survivors, finding me leaning against a shield. Samur's chest rose and fell as his eyes opened, pain wracking his own face.

"Jesus, did we win?" Samur's blasphemy was met only by silence.

Belisarius dismounted, ran to my position, and removed his helmet. Though I should have felt unrivaled joy at such fortune, all I could do was weep as the general approached, my tears melding the world around me into an unholy landscape of the dead and the dying. I cried out, begging forgiveness as Belisarius approached. The burden of my duties had been too great for me to bear.

"I'm sorry, Lord!" I cried. "I couldn't hold them, Lord, I'm sorry."

Belisarius took my head into his chest as I fell forward. Pulsing pain racked my limbs and chest, with screaming muscles tempting me to lay in the blood and mud for a desperate sleep. Yet I could not look Belisarius in the face, not with the deaths of so many of my men weighing upon my conscience.

"No, Varus, you were magnificent. I failed you... I couldn't break through when you needed me." Belisarius stood firm as I cried, ignoring all manner of muck that caked my skin and armor.

Behind me, a diverse array of armored horsemen and Thracian spearmen erupted into a cheer not heard in many years by a Roman army.

"*Roma victrix! Roma victrix!*" they shouted, the great victory cry of the Empire now carried by thousands of Roman voices at the northern edge of Rome's world. Others were chanting the general's own name, mixing in with the cheers for the victory of Rome. Belisarius smiled faintly, yet did not join in, staying with me as I sat in his embrace.

As I calmed myself, yet more riders pounded to us, carrying small contingents of my spearmen who had been scattered by the Avar assault. Cephalas still held our Imperial banner, its rust-stained golden eagle wrapped tightly in his broken fingers. Another man held Perenus upright as his horse walked smoothly along the grass, leading the Lazic man to weakly wave in my direction.

"Can you ride?" Belisarius asked, his eyes running over my body with concern.

"Slowly, Lord," I grunted, "but yes."

Belisarius gave a signal, and two ponies were summoned for Troglita and me. Samur waved off my concerns as he found Sunicas, and the Hun embraced my brother, chastising him for nearly getting himself killed. I offered a wave to Cephalas and Perenus, both men wounded yet awake and cheerful as they sat listless in the bloodied grass.

Belisarius brought us south, where we found a cowed circle of Avars near John's eastern lines. Several of the senior officers had already gathered, with others taking stock of their men and disarming the thousands of Avars who remained alive.

"Bring the prisoners," the general called to John, who nodded and passed along Belisarius' command.

Two shackled Avars dressed in Roman tunics were brought to Belisarius, and I identified such men as prisoners of Baduarius and Dagisthaeus. Belisarius beckoned the two chained Avars to follow, leading them into a ring of kneeling and surrendered Avar warriors. Dozens of Roman spearmen eyed the disarmed Avars warily, seeking out any hidden blade or sudden attack intended to end Belisarius' life. Thankfully, however, no such resistance emerged.

At the center of the ring, Belisarius and I found Kazrig, Khagan of the Avars, beloved of the Great God Tengri. But for a deep cut along his left cheek and his shaggy beard coated with gore, the Avar ruler showed no sign of discomfort as he sat in silence.

Kazrig moved to stand as Belisarius approached, but the general barked an order. "Kneel!"

Kazrig was visibly confused. One of Belisarius' prisoners translated the command into Avar. A defiant look flared on the Khagan's face, but, facing no other option than instant and uncompromising death, he complied.

Kneeling before the Roman general, Kazrig awaited his fate. We had learned that defeated lords of the plains expected to be slain, considering it a sacrifice to their dark god. If the lord died well, his people would only be enslaved by the victor, forced to toil in dung pits and carry firewood into the huts. If he did not, the lord's people usually followed him in that sacrifice.

"You will ride back to your people beyond Tauris, and you will never come this way again." Belisarius' commands were strained by a wild anger that was unlike him.

Kazrig spoke some reply, a lengthy statement in the growl of the harsh Avar tongue, and soon came the translation.

"Khagan Kazrig asks why you are letting him live. And why does this benefit him? His son and heir has died, and his forces are broken. Another steppe tribe is just as likely to sweep along and swallow the Avars whole," the prisoner said.

My interest sparked at the news of Shaush's death. Though I had dealt him a serious blow, I had assumed that the prince had been carried off into the safety of the Avar lines.

Belisarius' face drew close to Kazrig's, his voice low and chill.

"He can make other sons," Belisarius whispered. "And if he stays here, I will butcher every last Avar man. I still will, if he or his descendants return this way again. If I hear of any Avar crossing into Tauris, I will ride back with all of my men, and I will leave your bodies for the carrion eaters that fly over the plains." Then, he added, "I swear this on my God, and your own."

Many later questioned Belisarius' reasoning at such a mercy, yet its cause was a sensible one. Admittedly, I counted myself in their number, as I felt Kazrig to be the cause of unfathomable pain to thousands of innocents. As I grew older, however, I realized such unthinking vengeance rarely solved any conflict well, often spiraling into darker and more all-consuming outcomes with no victors, and many vanquished. With the wisdom of age, I see Belisarius' decision as one unsatisfying for a warrior, but the most prudent for the survival of Tauris. And, ultimately, such was the Emperor's desire—to create and preserve a modicum of peace in this distant land.

Though we had broken Kazrig's power, a small horde of women and young children remained in the steppes north of Tauris, who would have a blood vengeance with Rome's northern province after the death of their men and their khagan. By leaving Kazrig free, the Avars would live to fear Rome as they moved away from our lands, fearful of another horrific defeat by our spears. Belisarius also believed that an enemy once defeated could be defeated again, and that belief would haunt Kazrig's dreams for the remainder of his life.

We kept hundreds of Avar prisoners to be shipped back to Constantinople, a reward for the twin armies that sacrificed so much. Kazrig left with a thousand of his unarmed men, their black cloaks and furs fluttering in the wind as they fled north with all due haste.

Belisarius and I galloped toward the other senior commanders, finding Troglita, Mundus, and Germanus. Mundus hailed me as I approached and inquired after the state of our banda. Baduarius and Ascum joked lightly as they stood over a sea of corpses, while Belisarius and John discussed how we might leave this haunted place before the pestilence that follows all corpses sickened us.

From the west, Sunicas and Simmas approached slowly. With two other riders, the four Huns gingerly carried a prone figure between them. All joking ceased as Sunicas dismounted, laying the body to the ground and exposing his face to the other officers.

"Dagis?" Baduarius said. His eyes grew wide, and he made a mewling sound as he dropped his blade and dove beside his slain brother. Dagisthaeus' body bore a dozen gashes, yet in death, his expression was peaceful.

Baduarius cried out to the heavens, his screams startling the horses and drawing the attention of the men. Thick tears slid down his face as he touched his head to his brother's, his chest rising and falling as he moaned in agony. He spoke to the body in Gothic, his voice rising and falling in pain and anger.

Belisarius ran to Baduarius' side and squatted next to the giant of a man. He wrapped his hands around Baduarius' shoulders, and the Goth fell into the general's lap, his hand still clutching Dagisthaeus' motionless fingers. Baduarius screamed and cried as Belisarius rocked him gently, the other commanders gathering close and kneeling in a tight ring around the fallen Gothic leader.

The Last Dying Light

THRENODY FOR THE LOST

BELISARIUS' men set up camp a half mile from the battlefield, gathering the Roman dead and placing them on dozens of large wooden pyres. The next day, the corpses lay shoulder to shoulder in a wide square, with the lone body of Dagisthaeus laid privately in the center with a platform on its own. Dagisthaeus had been adorned with all of the finery that marked him a seasoned senior commander of Rome, and his armor had been cleaned and polished to shine against the sun's rays. The Goth's face had been left bare, his helmet resting at his side and his huge shield covering much of his body, as it had in life. Baduarius kept only his brother's sword, which now hung at his waist as he looked on over the funeral proceedings and dusk fell across the sky.

Atop a makeshift platform, Belisarius gained the armies' attention, the silence instantaneous.

"We honor our brothers, who kept their vows and fulfilled their promise to Rome," Belisarius mourned. "Leading them into the afterlife is Dagisthaeus of the Ostrogoths, *Dux* of the Roman Empire, who sacrificed his life in service of the Roman people. He will not be forgotten, and we shall not look upon another like him again."

Soldiers brought forth torches. Belisarius himself handed one great torch to Baduarius, who descended the platform and approached his brother's body. His eyes rimmed red, he kneeled and kissed his brother on the forehead one final time, and dropped the flames at the pyre's kindling.

Others followed suit, sparking blazes that consumed the bodies they held. Baduarius stayed close to his brother and was soon surrounded by his friends, whom he had served alongside for many years. Though I had only known Dagisthaeus for a few weeks, I grieved for his departing, seeing a flicker of Samur's own face upon the Goth's dead form. I shuffled next to Baduarius and offered what clumsy words may be conferred to one suffering from an incalculable loss.

"He was a kind man, and a brave warrior," I said. "Even though I did not know him long, he gave me hope that what we are doing is righteous."

Baduarius sighed. "Aye, he would have liked that. Of the two of us, he was always the one for ideals. One day, I will see him again."

"What would you say to him, upon that meeting?" I asked.

"That I'm sorry for so much blubbering." Baduarius chuckled, blotchy tears streaming down his massive cheeks and onto his scraggly beard. "He'll tease me for that, I'm sure."

We stood there well into the night, standing vigil over the fallen commander's body until it was nothing but ashes and twisted metal. Baduarius was guided back to his tent, and the men rested in preparation for a quick departure back to Scythian Neapolis and then Cherson.

Our march back was an uneventful if uncomfortable one, and my body ached from the rocking of the horse. As we rode, one of my men delivered to me a white wolf's pelt that had been lightly spattered in the blood of its previous owner. I nodded and carried Shaush's fur with me back to our camp.

Rosamund wept when she saw the state of my body, covered as it was in deep gashes and punctures, and my left arm and shoulder one sweeping bruise. The old priest, for his part, sighed in relief, and crossed himself as he thanked God for my deliverance. Curiously, Father Petrus soon sought an audience with Belisarius, though their meeting was private and such discussion unknown. Soon thereafter, the priest spoke a requiem for the departed souls, which even the many pagans in our armies attended out of respect for the Roman dead.

We walked toward Cherson, and its bells rang in triumph as we crossed through its stone gates. Throngs of citizens crowded the streets as we marched into the city, chanting Belisarius' name and showering gifts and praise upon our passing soldiers. Though broken and battered, many of my men drew visible comfort from such recognition, from Cephalas accepting a silver coin from a grateful cheese merchant to Perenus grabbing a gifted wineskin. For the first time in weeks, joyous laughter animated the Thracian Army, temporarily masking wounds seen and unseen, and relieving the burden of so many dead, whose ashes blew over Tauris' grasslands.

With its tighter quarters and fewer beds, Cherson's barracks could only support smaller contingents of spears and horses, and the dwindling Thracian Army and the senior officers were given preference, though many of the men departed for brothels and taverns regardless. I stayed near the barracks and let Rosamund follow Perenus and Cephalas into the town.

Yet, as with all things in life, our joy was fleeting. Later that evening, Cherson's governor sought an immediate audience with Belisarius, and entered the general's tent with brow furrowed and features grim. Shortly thereafter, Belisarius summoned his senior officers, and I followed the others as the heavy wooden door bolted tightly behind us.

Belisarius stood at the center of the room, his face grave.

"A message from Constantinople. The Persians have crossed the Tigris near Amida, and we are recalled with all haste," he said. "We'll be back on deployment by spring."

"Only the dead have seen the end of war," John observed darkly.

Little did we know, our struggles had only just begun, for Rome now faced a far greater threat, one from its mortal enemy. Rome had not won a victory against Persia in hundreds of years, and Persia's vaunted Shahanshah had since formed an army to rival those of Cyrus or Xerxes from a thousand years prior. Tens of thousands of men and horses, drawn from a dozen nations and peoples, bearing down upon the Empire's Mesopotamian frontier.

I kept that news to myself for one more night, giving the men time to enjoy their hard-won respite. In the morning, Baduarius was named *Dux Scythiae*, and ordered to remain in Cherson with a token force of riders to ensure peace throughout the province until the end of winter. Mundus later explained that, while some peacekeeping was in order, this was an honor intended to give the Goth more time to grieve for his brother before leaving the north for Armenia and Mesopotamia.

On the morning of our departure, fair seas carried us out, and we were back to Constantinople in just four days. Along the way, several of the men joined Perenus in games of idle gambling and wine, yet a mood of exhaustion and melancholy replaced much of the joviality of our earlier voyage north. Rosamund cleaned and bound my wounds each night, while Samur trained abovedeck with Troglita and Sunicas. The other officers had boarded one of the dozens of other ships to supervise the disparate detachments of the two armies, leaving me alone with my thoughts as I gazed outward onto the sea. I eschewed company where possible, preferring the silence of solitude. Yet, even in the darkness of the ship's hold, I could still hear the clangor of metal, the screams of the thousands of dying men, and see the blood of Avars and Romans alike watering the grasses of Tauris. Most of all, I saw the final moments of Isaacius and Godilas flashing in my mind again and again.

On the fourth day, our ship pulled into Constantinople's vast harbor, dropped anchor, and secured its gangway to an open dock. As a centurion and ranking officer aboard my vessel, I was one of the first to disembark, and I moved to organize the banda for its march back to the Imperial Barracks. A wharf master hailed me and approached, issuing orders with foul breath.

"Well met, centurion, and welcome back. But please tell your men to proceed immediately to the barracks, for no trade is allowed today," he said.

"No trade?" That was unusual.

"The old Emperor died in the night. Markets are closed for a week. They're saying his nephew will take over now, and his young wife with him," he said.

My jaw quivered, and I sank to the planks of the dock. Samur ran off the boat, and he fell to my side, soon joined by Rosamund and Perenus. I screamed my dominus' name as I wept one final time, wishing to God that I had arrived one day earlier.

For everything would be different once again, and Justin's vision would move on without him.

Since that day, I have wondered—would Justin still have looked upon me with pride? Had I truly grown into the man that he desired and hoped for? His final words to me offer some reassurance, yet a nagging uncertainty from so many unanswered questions allowed the specter of doubt to grow. It would only worsen in the days yet to come.

Even as a small boy, I wanted nothing more than to become a warrior, to carry Justin's runed sword into glorious battle against Rome's enemies. Yet now, with whatever success I have won, such unquestioning commitment seems far less illustrious given the cost of such victory. I have bled and taken lives. I have sacrificed and undertaken terrible acts of brutality for the Empire, and all its people. So perhaps alongside the question of Justin's approval, another concern snaked into my heart, corrupting the soul so recently deprived of its father.

What had I become? And, more importantly, why, given all the gifts, the friends, and the opportunities granted to me, did my path seem incomplete and ill-made?

In the aftermath of Tauris, I had few answers to such questions. All I knew was that Justin had died, and that my men and I had been called back to war. The Persian behemoth awaited us in Mesopotamia, and I had little choice but to obey the will of our new Emperor. God save us all.

AUTHOR'S NOTE

Above all else, this is a work of fiction. Characters are invented and events are adjusted to appear earlier in the historical timeline to fit the novel's narrative. *The Last Dying Light* has plenty of such artistic license, but I intended to keep to the spirit of the 6th Century Roman Empire as much as feasibly possible.

If they mention this period of Roman history at all, school textbooks often refer to the Roman government based in Constantinople as the "Byzantine Empire." Though the Eastern Empire sprung from the ancient town of Byzantium, the Romans of this period never referred to themselves as Byzantines, nor did they disassociate with their earlier heritage of Julius Caesar and the emperors who followed. Indeed, until the final Fall of Constantinople in 1453, the Emperors in Constantinople referred to themselves as Romans. Figures of the 6th Century Eastern Empire believed themselves the direct descendants of Augustus, Diocletian, and Constantine, and held the same dreams and enmities that had been borne by the broader Empire from previous centuries.

This is not to say that the Roman Empire of the 6th Century bore a close resemblance to the Republic or the Empire that followed. By Justin's time on the throne, the Empire had largely become a Greek-speaking nation, its Latin roots slowly fading away even as the official language of the Roman Court. Religiously, remnants of paganism were stamped out as Christianity took hold outside of the major cities in each province. Yet significant theological differences emerged that gave rise to movements deemed heretical by the state-sponsored churches in the east (Constantinople) and west (Rome). Even law and taxation in the Eastern Empire had begun to transform into an entirely new system, seeking to ease the difficulty behind largely unwritten Ancient Roman law into a codified system that all citizens could understand and follow.

Militarily, the Empire had transformed itself in a manner that would be unrecognizable to Julius Caesar or Trajan. The legions were eliminated, replaced by an interlocking system of field armies and provincial border guards that allowed the Empire's military leaders to be more efficient in response to an invasion or crisis. Infantry remained a large portion of the Roman military, yet emphasis in this period began to shift to horse soldiers as the Empire learned from the examples of the Huns and Persians. Emerging leaders like Belisarius understood this well, and sought to merge military equipment and tactics from their surrounding enemies to complement existing and battle-worn doctrine. This change was a logical one—the Eastern Empire had many large and well-resourced enemies, and had to be far more strategic and adaptive in its execution of battle to accommodate the reduced base of soldiers and supplies that could be levied from shrinking borders.

Following the final collapse of a decrepit Western Roman Empire, the 6th Century is occasionally used as the initial staging point for the infamous Dark Ages. Such a name implies an absence of knowledge or learning that, in popular imagination, left Western society in a relative cultural and technological slumber for several centuries. In the Eastern Empire, however, the 6th Century bore witness to a wide range of scholarship and achievement, many of which survive intact to this day.

Given such overarching ideas, a nagging challenge of writing about this era is the incomplete and biased record that remains to tell of the deeds of Belisarius, Justinian, Varus, and hundreds of others who shaped the 6th Century Roman Empire. There are an increasing number of second and third-hand sources that help explain the actions and motives of the day, yet primary sources are limited and laced with bias. Some specific events or actions are retold in explicit detail via Procopius or Agathias, while entire years pass with only the vaguest description of progress or strife. For a historical fiction novelist, this is simultaneously a great blessing and a considerable hardship. The blessing is in the capacity to shape characters with imagined traits, grudges, and aspirations, and the curse is the limited to nonexistent guide that tells us if we are doing the characters justice against their historical memory.

Little is known of Varus' life. Procopius tells us that he came from the Herulians (as *Pharas*), and led the mounted Herulian foederati into battle under Belisarius' leadership. Though Procopius dedicates little to Varus' memory, he characterizes the Herulian as a man of "truth and sobriety," painting him as an honest and straightforward individual in an age of intrigue. The few other details available indicate an extensive degree of trust that Belisarius conferred onto Varus, delegating him with pivotal activities on the battlefield and upon military campaigns. Though this novel and series recounts the broader story of Belisarius' exploits, it also expounds on how Varus and dozens of other men and women lived, loved, and died in the struggle to maintain the legacy of Rome.

Most (but certainly not all) of the characters in this novel are mentioned in the primary records from the 6th Century. Antonina, Theodora, Justin, and Liberius were all famous figures in their day, to whom the historical record provides greater insight of their characters and behaviors. Likewise, Mundus, Perenus (inspired by Peranius of Iberia), or Troglita (John Troglita) are less understood, with historians focusing on their military activities as opposed to their personal foibles and exploits. Others are but a footnote—mentioned in a dispatch or as participating in a momentous event, yet their origins or later life remain wholly absent from the record. I could not do justice to the thousands of individuals who helped reshape the Eastern Empire after the cataclysmic tumult of the 5th Century, nor fully capture the complex web of social, economic, and military figures that kept the Empire running. For the sake of storytelling, several of my characters serve as an amalgam of others from the historical record.

This book, and the intended series to follow, tells of the triumphs and tragedies of Belisarius. Until recently, Belisarius was a figure of little renown to popular Western memory. Yet his achievements under adversity stack strongly against any of Caesar or Scipio, and his steadfast nature was something of an anomaly in an increasingly politicized and vicious Empire. Whether by good sense or morality, Belisarius favored principles of fairness, protection of civilians and the weak, and safeguarding the lives of his men as much as feasibly possible. He was incredibly young when he rose to command—perhaps in his early twenties—yet demonstrated wisdom to anticipate his opponents and overcome grave odds. Belisarius was an equally flawed man, the details of which only make him a more compelling leader in a pivotal moment of the Empire's history.

Most of Belisarius' historical record focuses upon his role in command, particularly starting with the conflicts against Sasanian Persia. Only the barest footnotes describe his early life or progress through Rome's military ranks, the details limited to his service under Justin and continued promotion under Justinian. *The Last Dying Light* tells of imagined conflicts at the dawn of Belisarius' career, for someone entrusted with so much responsibility must have had a measure of demonstrated success on the battlefield. The Empire's conflict with the Avars came much later in the historical record (mid-6th Century), yet they are a useful device to demonstrate the struggle that the Imperial Army faced against a recurring battery of nomadic tribes. The reigns of Anastasius and Justin were characterized by lingering struggles of the Migration Period, when dozens of tribes moved throughout the former territories of the Roman Empire and engaged in all manner of skirmishing and destruction. In particular, controlling the northern border along the Ister River (modern Danube River) was a ceaseless task, where many tribes such as the Gepids, Herulians, Goths, and Huns preyed upon Roman towns for slaves and plunder. Though the Avars (also described as Pannonian Avars or Pseudo-Avars to differentiate from a separate yet possibly related tribe of Avars in the Caucausus) came later in Justinian's reign, their arrival continued the threat of invasion and destabilization within the Empire's northern provinces (Chersonesus, Moesia, portions of Dacia, Scythia, and much of Macedonia and Epirus). Fierce horsemen, the Avars would go on to carve out their own kingdom in later decades, waging war on the remnants of the Eastern Roman Empire, the Franks, the Huns, the Gepids, and many others.

The novel that follows *The Last Dying Light* will move toward more famous conflicts in the Iberian War, where Belisarius was transformed from a fortunate and well-connected military officer and into a legendary military commander.

The production of historical fiction is not simply the need to research and write a story. I owe considerable thanks to a team of dedicated professionals who brought this story to life, as well as a number of close contacts who served as test subjects for earlier drafts. Blair Thornburgh is a fabulous editor not only gifted in storytelling and craft, but also in a rich understanding of the early Medieval period that this novel strongly benefitted from. Crystal Watanabe of Pikko's House handled all proofreading and formatting. Zach Hoffman brought the novel and all its characters to life with his voice acting. Dusan Markovic provided the rich illustration of the novel's cover, conferring a level of detail and imagination that brings the 6th Century to life. The twin maps are productions of Cyowari, who constructed beautifully detailed works despite sparse records of the various peoples of the age. I am also blessed with a wonderful collection of test readers. *The Last Dying Light* is incalculably improved from their efforts.

The Last Dying Light

If you enjoyed *The Last Dying Light*, please consider leaving a positive review on Goodreads, Amazon, and other review sites. I am very grateful for your time in this—such reviews are critical to the series' success and continued production. Ultimately, Varus and Belisarius' tale has hardly begun. Far greater challenges remain ahead, with enemies not only in the vast and disciplined armies of Persia, but within the very heights of the Imperial government as well.

Made in the USA
Monee, IL
13 October 2022

3b1d1007-df35-448c-8277-5fe542468248R01